EMPIRE OF RECKONING AND RUIN

DRAGONS OF TIRENE SERIES

BOOK FIVE

NINA FROST

RoseHarbor
PUBLISHING

Copyright © 2025 by RoseHarbor Publishing

All rights reserved.

No part of this book may be reproduced in any form or by any electronic or mechanical means, including information storage and retrieval systems, without written permission from the author, except for the use of brief quotations in a book review.

❋ Formatted with Vellum

BOOKS BY NINA FROST

Dragons of Tirene Series

Kingdom of Shadows and Wings

Court of Secrets and Flames

Crown of Betrayal and Blood

Queen of Legends and Lies

Empire of Reckoning and Ruin

Description

Can love conquer all when the odds are impossibly stacked?

After weeks of chaos spent defeating the drachen and burning the dead god Narc's bones in a phoenix fire to save the people of Tirene, Lark eagerly awaits the culmination of her unexpected but extraordinary love story with Sterling. In one month, Lark will marry Prince Knox Sterling Barda, who will ascend the throne to become king of Tirene.

Yet happiness lies just beyond their grasp.

Strange occurrences interrupt Tirene's celebration of the impending nuptials. A mysterious wedding gift of dangerous magic that transforms water into diamonds. Stone statues coming to life and attacking people. Objects missing for years suddenly reappearing in their owners' homes. Not everyone is happy with the new normal...especially the gods...and they're sending a message.

Or a warning.

Lines have been drawn that leave Lark and Sterling with an impossible choice. War is coming again. And this time, Lark and Sterling will either change the world...or lose everything.

Impossible magic, breathtaking romance, and inescapable duty clash in Empire of Reckoning and Ruin, the climactic fifth and final installment of the Dragons of Tirene series by best-selling author Nina Frost.

Chapter One
Lark

In the palace's royal gift room, watery winter sunlight streams through tall windows, creating tiny stars out of the dust motes that dance between Sterling and me. His bronze, battle-scarred hand rests on my hip, warm and steady, like it's meant to be there.

And it is.

Dark brown eyes flecked with gold—so expressive I could drown in their depths—smile down at me. Add in the high cheekbones, square jaw, and confident swagger, and Knox Sterling Barda becomes too damn attractive for his own good. The fact that he's Tirene's crown prince does nothing to deflate his ego.

Though he rubbed me the wrong way when we first met, I've grown to love this man's enduring confidence.

It's still hard to believe he's all mine.

I lean into him, reveling in his hard, military-trained body as we weave around gift-laden tables, the weight of his touch anchoring me to this rare moment of peace after months of chaos.

My stomach flutters, not from nerves, but from the simple

pleasure of being alone with him. From this brief respite from my responsibility as Tirene's only dragoncaller in generations...and the savior of the kingdoms...and the fulfillment of an ancient prophecy.

For the afternoon, I don't have to be Lark Axton, born Ella Leona Hendrix, now Queen of Tirene.

I can simply be myself.

A young woman deeply in love, opening engagement presents with her betrothed during a desperately needed moment of normalcy in a world gone mad.

"Another golden goblet set." Sterling's voice rumbles through his chest. "That makes five."

I don't bother to hide my snicker. We could get through this pile faster if we separated, but where's the fun in that? "Now our company can get tipsy out of fancy drinkware too."

"By company, I'm guessing you mean Agnar, Leesa, and Bastian." Sterling's lips quirk up at the corners. His glossy black hair shines in the light, beckoning my fingers to stroke its silkiness.

An answering grin spreads across my face. "Exactly."

The gift room stretches before us, tables arranged in neat rows, each stacked with offerings sent to the palace in Windmyre, Tirene's capital city, from neighboring nations, noble houses, and dignitaries who want to curry favor with the kingdom's queen and soon-to-be-crowned king.

This small, out-of-the-way space is just one of many empty chambers that populate the palace. I'm pretty sure I never noticed it until we christened the place as the perfect spot to store our engagement and wedding gifts.

Many of the palace's extra rooms currently function as overflow housing for those who lost their homes before we finally destroyed the drachen. Though we've managed to repair some of the damage inside the palace walls in the last four months, parts of the capital city outside the barrier still resemble a war zone.

Rebuilding will take time.

Sterling's fingers trace lazy patterns against my side as we meander through the rows of packages. "Two months. Two months until you're officially mine."

"I've been yours since that first kiss in the stable at Flighthaven."

Heat rises to my cheeks at the memory of his hands on me, his lips. The taste of whiskey and danger. He served as my flight instructor, and students and instructors weren't supposed to fraternize. The first time we met, he struck me as arrogant as he was beautiful.

He gradually managed to lower my defenses. Little did I know he was only posing as an instructor at Flighthaven Academy. In reality, he was a soldier and Tirene's prince. He infiltrated the campus to verify the existence of the kidnapped dragoncaller raised in Aclaris and then win her trust so he could steal her back to Tirene.

He smirks as if he can read my thoughts. "And I've been yours. Soon the whole world will know."

Despite a rocky beginning, our story will finally culminate in a happy ending. The celebrations are set to last a full week. Sterling's coronation will follow our nuptials, with feasts and hunts and a masquerade ball sandwiched between jousts and tournaments and magical games.

Royals and nobles from the closest kingdoms have already confirmed their attendance, along with visitors from more distant lands who will cross seas and snowcapped mountains just to witness our union.

And we must host them all.

Considering the turmoil other kingdoms have experienced recently, I suppose I shouldn't complain.

"Do you think they're coming to see us get married, or to

see the woman who burned Narc's bones?" I try to keep my voice light.

Sterling's hand tightens on my hip. "Both. But mostly, they want to ensure Tirene's favor. Thanks to you, we're the strongest kingdom in the region."

I shift my weight uneasily. The reality of being the sole phoenix-born dragoncaller in existence and the strongest fire user in generations comes with plenty of downsides. My heritage granted me an isolated and ignorant upbringing and molded me into a pawn kingdoms squabbled over.

Sterling's gasp yanks me from my brooding. "Look, how original! A bird!" His voice rings with faux surprise as he lifts a delicate glass sculpture from a velvet cushion.

Rolling my eyes, I gesture around at the dozens of bird-related presents scattered across the tables. Some appear subtle, others ostentatious. All are intended to pay homage to my phoenix-blessed heritage.

"How many birds does that make?" As I do the math, I sweep a lock of hair behind my ear, the streaks of gold threading the brown glinting in the sun. "Seventeen?"

Seventeen glass birds. Just what everyone needs.

"Eighteen." Sterling sets the sculpture down carefully. "And technically, they're phoenixes. After all, you incinerated Narc's bones with your phoenix fire. People remember that."

With a sigh, I drag my fingers along the edge of a silver tray. "We all played our part."

"But you're the one who dropped into the broken earth." When Sterling recites the line from the prophecy about me getting buried alive, the mischievous sparkle in his eyes vanishes. "You torched his bones with phoenix fire to save us all. That's what people are celebrating. Hope rising from the ashes."

Rising from the ashes...the same way I did. Literally.

I rub my arms to fight off a shiver. I didn't just plummet

into the earth. I *died* down there, just like the prophecy stated I would. Then, I somehow came back to life on the ground above where I disappeared.

My gaze drifts to the window.

In the courtyard below, children play in the dappled shade of ancient umberheart trees. Among them, little Rose Lockwood, Agnar's six-year-old niece, runs in circles. Her blond curls bounce with each step, and a small dancing flame hovers faithfully over her right shoulder. The other children maintain a slight distance. Not enough to be obvious, but enough that I notice.

"I may have saved the world, but at what cost?"

Sterling watches Rose as her innocent laughter floats up to us. "You saved her too."

After Rose survived my phoenix fire, after she completely healed from the drachen's corruption, a small flame started hovering at her shoulder. The tiny blaze doesn't harm anyone or anything, not even the flowers she loves to pick, but its presence marks her as different. A mystery no one can explain. Maybe my grandfather could have helped solve this puzzle.

The pain—a sudden stab between my ribs—catches me off guard. Eldor Gentry's burial was over four months ago, just twenty-four hours after Dowager Queen Alannah Barda's. My grandfather and Sterling's mother died on the same day, murdered by the same traitors on the Royal Council of Tirene. Even though we were right there, we couldn't save them.

Not a single day passes where I don't feel the void created by the loss of my beloved, trusted family. So much loss concentrated in such a short time.

Too much.

"Rose is happy." Sterling wraps an arm around my shoulders. "Agnar says she and her mother are settling in well in the east wing. They'll stay until we find them a suitable home."

I nod, watching the girl spin in circles and the flame streak through the air like a comet. "A lot of places are filled with displaced survivors. Not just the palace. There's been so much destruction. So much death."

"We'll finish rebuilding. But first," Sterling pulls me closer, both hands now enveloping my waist, "it's time for celebrations. Something that will give hope to our people. Our queen's wedding."

I push up on my toes and kiss him, softly and sweetly. "And their king's ascension."

His pupils dilate. In a fluid motion, he sets me on one of the tables, knocking gifts aside with a sweep of his arm. Goblets and trinkets scatter, some thumping on the rug, others clattering against the marble floor.

I should care about the potential damage, but in a matter of seconds, his mouth is on mine, and suddenly nothing else matters.

He kisses me soundly, slowly, deliberately.

As always, my body reacts like this is our first time.

My blood heats as Sterling invades my mouth with his tongue, first tasting, then ravishing. His palms frame my face before sliding down to my neck, and his thumbs trace sensual circles on my shoulders.

He nips at my lower lip and pulls back, his expression contemplative.

I still. "What is it?"

The corner of his mouth rises. "You're going to have to practice dancing, you know."

"Dancing?"

I'm confused by the sudden shift in direction, but from the way he's smiling, he knew exactly what he was doing.

Two can play this game. I'll get him back later.

"For the wedding. The coronation ball. All the festivities where the kingdom will expect their queen to lead them in celebration." He strokes my hips. "Can't have you stumbling around like a newborn alicorn."

I narrow my eyes. "What makes you think I need to practice? I have plenty of experience dancing."

Sterling lifts an annoyingly cocky brow. "Dancing in the middle of a crowded ballroom and leading the dance are two entirely different things. It can be a little nerve-racking when all eyes are on you."

"Then by all means, let's practice." I slide off the table and extend one hand toward him while the other poises to rest on his shoulder. The opening stance of the first dance we shared.

"What's this? No arguing? Compliance?" Sterling's surprise lasts only a moment before he sweeps into the space I've created. He wraps his fingers around mine and molds his other palm to the small of my back. "You're full of surprises, my queen."

I toss him a wink as we begin. "Someone has to keep you on your toes."

We glide across the floor together, maneuvering between the tables. We dance like we're made for each other, just like we did at the ball Tirene's late king threw in my "honor."

My nose wrinkles. Honor. Please. More like a way for Jasper to flaunt his "prophesied dragoncaller." Ignoring the fact he planned to use me, breed me, and keep me captive to bolster his standing.

That feels like a lifetime ago.

Sterling draws me closer than necessary, and I suck in a breath as warmth blooms beneath my skin. Dancing with him is like making love upright with our clothes on. There's something about the way our bodies communicate without words...the push and pull, the give and take.

As Sterling leads me through a spin, my hips graze against his.

His pulls me flush to his body, and his eyes become molten. "Keep teasing me like that, and that gown will wind up shredded. You'll have to do the walk of shame back to our chambers naked after I spend the next hour worshipping every inch of your delectable body."

My lungs hitch, the heat in my cheeks mirroring the fire in his gaze. I stand on the tips of my toes and brush my lips across the corner of his mouth. "Tempting as that sounds, do you really want to subject the poor guard to that? He's right outside the door. Besides, we have more gifts to open."

Breaking away from the prescribed steps, I drag my fingers along his chest and circle him leisurely.

A feral growl escapes his lips. "I don't give a fuck who hears us. You should know by now that the only gift I care about is you."

My heart melts, and happiness blossoms in my chest. For these precious moments, the weight of the crown lifts, and I can temporarily set aside the responsibilities of repairing our shattered kingdom. There is only Sterling, the feel of his hands, the press of his body against mine, the softness of his lips.

"You always know just what to say to make me fall in love with you all over again."

He catches my hand, spinning me in circles until I'm wrapped in his arms and pinning me with his devious smirk. "Would it ruin the moment to say that you're also the only gift I care about unwrapping?"

His husky voice thwarts my attempt to fake offense. As we drift across the room, sharing slow, hungry kisses along the way, his sultry eyes mesmerize me. His hand tightens around my waist, and I'm certain he's going to set me up on a table again, spread my legs, and make good on his promise.

Sterling bump-guides me up against one of the tables near the high window, the gentle impact disturbing the piles of presents. His tongue finds that sensitive spot just below my ear, and I tilt my head to give him better access as my hands clutch at his shoulders.

Something tumbles off the table and drops at our feet with a soft thud.

He pauses, his breath hot against my neck. "What was that?"

I glance down and spot a plain package on the floor, wrapped in brown paper and tied with simple twine. No ribbons, no gold leaf, no official wax seal. Its simplicity stands out amid the ornate wrappings of other presents.

I reluctantly pull away from Sterling to bend and pick up the gift. "I don't remember seeing this one."

The package is heavier than I expect and about the size of a bread loaf. I find no card or note to identify the sender.

Sterling frowns. "That shouldn't be here if it hasn't been checked by security."

"Maybe it was." I turn the gift over in my hands. "Maybe they just failed to rewrap it in fancy paper."

"Lark..." Sterling's voice holds a warning, but curiosity has already gotten the better of me.

I pull at the twine, and the brown paper falls away, revealing a wooden box with intricate carvings along the edges. The lid slides open with a gentle push of my fingers.

Inside, nestled in black velvet, rests a bizarre artifact made of crystal and silver. It resembles a star caught in mid-explosion, the brilliant central sphere surrounded by delicate silver filaments that extend outward, each tipped with smaller crystals of varying sizes.

The way the light sparkles through the luminous object enthralls me. "What is it?"

Sterling leans closer, his shoulder brushing mine. "Some kind of art piece, maybe? At least it doesn't look like a bird."

I reach in and carefully lift the artifact from the velvet nest. The box must be heavy because the object itself is almost weightless in my palm. The crystals capture and fracture the sunlight streaming through the window into multicolored prisms that waltz across our faces.

My breath catches. "It's beautiful."

As I turn it to examine the craftsmanship, my finger accidentally brushes against a tiny silver lever hidden among the filaments. There's a soft click, followed by a musical tone so pure it vibrates through my bones.

Sterling and I exchange a glance, his wary, mine intrigued. He starts to caution me. "Lark—"

The air overhead shimmers like heat rising from summer stones.

A crack appears in the empty space, and hundreds of narrow, diamond-bright waterfalls tumble out. They cast glittering rainbows across the room as they cascade down, yet nothing gets wet. Like ghosts, the streams pass through solid objects—tables, gifts, our outstretched hands—and vanish just before they touch the floor.

"Sterling," I whisper, unable to summon more words. My pulse gallops in my neck.

Is this like the visions I had in the Lost City? The ones containing a memory of the past that replayed in the present?

We stand transfixed, watching prisms flow from nowhere, surrounded by the gentle tinkling of distant wind chimes.

Sterling's hand finds mine and squeezes tight. His face, illuminated by the radiance of the falling streams, is a mask of shock that must mirror my own, his lips set in a grim line. "I think we need to figure out who sent that to us."

I kneel to pick up one of the crystals. "What the...? It

doesn't make any sense, but I'm pretty sure these are real diamonds."

Sterling crouches and holds a stone as large as his thumbnail up to the light. "I think you're right."

Our eyes meet across the glittering floor, and his expression reflects my own growing bewilderment and nagging discomfort.

Something's wrong. Something's terribly wrong.

~

Three figures huddle in a circle in a stone chamber while the air around them thickens with palpable energy and ancient power. Shadows play along the walls, shifting and flowing like ghosts haunting the halls and attempting to cling to the threads of existence.

The figures gaze down at the silvery pool of water. Images slither through the depths, visions of things that are, were, and could possibly be. A myriad of potential outcomes, of rippling destinies that could intertwine with the lives of mortals.

The first figure, draped in a robe of deep indigo, hovers close to the pool's edge. He presses his palm flat against the surface, and a cascade of silver light bursts forth. "It is part of the pattern."

The second figure, garbed in shimmering white and tendrils of soft golden light, trails slender fingers through the liquid, disrupting the waters of what was. Scenes from the past emerge. Flashes of wars, love, betrayal.

"It has happened before." The second one's voice, though gentle, is heavy with a sense of history and experience.

The third entity studies the pool's contents. Her features twist with determination.

Her eyes smolder like coals, piercing through the surface into the depths of potential futures. "It will change nothing."

A thick, ancient silence stretches, broken only by the faint rippling of the water beneath their spectral forms.

Each god, a fragment of the cosmos, contemplates the events unfolding below. The mortal negotiations caught in the balance of unseen whims and twisted fates.

The pool stirs anew. Visions dance and flicker before them, reflecting the point in time where possibilities loom near.

The first being steps back. "This is not our concern. We must not interfere."

Another silence follows as the waters continue to stir.

CHAPTER TWO
LARK

My gown pools around me like ink on parchment as I pick up gem after gem, each one unnaturally cold to the touch. "How?"

"I don't know." Sterling rises and approaches one of the remaining waterfalls. The glimmering transparent substance ripples like liquid glass.

Sterling's eyes narrow in concentration until a faint blue glow emanates from his fingertips. The muscles in his jaw tighten. "If this were ordinary water, I could freeze it, direct it. But it's..." The tendons on his neck stand out as the blue glow intensifies and water vapor forms around his fingers. The prism shudders and curves away, like prey avoiding a predator. "It's resisting me. It's *aware*."

Aware.

The word hangs between us, heavy and wrong, while the hairs on my arms prickle.

Sterling sweeps his hand in a firm arc and tries again. The waterfall retreats farther and winks out of existence. The remaining falls vanish in sequence, like candles being snuffed out one by one.

The diamonds stay scattered across the floor, throwing in fractured rainbows.

Beautiful. Valuable. And freaking cold as hells. The temperature in the room has dropped enough for goose bumps to pebble my skin.

I straighten, remembering to pull my shoulders back like a queen rather than slump like the girl who still sometimes wakes screaming from nightmares. "We need to gather the palace guards. And the others."

"Agreed." He steps to the door and issues clipped orders to the guards stationed outside.

Within minutes, Captain Griffin Fitz strides in and bows. Sharp brown eyes regard me from beneath a scarred left eyebrow, the flaw a white slice through his mahogany skin. His leather armor is covered by a tabard bearing my sigil, the phoenix and dragon. "Your Highness?"

Sterling points to the wrapping that covered the gift. "Find anyone who saw this package arrive. Who delivered it, when, and on whose orders."

"Yes, Your Highness." I catch the slight widening of Fitz's eyes as they sweep over the diamonds. "We'll begin immediately."

Agnar Kerrin arrives next, a little out of breath and with sweat glistening on his battle-scarred face. Coppery hair flows untamed around his broad shoulders as he scans us from head to toe. Once he reassures himself we're both unharmed, a relieved smile softens his mouth. This man is like a brother to Sterling. Closer even, considering they served as soldiers together.

His smile quickly fades when he takes in the rest of the scene.

"Well," he rakes a hand through his unruly hair, "that's not something you see every day. If those are the kinds of gifts you get, it's almost enough to convince me to get married."

Leesa and Bastian enter together with linked hands that quickly separate once they see the assembled group. Leesa's dark golden blond waves bounce as she hurries to my side. My adoptive sister and the half-brother I've only met this year make the perfect couple. Their love produces adorable displays of affection and lots of blushing on Leesa's part.

"What happened?" Her olive complexion pales as she surveys the diamond-littered floor. "Are those real?"

"Very." I nudge a gem with my toe. The icy chill seeps through my leather slippers. "And no one knows where they came from."

Astrid Fleming slips in last, quietly and efficiently as always. Her honey brown eyes miss nothing as she absorbs the situation.

I raise an eyebrow, but she shakes her head, sending her short chestnut waves flying. As my personal scribe and assistant, Astrid is the one who catalogued all the delivered presents. Yet even she has no idea who's responsible for this particular present.

"The servants report no unusual deliveries." Fitz returns from his initial inquiries. "No packages, no messengers."

"The sentries?" Sterling's voice is tight.

"Nothing, Your Highness. No strangers approached the palace today."

I examine the diamonds again as the chill from my feet spreads to the rest of my body. "So whatever...whoever...sent this either has access to the palace or—"

"Or can bypass our security entirely." Sterling's lower lip curls in.

I address Astrid. "Whatever this is, it started out as water and recoiled from Sterling's magic. Almost as if it were sentient."

Sterling's eyebrows dip. "Before transforming into these,"

he gestures at the diamonds, "I got the sense that the water was aware."

Bastian squats to examine a handful of stones with troubled hazel eyes. "This isn't just complex magic. This is impossible magic."

"Who could afford to gift this many diamonds?" That's Agnar, practical as always. "Assuming they're real, we could buy everything we need to rebuild a few countries. Or have three hells of a wild party."

"They're real." Leesa and I speak simultaneously. My adoptive mother—Leesa's birth mother—taught us how to identify genuine gemstones.

My chest aches. Her death is still fresh in my mind. Another casualty racked up by King Xenon. Thanks to his relentless quest for power, Leesa will forever bear the scars of killing our mother while under the drachen's influence.

Astrid steps forward and picks up one of the larger diamonds. She examines the gem, then places it on the floor. A small flame appears on her fingertip, which she touches to the stone. The diamond absorbs the heat without changing. "Real. And this small pile is worth more than some small kingdoms."

Bastian glances at the plain wrapper discarded on the floor. "Aclaris?"

Leesa's already shaking her head before he can finish. "No, they're still recovering from King Xenon's tyrannical drachen occupation. They barely have enough to rebuild…"

Sterling nods. "They have a green provisional ruler too, and their new government is still finding its footing."

"The Free Cities?" Fitz offers.

"Collectively, maybe, but they rarely agree on anything, and I doubt they could coordinate such a gift. None of them are powerful enough for this." I sweep my arm over the glittering floor. "Their magic is practically nonexistent now."

The truth sits heavy in the room.

Tirene alone still possesses magic. Following Narc's destruction, the elemental powers in every other kingdom faded away. To kill the god and prevent his return, the eyril plants were destroyed. And without distilled eyril to bolster non-Tirenese magic, their powers are close to extinct.

I shudder, recalling how my blood dripped onto the altar where Narc's bones rested, courtesy of a drachen's talon. The scar from that shoulder wound still aches sometimes, especially whenever nightmares yank me from sleep.

Those tiny drops of dragoncaller blood were enough to revive him. Give him flesh.

Once I found my phoenix fire, buried deep inside me, I managed to purge the land of his taint. He died in the process...or something like that. The details of that night feel like a distant dream.

Freedom from corruption came at a price—the loss of other people's magic. A price I never meant to exact when I destroyed the eyril to eliminate the drachen.

Even so, I'd do it all over again in a heartbeat to rid the world of Narc and his hideous monsters.

"That leaves us with no suspects," Sterling crosses his arms over his chest, "and impossible magic."

"Someone is clearly eager to show us they can do the impossible. That's not a gift. That's a threat." I bend down to sweep my fingers across the stones. They remain cold, as if they've been buried in ice for centuries. "Something much bigger than diamond waterfalls is happening here."

"Agreed. We'll quarantine this room until we know more." Sterling addresses the captain. "Double the guard rotations. No one enters or exits the palace without being verified by at least two guards who personally know them. Every package is to be inspected before being brought inside the palace."

"Yes, Your Highness."

"And these," Sterling gestures at the gems, "remain here until we determine whether they're safe."

"Safe?" Agnar raises an eyebrow. "They're diamonds."

"Diamonds that were water mere minutes ago. Water that left nothing wet. And they're still cold." I wave a fire-wreathed hand over them. "We don't know what they'll be in twenty minutes."

Guards are summoned to seal off the room. As we leave, Leesa studies the diamonds with a mixture of awe and fear. "They're beautiful."

"So are many other deadly things."

We stride down the long corridor, flanked by open windows that allow the crisp winter wind to chase away the staleness. Sterling sticks beside me. Agnar, Bastian, and Leesa follow. Captain Fitz and his guards form a protective barrier around us all.

City sounds echo through the open windows and partially repaired palace walls. Market vendors call their wares. Children laugh. These are the everyday noises of a kingdom at peace.

Then angry shouting reaches our ears.

"Now magic is gone in all the lands but Tirene?" The voice rises in pitch, trembling with outrage. "Such inequities! The gods despair at the imbalance."

I pause at a window to peer down at the crowd gathered around a thin man in a dark robe.

His arms wave wildly as he preaches to the growing audience. "The old ways are forgotten. The balance is broken. How can any kingdom survive when Tirene hoards magic?"

The crowd murmurs in response, some nodding, others shaking their heads and arguing. Even from this distance, the tension is palpable.

The warm hand Sterling places on my shoulder steadies

me. "Don't worry about him. People always find ways to blame others for their unhappiness."

My chest feels tight, constricted by the weight of desperate decisions. Guilt writhes in my gut.

"What else were we to do?" I'm not really asking Sterling, but the universe itself. "Let Narc's evil seep into the land? Let him and Xenon and the drachen take over and corrupt us all?"

Sterling says nothing. Probably because there's no answer that doesn't somehow taste of ash.

We continue walking, and eventually the city's hum swallows the preacher's voice. Every day, the fallout from our victory becomes clearer. People are growing more desperate. Angry. Scared. A world without magic, save for one kingdom, is a world fundamentally altered. The balance of power has shifted.

The patter of running feet breaks the quiet.

A woman in the simple gray, tunic-like dress of a temple acolyte races up the stairs, nearly tripping on the length of her drab garb. Her face, young and nondescript, is flushed with exertion, or maybe fear. Guards draw their swords, moving to intercept her, but she falls to her knees before they can reach her.

"Your Majesties!" The words are torn from her throat between desperate gulps of air.

Beside me, Sterling's silver wings snap out, as if he's preparing to take flight at the first mention of bad news.

Alarm needles my scalp as I release his hand and step forward. "What is it? What's happened?"

The acolyte's eyes are wide with terror, and her hands shake as she raises them in supplication. "The Victory Goddesses' temple. The stone warrior statues. They've come alive!"

Agnar's eyebrows nearly meet his hairline, disbelief plain on his handsome face. "Alive?"

The woman nods while drawing in ragged breaths. "They're attacking people. The stone moves like flesh, but it's impenetrable. Swords shatter against the warriors, and they feel no pain." Her voice breaks. "Everyone is dying!"

The blood drains from my face. This is no coincidence. First the strange water that resists magic and transforms into diamonds, and now stone statues coming to life.

There must be a connection.

Horror floods my veins with ice water. Reaching into the pocket of my dress, I open the hidden slit, withdraw the short sword strapped beneath my gown, and expand my wings. "Agnar, assemble the guards. Have a few of them gather medical supplies and meet us at the Victory Goddesses' temple."

Time to defend our city against a brand-new threat.

I can only pray this one is easier to eliminate than the drachen.

Chapter Three
Lark

Less than fifteen minutes later, the Victory Goddesses' temple rises from the horizon on the far side of capitol. The structure is just barely visible with the heightened eyesight I acquire when my wings are out.

As soon as I focus in, I wish I could retract my wings and clamp my now-golden eyes shut to block out the devastation.

Red streaks the white marble steps and walls, and debris litters the ground.

No, not debris. *Carnage.*

My heart pounds as I put on a burst of speed. Below us, people run around like scattered ants, the chilly winter air carrying their screams upward.

When I spot a massive entity moving within the crowd, my heart ceases beating entirely.

"Sterling!" I shout over the wind. "Look!"

Sterling's jaw drops as he surveys the scene. "What in the three hells?"

Gleaming copper-colored feathers enter my field of vision as Agnar appears at my other side. Captain Fitz and his guards assume a protective formation around us.

As we approach, the picture sharpens.

Ziva save us.

The massive stone warriors sculpted centuries ago that stand outside the temple walls and symbolize the Victory Goddesses' protection have come alive.

Granite limbs swing with speed and precision, cutting into the fleeing crowd like a scythe through wheat.

"The military should be right behind us." In the face of such chaos, the words feel hollow. "The healers too."

As we descend, a man unfurls his wings and attempts to soar upward. A giant fist immediately knocks him from the sky, and he plummets to the road below.

"Fuck," Sterling growls.

My thoughts exactly. Help might be on the way, but we can't wait.

People are dying.

As we near the destruction, the primal, raw-throated shrieks grow louder. They mingle with a harsh, stone-on-stone scraping noise that sets my teeth on edge.

The smell hits me next.

Dust, blood, and fear. A combination that flares my nostrils and stirs the magic beneath my skin. The reek of battle.

We take care to land well beyond the monsters' reach. The temple courtyard stretches before us, the pristine white marble steps now slick with blood. Bodies lie crumpled at unnatural angles. Some twitch, reaching out with feeble limbs as we pass. Others are deathly still.

A knot forms in my throat.

"This isn't right." My voice cracks. "The Victory Goddesses always choose glory over bloodshed. They're fierce but fair and favor honorable combat."

Agnar tucks his copper wings in tight behind him and draws his sword. "Maybe someone needs to remind them, then, because they seem pretty bloodthirsty to me." We watch a stone warrior pursue a group of fleeing pilgrims.

A thunderous crack rattles the earth.

With our weapons raised, we whirl as one to find another stone warrior shuddering to life. Then another. Cracks spiderweb across their immense bodies as the warriors wrench free of the pedestals that served as their centuries-old posts.

The ground trembles beneath my feet as the stone giants leap off those pedestals. Dust cascades everywhere. A fresh wave of shrieks pierces the air as townsfolk scatter in renewed panic.

Stone fists the size of newborn foals smash into the temple's outer walls. Shattered masonry rains down and pelts the ground.

Another warrior stomps forward and backhands a knot of armed townsfolk escaping for the town gates. Their bodies fly through the air like broken dolls.

"Get inside!" Sterling gestures to the absconding crowds. "Any building! They're only attacking people they can see."

Huddling against a vendor's cart, a mother clutches an infant to her chest and clings to a toddler's hand. The father stands in front of his family, protecting them with his own body as a warrior pivots toward them.

Somehow, its featureless face manages to radiate malice.

The man attacks with strong air magic, but the powerful gust does nothing to slow the monster.

Heat rushes from my blood to my skin, and I thrust my hands forward. A blazing torrent of fire streams from my fingertips. The inferno strikes the warrior square in the chest, the heat so intense that it draws sweat to my own face.

I hold my breath as the warrior staggers, my flames licking across its granite body.

Please, please, please...

The creature doesn't fall.

23

Instead, it swings toward me, blank eyes now gleaming with pinpricks of starlight arranged in patterns similar to those in the diamond waterfalls.

"Look at its eyes!" Sterling lunges forward, his hands slicing through the air to summon his water magic.

A stream disgorges, hammering the warrior with the force of a battering ram. The warrior totters backward, off-balance from the sudden pressure.

Sterling's face contorts into a grimace I've never seen before. He stumbles, nearly losing his footing, and the water stream falters. "Something's not right. The water, it's—"

"No! Stay back!" Agnar's horrified shout cuts through the battle, and the note of raw fear freezes my bones.

I spin, and for a moment, I can't process what I'm seeing.

As Kaida takes off, a small figure squirms free from the enormous pack of emergency supplies on the ground. I was so intent on the stone warriors wreaking havoc, I didn't even notice the black and blue dragon land.

Tousled blond hair flies as Rose skips into the gore-splattered street.

Directly into the path of an advancing stone warrior.

The flame over her shoulder flickers merrily, as if unaware of the impending danger.

"Rose!" I shout. "Watch out!"

I launch into a desperate sprint, already knowing I'm too far away to reach her in time. As I race toward her, I grasp for my dragonbond and convey my terror to Kaida. He turns mid-flight and heads back toward the battle.

The warrior raises a wicked blade, the edge glinting above Rose's head.

Her eyes, though wide, stay oddly calm.

Then something happens that almost stops me in my tracks.

The flame familiar that hovers over Rose's shoulder, that

tiny sprite of living fire that follows her everywhere, suddenly expands. With an explosive burst, a shield of protective flames cocoons the child and blazes upward like a miniature inferno.

The stone warrior recoils.

Where the flames touch its arm, the stone thins and becomes almost transparent, revealing a void beneath. Not flesh or machinery, but a hollow space brimming with starlight and shadow.

Just like its eyes.

Rose remains motionless in the center of her fiery shield, her small face eerily peaceful amid the chaos. "They're stone and yet not." She speaks with that same serene tone she's often used since I freed her from corruption with my phoenix fire, like an old soul trapped in a little girl's body.

Sterling rushes to my side, his face pale with exertion. He aims his magic and creates a dome of water around Rose.

Instead of extinguishing her own personal flame, the fire expands to fill the dome, creating a shimmering, comingled barrier of water and blaze that shouldn't be possible.

Another warrior lunges for the barrier.

The moment the stone fist strikes the water-fire shield, the creature rears back as if scalded. Cracks zigzag across its exterior, revealing more of that starlit void beneath.

"Get her out of here!" I pivot to find Agnar waylaid by two stone soldiers as he struggles to reach Rose.

"Can't." He's battling both at once, his blade sparking against their giant bodies. "She's safer with us than trying to run." He ducks under a giant arm. "Fancy a merge? Earth and fire together should smash these fuckers."

Merging magic strengthens the elements beyond their individual power. Merging also allows for blended types of elemental attacks. That's how I managed to destroy Narc mid-resurrection.

That and my phoenix fire.

"Not yet!" Sterling's strained voice interrupts us.

My heart seizes when I see the expression on his face. Pain mixed with confusion and more than a hint of fear.

"Are you hurt?"

My sense of foreboding rises when I watch him create a massive wall of water between a group of fleeing townspeople and their pursuers.

What's he doing? Ice would form a much better barrier. And his water is moving strangely, almost sluggishly. Sections are shimmering.

Temporarily leaving Agnar to fight on his own, I battle my way to Sterling's side, dispatching an attacker with a concussive blast of fire. "What's wrong?"

At first, he doesn't respond. The statue before him stumbles back, crushed by a torrent of water. Sterling stares down at his hands in horror.

They look normal enough to me. Strong and calloused from years of swordplay. "Sterling?"

"The water." His wild eyes connect with mine. "It no longer belongs to me."

Chapter Four
Sterling

The second the words leave my mouth, Lark's hair catches on fire.

Not just her hair. All of her. Flames spew from her body, wreathing her in radiance. The fire devours one of the massive stone assholes and lights the dust-clogged battlefield with a flash of crimson.

Yet the woman who owns my heart remains unscathed.

Her flames cradle us while she attacks. She spins a web of heat and destruction, and my gut clenches with both awe and desire.

My duchess. My warrior queen.

Lark requires no crown, or fancy gowns, or anything except herself to appear majestic. She simply *is* majestic. Every day, I think it's impossible to love her more, and then she shows me yet another reason.

She's magnificent.

If only I weren't floundering.

I dig deep inside myself for my ice magic and curse when I slam into the resistance again. The shock of losing control is akin to falling off a cliff and slamming into the ocean far below.

Since I was old enough to wield, I never once lost command of my own godsdamned element.

Until now. Can't say I'm enjoying the experience.

I batter the internal wall in an effort to reclaim my power as people continue to flee the courtyard. A hand grabs my arm, and I nearly punch Agnar's cheek before I realize who's shaking me.

Despite the dirt-streaked blood smeared all over his face, his mouth twitches. "Taking a little break while you put your honey to work? I think that crown's turning you lazy."

I can tell he's joking, but my chest tightens with guilt anyway. Lark's taken on far too much responsibility and suffered far too much because of me. First with the drachen corruption, and now this new clusterfuck with my elemental abilities.

Agnar squeezes my arm, grounding me just in time to watch an enormous stone fist swing at Lark's head.

White-hot rage courses through my veins. Instinctively, I reach for my water with every fiber of my being, only to encounter more resistance. Like someone's tampering with my element.

I grit my teeth and try again.

A cold more frigid than ice pierces me as I finally manage to tear through the internal resistance and blast the stone warrior with a water cannon.

I stumble as water crashes through the barrier like a broken dam. Relief bubbles inside me. Thank fuck. My element is back under my command.

Still, the thought of losing my power again—of losing *her* —punches me in the gut.

Keep your shit together, Barda. "This isn't just an attack."

"Sure feels like one to me," Agnar shouts as he tosses boulders at our enemy.

"They're trying to herd us."

My friend lobs another builder, this time tripping a giant. "Why?"

"I don't know why, but I do know where."

"Where?" Lark's breathless as she scans the area. Her gaze lands on Rose, still shrouded by her flame familiar, then on Kaida. The dragon lands beside the child, tucking his wings in to stand guard over her.

Seemingly satisfied that Agnar's niece is safe, Lark focuses her attention on me.

"To Valk's war shrine." She takes a beat to track where I'm pointing.

"Sure." Agnar erects a wall of earth around an advancing warrior. "Makes sense. 'Please visit our temple' doesn't have the same ring as 'Visit or die.'"

Lark and I simultaneously topple another statue with dual jets of water and flame while Rose claps her hands and giggles over my buddy's lame joke. Kaida chuffs, as if amused by the tiny human's antics.

Lark groans and gestures for us to regroup as a triangle with our backs together. "You two are insane."

Agnar and I trade a glance over her head.

"Possibly." Agnar shrugs, as if his sanity or lack thereof doesn't faze him in the slightest. "Ready to merge? We'll do more damage together."

Lark presses her mouth close to my ear. "Can you?"

My fists clench. I hate that she feels the need to give me an out...just in case I don't have my shit together yet. "Absolutely. Take the lead, Dragoncaller."

Though she grins at the title, worry clouds her hazel eyes. "Then let's do this."

Battling rising doubt, I pulse my magic until it touches

theirs. Our three-way connection energizes me, and the heady sensation swoops into my very core.

Earth, fire, and water meld together as one.

A whirlwind of red magma and molten mud immediately circle us.

Lark steps forward.

"Hit 'em hard!" Agnar points at a cluster of stone warriors, but his eyes dart to where Rose huddles next to Kaida.

Lark doesn't answer. Not with words. Instead, the boiling substance surges ahead.

Shit.

We've practiced this maneuver, but never under pressure.

The fiery mud launches at the first giant, encasing and cementing the fucker to the ground.

Disappointment rips at me, followed by worry.

That's her fire, and Agnar's earth, but no water. What the hells is going on with my abilities?

As their magical compound races past the first captured enemy, a stream of water washes over it. Both mud and stone crack and disintegrate, leaving nothing but dust behind.

I expel a relieved breath while watching the fog roll out and the stone giants crumble.

The seconds dragging by turn to minutes as I struggle to control my magic enough to keep feeding the element to Lark.

Then it's released, and I can finally breathe again. Agnar looks like he's going to pass out, but he doesn't. He sits in the middle of the courtyard, shaking his head as well as the dust off his clothes. "Temple sucks, in case you were wondering."

I shoot him a dark glare. "Tell me something I don't know."

After a short period of silence, people start poking their heads out.

Lark sways on her feet from the aftereffects of using borrowed elements. She'll also be thirsty. I'm already freezing, and I stumble as I catch her. We lean on each other while the exodus of people dwindles to a stop.

A handful return, but others call out, insisting it will be safer at Valk's shrine.

Right now, I'm happy to follow someone else's lead, because I don't have a fucking clue which path is right.

I don't even know what's happening with my own magic.

CHAPTER FIVE
ROSE

The sun looks like a big orange ball getting squished against the edge of the world. It makes the sky all pink and purple, like when I mix my paints together. Uncle Agnar holds my hand as I watch the people of the town carry their dead friends and family.

They're all floppy like my dolls when I drop them, but I'm not supposed to stare because staring is rude. My flame sprite dances over my shoulder, forming little shadows that wiggle across the ground.

"Hold still, Rosie." Uncle Agnar sounds tired, the way my papa used to when he worked too hard, back when he was still alive. "And don't look over there."

Oops. Too late.

I already saw the carts with all the dead people. Arms and hands hang off the sides as if they're trying to wave goodbye. I know what that means.

It means they're never coming back.

Uncle Agnar said my papa got killed trying to save me from the drachen. Then Lark saved me after I was corr-up-ted.

Even though she's the queen now, I usually just call her

Lark. She claims she's still the same person and doesn't care about fancy titles anyway.

Uncle Agnar scolded me when I told him how I'd crawled into the big leather pack and hid after hearing one of the guards say he was sending supplies to the battle zone. Knox tried to appear stern, too, but I could tell he wanted to smile.

Lark just sighed, shook her head, and hugged me.

"We'll send aid from the capital." Lark sounds soft but strong at the same time. "Food, medicine, whatever's needed."

"Absolutely." Knox rotates his huge silvery wings before rolling his neck from side to side. "They'll need grain too."

I tug free from Uncle Agnar's grip, and my flame sprite drifts closer to my ear, tickling me. I giggle, but nobody notices because they're all busy talking about important adult stuff.

Lark nods. "We'll make sure they have enough."

Bored, I pull out the rocks I found before Uncle Agnar grabbed my hand and refused to let me go. He was so angry with me after the loud fight that I hid them in my skirt pockets.

Now, I flip the rocks and rub my fingers over them.

They're not regular rocks. They're smooth and have all these neat shiny lines running through them, as if tiny lightning bolts are trapped inside. I stack them, one on top of the other, to build a little tower.

"The town well's intact, at least." Uncle Agnar points to the spot beside him, silently instructing me to stay put before he pivots to talk to the others.

"Look." I hold up one of the stones so it catches the last bit of sunlight. "They're pretty inside. They glow like swimming stars."

Uncle Agnar spins around fast. When he sees what I'm playing with, his eyes get really big, and his face does that thing where his eyebrows scrunch together.

"Rose! You don't know where those things have been." He scoops them up and drops them into a pouch attached to his belt. "Hands out."

I show him my palms and...oops. They're dirty and sparkly with dust from the stones. Uncle Agnar strides over to the well, motioning for me to follow. He pulls up a full bucket, pours water over my hands, and then tells me to scrub them together.

I'm sad as I watch the glittery bits wash away. "Is that stuff bad?"

"Could be."

Which is grown-up talk for, "yes, but I don't want to scare you."

After I've cleaned my hands, Uncle Agnar uses the wooden ladle hanging on the side of the well to scoop up more water. He drinks so quickly that water runs down his chin and neck, and he swallows with these funny gulping sounds that make me giggle.

He passes the ladle to Lark, who seems just as thirsty as my uncle. Her fingers are long and pretty, even with dirt under her nails and that red cut across her knuckle.

The skin beneath her eyes looks purple, like maybe she's tired. Her legs wobble when she hands the ladle back too. I want to shout, "sit down," but I know for a fact that adults don't usually like it when kids tell them what to do.

Knox doesn't move at all. He stands all stiff and straight. Just like the soldiers do when they line up in rows in the town square and stare ahead at nothing while other people yell orders.

My stomach wobbles a little. I don't like the way he's standing there. It's as if someone turned him into a statue.

"Sterling." Lark's voice when she says his name reminds me of how soft Mama's used to be sometimes when she talked to Papa. Especially when she thought they were alone.

"You said something about your water magic not working right?"

I rub my chest. I try not to think about Papa too much because it hurts my heart and makes me miss him even more. Whenever that happens, Mama gets even sadder.

Knox's shoulders jerk before he shrugs. "Everything's okay. Just difficult to focus with animated stone warriors trying to bash in your skull."

Uncle Agnar grunts as he pulls his tunic over his head and stands with a naked chest in front of the gods and everyone. He uses his tunic to wipe sweat off his face and neck.

Mama would be so mad at him if she were here.

"Can't say we don't know how to have a good time." Uncle Agnar sounds tired too.

Knox gives a little nod, but he's looking at something far away. A big cliff with a building on top. "The fun never ends in Tirene."

My nose wrinkles. I'm pretty sure this is one of those times when adults say one thing but mean another, because I don't see how getting attacked by giant statues would be very much fun.

Lark glances up at Knox. "What do you think?"

"I think I'm pissed off."

I pipe up. "Uh oh. If Mama heard me say that, she'd wash my mouth out with soap."

Knox smiles at me. "Sorry, pipsqueak."

"S'okay."

Lark tucks a loose strand of hair behind my ear before turning back to Knox. "I think we should talk to some gods."

Excitement bubbles inside me. "Talk to gods? Real gods? You can do that?" I've only ever seen the little statues of gods in our house and the big ones at the temple. Mama says gods are always watching from way up above, but I never knew we could talk to them in person.

Lark lifts a shoulder. "I don't know yet, but I think we should try."

"Agreed." Uncle Agnar narrows his eyes as he stares at the broken wall where the bad statues came from. "At the very least, we need to inform the Victory Goddesses of what's happened."

Sterling peers up at the cliff again. "Pretty sure they already know."

"But we don't have confirmation yet." Lark sounds a little like my teacher when she's trying to make a point. "And we need that."

"I've got the goddesses." My uncle puts his dirty tunic back on, which is kind of gross since he wiped his sweat all over it. "Stone is my thing, and their stone warriors created this mess."

The pink and purple sky catches my eye. I love those colors. I sigh as they change to dark blue and leave only a thin line of orange behind where the sun vanished. The darker the sky becomes, the brighter my flame sprite glows. People in town always stare at me now, but I like having my sprite. I don't have to be scared of the dark anymore.

"We should also try to talk to Valk and get the little one back to the palace." Lark glances at me with kind eyes. "It's getting late."

"I'm not tired," I fib. My eyes feel heavy, and my belly keeps grumbling, but I'm glad I didn't miss the excitement.

Uncle Agnar reaches for my hand again. "Time to go, Rosie. Your mama will skin me alive if I don't get you back soon."

"Can I come with you to talk to the goddesses?" I clap my hands together and round my eyes. "Please? I'll be super quiet. I promise."

He studies my face for a moment before groaning. "Fine, but you're not to say a word. Understand?"

I slap my hand over my mouth and nod, laughing when he snorts.

My giggles soon stop. "Uncle Agnar, are the gods mad at us? Is that why the stone warriors attacked?"

"Don't worry about that, Rosie. The grown-ups will sort it out."

"But you'll beat the bad people, right? You, Lark, and Knox?"

Uncle Agnar smiles, a real smile that pushes his cheeks up and crinkles the corners of his eyes. "That's the plan, little one. That's always the plan."

Feeling better, my belly unclenches a little.

If Uncle Agnar says they'll beat the bad people, then they will.

He never breaks promises, not even small ones like bringing me candy from the palace kitchens or telling me an extra bedtime story.

My flame sprite dances in the air, creating circles of light. I'm no longer as scared.

Uncle Agnar and his friends will fix everything.

He promised.

~

Lark

Rose, blissfully unaware of the weight of our fears, dances among the night-blooming flowers, her flame flickering brightly as if to combat the encroaching darkness.

The temple's ruins stretch before Sterling and me, dark and foreboding against the night sky. Crumbled stone walls jut into the air like broken teeth. After a quick discussion with Agnar and Sterling, we all agreed not to head down to Valk's temple where people are still recovering. Summoning the gods is best done in privacy and solitude, because Ziva only knows what could go wrong.

The trip back to the palace goes on the back burner for now. I kneel beside Sterling and clutch tufts of grass, a desperate prayer lodged in my throat as I gaze toward the remnants of what was once a sacred place of worship.

"Valk, Goddess of War. We need your guidance."

Rose's familiar illuminates the girl's small form as if she's a flicker of hope meandering through the remnants.

At the far edge of the destruction, Agnar rests his hand on one of the few remaining pillars. He bows his head, still pleading to the Victory Goddesses.

I wish I could bridge the distance between us and eradicate the shadows that threaten to swallow our faith whole.

"Come on, Valk." Sterling dips his head, too, his tone laced with urgency. Rose begins to hum softly, her sweet voice weaving through the layers of desperation and tension.

Still, as the night thickens, so does my doubt. What if our prayers go unanswered? What if our goddesses see us as nothing more than tiny specks of dust in the wind? As just another set of insignificant voices to add to the cacophony of prayers from the rest of the city?

The air shifts, charged with an unworldly energy that raises the fine hairs on the back of my neck. I barely have time to exchange a glance with Sterling before she materializes.

A wispy, ethereal figure shimmers like heat haze in the summer. Full armor covers Valk from the ridge of her helm to the pointed metal boots on her feet. Not a single inch of flesh shows, and vibrant red light glows from the eye-slit in her helmet.

I want to call out, to explain, to implore her for understanding, but before I can gather my thoughts, her imperious voice slices through the night.

"Well, what do you want me to do? It wasn't *my* shrine."

Sterling stiffens. "No, but—"

"Humans can pray to whomever they choose, however weak those gods or goddesses may be. Isn't that what you want?" Her unearthly gaze shifts to Rose. "Silence that child."

I jerk, heart galloping. Rose appears confused and hurt by the goddess's words, and a spark of anger flares to life in my chest.

I glance at Sterling. We both know the divine have their own set of rules, their own terrifying reasons and codes. "The stone warriors were driving people toward your shrine—"

"How dare you question godly matters, mortal. Know your place." Valk's words stab me with unexpected fury before she vanishes into the shadows.

The uneasy silence that follows vibrates with our confusion and disbelief. Sterling and I stare at each other, both reeling from the sheer audacity of the goddess's dismissal.

"That was about as helpful as a spear to the eye," Sterling grumbles.

As I pivot toward Rose, I notice Agnar heading toward us, his long limbs moving with purpose. My stomach sinks at his grave expression.

When he finally reaches us, I'm afraid I already know the answer before I even ask. "Well? What did they say?"

He runs a hand through his coppery hair and directs a flimsy smile at his niece. "Both goddesses showed up... eventually. I tried to explain what happened at the temple, but they claimed they already knew."

"And didn't care?" Storm clouds gather on Sterling's handsome face as he surveys the damage.

"They cared...I think. But they were dismissive. Like politicians dodging questions." Agnar shakes his head, frustration burning bright in his cerulean eyes. "Belda recited their mantra a few times, 'We seek only glory, not conflict,' which was fun. Eventually, Fennelsa cut in with, 'We have no comment on today's events.' Like I was some damned chronicle-keeper or something."

Rose interrupts by raising a bouquet of flowers. Her familiar glows above her shoulder, casting strange shadows on her face.

"Look, Uncle Agnar!" She beams. "I picked them for you."

My heart warms at the sight.

For a moment, the weight of our fears feels distant, replaced by the simple joy of a child who gives without expectation. Agnar makes a big show of thanking Rose for the flowers and asks her to hold on to them until we get back to the palace.

An ache stirs within me at the stakes we face. "If the celestial attacks are directed at mortals, we're in big trouble. Even if this has nothing at all to do with mortals, we're still in big trouble."

Agnar clucks his tongue. "Your pep talks could still use some work."

I elbow him in the ribs before crossing my arms over my chest and gazing out across the sky. Near the horizon, the shadows deepen. "Either way, waiting for the next disaster isn't an option."

Agnar nods his agreement, but Sterling's attention fixes on Rose, who's tilted her head back all the way to peer up at the sky.

Her wide blue eyes reflect the starlight as she sighs. "The stars are swimming."

A chill creeps into my bones. No one has any idea what she means, but I can't shake the feeling that she senses things the rest of us miss.

I hesitate before asking the question. "Is that a bad thing or a good thing?"

Rose sighs again. "I don't know yet."

CHAPTER SIX
LARK

Arguing voices echo down the winding stairwell of the Council Tower as I climb, my boots scuffing against a surface worn smooth by centuries of footsteps. I'm not even there yet, but my temples already throb from the tangle of overlapping complaints.

Another day, another crisis. Lucky me.

Though yesterday's crisis involved a grisly attack by murderous, animated statues, so at least dealing with cantankerous council members is several notches down on the scale of horrific things.

For the most part.

Sterling and Agnar trail at my heels, deep in discussion about proper sword technique.

"Because the Northern Grip gives you better control during the backswing." Sterling curves his fingers in demonstration. The early afternoon sun streaming through the arrow slits illuminates his profile, highlighting the sexy but oh-so-stubborn set of his jaw.

Agnar's scoff bounces off the walls. "Only if you want to

41

proclaim your next move to everyone in the kingdom." He mimes an exaggerated sword swing. "Southern Grip. Always. Unless you enjoy getting gutted."

Sterling's mouth quirks up at one corner. "That explains a lot. Exactly the sort of opinion I'd expect from someone who breaks in his riding boots by wearing them into battle. In the rain. Against the corrupted."

"They were perfectly broken in by the time the fight was over, during which I was too busy to even notice my feet." Agnar's grin reveals a hint of white teeth. "At least I don't spend twenty minutes folding a map into tiny precise squares. Tell me, do you align the creases by constellation or compass point?"

"Neither." The silky edge in Sterling's voice warns me to brace myself for something spectacularly vulgar. "I organize them by your mother's—"

"Enough! What are we, nine?" I tsk at them like a disappointed instructor. "It's a matter of personal style. Each of you should use the grip that works best for you."

By shoving open the heavy oak doors, I undoubtedly cut off one of Sterling's foul-mouthed defenses of his meticulous map-folding system.

Secretly, though, I think there's something endearing about his need for order in a fundamentally chaotic world.

When the doors swing open, the debate about swordplay techniques is forgotten. Flames crackle in the hearths of twin fireplaces, saturating the drafty space with cozy warmth. Two of the large windows are cracked open for ventilation. Candles flicker from low-hanging chandeliers and a few ever-lights glow from sporadic lanterns, shedding ample light on the papers scattered across the large round table. Though the chamber lacks the rest of the palace's grandeur, the space is comfortable and efficient.

The six council members sitting at the table shift to face us, their expressions holding varying degrees of amusement that quickly morph into composed deference.

Wonderful. They probably heard every word of our conversation...particularly the part where I cut off Sterling's commentary about Agnar's mother by scolding them like a pair of schoolboys.

Duchess Breann Farlow smiles first. A thin woman with hair that recently turned more white than gray, the duchess has been in my corner since my arrival in Tirene. Rafe Bennett just shakes his head. A lock of wavy brown hair topples over one eye as he directs a pointed look at the two men beside me, basically confirming that the merchant guild master and the rest of the council overheard our conversation.

Nira Vipert arranges the skirt of her stunning burgundy gown and leans in to whisper to the man beside her. Always impeccably dressed, the beautiful woman resembles a queen more than I do considering I opted for a cream-colored tunic, black breeches, and my short sword.

After yesterday's battle, I decided against wearing another dress.

Though I've visited this room many times over the past four months, I still envision the faces of the council members who betrayed us whenever I walk inside.

Not because I feel bad—I firmly believe that the world is a better place with those three gone. It's just a shame that their passing also stole my grandfather and the dowager queen.

My chest aches at the sight of those empty chairs. Queen Alannah can never be replaced. We haven't filled the other spots yet, though Bastian, who's standing near the windows, is a welcome presence due to his extensive knowledge of the archives and the kingdom's history.

I slide into an open seat as Sterling rounds the table, briefly running his hand across the back of what was once his mother's chair, the one covered with thick cushions and closest to the fire. He quickly represses the flicker of pain on his face, a spasm of grief that squeezes my heart.

I recognize that look. I've worn it myself on too many occasions.

While the chamber holds its usual mix of afternoon light and lingering shadows, today's air feels heavier, charged with tension that needles my skin.

"Your Majesty." Ever the gentleman, Fenton Wick greets me with a polite smile that deepens the wrinkles around his eyes. "We were just discussing yesterday's attack."

I nod to him, then glance at Agnar. "Please give the council a full report."

Agnar sinks into an empty seat across from me. "As most of you have heard, we were assaulted by the warrior statues. One moment they were stone, and the next they were moving and fighting. We were at the Victory Goddesses' temple when one came alive, tearing free of the wall to walk like a man. Then the cursed thing started smashing any human it could reach. Weapons were ineffective and just skittered off the surface without even chipping them."

"What of magic?" Other than a raised eyebrow, Dalya Ungar's face reveals no hint of emotion. Over the last several months, the unshakable magenta-haired woman has proven to be a voice of reason many times over.

"Water had minimal effect, though Crown Prince Knox's first attack seemed to knock one back momentarily." Official meetings are usually the only time Agnar calls Sterling by his first name. "It wasn't until Queen Lark unleashed her fire that we started to see results. The flames revealed something strange beneath their facades...some sort of light that resembled distant stars."

We agreed beforehand not to share that Rose's flame

familiar revealed that oddity. If at all possible, we want to keep her out of the discussion entirely.

Duke Bron Dolf leans forward, a swoosh of blond hair falling across the young noble's forehead. He bats it away with an impatient hand. "I've heard of such things happening in the Northern Kingdoms."

Nira presses her lips together, her attention shifting from the duke to me. "I wonder if this relates to an ancient prophecy about walking stone."

All I can do is shrug as I try not to shudder. Gods save us from any more prophecies. I've had enough destiny and fate to last several lifetimes, thank you very much.

"Crown Prince Knox," Rafe dips a quill in ink and pulls a clean piece of parchment from the stack, "was there an issue with your water magic...faltering? Tell us more."

Sterling's lips ease into his lazy smile...the one that charms people into believing every word that emerges from his sinful mouth.

I know that smile all too well.

It's a shield.

"The only issue was with stone warriors coming alive and attacking people." He leans back in his chair with practiced ease. "Fighting living stone with water is not an easy task. I'm sure you'd encounter the same difficulties with your air magic. Everything worked just fine when we merged and added Agnar's earth element."

I bite my cheek, battling the urge to rush to Sterling's defense. So far, I'm the only one who truly knows about his magic's attempts to resist him.

We're interrupted by new disturbances that waft through the open windows: the clatter of carts, shouts from merchants, and a passionate voice rising above the rest.

"Sacred springs run black in Westcliff! Only the faithful will be spared when—"

"Fucking Devoted," Rafe mutters, loud enough for me to hear.

I frown. "Devoted?"

Rafe scowls, his dark brown wings shifting with his irritation. "A cult-like group of religious zealots who've been crying about the end of the world and appeasing the gods. I've seen them in the coastal cities, but this is the first one I've heard in the capital. They must be growing in number."

"Ah, so that's what we're calling them." Ever since Tirene's first encounter with the drachen, we've all noticed the gradual rise of street preachers. Kind of annoying sometimes, but considering we were fighting against the remnants of a dead god—Narc—who wanted to control the entire world's population, the newfound devotion is understandable.

Strange times tend to prompt people to seek answers and help from a greater power. Even I prayed more during that time period than ever before.

In fact, I met several gods face-to-face. Those experiences still feel like fever dreams some days. "What do they want?"

"Fear." Dalya isn't one to mince words. "They spread fear and collect coin from the frightened masses."

So, probably not an urgent concern compared to our other issues. Though I still intend to instruct the guards to find out why that idiot's proselytizing so close to the palace.

I turn to Bastian, who remains by the window while quietly absorbing everything. "We need every historical record of similar divine manifestations." Then I address the council. "And I want scouts positioned near all major temples in Tirene to report any unusual activity."

The council members nod. Across the table, Sterling rises, striding to the window to speak to my brother in hushed tones. Bastian's eyebrows lift, and then he nods.

When I try to catch Sterling's attention, he gives me a brief shake of his head.

Another secret. Another thread I'll need to pluck at later.

"There's more, Your Majesty." Bron tugs my focus back to the council. "Reports of other strange events happening across Tirene."

"What kind of events?" I already dread the answer.

"Guardian cave cats spotted roaming beyond their usual territories." Duchess Breann glances at the shadow in the corner, as if concerned she might find Nyc eavesdropping on our discussion about the goddess's sacred animals.

Or who knows, maybe Breann's hoping the goddess will respond.

"Northern villagers report that it seems more like prowling." Nira points to little colored flags marking the map of Tirene on the wall. "Though none have complained of any attacks. Not even against livestock."

Bron gestures to the papers in front of him. "Then there's the matter of the lost items."

"Lost items?" I cock my head.

"Yes." The young duke scratches his chin. "A spate of long-lost objects, missing for years, have suddenly reappeared in their owners' homes."

I frown. "That seems odd but harmless. The return of missing items? Isn't that a good thing?"

Duchess Breann dabs at her nose with a handkerchief. "They claim the God of Lost Things is including messages with the items. Divine messages."

Sterling returns to his seat. "What kinds of messages?"

The council members exchange glances.

Bron sighs, impatience tightening his features. "One scholar reports that his quill now writes on its own when left unattended. Strange sayings like, 'Even stars die.' A merchant reports a valuable ledger where the numbers rearrange themselves to form words when moonlight hits the page.

'Count your prayers as you do your coin. Riches await...or beggary.'"

Ziva's flames, that's bizarre.

But is it harmless? Or ominous?

Are the gods assisting us after we helped them? Or should we consider these communications threats?

The duke shuffles some papers before continuing. "In consequence, the merchant has made a substantial donation to his local shrine, money his family simply cannot afford to give. Odder still, people have begun throwing valuable items into temple wells and fountains, hoping for some celestial response. Like children tossing coins in a wishing well."

"Except they're throwing in family heirlooms and precious vessels." Fenton shakes his head, and his gray curls bounce. "And then everyone fights over the returned items, claiming they belong to their family. An entire black market has sprung up for 'divine lost things.'"

Rafe's caramel-colored eyes meet mine. "And the Devoted are trying to capitalize on it. Preaching about divine retribution and redistribution in the streets. They're scaring people."

Angry heat rises in my chest. "We didn't defeat Narc just to be playthings for the rest of the gods."

"Exactly." Sterling's expression hardens, mirroring my resolve. "We can't sit here while people suffer."

"If these are attacks, we need to defend ourselves." I mull over the possibilities. "If they're warnings, we need to understand the message. If they're blessings or portents, we need to be properly thankful."

Rafe crosses his arms. "Ideas?"

I wish. "I could travel to Westcliff to see these black springs myself. Or maybe—"

"Your Majesty, you cannot be wandering the countryside

with animated statues on the loose." Fenton's patronizing tone sets my teeth on edge.

"The queen will go wherever she's needed. With purpose, not wandering. No permission needed." Sterling's icy stare could freeze water. *Literally*, if he wanted. "Understood?"

Fenton blanches. "Of course, You Highness. I meant no disrespect."

I have no doubt the older man speaks the truth, that he was only worried for my safety. Sterling merely nods.

"Perhaps we should send scouts first." Nira's suggestion softens the tension in the room. "Gather more information before acting."

"While the Devoted spread their poison?" I wave to the window. "Maybe I should find one of their street preachers and—"

"Punch them in the face?" Rafe brightens as if he enjoys that idea a little too much. "Though it might not be the most diplomatic strategy, Your Majesty."

Before I can defend my not-entirely-violent intentions, the chamber doors burst open. A petite woman with papers clutched to her chest rushes in, her face flushed and her gray eyes wild. Pale blond tendrils escape a complicated updo.

It takes me a moment to recognize her as our wedding planner. Crap, what was her name again? Lady Odetta? Lady Odelia? Lady Oh-why-the-hells-can't-I-remember-her-name?

I dig through the depths of my memory and almost collapse in relief. Odessa! I'm pretty sure that's it.

"Your Majesty! Your Highness!" She gasps. "Forgive the interruption, but we have a wedding crisis."

The council members trade glances that range from amusement to irritation. Rafe coughs and ducks his head to hide a smirk while I arrange my own face into a carefully blank expression.

"The flowers you selected are now unavailable." She barely

pauses for breath. "A strange blight has withered all the flora in the Eastlands. All of them! And the pavilion tents are back-ordered because a river flooded in the South and knocked away the bridges used for deliveries!"

And here I thought there was nothing worse than sitting through an hours' long council meeting. Wedding planning with a frazzled assistant just might top that.

She flings her arms wide, sending papers fluttering. "But that's not the worst of it. I'm not sure if the wedding fountain is designed to best suit the ancient water ceremony. The royal artificers are at an impasse, and if we don't decide soon, the artisans will miss their deadline, and then where will we be?" Her voice rises to a near-wail on the final question.

I listen, first astonished, then dazed, then a little empathetic. The poor woman looks like she hasn't slept in days.

Bewilderment soon sets in. Ruined bridges sound noteworthy but not in terms of delayed flower deliveries, and is a fountain really this important? Do any of these things matter right now compared with animated statues and religious cults?

Then I remember the calamity that ensued when I refused to partake in council talks about my own coronation and bite my tongue. From here on out, I will be present for any meetings revolving around ceremonies that involve me.

I feel Sterling's stare burn into me from across the table and shoot him a warning glare that he willfully ignores.

He stands, the epitome of grace and charm. "I'll help with the water fountain." He tosses me a grin. "And the queen will too. Won't you, my love?"

I swallow the curses rising to my lips and force my eyes not to roll. In the process, I meet Agnar's gaze.

My love, Agnar mouths while tossing me a wink.

Subtly, I scratch my neck with my middle finger before

answering Sterling with faux sweetness. "Of course." I climb to my feet and circle the table, leaning over to murmur in Agnar's ear. "Guess who just got out of a council meeting? That means you get to stay and take notes for us...*my love.*"

Agnar's groan follows me as I join Sterling and our harried wedding planner by the door.

Some days, it's good to be queen.

CHAPTER SEVEN
LARK

Odessa's heels clack against the stone as she guides us down five flights of stairs and into the palace courtyard. Sterling walks beside me, and our shoulders occasionally brush. Each contact sends a familiar warmth rushing through my veins that has nothing to do with my fire magic.

Beneath the inscrutable mask, I notice the slight curve of his mouth. The bastard's entirely too pleased with himself for roping me into this.

The courtyard opens into a sprawling space that's currently being used as a workshop. Scaffolding surrounds a tiered fountain with stone cherubs perched along each level like decorations on a mutant wedding cake. Craftsmen hover around it, tools in hand, pausing their work as we approach. They bow hastily while clutching chisels and hammers.

"Your Highnesses, the fountain is nearly complete. The craftsmen have been working day and night to ensure it meets the royal standard. The Traditional Fountain of Eternal Union." Odessa heaves a happy sigh.

Sterling settles into the mask of polite interest he wears at court. Unfortunately, mine isn't half as good as his.

The craftsmen scatter, clearing a space around the fountain. Sterling approaches with the lazy confidence I've come to love and envy. His movements are unhurried yet purposeful, like he has all the time in the world but refuses to waste any second.

"If you could just fill it with water, we could make sure everything works the way it's supposed to, Your Highness." She clasps her hands together and gazes at the fountain like it's the greatest thing in the world.

I have to admit, the artistry is exquisite.

Sterling nods and positions himself. I hang back, arms crossed, watching the way his back straightens and his fingers spread. The water in the base tier stirs, responding to his presence even before he begins the formal magic.

When he raises his hands, the water leaps to obey.

The dance is beautiful. The water rises in perfect spirals, defying gravity and streaking through the air like liquid silver. It foams gently through the first tier, spelling out "Love" before regathering to climb higher.

"The first tier represents the passion and devotion that bring two souls together," the wedding planner narrates, and I cover my involuntary snort with a cough.

That earns me raised eyebrows from Odessa.

The water curves through the second tier, "Fortune," splitting into delicate arcs that intertwine before separating again.

"The second level symbolizes how prosperity and abundance flow from a harmonious union." Odessa sighs yet again, dimples popping out in her cheeks as she smiles.

Sterling's hands move with practiced grace, each gesture fluid and deliberate. His focus is absolute, his breathing measured. This is Sterling in his element, the soldier's discipline applied to artistry.

As I watch him work, my skin heats. I probably shouldn't find this hot, but I definitely do.

The water reaches the final tier, "Fertility."

Odessa mercifully skips her explanation as the water gathers above the fountain to form a shimmering sphere that hangs suspended in the air. Sunlight hits the droplets, casting prisms of color across the courtyard stones.

"Perfect!" She claps her hands together in delight, and a few of her papers go flying. "Absolutely perfect."

Except it's not.

From where I stand, I don't miss the slight tremor in Sterling's right hand or the tightness around his eyes.

Something's wrong.

Normally, he could fill a fountain with his eyes closed and his hands behind his back. No concentration necessary.

I instinctively step forward, my own magic stirring beneath my skin. Not that fire would help with this task, but the protective impulse rises anyway. Sterling and I have always been opposites. His ice and water to my fire and heat. Complementary forces.

At least, that's what the court poets say.

The sphere wobbles, its perfect form distorting for just a moment. Sterling's lips turn white, and I can tell his usual confidence is faltering. His fingers twitch as he tries to maintain the water's flow.

A sharp pang of worry shoots through me.

Is Tirene's magic fading too? The reports from some of the provinces have been troubling. Magic users losing control. Strange anomalies. But the native Tirenese have always possessed stronger magic than people born in other kingdoms. No eyril needed here.

I haven't sensed any problems with my fire magic, but as a dragoncaller, I'm not exactly the norm either.

"Sterling?" I murmur, too quietly for the wedding planner and guards to hear.

He doesn't respond, his attention fixed on the water sphere. The edges start to warp, and smooth curves become jagged. Ice crystals form dripping cascades where only water should flow. "Not again..."

My throat tightens. Again? His elemental magic is fighting him.

I position myself behind him, my muscles tensing in anticipation of needing to...what, exactly? I have no idea what's going on or how to help. My fire magic would only worsen the situation.

My gut clenches when I realize...there's absolutely nothing I can do.

Sterling extends his magic toward the crystals, clearly trying to melt them back into the water. Instead of dissolving, they pulsate with a faint inner light that appears blue at first before shifting to a purple so deep it's almost black.

Caught up in her excitement, the wedding planner misses the change in Sterling's demeanor. "Oh, I don't recall that from the manual, but it's gorgeous—"

One of the cherubs adorning the fountain turns its head with a stone-on-stone grind.

Its blank eyes fixate on us before sweeping across the gathered craftsmen. Another cherub moves, and another, until all four of them stare at the assembled crowd. The clink of crystals falling and striking each other creates a discordant tune.

Sterling's shoulders tense. "Holy shit."

Agreed.

So much for a dull afternoon full of minute wedding details.

Instinctively, I reach for the short sword at my waist. But what's the point? If weapons didn't work against the stone warriors, I doubt they'll be any more effective against the cherubs.

One cherub opens its mouth.

Instead of stone teeth, diamonds reflect the light in painfully bright flashes.

Odessa skitters backward on her heels, her composed demeanor cracking. "Oh, I don't like this." Her high-pitched tone squeaks with the beginning of panic. "Not one bit."

Preach, sister.

Fire gathers in my hands. Water or not, if those things attack, I'm incinerating them.

Raising their open palms to the sky, the cherubs begin to sing.

I flinch. Singing might be the wrong term for the jarring pitch that pours forth. As the collective screech rises and falls in words I can't understand, splinters slice through my head.

My skull vibrates.

One at a time, my ears pop.

Pressure builds in my jaw.

My nose burns, and tears prick my eyes.

Craftsmen collapse to their knees even as they try to flee. Trees twist, whether from the musical assault or to continue the supernatural attack, I can't tell.

Dread sours my stomach as I meet Sterling's eyes and see my own anxious question reflected back at me.

What now?

CHAPTER EIGHT
STERLING

Too damn many. We've experienced too damn many attacks and bizarre occurrences in a short span of time. And we still have no clue what's causing all this.

Leaves fall and spin as if there's a vortex around each tree. My stomach dips.

I grew up watching my mother use air magic, so I know how lethal it can be.

My fingers prickle as I summon my own element.

The stone cherubs writhe and twist on their pedestals. Their once-benign faces split into grins that reveal those fucked-up rows of sharp diamond teeth.

Beside me, Lark shifts her weight in a subtle movement that I've learned to read better than any battle map. I can sense her fire gathering, prickling my skin with more than just magic. Standing here, confronting an opponent we know nothing about, I should feel a lot more worried.

It's my faith in her that keeps me grounded.

Every single time. Every fight.

The woman who survived kidnapping, war, and betrayal

never fails to steal my breath when she prepares for a fight. Wrapped in shadow and flame, she's magnificent. The fire enhances the glimmering golden hues in her eyes and also her wings as they expand behind her.

Scattered across the courtyard, nobles and servants alike freeze in horror.

"Your Majesty, get back!" A guard rushes forward, sword drawn.

Useless. Steel won't help against animated stone.

The cherubs stretch to their full height. Crystals form beneath them on the tiers.

Leaves continue to spiral and lash out in all directions.

The courtyard dissolves into chaos.

Servants disperse like startled birds, their clothing flapping as they flee. Guards curb their fear to form a perimeter. The wedding planner stands paralyzed, mouth agape.

"Sterling?" Lark's voice is calm, measured. "You ready?"

I lurch forward, calling forth the water from the fountain. The fluid spirals around us, forming a translucent shield that distorts the world beyond like warped glass. "Already on it."

Lark doesn't hesitate.

She summons her fire, sending it into my water shield. The elements don't fight. They meld together in a heady rush. Fire dances over the water without extinguishing, and water encloses fire without evaporating. The combined magic hurls fractals of light across the courtyard. The brilliant patterns shimmer and pulse with our shared power.

The cherubs freeze before slowly pivoting their heads to aim their diamond-laced grins at the light show.

Stone heads tilt in unison, as if listening to music only they can hear.

"What the hells are they doing?" I mutter.

"Being creepy as fuck."

I grunt my agreement.

One of the stonemasons hired to create the monstrosities releases a scream that curdles my blood.

I track his pointing finger.

The fountain casts forming and reforming shadows that dance across the ground.

Cold, choking, unreasonable fear crawls down my spine.

Shadows writhe like living beings, like liquid darkness solidified.

Like drachen.

Memories crash over me, and a slimy sensation invades my gut.

Those vile creatures of darkness...enrapturing people with fear, leaving corruption and death in their wake. Narc controlled me, used me against my own people, against Lark. Forced me to murder innocents.

I nearly choke while swallowing down my panic and telling myself to pull it together.

The drachen are gone. Lark destroyed them months ago, along with the God of Nightmares.

Shadows are just shadows now. They can't hurt anyone ever again.

Sucking down a lungful of air, I shove aside the memories.

"Everyone stay within the shield." I circle my free hand, drawing more water from the fountain. The liquid responds by spiraling around each cherub like transparent snakes. With a flick of my wrist, I drop the temperature and freeze them in cocoons of ice.

Relief washes through me as my magic works exactly as intended.

About damn time.

The cherubs fall back to their pedestals, still somehow singing through their diamond teeth in a high scraping sound akin to grinding crystal.

Shadows arrange themselves in symbols that begin to glow.

The air crackles with the energy of an approaching thunderstorm, the scent of magic rising.

I check on Lark to ensure she's okay.

Her golden gaze meets mine, and in that instant, we hold an entire conversation without words. We've fought together enough times to understand each other's intentions.

My water magic surges through the fountain again, not fighting the crystals, but flowing around them, containing them. The crystalline formations beginning to grow from the cherubs' icy prisons shudder. They try to spread, but they're trapped in shells of swirling water that I control.

My muscles strain with effort.

Sweat beads on my forehead despite the chilly temperature. Despite the cold emanating from my palms.

Lark calls up precise bursts of fire, not to destroy but to illuminate. Her flames prance along her arms, curling from her fingertips in tight, controlled spirals. The fierce flare catches in my water spheres. Prisms form, spilling radiant rainbow fragments across the courtyard.

The cherubs' song wavers. Their diamond teeth begin to crack.

"It's working." I can't explain how I know. The magic just feels right, like a puzzle piece clicking into place.

Confusion blooms behind Lark's determined expression. She intensifies her fire, careful to work with me, and the flames within my water create beautiful and complex patterns.

All the cherubs fall silent.

Their teeth dissolve into ordinary stone. Twisted shadows snap back to natural angles. The crystal formations inside my water spheres melt away, leaving nothing but ordinary fountain water that splashes to the ground when I release my hold.

"Well, I don't," Odessa clutches her papers to her chest, "know how I feel about that!"

I keep my face impassive. Flexing my fingers, I stretch out the stiffness from channeling so much magic.

"Did you see it?" Rafe's voice spins us around. He stands at the courtyard entrance, his tall frame silhouetted against the palace hallway. His sharp gaze takes in the scene—the frozen cherubs, the scattered nobles and craftsmen now cautiously returning, the guards still at attention—and then snaps to Lark. "Did you see the shadows?"

Good to know I wasn't losing my damn mind.

Lark's face falls. "What shadows?"

Odessa edges forward, eyes wide with alarm. "Shadows? Surely, you don't mean..."

"No, not drachen." Rafe gives the near-hysterical wedding planner his version of a reassuring smile before gesturing to us. "If you'll excuse us, I need to have a word with the queen and crown prince."

"Of course." Odessa wrestles her stack of papers into control and turns to Lark. "We'll meet again later?"

"Can't wait," Lark lies as she retracts her wings and pats the short sword at her side, as if confirming her weapon is still there. "We really appreciate all that you're doing. We trust your judgment. So depending on what else comes up in the next few days, if we're not able to meet for a while, just keep doing what you're doing. Thanks to you, the wedding will be fabulous."

Beaming at Lark's praise, the wedding planner scurries away.

Rafe crosses his arms. "Before you dealt with the cherubs, the shadows were spelling words."

Lark rubs her temples, and I read the weariness in her eyes. "What words?"

"'Follow the signs.'" Rafe's chin juts forward with the importance of this revelation.

Lark's eyes widen. "That's it. That's what's happening. The gods are leaving us breadcrumbs. Not attacks, but messages."

"Or maybe messages along with attacks." I gesture toward the frozen cherubs. Those diamond teeth seemed plenty capable of piercing flesh.

Around us, the courtyard begins to return to normalcy. Guards escort shaken nobles back to their quarters, and servants rush in to clean up the damage.

Face set with grim determination, Lark addresses Rafe. "We need to document every strange occurrence, no matter how small. The gods are trying to communicate through chaos. Or hurt us through it. I'm going to try to reach out to some directly."

～

Lark

I slip out to my private patio holding a small open flame in my palm. Sterling waits inside. Nyc, the Goddess of Night, has spoken to me several times, but never where he can hear.

The crisp night air carries the scent of damp earth and distant gardens. My fingers trace the cool railing as I climb the narrow stairs to my private rooftop balcony. Tonight, I need answers, and there's only one being I know who might provide them.

The royal guard stationed at the top of the stairs stiffens at my approach. Even in darkness, his training is impeccable.

"Your Highness." He bows and begins to back away. "I'll give you privacy."

I nod, grateful for his discretion. "Thank you."

He vanishes into the sky, leaving me alone beneath the vast expanse of stars.

I move to the center of the balcony, where the stone is worn smooth from years of use. Though I brought nothing to sacrifice, I plan to try contacting the goddess anyway.

Snuffing the flame in my hand, I let the darkness wrap around me like an old friend.

"Nyc, I seek your guidance."

Usually, when the Goddess of Night answers, there's a peculiar warmth to the darkness. A contradiction that makes perfect sense in the moment, like the comfort of the womb. Her presence feels like a smile you can't see but somehow know is there.

Tonight, something's different.

The darkness coils around me, carrying an inexplicable sense of wrongness. There's a frigidness that has nothing to do with temperature. A sharpness in what should be soft.

I fight the urge to pull back and break the connection. "Nyc? Will you heed my call for clarity?"

The darkness around me tightens, and I sense her presence crystallize. But the soothing warmth I've come to expect is absent, replaced by something that has my skin crawling.

"The old alliances shift." Her voice whispers directly into my mind, and each word scrapes like broken glass across my thoughts. It's nothing like her usual velvety tone. "Choose carefully where you stand, mortal queen."

The words themselves unsettle me enough, but it's the cold contempt behind them that stutters my heart. Nyc has expressed her frustration with me before, particularly over my failures to destroy her son Narc's bones during my first few attempts.

But this...isn't frustration.

This feels more like a threat from someone who used to be an ally.

My hand presses against my temple, where a dull ache has taken root. What just happened? What did she mean by old alliances? And why would the goddess who's guided me, however reluctantly at times, now treat me like an enemy?

Calling flames to both hands, I unfurl my wings and jump down.

Retreating to inside the palace seems like the safest option.

Just like hiding under my blanket kept me safe from monsters in my childhood bedchamber.

Right after my feet hit the ground, the door to the patio swings open with a soft creak. Sterling's silhouette fills the opening.

"What's wrong?" He stares at the twin flames I'm using to keep the darkness at bay.

I blink, still trying to process what just happened. "Nyc. She was...different. Cold." My fingers tremble, and I clench them into fists. "She threatened me."

"What did she say?" He doesn't reach for me, instead maintaining that careful distance he reserves for times like this. As if the soldier in him needs to assess the situation before acting.

I shake my head and repeat Nyc's message. "As if she expects me to pick a side in some conflict I don't even understand. Is she telling me to choose between magic users and those without power? In that case, of course I'll pick magic. I'm Tirenese. I don't want us to lose the magic we still have."

Sterling remains quiet for a long moment.

The silence stretches between us, filled with unspoken concerns.

"Speaking of magic, mine has been...different." Those capable, strong hands that have held both swords and my body with equal care flex and relax. "Not just difficult to control.

More like it's actively resisting me. Like it's already been commandeered or pre-claimed by something else."

This, I understand.

As a dragoncaller, I've wrestled control of fire from other users before. Even dragons. Dragonfire flames are heavier and denser than what humans can channel. Wielding them is like trying to divert a river. This rare skill marks me as unusually powerful and dangerous.

Still, the idea that someone or something could do the same to Sterling, whose control over water has always been exceptional? That thought terrifies me.

"Why didn't you tell me?" I try to keep the tremor of hurt from my voice, but when his jaw tightens, I know I've failed.

Sterling's shoulders tense in a barely perceptible motion that speaks volumes. "Because I didn't want to worry you. Because I thought maybe I was imagining things." He shifts to face me with a glimmer of vulnerability in his eyes. "Because I didn't want to admit that something could take my magic from me."

The admission costs him.

For Sterling, control is everything. Control of his emotions, his magic, his kingdom. To have that threatened must shake the very foundation of who he believes himself to be.

Hot, fierce protective instinct flares inside me.

I close the distance between us, wrapping my arms around his waist and pressing my face into his chest. His steady heartbeat soothes the worries still racing through my mind.

"We'll figure it out. Track down answers. We'll question everyone." I pull back just enough to meet his eyes, allowing my own determination to show. "No one gets to take from you what the gods have given."

Sterling tips his chin down, his mouth quirking in that half-smile I love so much, the one that transforms his serious face by softening the hard edges. "Now that sounds like my queen."

His strong arms cocoon me. In this embrace, the threat of Nyc's warning feels temporarily distant, though not completely forgotten.

Something is happening in our world. Something that affects even the gods and our relationship with elemental magic.

CHAPTER NINE
STERLING

I stare at the map until my eyes burn, as if I can somehow force the red wax markers to rearrange themselves into a pattern that makes sense with the power of my mind. Over the last five days, we realized we needed more than just our original map of Tirene. We had to dig through storage to find a map of the entire known world, which I've pinned on the wall in front of me.

I'm drowning in reports of bizarre occurrences with no obvious connections.

Aclaris and Kamor on the continent to the south. The Havens and Meridia to the east. Tír Ríoga, Northern Volox, and the Withered Undulations on the continent north of Tirene. And so many around our capital that the paper is completely covered.

The candles in the council chamber have burned low, their flames casting long shadows across my kingdom, my responsibility. I roll another ball of wax between my fingers, letting my magic warm it just enough to become malleable without melting.

The heavy oak door creaks open behind me, and I know

who's entered without looking. The purposeful yet quiet footsteps belong to Sterling. Even with my back to him, my body's viscerally aware of his presence.

"Find any patterns yet?"

"If by patterns, you mean absolute chaos and no answers, then yes. We have lots of those." I gesture at the map with wax-sticky fingers. "I'm starting to think the gods are just rolling dice with us."

I pivot to find him balancing a stack of scrolls, his face partially hidden behind the pile. Even after everything we've been through, my heart performs the same ridiculous jump as always.

"Temple attacks here and here." I point to red markers near our western borders. "Water behaving oddly there." My finger traces the coastal regions. "And reports of strange star patterns visible only from this mountain pass." I tap a spot in the northeastern reaches of Tirene.

Sterling sets the scrolls on the table before coming to stand beside me. "You missed one." He reaches past me, his sleeve brushing mine as he indicates an unmarked spot. "One of the scouts just arrived. The white stags of Aurora Grove have turned obsidian black."

"What?" I blink. "That's—"

His mouth quirks. "Impossible? Like water flowing uphill or temple doors sealing themselves shut with no one inside?"

"Every temple official Rafe and I spoke with this week had the same sort of stories. Such strangeness, and no clear response from the gods." I rake my fingers through my hair, unable to summon energy to care about any traces of red wax I'm leaving behind. "Something must be connecting these events. If we understand what the gods want, maybe we can put a stop to all of this."

Sterling studies the map in silence, his expressive brown eyes narrowed in concentration. The shadows highlight his high cheekbones and square jaw. He stands perfectly still, the way he often does when thinking.

"I've sent messengers to the temples of Aletheia and Cyphero." Unable to remain still any longer, I begin to pace. Outside, the weather is chilly and the gray clouds covering the sun cast the room in gloom. "If anyone might give us straight answers, it's the Goddess of Light and Truth or the God of Hidden Knowledge."

Sterling's eyes track me, his stillness a contrast to my restless motion. "And if they don't?"

"Then we keep pushing until someone breaks." I cross to where I left my pack earlier and grab the worn leather strap. "I'm going to head out and speak to—"

The doors to the chamber swing open. Rafe enters first, his thick eyebrows drawn together. The remaining council members drift in behind him like a reluctant tide, their faces a mix of determination and exhaustion that probably mirror my own.

"Your Highness." Rafe nods at me, then Sterling. "We're ready to discuss supply lines for the Southern Shore reinforcements."

Repressing a groan, I release my grip on my satchel. Another three hours, at minimum, of debating stone quality and labor distribution when more urgent matters demand attention. But the barriers require strengthening before the spring storms hit mere months from now.

Royal duty never ends.

I bite back a groan and force my features into polite interest.

Sterling shifts beside me. "Unfortunately, Lark and I have another engagement."

Hope springs to life. He could tell me he's taking me to count ants as they parade in and out of their colony and I'd gladly agree. Anything to get me out of this room for a while.

I manage a serious nod. "Yes, very important. Can't be rescheduled."

Before anyone can question us further, Leesa pops her dark golden blond head through the open doorway. Perfect timing.

Suspiciously so.

"Sorry to interrupt, but Lark, that important appointment..." She pauses for dramatic effect, and I almost snort. "You and Knox? Remember?"

I fight a smile as I arrange my features into an expression of dismay. "I completely lost track of time. My sincerest apologies, council members, but this particular matter..."

To my utter surprise, they all nod in understanding. Every last one of them.

Rafe waves a dismissive hand. "No problem, Your Highness. We'll handle preliminary discussions and present options tomorrow."

Relief floods through me as I gather my things, trying not to appear too eager to escape. Placing a hand on the small of my back, Sterling guides me to the exit. As always, the casual gesture spreads warmth across my skin.

"What is our oh so important appointment?" I whisper as the chamber doors close behind us.

Leesa falls into step with us as we descend the staircase. "Flowers."

Sterling's low laughter echoes. "Flowers?"

"Yes. Flowers." Leesa grins. "The palace gardens are in full winter bloom, and if we don't select the arrangements for the wedding and coronation soon, the royal gardener might collapse from anxiety. Bastian's there with him, to keep him calm."

I glance at Sterling, finding his amused gaze already on me. "Well, we can't have that on our conscience now, can we?"

"Definitely not." Leesa nudges my shoulder. "See? And

here you thought it was a waste to use all those earth elementals to resuscitate the gardens so quickly after the fire."

I huff. "Not sure the need for wedding flowers changes my mind. Although, on second thought, if it prevents another Odessa freak out, then it was definitely worth the effort."

As we stroll toward the gardens, I can't help but nibble my lip as an image of red marks with no discernable pattern on a map reappears in my mind. The mystery of bizarre occurrences continues, and somewhere in Tirene, white stags have become black. But for the moment, apparently, we must focus on flowers.

I shake off the persistent sense of unease.

Honestly? Flowers sound wonderful right about now.

≈

Lark

Past the vine- and moss-covered stone wall, the royal gardens sprawl in artful wildness, a choreographed chaos of color and scent that's somehow both overwhelming and perfectly balanced.

Sunlight filters through the ornamental fruit trees and umberhearts, dappling the cobblestone path with shifting patterns that remind me of that stupid map.

With annoyance, I push the thought away.

For just one afternoon, I want to slip free from the weight of the kingdom on my shoulders. I want to think about something beautiful and hopeful instead of ugly and ominous.

The royal guards trail us at a respectful distance, their weapons at the ready despite the peaceful setting. Elijah Durand's presence among them is still strange when I stop to think about it. Not that long ago, when we were both students at Flighthaven Academy, the Aclarian noble hated me and strove to make my life miserable.

How things have changed.

"What do you think of these?" Leesa stops to admire a cluster of bluish purple blooms that tumble over a trellis. Her fingers hover just above the petals, not quite touching. "They'd make gorgeous centerpieces draped over little stands. Like colorful waterfalls."

I tilt my head, contemplating. "I'm familiar with those. They're beautiful, but aren't they the ones that caused half the court to sneeze uncontrollably?"

"I've heard that was at last year's reception for the Southshore delegates." Bastian chimes in with a small smirk. "The head cook still complains about all the plates that went back untouched."

"Right. Let's avoid flowers that might clear the room before we finish our vows." Sterling moves beside me with that fluid grace that always reminds me of a predator, though his expression remains soft as he surveys the flora.

A royal gardener hovers nearby, practically vibrating with anticipation. Shaggy brown hair that curls around the edges, brown eyes, and a brown beard blend right in with his dirt-stained apron. He's nearly as tall and broad as Agnar.

"What do you think about these, Henry?" I point to a cluster of elegant white blossoms with golden centers reminiscent of stars against a night sky. "They're lovely."

"An excellent choice, Your Highness." Henry comes forward eagerly, brushing his work-roughened hands against his apron. "Midnight Stars. They symbolize hope and new beginnings."

"Perfect for a coronation and wedding." Leesa grazes her lips over her knuckles and peruses another cluster of flowers. "Though we'll need something with more color to balance them."

I glance at Sterling, who's studying a crimson bloom nearby. "These would look beautiful in your hair, Sterling." I pluck one and hold it up to his shiny dark locks.

His mouth twitches. "I was thinking for my beard."

Leesa raises an eyebrow. "You don't have a beard."

Sterling swipes a thoughtful hand over his jaw. "I'm considering one for the coronation."

I try to picture him with facial hair and find myself smiling. "I don't know if I'd recognize you."

"That's part of the appeal." His voice drops lower, intended only for me. "Sometimes it's good to be unrecognizable."

At his tone, a strange shiver dances over my skin.

"What about including some of the Fusion Root Vine?" Bastian gestures toward a section of the garden where we replanted the peculiar flowers we rescued from the dowager queen's garden. The color gradient of their petals shifts from deep purple to ebony streaked with blood-red, and their velvety leaves dance in the faintest breeze. "It would be a fitting nod to past events."

My mind flashes to Dowager Queen Alannah, and my chest squeezes. Sterling's mother will be missed for a very long time. I can envision her tending to the sometimes-fractious flower, and I ponder how important it became to our success in merging elements. "Isn't that a waste? They're so useful for medicine. Fevers, dehydration, merging...seems frivolous to use them for decoration."

"The flowers and the medicinal parts are different." Bastian is the one who did all the research after my grandfather's death, so he would know. "The blooms could be harvested without harming the rest of the plants."

The thought of featuring the delicate flowers in the wedding brings a smile to my face. "That would be—"

Muffled shouts echo from beyond the far side of the gardens.

Sterling tenses beside me, his relaxed demeanor vanishing in an instant. His hand drifts toward the dagger at his waist.

"What now?" Leesa sighs, and a wariness appears in her eyes that wasn't there a moment ago.

Without discussion, we head for the commotion, the royal guards closing ranks around us. Elijah's hand rests on his sword hilt, his fingers flexing as if eager for trouble.

If I were trouble and Elijah had that gleam in his eye, I'd fucking run. Even though I know he's on my side now, I'm still sometimes leery of the burly brown-haired guard.

Several guards fly ahead, but Sterling, Bastian, and I remain on foot with Leesa and Elijah.

On the far side of the gardens, just outside the walls, lies Viridian's temple, a structure unlike any other in Tirene.

Verdant vines and flowering plants that shouldn't thrive together drape the walls on all sides in a living blanket. Where most temples are built of stone and wood, Viridian's sanctuaries grow, constantly shifting, renewing, dying, and being reborn in endless cycles that mirror the goddess's domain.

Two massive drakewood trees frame the entrance, their trunks gnarled with age, the branches reaching upward before curving to intertwine above the doorway. Water trickles down the bark, feeding the moss and ferns that carpet the ground beneath.

On a normal day, this place emanates tranquility.

Today, it resembles the center of a brewing storm.

In front of the temple doors, the voices of a growing crowd rise in a jumble of concern and accusation.

A short man with more hair on his face than his head stands at the forefront, his finger jabbing at the vines. "They're moving on their own! The patterns changed overnight. Tell me that's normal."

I nudge my way forward, the crowd parting when they recognize their queen and crown prince. Murmurs of "Your Majesty" ripple outward like stones dropped in still water.

Now I can see what's caused the disturbance.

Across the temple's moss-covered walls, water flows upward in weird, deliberate patterns. The paths seem to form words.

In a language I don't understand.

A middle-aged priestess hurries out from inside, her robes dyed a vibrant green at the shoulders and a rich earthy brown at the hem. Her expression flickers with genuine alarm. "They're just water stains. The goddess blessing her plants. It's nothing to worry about."

"Then why are they changing?" An older man with the calloused hands of a craftsman leans closer. "And why do the vines move to cover them when too many people gather? Why are they forming messages—"

"There are no messages!" The priestess steps back toward the open doorway. When her eyes dart to me, they widen in recognition. Before I can address her, she retreats inside, slamming the door shut with a finality that silences the crowd.

Briefly.

"Water?" Sterling kneels to examine the markings where they pulse between unfurling leaves. His fingers hover just above the surface, not quite touching, and I can sense the chill of his magic reaching out.

I crouch beside him. "What is it?"

He shakes his head, brow furrowed. "I don't know. But it's deliberate. This water is moving against gravity."

I study the wall where the water flows. If the marks once spelled out words, they no longer do. Instead, they appear exactly as the priestess said. Like water stains.

Still, the patterns seem almost familiar. A distorted reflection of something I should recognize.

Once again, a hush falls over the crowd. A small cluster of people in dark cloaks slithers up the garden path, their faces obscured by deep hoods. The crowd parts for them, some with expressions of interest, others with unmistakable distrust.

"The gods weep." The other cloaked figures nod with the speaker in unison, the motion eerily synchronized in a manner that prickles the hairs on my neck. "These are their tears."

"Street preachers," Bastian mutters. "The Devoted."

Leesa leans closer to me. "See their hands?"

I follow her gaze and catch what I'd missed before. They have matching tattoos on the backs of their hands, constellations that trail up their wrists before disappearing beneath their billowing sleeves.

"Ah." Sterling's lip curls in disgust. "It's them."

One of them lunges forward, his voice rising above the murmurs. "I see the divine tears. The gods weep for our arrogance. For keeping magic while other kingdoms go without. And what are the royals of Tirene doing about—"

"Oh, shut it." A man in the crowd shakes his fist. "You see divine tears in every puddle. Viri brings the cycles of life, not your doom prophecies!"

The air vibrates with tension.

Instinctively, I lurch forward.

Sterling catches my arm. "Watch the water marks."

I focus on the temple wall again, and goose bumps skitter down my spine.

As the argument heats up, the water stains appear to... respond. They ripple and shift, like a lake surface disturbed by a passing breeze.

The patterns elongate, contract, and rearrange...as if trying to form words before dissolving back into randomness.

I keep my eyes locked on the strange sight. "That's not something you see every day."

Sterling's fingers tighten on my arm. "It's magic. But not like any I've ever felt."

The crowd grows louder, their collective anger mounting.

One of the Devoted pushes ahead, his star-marked hand raised in accusation. "The gods are calling us to account! They've sent signs throughout Tirene—"

"The only sign I see is that you lot need to find proper work instead of scaring the shit out of people!" a woman shouts back.

What happens next unfolds in heartbeats.

The Devoted member lunges at the woman. Someone else shoves back. Bodies collide, tempers flare, and the peaceful temple grounds erupt into pandemonium.

Elijah and the royal guards lurch forward, creating a barrier between me and the scuffle.

Behind them, I glimpse the temple guards reluctantly intervening, their living armor of woven vines and bark flexing with each action. They seem hesitant to engage, as if they'd rather retreat inside with their priestess.

A wisp of flame curls from my fingertips, and the crowd freezes. "Enough!"

Sterling stalks forward, exuding dangerous power. "Now. Take your grievances to the proper channels."

Slowly, begrudgingly, the crowd thins, with most dipping their heads to their queen and crown prince.

The Devoted retreat last. Their leader's intense eyes find mine before he turns away, the constellation on his hand shimmering in the afternoon light.

"Did you see?" Leesa whispers beside me. "When the fight broke out, the water looked like it was trying to spell something."

Tension tautens my muscles. "I saw."

77

My gaze returns to the temple wall where the water marks have once again settled into innocuous stains.

Another bizarre event in a series of oddities, yet we still have no clue what any of this means.

Or what we need to do to stop it.

∼

Lark

By the time Sterling and I return to the now quiet temple, night has fallen. The paths are deserted except for the occasional guard.

Agnar accompanies us, his tall frame providing additional security. "The priestess wouldn't let anyone in after the disturbance. Said the temple needed to rest and heal from the negative energy."

I study the living walls in the moonlight as a crisp breeze ruffles my hair. The water stains changed again. The patterns disappeared, leaving only ordinary moisture marks. More tellingly, the temple's plants have shifted since the afternoon, the vines and leaves growing to cover the exposed areas.

Sterling paces the length of the wall. "This temple is definitely hiding something."

We study the structure for another long moment before retreating for the palace.

"It's almost like someone's trying to communicate with us." I'm glad I wasn't alone when I saw the patterns. Otherwise, I would think I was losing my grip on reality. How many other witnessed miracles go unreported because people fear no one will believe them?

Agnar's battle-scarred face is solemn. I guess even he takes dispatches from the gods seriously. "And someone else is making very sure we can't read the messages."

Who could be strong enough to do that?

"The water felt like it was being pulled in two directions. Like two users fighting for control. With that kind of strength, it has to be the gods." Sterling stops at the palace entrance and waits for the guards to open the doors with practiced efficiency.

Inside, warmth and light await, but the comfort feels hollow compared to my growing anxiety. "I think it's time to see if the reports are true and find out if this is happening in other kingdoms."

Sterling's expression hardens. "If it's just Tirene, that tells us one thing. If it's everywhere..."

He doesn't finish the thought. He doesn't need to.

"We need allies and information."

The flowers and wedding plans will have to wait. I won't feel safe until we understand what the gods are trying to communicate...and who's trying to silence them.

CHAPTER TEN
ROSE

I press my nose against the big window in Lark and Knox's sitting room, leaving smeary marks that someone will probably lecture me for later. But I don't care because dragons. Dragons are in the courtyard!

Their scales catch sunlight and turn it all kinds of colors. Like when Lady Rhiann let me play in the jewelry box and I accidentally spilled all the pretty sparkly necklaces and earrings. Mama says I'm "not to be left alone." Which is silly because I'm already six and can take care of myself.

That's why I'm here watching Lark and everyone get ready for their important trip.

My flame—it doesn't have a name yet because it's still deciding—hovers over my shoulder and makes tiny glittery circles in the air. Uncle Agnar says most people don't get familiars. He says it's special, like me.

I may not have my wings yet, or elemental magic, but at least I have something no one else does.

"Rose, get your face off the glass." Uncle Agnar scolds me without even looking. I swear, he has eyes in the back of his head.

I rub away the smudge with my sleeve. "How long 'til you come back?"

Uncle Agnar counts the swords laid out on the large table. He picks each one up, swishes the blade through the air, and puts it back down again. "Five, maybe six days if the negotiations take longer. Shouldn't be more than a week."

"That's forever." I huff and flop onto a giant chair. My feet can't reach the floor, so my legs stick straight out. My flame zooms around my head, trailing light behind it.

On the other side of the room, Knox holds a piece of paper. "Thirty-seven waterskins. Twelve tents, winter-weight. Fifty rations of dried meat."

Bastian nods. He resembles Lark, with the same hazel eyes and shiny brown hair, only his chin is pointier. "I've doubled the blankets. The mountains of Tír Ríoga are colder this time of year."

Blah blah blah. Blankets and tents are boring.

I slide off my chair and tiptoe closer to where Lark is talking with Councilor Bennett, who usually looks like he just ate something sour. "The Northern Passage will be guarded by six of our strongest air wielders. We've stationed lookouts at various intervals."

My flame friend drifts toward them, just as curious.

"And the contingency plans if we're separated?" Lark's voice is quieter than the others', but I can still hear her just fine.

"Rendezvous at the Eastern Ridge." The councilor studies a big scroll on the table, tracing the words with his finger. "I've briefed every guard personally."

"Excellent." Lark strides over to Sterling and whispers in his ear. He grins before whispering something back that turns her cheeks red.

I love looking at Lark. Her wings are tucked away now, but I've seen them when they're out, and they're so pretty.

The dark brown feathers have burgundy streaks and little bits of gold.

She only got her wings in the last year. I really hope I don't have to wait that long for mine.

She notices me staring and smiles. "Hey there, Rose."

I feel like I just swallowed sunshine. "Hi."

Lady Leesa calls out from across the room and holds up cloaks. "Lark, do you think the blue or the green will be more appropriate for the welcome ceremony?"

The green cape is so dark it's almost black and has little shiny pieces sewn all over it. The blue one has fuzzy bits around the collar that would probably tickle your chin.

Queen Lark points at the green one. "The blue doesn't look very warm."

Leesa nods and folds the green cape carefully.

My eyes wander the room for something to do until I spot my uncle by a table of bows and arrows. He pulls each bowstring until it twangs and then checks every arrow.

I creep over and watch him work. "Can I help?"

His brow crinkles. "These aren't toys, Rosie."

"I know that." I roll my eyes. "I'm not a baby."

Uncle Agnar's mouth twitches like he wants to smile. "Hand me that polish, then."

I pass him the little jar, and he dips a cloth inside before rubbing it over a curved piece of metal on one of the bows. The sharp odor wrinkles my nose. "Will you have to shoot anyone?"

"I hope not. This is a diplomatic mission, which means we're trying to make friends. But we always prepare for trouble, just in case."

I nod like I understand, but I don't.

Whenever I try to make new friends, I don't take a bow and arrows just in case I have to shoot them.

Adults are weird sometimes.

I squeal at the sound of dragon wings flapping outside the window. More dragons are landing in the courtyard, their riders jumping off and leading them to others.

"Where's Dame?" Even though Lark is one of the few people she lets close to her, Dame is my favorite dragon. She's a reddish-brown color, sort of like the glossy flower vase my mama bought at the market.

"Probably in her cave." Knox is so tall I have to tilt my head way back to see his face. "Her eggs are about to hatch."

"Baby dragons!" I bounce on my toes. "Can I see them when they do?"

Knox ruffles my hair. "Perhaps. If Dame allows it."

I gather all my courage and take a deep breath. "I want to come with you to Tír Ríoga."

The room gets extra quiet, the way it does when I drop something breakable.

Knox stares at me for a long, long moment. "You're very brave, Rose." Something in his voice leads me to believe he might actually say yes.

My heart beats faster. My flame familiar glows bright with hope.

But then Lark steps forward, shaking her head. "I'm sorry, Rose, but there won't be other children there."

A lump clogs my throat. "But I'm brave! Knox just said so!"

"You are incredibly brave." Lark kneels down so her eyes are level with mine. "But Tír Ríoga is most likely going to end up being terribly boring. The negotiations themselves could become...complicated. Which means we'll do nothing but sit around, listening to people complain for days and days." She sighs, her shoulders drooping. "I don't even want to go, and I'm the one who set this all up."

Knox's eyes soften. "Lark is right, little warrior. Perhaps another time."

My flame familiar dims, sharing in my disappointment.

I glance at Uncle Agnar, hoping he'll take my side, but he crosses his arms and gives me *the look*. "In. No. Uncertain. Terms. You are not coming on a sensitive diplomatic mission. I've got to watch over these two. I can't watch over you too."

He stares straight at me, and I stare right back. Just because I'm not allowed to doesn't mean...

"And if you try to stow away again, I'll pluck you out of the saddlebag myself and drop you mid-air."

I gasp, and the flame flickers. "You would not!"

"Try me." Uncle Agnar's eye twitches.

My flame familiar pulses sharp and bright, like it's saying bad words in fire language.

"You're joking." I narrow my eyes and point at him. "You're just worried about me."

Uncle Agnar's eyebrows shoot up so high they almost touch his hair. "Of course I'm worried about you. You're six!"

"Six and three-quarters." I put my hands on my hips like Mama does when she's correcting him. "And I came through phoenix fire, remember?"

The twitch near his eye gets bigger. "Yes, and you nearly gave everyone heart failure!"

Everyone's looking at me now. Leesa's smiling behind her hand. Bastian glances at me and coughs before staring at his feet. Queen Lark's gentle eyes make me feel worse about getting mad at her.

I stick my nose in the air and spin around. "Well, I'm not worried at all. And neither is my familiar."

My flame brightens and shows off by doing a little loop-de-loop.

"Have a nice boring trip without me." I stomp toward the door. "I'll just stay here and do boring things like...like eating cake and playing with Dame's babies when they hatch."

Uncle Agnar chokes a little. I bet his face is all scrunchy. I skip out of the room, my familiar trailing golden sparkles behind me.

Maybe I *will* check the packs in the dragon enclosure. Just to see if there's enough room for a six-and-three-quarters-year-old girl who's good at holding her breath and staying quiet.

Uncle Agnar can't drop me mid-air if he never finds me.

~

Sterling

I pause at the threshold of our bedchamber, my hand still on the ornate door handle. The space is about the same size as the sitting room, with wall-to-ceiling windows and a door that leads to the private patio. Two giant chandeliers hang overhead, and a large fireplace spans one wall to keep the chill at bay on crisp winter nights.

The unexpected sight before me prompts me to halt my stride at the two cushioned chairs next to the door. On the other side of the room, Lark stands ramrod straight before a potted fern that sits between her vanity and the door to the bathing chamber. Her voice is pitched in a formal cadence so unlike her normal tone.

My lips twitch with amusement, but something in the rigid set of her shoulders tugs at me. This kind of tension doesn't belong in our private sanctuary.

"Furthermore, the crown must consider the long-term implications for our agricultural interests." She nods her head to the indifferent plant, each syllable weighted with practiced solemnity. Her hands move in stiff, rehearsed gestures that seem borrowed from the court advisors rather than flowing from her natural grace.

This is a side of my queen I've never witnessed.

My Lark, fierce dragoncaller, savior of the realm, the

woman who once set an entire battlefield ablaze with her fire magic when she was cornered, is practicing courtly speech on a houseplant.

"The delegation will expect precise accounting of the Southeastern Border Patrols." She drops into what I recognize as an imitation of Lord Dunfell's self-important drone.

The smile pulling at my mouth fades as quickly as it forms.

Understanding settles in my chest. Politics, where words become weapons and smiles turn sinister, holds its own danger. It's a battlefield where you can never truly know what the other party has planned. And Lark, for all her strength, has always hated the diplomatic side of governing.

She lifts a silver-handled hairbrush from the vanity. "Your Excellency, Tirene appreciates your gracious hospitality and looks forward to strengthening the bonds between our nations."

I can't watch this anymore.

Stepping fully into the room, I allow the door to close behind me with a soft click. "I'm sure the hairbrush is thrilled over your consideration of its trade concerns."

Lark whirls, clutching the brush to her chest like a shield. Her face flushes crimson, and her eyes widen with mortification. "Sterling! How long have you—"

"Long enough." I cross over to her, my footfalls heavy on the thick rugs.

"I was just..." She makes a vague gesture with the hairbrush before dropping her hand with a defeated sigh.

"Practicing being someone else?" I reach out and gently extract the hairbrush from her grip. When my fingers graze hers, a familiar jolt of awareness zips through me. "Someone you think you need to be?" I set the brush aside.

Her shoulders slump, the formal posture dissolving like frost under the afternoon sun. "Is it that obvious?"

"Only to someone who knows exactly who you are." I

draw her into my arms. She melts into me, pressing her forehead against my chest.

"We leave tomorrow." Her exhale ruffles my shirt. "They'll expect a queen who knows how to navigate diplomacy. If I'm going to be an effective ruler, I need to be that. I need to be better than what I am."

The statement hangs between us, and unexpected anger courses through me. Not at her, but at the assholes who convinced her of such nonsense. "I wish you could see what I see when I look at you."

"And what's that?" There's a hint of defensiveness in her tone.

"A queen who leads from the front, who inspires through action rather than empty words." I slide my hands to her shoulders, admiring the latent strength in them. "A warrior who trusts, a lover who incites, a protector of people and dragons. They'll expect to meet Tirene's queen. The woman who burned the eyril field and destroyed the God of Nightmares. Not some stiff imitation of what you think royalty should be."

Her gaze drops, and I don't miss the shadows beneath her eyes, evidence of many fret-fueled nights. My heart aches at the sight.

She fists the fabric of my shirt, her warmth seeping through the material and into my skin. "What if they just think I'm some pampered noble turned queen?"

"If they think they're going to get some stiff-backed, pampered princess, then they haven't been paying attention to recent events." I lift her chin with gentle fingers. "You are exactly what the world needs, what this kingdom needs, what I need. There is not a single fucking thing I would change about you even if I could. What is it going to take for you to understand that?"

"Those are pretty words," she steps back and traces my

bottom lip with her thumb, "but I've always learned best by doing."

The desire in her beautiful hazel eyes and the silkiness of her skin against mine nearly short-circuit my brain.

I catch her thumb between my lips, sucking before I release it. "Is that a fact?"

Her breath hitches, color saturating her ivory cheeks. "Yes."

"Then I guess I'll have to show you just how perfect you are." I draw her toward the ornately carved bed, where the cool wood meets warm silk bedding.

When she follows without hesitation, my chest tightens in a familiar way. With the constant wonder that this extraordinary woman chooses me, again and again.

"Sterling." The way she says my name pulses warmth through me that has nothing to do with her fire magic.

I cradle her face with both hands and rest my forehead against hers. "Gods, yes. You are precisely what I need."

My lips meet hers in a kiss that starts soft but deepens with each heartbeat. I pour everything I cannot say into this kiss. My faith in her, my love, my unwavering belief in her strength.

"You always say the right thing." Her hands find their way to my shoulders, her fingers digging in with an urgency that matches my own. "What did I do to deserve you?"

I relish the subtle heat that always emanates from her skin when her emotions run high, the precursor to her magic flaring. In response, the coolness of my own nature rises to meet it, creating that perfect balance of fire and ice between us, with neither overwhelming the other.

"It's the other way around, Duchess." My lips dance across hers. "I'm the one who doesn't deserve you. But I'm going to spend the rest of my life striving to be worthy of your love. Worshipping you. Showing you just how perfect every inch of you really is."

"Mmm," her eyes flutter shut, "every inch of me, huh? I can't wait to learn what that entails."

"It involves tasting, sucking, kissing, pleasuring. Making you come so hard the only thing you can remember is my name as you scream it." My hands slide down her back, tracing the ridges where her wings emerge when she calls them forth. "But don't let me bore you with my pretty words."

"Smartass." She shivers at my touch, arches closer, and opens those beautiful eyes.

The desire in them—no, the need—is undeniable. It mirrors my own.

"Careful." I guide her backward until her knees hit the edge of the bed, and we sink together onto the plush surface. "Wouldn't want to have to punish you instead of worship you for that sassy mouth of yours."

"Is there a difference?"

"Keep smarting off, and you'll find out." I bite the sensitive spot where her neck meets her shoulder. Not hard enough to hurt, but enough to startle a yelp out of her.

Her silky dress rustles beneath my palms as I explore the familiar curves of her body. Every time, each touch feels like a revelation. I plant kisses along her jaw, down the elegant column of her throat, and linger at the pulse point where I can feel her heart racing.

"I need you just as you are. Not as some court-crafted version of a queen."

"Need me, hmm?" Her fingers tangle in my hair, guiding my mouth back to hers. "So you've said. Why don't you stop talking and show me?"

I smile against her lips. This is my Lark. Commanding even in vulnerability, fierce even in surrender. "Take my clothes off, and I will."

We quickly undress each other until we're once again nestled in the bed, my body covering hers.

"Look at me." When her eyes meet mine, I capture her gaze. "This is who you are. The woman I love. A warrior who loves without reservation, who fights despite fear, and who never backs down, even in the face of the gods. This is who Tirene needs. Not some practiced performer." Swiveling my hips, I tease her. I trail against her opening, holding back when she arches and tries to capture me.

"Sterling..." The desperate yearning in her raspy voice is all I could ever hope for.

"The way you just said my name," I stop teasing and bury myself in her, "that's how much I always need you.

She answers with a moan, and the sweet sound fuels my burning desire for her. The world narrows to just the two of us as we settle into a rhythm, our bodies moving together in perfect harmony.

Time loses meaning in the charged atmosphere of our bedchamber. Each caress is both familiar and new, an affirmation that transcends words. I watch her every motion, every gasp, every time she bites her lip or twists her head and tangles her hair against the pillows.

My love. My queen. My warrior.

This woman is everything to me.

I feel the moment she lets go, surrendering not just to pleasure but to trust. Her fire magic flares, warming the air around us as she cries out my name. Skin hot against mine, she runs her nails down my shoulder to my back.

Her body trembles underneath me, moving with my thrusts. And as always, she doesn't back down. Instead, she urges me on. Her knees clamp at my sides, body dancing upward to meet me as I follow her over the edge.

Limbs entwined, I keep her tucked to my chest while our breathing slows.

Her fingers trace idle patterns on my skin, following the

lines of old battle scars. "Do you really think they'll respect me more if I'm authentic?"

I press a kiss to her forehead. "I think they'll fear you more. And in diplomacy, that's often more valuable than respect."

As Lark nudges closer to me, I make a silent vow.

I will never let her forget the incredible woman she truly is, even when the weight of the crown threatens to reshape her.

CHAPTER ELEVEN
LARK

After flying through half of the night, the dragons we're riding bank right beneath us, their massive wings cutting through the air as we near Tír Ríoga. My knuckles whiten against the ridges of Ryu's neck, not from fear of flying—that's become as natural to me as breathing—but from the knowledge that I'll soon have to speak.

Not fight. Not strategize.

But engage in the delicate dance of diplomacy that twists my stomach like I've swallowed live eels.

The sunrise paints the snow-covered landscape below in watercolor grays and pinks. Below, the countryside unfolds like a fever dream. Prayer circles spiral outward instead of forming traditional rings, their stones arranged in patterns that hurt my eyes if I stare too long. Weathervanes spin against the wind, twirling in defiant opposition to nature's currents.

Sterling flies slightly ahead on Tanwen, the green male dragon that's often his mount. His back is rigid, his eyes fixed on an ice-covered lake we're passing. "That lake is grieving."

The words permeate the air, senseless yet somehow chilling.

No one responds.

What do you say to that?

Agnar, who's flying to my right, stops checking the pack strapped to Nailah, an orange and yellow female dragon, long enough to capture my attention. His eyebrows lift in a silent question.

I give a tiny shrug in response. What can I do?

Agnar forces a laugh. "You sound like Rose. She's been saying the trees are hungry and the rocks are angry. Thought it was just a child's fantasy."

Sterling blinks a few times, like he's coming up from underwater. "What? Sorry, I was..." He shakes his head. The momentary fog lifts from his eyes, replaced by the sharp intelligence I know so well. "We're nearing the capital. Remember, we need to appear both respectful and formidable."

"Yes, because bringing several dragons and a squadron of elite soldiers doesn't already demand that.'" I run a hand over Ryu's smooth scales.

Agnar snorts. "Diplomacy, Your Highness. It's all about the silent threat packaged in pretty words."

"That's why I'm terrible at it." I release a breathy sigh. "I prefer my threats loud and my actions straightforward."

We crest a small set of hills, and my breath catches in my throat. The heart of Tír Ríoga, a kingdom forged among snowcapped mountains and expansive forests, spreads before us.

"Look there." Rafe flies up to my left atop Kaida and points toward a massive black stone temple rising from a clearing.

Hundreds of people orbit it, their bodies flowing in unnaturally synchronized patterns. From this height, they're reminiscent of insects swarming around spilled honey, but there's something deeply unsettling about the precision of their movements. They rotate and shift in perfect, eerie unison.

"I've seen battle formations less precise." Agnar shakes his head in wonder, his coppery hair rippling in the wind.

As we fly closer, Ryu banks hard to the right, nearly upsetting my balance. The other dragons follow, wings stiffening as they veer away from the temple.

Sterling, who's lying low against Tanwen's neck, tenses. "What's wrong with them?"

"They're spooked." I send soothing thoughts and questions to Ryu and the rest of the dragons. None of them have a real answer other than a disturbed feeling about that place. "There's something down there they don't like."

We watch as our entire formation arcs wide around the temple, not a single dragon willing to fly directly overhead. Even the alicorns carrying the small military unit behind us veer around.

"There are more of them." Rafe points to another temple in the distance, where similar synchronized movements are taking place.

The dragons' resistance is palpable, their muscles tensed beneath our legs. Ryu actually trembles when I try to guide him back on course, so I immediately relent. I trust his instincts more than my diplomatic timetable.

Ahead lies Emraldae Keep, Tír Ríoga's capital city. Unlike Aclaris with its rigid stone structures or Tirene with its sprawling, ancient architecture, Emraldae Keep was built in harmony with the landscape. Buildings rise organically from black stone, their surfaces gleaming with inlaid precious metals that contrast with the bright white of the powdery snow-covered ground. In the center stands the Great Keep, a structure that seems to spiral upward like the prayer circles we've witnessed on a more massive scale.

"Gods." I momentarily forget my anxiety. "I forgot how beautiful it is here."

We begin our descent, the dragons angling toward the enormous courtyard where swirling patterns on black stone gradually solidify into the shape of a giant eye.

I wrinkle my nose. "And creepy."

Ryu lands with practiced grace despite his formidable size, folding his blue wings neatly against his sides. Around us, our entire diplomatic party follows suit. Four dragons with their riders, plus additional soldiers who dismount from the alicorns. We take up the entire landing area, the dragons crowding nearly half of it by themselves.

We're an imposing force by any measure. The display is meant to demonstrate both respect, in that we sent our best, and power.

The dragons, clearly enjoying the attention they're getting, arch their necks and preen slightly. Kaida huffs a small flame, showing off for the gathered Tír Ríogan guards who stand at attention around the courtyard periphery. Tanwen watches everyone, his agile mind checking for any show of disrespect among these unknown humans.

After the four of us dismount and unload our gear, the dragons take off. They'll search for a remote area to hunt while remaining close enough to still feel our connection.

From the ground, the grandeur of the city is even more overwhelming. Buildings tower above us, their glass-like black surfaces reflecting sunlight in prismatic bursts. Everything comes across as both ancient and foreign, familiar elements arranged in ways my mind struggles to process. My hands grow clammy inside my gloves.

I'm so out of my depth here, it's not even funny.

The keep's expansive doors swing open, and the king and queen of Tír Ríoga stroll down the steps. King Mihel Lennox walks with deliberate strides, rows of golden blond braids swinging and his tall, lean frame draped in garments that shift colors with every motion, like oil on water. Though the eclectic ensemble screams court jester rather than royalty at first glance, he's rocking the look like he's dressed this way all his life.

Damn. That's the kind of confidence I need.

Beside him, Queen Maeve oozes dignity and poise. She glides with fluid grace, her dark hair cascading down her back in loose waves. A velvety black cape covers the upper half of her long-sleeved crimson gown, smooth ebony skin peeking out of the high collar.

This is it.

The moment I've been dreading. I step forward, feeling every eye on me.

"Beannachtaí Tír Ríoga." I attempt the formal greeting I've spent weeks memorizing. "Nílim...nílimid..." The words tangle on my tongue. My brain knows them, but my mouth rebels. Heat rises to my cheeks.

Mihel's eyes crinkle at the corners. With amusement? Contempt? I have no idea.

I shift gears into the easier protocol I've studied from books. "Your Majesties, we bring greetings from Tirene. We are honored by your welcome and hope that our nations may find common purpose in these challenging times."

My voice sounds stiff even to my own ears, like I'm reciting a script rather than speaking. Which I am, so I guess that tracks. Sterling comes forward, adding a natural warmth to the exchange that I couldn't manage.

I watch everyone closely. Nothing can move forward until every delegate is introduced. Rafe keeps his responses tempered, thoughtful, and void of the barbed quality his voice often carries in council meetings. He stands with his feet apart, hands relaxed but visible. A stance that projects both confidence and openness.

I try to mimic the guild master's measured manner, keeping my face composed as the first part of the formalities concludes and we're welcomed to join the king and queen inside.

As we follow our hosts up the black stone steps, Sterling takes my hand and leans close. "You're not Rafe. Stop trying to be."

I nearly stumble on the steps. How did he—

"Why are you so anxious?"

My jaw drops. "Why? Oh, I don't know," I whisper. "Maybe because I'm pretending to be a queen? Or because these people probably blame us for destroying their magic? Or because I have the diplomatic skills of a hammer?"

"Just be your fiery, clever, engaging self, Lark. Not some standoffish parrot." His eyes soften. "A parrot of Rafe, for the gods' sake."

I clamp my mouth shut, anger building in response to the insult. Then I note the slight upturn at the corner of his mouth and the spark in his eyes. That was his intention. To shock me out of my rigid formality. "You're an ass."

That earns me a wink as Sterling's lips curve in a conspiratorial half-smile.

Agnar catches up, popping his head between us. "Just imagine them all naked. Works for public speaking." He wiggles his eyebrows. "Do you think the king is as well-endowed as the Tirenese? Or is this fancy city his way of overcompensating?"

"Not helping, Agnar." I groan as I picture the king and queen stripped of their finery and standing before us nude. That's an image I'll never be able to scrub from my mind.

"Okaaay," Agnar draws out the word, "then imagine they're all Rose asking you about your dragon for the hundredth time."

A reluctant laugh escapes me at the memory of little

Rose's persistent questions about Dame. "Does she sleep upside down? Can she breathe underwater? Will she make more eggs filled with baby dragons soon?"

Sterling's warm, steady hand presses against the small of my back. Ahead lies the diplomatic breakfast, the next test in what will no doubt be a challenging day.

～

Lark

The others are shown to their rooms to eat a hot meal and rest after flying much of the night. Sterling and I are expected at breakfast with the king and queen, so we quickly change our clothes before heading out to meet them.

I stand at the massive arched doorway that leads to their royal dining hall, my mind a jumble of memorized phrases and rules of etiquette. Because of course the formality doesn't end after the initial greeting. I'm so frazzled, I almost smack into the back of my chair.

In Tirene, many of the chairs have low or no backs to accommodate our wings. But these people don't have that consideration. Looking up, I spot even more differences. While the ceilings are still high, there are windows at the top that open on horizontal hinges.

Focusing on the murals painted on the walls, I take a moment to admire my surroundings rather than think about what comes next.

Hand on my arm, Sterling leans close, his breath tickling my ear. "Remember, just—"

"Be myself. I know." I mentally pat myself on the back for managing not to roll my eyes. "Easy for you to say when you were born in a court. The first time I participated in a royal setting, it was as a hostage." The part I don't need to add is that it was his brother's court, that Sterling was my abductor, and that I eventually ended up a prisoner in the palace's dungeon.

A herald announces our names and titles with elaborate flourish. I inch forward, intent on not tripping over the hem of my formal ice blue dress.

King Mihel and Queen Maeve wait at the near end of a table long enough to seat fifty but only set for about twenty. Though their smiles seem genuine enough, I've learned that royal smiles reveal precisely nothing.

I take a deep breath and attempt the traditional greeting again. "Beannaektee..." My tongue twists around the unfamiliar syllables. I try again. "Bea-natch-tay Teer Ree-oh-gah..."

Gods, I'm butchering this. Once again, heat floods my face.

Queen Maeve's dark eyes crinkle at the corners. "Beannachtaí Tír Ríoga. May our hearths warm you and our walls protect you." She makes the subtle hand gesture that accompanies the greeting. A flowing motion that mimics the spiral patterns we've seen throughout their kingdom.

While I attempt to copy the action, my hands feel clumsy and artificial. In response, I fall back into rigid protocol, holding my posture too straight and allowing my words to come out stiff and rehearsed. "We are most grateful for Your Majesties' generous hospitality and look forward to fruitful discussions regarding the mutual challenges facing our kingdoms in these unprecedented times."

If I sound like I'm reading from a diplomatic handbook, it's because mentally, I am.

Sterling steps in smoothly, guiding me toward our assigned seats with practiced ease. Under the table, his hand rests on my thigh. The simple touch grounds me despite my embarrassment.

The breakfast spread overwhelms me.

Dishes I don't recognize crowd the table. Vibrant fruits cut into intricate shapes, pastries arranged in spirals, and what appear to be fish gleaming with an iridescence I've never seen before. Crystal decanters contain liquids in improbable colors. One shifts from purple to blue as a servant pours it into goblets.

I study the others covertly, mimicking their movements with the unfamiliar utensils. There's a spoon with holes that is used solely for the fruit, and a three-pronged fork that seems designed specifically to torture foreigners.

"The Galwaen fruit is particularly succulent this season." Queen Maeve gestures to something akin to a star-shaped orange with blue speckles. "Though we've had to import it from the Southern Provinces now that our northern orchards are struggling."

I nod even though I have no idea what a Galwaen fruit is supposed to taste like.

"It's delicious," I lie after taking a cautious bite. The fruit is actually bitter and slightly metallic, but I'm not about to break diplomatic breakfast rule number one. Never insult the food.

Small talk drifts around us. Weather patterns, fashion trends in our respective kingdoms, harmless gossip about nobles none of us really care about. I maintain my careful composure, responding with appropriate affirmations and brief comments.

Sterling carries much of our side of the conversation, drawing out Queen Maeve with gentle questions about Tír Ríogan architecture that actually seem to interest her.

"Our sacred temple wolves have been acting strangely, abandoning their usual posts to patrol the city walls instead." Now Maeve has my full attention. "And our shrine eagles have been flying in bizarre patterns, making shapes in the sky we've never seen before."

I straighten right out of my rigid posture. "We've had similar occurrences in Tirene. Birds flying in formations that look…" I hesitate, not wanting to sound foolish.

"Like written languages?" King Mihel dips his head, his pale blue eyes sharp.

"Yes!" In my excitement, I realize I'm a little too loud and quickly modulate my voice. "Exactly like that. Scripts no one recognizes."

The Tír Ríogan royals share a meaningful glance.

"The temple guardians say it began the day we lost magic." The queen keeps her eyes downcast.

And there it is. The massive dragon in the room. The day I torched Narc's bones.

"I—" My practiced diplomatic apology sticks in my throat.

King Mihel raises his hand. "You need not tread carefully, Queen Lark. We understand the choice you faced. Had Narc's power continued to grow unchecked, we might all be slaves now, magic or no magic."

I blink, surprised by his candor. "Then you don't blame Tirene?"

Queen Maeve offers a smile tinged with sadness. "We are grateful you burned Narc's bones. The loss of magic is a heavy price, but to be puppets to a mad god's whims?" She shakes her head. "That would be intolerable."

Sterling's leg presses against mine under the table, silently communicating his relief. The conversation flows more easily after that, though bumpy moments still punctuate the exchanges. We discuss the strange happenings in both our kingdoms, not just animals behaving oddly, but people too.

"There's been a marked increase in territoriality." Sterling picks out a puffy pastry and puts it on his plate. "People fighting over matters they would have laughed off months ago."

"We've seen the same." King Mihel sips from his crystal goblet. "Families who've lived peacefully for generations suddenly disputing property lines...merchants squabbling over minuscule price differences."

"Fear." Queen Maeve dabs her mouth with a napkin. "When people lose something they've relied on their entire lives, they grasp more tightly to what remains."

"We've had reports of dangerous experiments." I watch carefully, wondering how they'll respond to my words. "People attempting to recreate magic through alchemy, blood rituals, even sacrifices."

"Again, we've experienced similar problems." King Mihel's hands tremble as he sets down his goblet. "Last month we had to dispatch guards to a northern village where a self-proclaimed prophet insisted he could restore magic through human sacrifice."

The table falls silent, the weight of these shared issues pressing down on us all.

Then the conversation shifts to more pragmatic matters, and I find myself truly engaging for the first time.

"The Eastern Provinces lost nearly half of their summer crops." Creases form between Queen Maeve's eyebrows. "Without earth magic to nurture the soil through drought, the farmers have been desperate."

"And trade routes have become treacherous." King Mihel's features are grave. Though these royals claim they don't blame us for their lost magic, I can't help but wonder if there's still a little underlying resentment. "Without air magic to calm sudden storms, we've lost three merchant vessels in the past month alone."

Now we're discussing something concrete, something I

understand. The stiff political persona I've been forcing myself to maintain melts away as I lean forward, genuinely invested.

The conversation flows naturally, and I'm so engaged that I barely notice when Sterling's hand moves from my knee to rest lightly on my thigh. His eyes sparkle with pride when I catch his glance.

The great doors to the dining hall burst open with a bang that causes everyone to jump. Queen Maeve actually shrieks, her goblet toppling and staining the white tablecloth.

Armed men march in, their stiff-backed posture and distinctive layered vestments immediately identifying them as Kamorian. Five guards flank a tall, broad-shouldered man with a shaved head that sports intricate designs on the sides. An elaborate metal collar marks him as a high-ranking official.

King Mihel rises, his expression morphing from shock to controlled tactful neutrality. "Prince Torach. We were not expecting Kamor's delegation until tomorrow's session."

The Kamorian royal's cold eyes fixate on me before sliding over to Sterling. His lips curl into something that resembles a smile only in the technical arrangement of facial muscles. "So this is where the magic-killers hide. Playing at diplomacy while our world crumbles."

CHAPTER TWELVE
LARK

The breakfast room freezes in an instant, as if the air has solidified. No one moves. My muscles tense, my body instinctively preparing for a fight while my mind races through political protocols I've barely mastered. The maid near me stops pouring, the pitcher suspended at an awkward angle. Wine trembles at its lip like a drop of blood hesitating before a fall.

Queen Maeve pushes up from her seat, strain evident on the lines of her face. Even from across the table, I don't miss the pulse jumping at her throat.

King Mihel's hand lands atop hers, heavy and restraining. His face transforms into something stormy and dangerous, deep lines carving themselves around his mouth.

Instinctively, I reach for my short sword.

Which isn't here.

I'm dressed in diplomatic finery, not battle leathers. The absence of my weapons sends an uncomfortable prickling sensation down my spine. I sit rigid, vibrating with tension, feeling simultaneously naked and trapped in these formal clothes.

But Sterling...smiles.

One I recognize from a hundred encounters, from council meetings to battlefields. The one that means someone has just committed a grave error.

My own pulse quickens.

Shit is about to get real.

Like he's got nothing but time, Sterling saunters to his feet, his gaze locked on the Kamorians who've just entered uninvited. He straightens to his full height, shoulders square, hands relaxed at his sides. The posture of a man who doesn't need to reach for a weapon to be dangerous.

King Mihel rises far more quickly, nearly knocking his chair backward. His expression is a thunderous storm of barely contained royal rage. "Prince Torach, you forget yourself. Queen Lark and Prince Knox are honored guests. In my home."

My spine stiffens, and I stand with the others. Beside me, Sterling subtly shifts his weight.

Prince Torach, a man not much older than I am, who possesses the arrogant bearing of inherited importance, flashes a sardonic smirk. Then he yanks out a chair at the table as if he's been asked to the most casual breakfast. "Your Majesty." He nods to King Mihel, but it's hardly polite. The slight incline of his head mocks the gesture it's meant to represent. Insulting. Presumptive.

I scan the room, cataloguing escape routes, noting which windows would shatter easiest, which of the soldiers look most ready to draw weapons. Three by the door seem particularly twitchy. Trained, but young. Eager.

The most threatening kind.

"Why are you here?" King Mihel's hospitality has clearly been stretched to its limit.

Torach sprawls out in his stolen seat. "You were meeting with the magic-killers." He grabs a piece of bread from a nearby basket, ripping into it without ceremony. "We took it upon ourselves to arrive early. Wouldn't want to miss anything important."

Sterling regards him with the clinical detachment of a man assessing whether someone is worth killing. "You are the son of Aldrin, the King of Kamor."

The man nods.

"So as the Kamorian prince, you understand what it means to insult a monarch in their own home." Sterling's tone adopts a menacing edge, like a dagger wrapped in velvet.

I suppress a smile. Sterling's dangerous voice. The one that sounds polite while promising consequences. That's what I need to learn to mimic. Not Rafe's formalities.

Torach's smile falters, the bread suspended halfway to his mouth. He says nothing.

"And I'm sure you know what could happen if word reached your father that you'd endangered Kamor's trade agreements with both Tirene and Tír Ríoga through," Sterling pauses, allowing the silence to stretch uncomfortably before finishing, "undiplomatic behavior."

A muscle twitches in Torach's jaw. His soldiers start scanning the room, no longer quite so confident. One swallows hard.

I lean close to Sterling, muttering so no one hears but him. "Forget trade. Let's talk about how fast his soldiers can run."

The tiniest flicker of humor touches the corner of Sterling's mouth, though his eyes remain fixed on the offending prince. "No matter, Prince Torach. I know you came to discuss solutions, not to create problems. I'm sure it was merely the...excitement of the moment." His eyebrows lift, offering the young man a graceful exit from his own lack of manners.

Torach sets down the bread and straightens his shoulders

as if trying to recapture his dignity. "Indeed...Your Majesty. Peaceful solutions are always preferable."

But setting the dragon fucker on fire would be so much more fun.

Sterling's gaze flicks to me for a heartbeat, causing me to question whether I voiced my thought.

Torach's jaw clenches as he addresses me. "Queen Lark of Tirene. Your...reputation precedes you."

He says "reputation" like it's a disease. I offer him my most tactful smile, which probably looks more like I'm baring my teeth.

Sterling turns to King Mihel. "Your Majesty, shall we all talk?"

Awe fills me at how easily Sterling defused what could have been a bloody situation and put the arrogant Kamorian prince in his place.

I sink back into my chair, arranging the damned formal dress so it doesn't get too wrinkled.

King Mihel nods, the tight lines around his eyes betraying his displeasure even as he offers the gesture of peace. He motions for Sterling to take a seat again, and they sit at the same time. It's a subtle dance of equal respect that doesn't escape my notice.

Or Torach's, judging by the other royal's not-so-subtle scowl. "Tirene destroyed magic deliberately. You've stolen what makes us equal."

Wow, guess he isn't interested in diplomacy. He doesn't even pretend to be.

"Not only is that incorrect, it's also impossible." Sterling's voice hardens, his polite veneer thinning. "We only did what the gods asked of us. To destroy the corrupted remains of a dead and forsaken god. It was eyril fertilized with dragon blood that grew the plants used to control human minds. And everyone knows what happened to people who ingested too much eyril even before the drachen rose and started slaughtering or corrupting every living thing."

"It seems everything is changing." King Mihel hesitates, as if measuring his words. "Including the gods themselves."

Torach leans back, something unpleasant flickering across his features. "Maybe the Devoted are onto something. Maybe we should be asking for the gods' aid in regaining magic."

Queen Maeve reacts with horror, her regal composure cracking for the first time. I can't blame her. The Devoted have been causing violent unrest throughout the kingdoms, stirring hatred and division. Their brand of faith demands blood and submission, not healing.

I can't maintain my tactful silence any longer. The mention of the Devoted churns my stomach. "The gods have nothing to do with magic. Magic was always ours."

Torach regards me, his gaze cold and contemptuous. "Magic is yours. Not ours. And you stole it from us."

∼

The Chronimūrti

Darkness envelops the chamber, cut only by the glimmer of starlit moments. Tiny fragments of what was, is, and will be, float like motes in an ancient abyss.

The Gods of Time stand motionless around a small pool. Their reflections shift between youth and age, formation and decay, possibility and certainty.

Chronir, God of the Present, leans over the water. His eyes contain the intensity of the now, the singular focus of the moment being experienced.

His palm hovers just above the pool's surface, fingers splayed as if conducting a symphony. "Seeing the pattern now."

Chronoth, God of the Past, stands to his right, his body seemingly carved from memory itself. The edges are soft, blurred like paintings faded by centuries of sunlight. His beard flows down his chest, each hair a timeline of past moments.

His eyes carry the weight of every mistake ever enacted. Every triumph ever celebrated. Every life ever lived. "Seen it before."

Chronira, Goddess of the Future, shifts between innumerable possibilities with each breath, sometimes tall and formidable, sometimes delicate and precise.

Her eyes never settle on one color or shape, moving instead between potential outcomes as one might flip through pages of a book. "Will see it again."

"They always turn on each other." Chronoth trails weathered fingers through the waters. Where he touches, the visions shift. The same palace razed and rebuilt across centuries, the same conflicts arising under different banners. Different rulers with the same desires.

"Always." Chronira's form solidifies as one scenario gains strength in the waters. A scene of treachery. Of a sword raised in a throne room and a broken crown.

"The patterns repeat." Chronir's ageless voice demands attention.

The water beneath his palm ripples with images of a palace, of a woman with gold- and burgundy-streaked wings. She stands as more people enter the dining room, clad in the red and yellow of Meridia. They join the fight, pointing accusatory fingers at the winged people.

Chronira's face reflects the aftermath of decisions not yet made. Tears of betrayal and loss flow down her cheeks. She shakes her head. "Always."

The sorrow in her voice draws glances from her brothers before they return their gazes to the waters.

Chronoth peers closely into their depths, watching

ancient civilizations rise and fall in the blink of an eye, each believing itself immortal, each crumbling to dust within a breath, within the blink of an eye. "They never have vision. Only blame."

Chronira closes her eyes, blocking out the vanishing potentialities. "True."

The number of choices will continue to shrink until only violence and destruction remain.

Until history repeats itself once more.

≈

Lark

King Mihel's knuckles are white where they grip the armrests of his chair. I sympathize with him. In a kingdom where manners are so crucial, having two groups of guests who barge in and start yelling is a grave insult.

Shortly after Prince Torach and his entourage of guards burst through the doors, a small group from Meridia arrived. Almost like they planned the ambush.

"Your queen hoards magic like a squirrel hoards nuts in the winter!" The Meridian delegate whose name I've learned is Ronan has gone purple with rage, spit flying from his lips as he jabs a finger in my direction.

I cast a sidelong glance at Sterling, whose perfect posture hasn't faltered despite the accusations.

His eyes meet mine. "Queen Lark cannot possibly control the distribution of magical ability across kingdoms." Sterling's words remain measured, but there's tension in his jaw. "The changes in magic have affected everyone, including those in Tirene."

"Yet your queen burns brighter than ever." A Meridian woman with steel gray hair pulled back so tightly it gives her the appearance of a permanent scowl glares at me. Her face is nearly as red as her tabard, which also features yellow lining and an image of a wheat sheaf. "While our people can no longer manifest even the simplest magic."

I look the irate woman in the eyes, refusing to let her anger intimidate me. "I understand your concern. Truly. But accusing me of hoarding magic is like accusing me of stealing the rain. It's not something anyone can control."

"Convenient," Prince Torach mutters loud enough for everyone to hear.

Digging my nails into my palms, I silently count to five. "No. What's convenient is blaming me for things I cannot control after I risked my life and those I love in order to save the world. Tirene lost many people in the battle against Narc and the drachen." I gesture between Sterling and me. "So while other kingdoms no longer possess magic, we lost something infinitely more valuable that we have no chance of reclaiming...human lives."

"Like I said," Torach leans closer, malice evident in every line of his face, "convenient. For you."

This entitled bastard is itching for a fight.

And I'm more than happy to give him one.

"Perhaps," Queen Maeve raises her hands, her palms out to both Torach and me, her delicate brows furrowed in frustration, "what we need is unity, not division."

All eyes settle on her. Her king has steepled his fingers, his knuckles white with strain. He nods to his queen.

"This is our home. You will at least pretend you have some manners while you sit at my table." She lifts her chin. "The absence of magic concerns us all. Pointing fingers will not restore balance."

King Mihel nods, genuine hope crossing his features. "Indeed. Perhaps a more...traditional approach is required." He folds his hands to hide his anger.

The Meridian delegates exchange nervous glances.

Even Prince Torach seems to hesitate, something almost like interest flickering in his eyes. He straightens, removing his elbow from the table. "What do you propose?"

The tension in the room sings like a broken gittern's string.

Discordant. Jarring. Lingering.

Like a true diplomat, King Mihel spreads his hands in a gesture encompassing all present. "A ceremony. At dawn tomorrow. At our great temple, the Divine Commons, with four kingdoms participating. An attempt at unity through traditional worship."

I resist the urge to roll my eyes. More ceremonies, more rituals, more conversation when we should be investigating, testing, and experimenting with the actual magic itself. But I hold my tongue.

"The gods have abandoned us," Ronan slams his fist against the table, "just as magic has."

Maeve purses her lips but doesn't get a chance to reprimand him.

"Then perhaps it's time we remind them of their obligations." King Mihel glares at the clenched fist on his welcoming table. "The Divine Commons was built to honor all deities, great and small. If the gods are changing, as some believe, then maybe we need to address them directly. Together."

I'd rather force everyone to run laps around the castle until they're too tired to argue. Like naughty children. But I'll try anything at this point. We don't have any other options. While I'd love more than anything to put these pompous asshats in their places, Tirene is still recovering from all the drachen attacks. The last thing we need is a war on multiple fronts.

Queen Maeve leans forward, her soft voice reaching every corner of the room. "The Divine Commons stands at the highest point in Emraldae Keep. At dawn, the first light touches the central altar in a way that has been considered auspicious for centuries."

"Very well." Prince Torach slouches in his chair like a child. "We will participate in your ceremony." His tone suggests he's granting an enormous favor rather than agreeing to a perfectly reasonable request.

I nod in acquiescence, not trusting myself to speak politely. There's no way I can match Queen Maeve's calm demeanor and polished speech. The Meridian delegates follow suit, though the steel-haired woman looks far from convinced.

"Excellent! We shall meet tomorrow at the Divine Commons before first light." King Mihel rises to his feet, signaling the end of the discussion. "I suggest you all use the time until then to meditate and pray to the gods in your chambers. My guards will show you the way so you don't get lost."

A dozen or so guards peel away from the wall, finally able to do something. Escorts step up to each group, ready to lead us all away. The meeting dissolves as the various delegations drift out the doors.

Sterling stands, offering me his hand. "We will be honored to join you at dawn."

King Mihel dips his head. "My wife has made a room available to you that is completely dark, should you wish to pray to Nyc. We know you have a special bond with her, Queen Lark."

"Thank you for that, King Mihel, Queen Maeve." I return the head dip, one reigning monarch to another. Except this is their home ground, not mine.

Once we're clear of the chamber, without guards needing to help us along, a servant steps forward to guide us back to our assigned quarters. I walk beside Sterling in silence, conserving my energy and holding my thoughts until we're alone.

I'm impressed by the castle's guest wing. All smooth stone and intricate tapestries depicting Tír Ríoga's rugged mountains, forests, and seascapes. Our group has been given an entire corridor, with Sterling and me in the largest chambers at the end. The rest of our people create a buffer between us and potential threats.

As soon as the door closes behind us, I release a groan that's been building since breakfast. "I need to wash the diplomatic slime off me. Have you ever seen someone as rude as Torach or those jackholes from Meridia?" I start pulling at the fastenings of my formal attire.

"Unfortunately, yes." Sterling prowls through the room, checking every door. "The servants have already prepared a bath."

I shoot him a grateful glance before disappearing into the bathing chamber. Steam wafts from the large copper tub, and scented oils float on the surface. With a contented sigh, I sink into the hot water, feeling my muscles unclench for the first time in hours. Taking my time, I scrub away the day's tension and frustration.

When I eventually emerge, wrapped in a soft royal blue robe provided by our hosts, I feel almost human again.

Sterling has removed his formal jacket and opened a window, allowing the chilly breeze to sweep through the room. He turns as I enter, his eyes softening in that way they do when we're finally alone. "Better?"

"Getting there." I drop onto the bed and arrange myself against the pillows. "I think I need a nap before I can face any more diplomacy today."

He smiles. "Rest. You have plenty of time before dinner."

I close my eyes, allowing exhaustion to pull me under.

When I wake, the light has shifted, and late afternoon

shadows reach across the floor. Sterling sits in a chair by the window, reading a slim volume bound in dark leather.

I stretch, feeling more clearheaded. "What time is it?"

"About an hour before dinner." He closes the book. "You slept the whole day away. You must have needed the rest."

I swing my legs off the bed, moving to the wardrobe where my clothing has been unpacked. I select a formal gown suitable for a foreign court. More ornate than the tunic and breeches I'd rather wear, but I want to make a good impression.

As I dress, I feel Sterling's eyes on me, appreciative but thoughtful.

"You're worried." It's not a question.

I nod while fastening the last clasp. "I'm not built for this, Sterling. I want to hit something. Or stab something. Or set something on fire."

"I've noticed." The corner of his mouth quirks upward. "Your right hand twitched toward your nonexistent sword approximately every three minutes at breakfast."

I grimace. "That obvious?"

"Only to me." He catches my hand as I pass him and gently gathers me into his lap. "Lark, you're doing great. Better than anyone else would in your position."

"Thank you. But I still wanted to pitch those arrogant fuckers out the window, one by one." I relax enough to wrap my arms around his head and hug it to my chest. "Perhaps in small groups, for efficiency."

Sterling chuckles while extracting himself from my hold. "How many do you think you could handle at once?"

The question brings me back to reality. I'm not actually going to decapitate foreign dignitaries, no matter how tempting. "It would be easier just to feed them to the dragons. All I'd have to do is stop dampening so the dragons can feel everything I'm feeling, and then..."

A knock at the door interrupts us. Sterling's arms tighten briefly before releasing me. "Come in."

I settle into my own chair as Agnar enters, followed by Rafe.

"Guards at the door hassled us. Insisted that we knock." Agnar heaves an exaggerated sigh. "But based on the way you two split apart when we came in, now I'm thinking I should thank them. There are some things that my delicate eyes just don't need to see."

Rafe snorts, tugging at his collar in discomfort. He's still getting used to Agnar's blunt comments.

"Actually," Sterling's lip curls in amusement, "Lark was talking about the most practical way to take out some troubling individuals."

Agnar stops in front of me. "Has anyone ever told you you're violent? I don't know if having that much rage inside is healthy. Maybe you should work on that."

"Has anyone ever told you you're a pain in the ass?" I offer my sweetest, most innocent smile.

Agnar roars with laughter while Sterling shakes his head.

Rafe mumbles something I can't quite parse before clearing his throat. "So sorry to intrude on whatever it is you were really doing. But we came to ask about the meeting. We heard some servants gossiping about a scene between the Kamorians and Meridians. How bad was it?"

I reach for the side table where a decanter of amber liquid sits alongside crystal glasses. "Anyone care for a drink?"

When everyone nods, I pour a measure into each glass and pass them around. I take a healthy swallow from my own glass.

The spirit burns pleasantly going down, warming me from the inside. It's a local specialty, distilled from a grain that grows only on the rocky slopes of Tír Ríoga. As the others drink, Sterling and I relay how the first meeting with the other delegates broke down before it could even officially start and how we've agreed to attend a prayer meeting tomorrow morning to seek guidance from the gods.

Agnar settles into a chair, stretching his long legs out before him. "The ceremony tomorrow...you think it will help?"

I snort. "About as much as spitting on a forest fire."

"We need answers." Sterling swirls the amber liquid in his glass. "The ceremony will offer pageantry, not solutions."

"Agreed." Rafe nods, his expression grim. "These people are scared. Eyril has been their equalizer for centuries. Without it, the balance of power shifts completely in our favor."

I tap my fingers against my glass as an idea forms. "While we're praying at dawn, we need to know what's happening outside the temple. Do some discreet exploration of the city instead."

Agnar straightens, intrigued. "You want us to eavesdrop on the locals?"

"I want you to take the pulse of Tír Ríoga," I clarify. "Visit the markets, the taverns, listen to what ordinary people are saying about magic. About us."

Rafe's eyes narrow in thought. "You believe there's more happening than diplomatic posturing."

"There's always more happening than what we see in court." I sip more of the strong liquor, careful not to drink too much at once on an empty stomach. "And we need to understand the full picture before we can find solutions."

Sterling shoots me an appreciative glance that warms me more than the alcohol. "Good thinking. What we need to know won't be shown in front of the king, queens, and prince."

"Meanwhile, you'll be sitting through a meaningless ceremony." Agnar grins. "This is why you're my favorite monarch."

I smile despite myself. "Just don't get caught or do

anything to draw attention. The last thing we need is to be accused of spying on top of everything else."

Rafe downs the rest of his drink in one swallow. "We'll be inconspicuous. I know how to blend in."

Agnar winks. "I'll teach him. By tomorrow, he'll be swearing like a dockworker and walking with a proper commoner's slouch."

"I am the Master of the Guilds." Rafe raises his chin, peering down his nose at Agnar. "I know how to talk with the common man. And I dine with them at least once a year."

Another laughing fit overtakes Agnar as he claps the man on the shoulder and leads him out.

I worry that these diplomatic tensions may be just the beginning of a much larger conflict. One that none of our kingdoms can afford to fight.

I frown when I catch Sterling watching me, his expression pensive. "What's wrong?"

"Nothing." He shakes his head. "Just thinking that Tirene has the right queen for these troubled times."

"A queen who fantasizes about murdering diplomats?"

"A queen who looks beyond the obvious." He rises to stand before me, coasting his fingers down my arms and trailing featherlight kisses down my neck. "Who sends her people to find the truth while others give in to fear."

A thrill zips down my spine just thinking about what those fingers can do. "Careful. We don't have much time before dinner."

Sterling's warm, spirit-laced breath tickles my ear. "Then consider what I'm about to do to you an appetizer."

CHAPTER THIRTEEN
LARK

My neck aches from the effort of keeping my chin level, my spine straight, and my shoulders back. The blustering predawn air feels thick with the unknown. It hums with expectation as eyes track our procession toward the Divine Commons. Much of yesterday's snow melted into slush, and I've never been more grateful for my heavy leather boots.

No fancy slippers in this climate. At least not outdoors.

Beside me, Sterling marches with the measured pace of a soldier, but his attention keeps drifting to every fountain, every well, every frozen body of water we pass. It's not like him.

Not during something this important.

And that tiny deviation from his usual focus gnaws at my already frayed nerves.

I try to match Queen Maeve's graceful stride, the way she seems to glide rather than walk, feet barely disturbing the ancient stones beneath us. These pathways have been worn smooth by centuries of pilgrims' feet, and now they bear the weight of four kingdoms' diplomats and royals.

I should be honored. Instead, I feel like an imposter. A Tirenese noble child raised in Aclaris who's somehow become Tirene's queen.

The nobles trail behind us in their finery, their faces carefully arranged into political masks. We encounter citizens along the route with far more honest expressions. Some hopeful, some suspicious, many simply afraid.

Most of all, I keep an eye on Sterling, on the way his dark eyes track to yet another decorative fountain.

When his gaze briefly meets mine, I raise my eyebrows in silent question. He shakes his head, almost imperceptibly. The small gesture promises that he'll tell me later.

We proceed through the enormous dome of a greenhouse and a temple garden that should be lush with pre-harvest offerings but instead stands withered and neglected. The soil is cracked, the plants shriveled. No one tends the sacred spaces anymore. This is the third empty garden we've seen.

The bare fish markets come next, stalls swept clean of their usual morning catch. Even the weather-shrines stand abandoned, their offerings of colored glass and polished stones scattered by the wind, or perhaps by desperate hands. Trade caravan wagons cluster together in defensive circles rather than spreading out to display their wares.

Unable to contain my growing unease, I finally turn to Queen Maeve. A ruby-studded clasp sweeps her dark hair off her face. "Why do you think this is all happening?"

For the first time since we began our procession, the queen's composure cracks. She doesn't quite meet my eye, her obsidian gaze floating somewhere over my shoulder. "The loss of magic has scared people. They cluster in small groups to hide and build defenses."

Fear sounds like an understatement. They're acting like cornered prey. Boxing themselves in. This creeping dread has reshaped an entire kingdom's behavior. Tír Ríoga isn't just troubled.

It's terrified.

Is this my fault?

This is what we'd helped create. What I'd caused by destroying Narc's bones. The act meant to free us from tyranny has instead unleashed a different kind of oppression. One born of uncertainty and powerlessness.

This is why Maeve won't meet my eye.

Never in my life have I worried about not having magic. My magic has always been too strong. As a Tirenese child raised by Aclarians, my first accidental attempts at using my fire element were wild and uncontrolled. For most of my life, my mother forced me to consume tablets that weakened and managed my power.

Now these people have been stripped bare of their abilities. They're having to relearn life without the magic they relied upon.

We climb higher, and the Divine Commons finally comes into view, rising atop Emraldae Keep's highest hill. The enormous amphitheater's black stone gleams in the morning light, the unity of its design now feeling like a hollow promise. Massive stairs sweep up in three curved sections, each representing one of the great visiting kingdoms and meeting at a columned entrance hall.

"It's stunning." Sterling's voice is laced with awe.

Maeve accepts the compliment with a dip of her chin. "This was built two centuries ago when Tír Ríoga positioned itself as neutral ground. Our ancestors wanted to promote religious harmony." She sweeps her arm toward the structure, jangling the gold bangles on her wrist. "All the gods honored in one place."

King Mihel nods, love and respect for his wife shining in his eyes.

The queen is right. As we approach, I can see how the architecture pays homage to the pantheon. Stone and marble pillars for Hallr, the God of Stone and Mountains. Constellation markings on the archways for Zeru, who governs the stars and heavens. Fountains flow in graceful arcs to honor Rivlan, God of Water. Neglected gardens that once showcased flowers and fruits for Viridian's climb both horizontal and vertical surfaces.

We begin ascending the wide, curving staircases, then we pass through a high-ceilinged entrance hall. The space should feel sacred, solemn. Instead, it harbors the breathless tension of a room where something valuable has been stolen, but no one wants to acknowledge the theft.

As we near the heart of the complex—the central, open-aired stadium—a strange glimmer catches my eye.

Crystalline growths, strange and intricate formations that glimmer with an almost grotesque beauty, creep up the walls and pillars. Most people breeze past without noticing. Or perhaps they're choosing not to.

My stomach clenches into a knot. The formations are identical to those from the wedding fountain in Tirene.

Sterling picks up on my hesitation and tracks my gaze. His body goes rigid beside me. "Those fucking things again."

I grip his arm tighter than I intend. "What are they?"

The shimmering structures crawl up the shrine wall like frozen lightning, beautiful and wrong at the same time.

Before Sterling can answer, we're swept into the vast amphitheater ahead of the crowd of citizens.

The curved tiers of seating already hold thousands. Smaller worship spaces appear between sections, each one dedicated to different gods. The central platform gleams with ritual objects, censers for incense, bowls of sacred water, ceremonial daggers, and offerings of grain and wine.

For a fleeting moment, as we take our positions, hope flickers.

The high priestess comes forward, her dark purple robes swirling with embroidered symbols of unity. Her voice rings out across the amphitheater, calling for peace, for cooperation, for a return to harmony between the kingdoms.

I almost let myself believe this could work.

Then I spot the cave cats lurking in the shadows of the temple, their emerald eyes glinting in the light. They tend to shun cities, so their presence likely indicates that at least one god retains power in this domain.

In light of that, I'd expect them to act like ceremonial guardians. Instead, they pace and prowl around the perimeter, their black coats gleaming, their eyes watchful. One snarls, showing glinting white teeth, and the priestess falters in her invocation.

The flames at Ziva's shrine flare, shooting high into the air. They turn black, belching smoke that reeks of sulfur and rot.

There's a tug in my chest, a familiar heat that tells me my fire magic is responding to something. But I can't control this. This isn't my fire.

"Sterling, something's wrong."

He's already tensed beside me, one hand resting on the sword at his hip. "Stay close."

Around us, fountains begin to crystallize. The clear water hardens into jagged formations that crack and split and spit pellets across the arena. People yelp as the shards strike them, their tiny wounds beading with blood.

Panic ripples through the crowd.

People begin to back away and push against each other. Children cry. The priestess raises her hands, calling for calm, but the compounding chaos drowns out her voice.

From the edges of the amphitheater, figures in dark cloaks

emerge. Each bears a star-mark on their hand, a constellation image that snakes up their wrists and disappears beneath billowing sleeves.

The Devoted.

Worshippers of Zeru who've weaponized their faith.

One points directly at me, then at Sterling. "See what happens when the magic-killers dare participate in sacred rites?"

The accusation acts like a slap to the face. Magic-killers. Is everyone outside of Tirene calling us that now?

"Better magic-free than god-stuffed!" a woman in the crowd yells back.

I've never been so glad to hear someone shout in my life. It seems not everyone blames us.

A young man with cropped black hair glares in the direction of the Devoted. "Go crawl back to your shrine!"

The tension snaps.

Arguments break out across the amphitheater, which quickly escalate to shoving matches. The guards swoop in, attempting to separate people, but they're overwhelmed by the sheer numbers.

The Devoted spread through the crowd like ink in water, their accusations becoming louder and more specific.

"They burned the sacred plants!"

"They poisoned the magic!"

"The false queen brought this curse upon us all!"

I stand frozen as the careful diplomatic event we'd agreed to participate in crumbles into shambles.

A rock sails through the air, missing my head by mere inches.

I flinch, and in an instant, Sterling is stepping in front of me, putting his body between mine and the growing mob.

"We need to move." He scans the area for an escape route. "Now."

But the crowd surges like a tide, cutting off our retreat.

I reach for my fire magic and feel it stir beneath my skin, hot and ready. If I have to defend us, I will. But using magic in this already volatile situation might only confirm their suspicions.

CHAPTER FOURTEEN
LARK

Sterling stands rigid beside me, his hand hovering near his sword. But we both know weapons won't solve this. I step around him, drawing breath into lungs that feel vast and ancient.

Something shifts inside me. Not in my stomach where anxiety usually coils, but deeper, resonating through my bones like a plucked string.

It's anger at seeing things that shouldn't be. People turning on each other because they fear what they don't understand.

"What are you doing?" My voice carries across the Divine Commons with a resonance that gives people pause. "Look at each other! These are your neighbors, your friends."

A few heads twist toward me. Like a wave encountering resistance, the fighting slows. The enormous amphitheater, with its soaring columns and intricate stonework honoring every god, shouldn't be filled with violence. This sacred space, meant for unity, reverberates with condemnations and fear.

I take another step forward.

Sterling's fingers brush my elbow in a warning, a reminder of danger, but I shrug him off. The crowds that were pushing toward us, waving fists and shouting about lost magic, begin to fall back.

"I understand your anger." The words tumble out, honest and unpolished, so unlike the careful speeches I've been rehearsing since becoming queen. "We never intended to destroy magic. We intended to destroy Narc and the drachen, who were spreading corruption through our lands like poison."

A man with a bloodied lip snorts. "Convenient excuse, Your Highness."

I meet his eyes, unfazed by the smoldering hatred in his gaze. "It's not an excuse. The gods themselves helped me find what we needed to purge Narc's tainted existence from the soil. Nyc, Narc's own mother, asked me to burn his bones and return him to her so he could finally rest. Otherwise, the corruption would have devoured our world. We did only as the gods demanded. What needed to be done."

The crowd ripples with uncertainty. Doubt replaces rage in some faces, especially those older citizens who remember the teachings about the gods before the Devoted began twisting them.

"How many of you knew someone who was corrupted? Someone whose body and mind were enslaved to Narc and his drachen and his obsession with 'perfected humans'? People who were stripped of their free will? My own sister killed a dear friend under Narc's control." And our own mother. "Thousands more would be corrupted by now if the drachen were still here. I'm truly sorry for the loss of magic, but I will not apologize for doing the right thing."

The fighting stills completely.

A woman with black hair and a scythe at her waist raises

her hand and blanches. To my right, a virtual giant hunches his shoulders while others exchange glances heavy with shared grief.

They know. They watched the monsters imprison their loved ones' minds and use their bodies like puppets.

"My husband," the woman with the scythe whispers. Yet in the strange acoustics of the Divine Commons, her words reach everyone. "He came back changed. Spoke of perfection, of a new world order. When I refused to follow, he—" She stops, touching a scar that runs along her jaw.

For a brief second, understanding bridges the gap between Tirene and Tír Ríoga. Between every kingdom present. Between those with magic and those without. Between queen and subject.

Then a voice cuts through the momentary peace.

"Pretty words from Tirene's queen, who can stay safe in her magical kingdom." A sandy-haired woman in the dark robes of the Devoted comes forward, the star-mark on her hand glinting in the light filtering through the amphitheater's open ceiling. "While our children grow weak and our crops fail. While our people suffer."

My skin crawls from whatever drips from her voice. Not just hatred, but something calculated. Manufactured. I've heard this exact cadence before, from street preachers in Tirene's market squares trying to sow division.

The uneasy crowd stirs again.

"Magic sustained us for generations." The Devoted woman squares her shoulders. "And now it's gone."

"That's not—" I snap my mouth shut, because what more can I say? The damage is done.

Her words ripple through the gathered masses, reigniting the anger that had just begun to cool.

The crowd surges worse than before as people begin shoving toward us from all sides. Sterling inches closer to me.

Guards struggle to maintain a perimeter around us. I reach for the short sword strapped to my side.

That's when I feel it.

A tremor beneath my feet.

The ancient stone floor of the Divine Commons shudders. The immense pillars supporting the vaulted ceilings tremble.

"Sterling. Do you—"

"Yes." Hand on his own weapon, he scans the amphitheater.

The rumble grows, no longer subtle. Confusion transforms to fury and then fear as a violent shake sends people stumbling.

A crack rips through the stone near one of the worship alcoves.

People shriek and rush toward the exits, but the falling debris blocks several pathways.

Sterling's eyes meet mine, and in that moment, I know what he's thinking.

I reach for his hand. His fingers are cold against mine, but when our skin touches, the elemental magic within us recognizes its counterpart.

Our magic merges.

On your lead, he whispers in my mind.

That's all the confirmation I need.

Stepping forward, I direct a wave of ice toward the entrances to fortify them.

More screams. People thrust their arms up as if to defend themselves.

My fire curves a protective arc above the fleeing Tír Ríogans, vaporizing raining debris before it can crush them. Sterling's ice creates temporary supports, beautiful crystalline columns that brace against collapsing sections of wall. Fluttering mist knocks the choking dust from the air.

"Stand up and run!" More walls waver, and I hurl another layer of ice to cover it.

"Almost there." Sterling grinds his teeth, either frustrated at the people who spend more time staring at me than running or at his struggle to maintain his water magic.

The last family rushes through the opening we've maintained.

King Mihel and Queen Maeve regard me with wide eyes, their clothing already coated in fine rock dust.

The pressure on the ice mounts, and I have to fill the fissures. "Go!"

"Not without you!" Maeve darts forward to grasp my hand while Mihel throws Sterling's arm over his shoulder.

Together, the four of us make it through the ice-braced arch. Guards surround us, their attention fixed overhead as we stumble on the uneven ground.

The rumbling stops as suddenly as it began.

The Divine Commons stands damaged but not destroyed. And we've managed to prevent extensive loss of life.

Outside in the main square, the crowd mills about in shocked silence. Some clutch each other, checking for injuries. Others stare back at the ancient building, disbelief evident in their expressions. A few glance toward us with begrudging acknowledgment.

"Thank you." A father cradles his young daughter to his chest. "You saved my child."

A spark of hope ignites in my chest.

"Ah, yes. We needed Tirene's king and queen to save us." The Devoted woman appears unscathed, her robes barely dusty. "Since they're the only ones with magic. Wouldn't it be wonderful if such power were available to all of us again? If, rather than depending on the mercy of Tirene royalty, we could have saved our children with our own hands?"

The spark flickers out, doused by the Devoted's taunt.

Murmurs start up again, this time underlaid with resentment rather than gratitude.

Maeve and Mihel release us and back away.

I need to understand this fear. This loss. This desperation that lends the Devoted's words so much power.

And then I need to do something about it.

~

Lark

The door to our guest quarters closes with a heavy thud. I sink onto the edge of a plush chair, my limbs buzzing with the aftermath of adrenaline. Sterling paces by the window. Agnar leans against the wall near the door, his skin ashen with exhaustion, while Rafe stands with his arms crossed, thick eyebrows drawn together like storm clouds about to collide.

"Well," I break the silence that's stretched between us since returning to the keep, "that could have gone better."

Agnar's snort is somewhere between amusement and disbelief. "I would have called it a shit show, but that's one way to put it."

Sterling stops his pacing to pour water from a crystal decanter. He passes me a glass first, always thinking of me before himself, before distributing glasses to the others.

I catch his eye and find a silent question there. *Are you all right?* I give him the barest nod in response.

"What did you discover?" I turn to Agnar and Rafe. "Before the Divine Commons attempted to murder us, I mean."

Rafe clears his throat, arms falling to his side. His wavy brown hair is disheveled, and there's dust on his clothing from wherever he and Agnar had been investigating. "We headed out last night, thinking we'd finish up at the Commons. Trust me when I say we double-checked everything. It's worse than we thought."

I sip my water, buying time for my stomach to settle. "Let's hear it."

Agnar pushes off from the wall to stand beside Rafe, and my heart squeezes with dread over the glance they share. "We found evidence of failed restoration experiments, just as you feared."

Sterling stills. "What kind of experiments?"

Rafe's throat works on a swallow. "Sacrificial ones."

The water catches in my throat. "Sacrificial?"

Oh gods. If children are being sacrificed...

Spotting my horrified expression, Agnar quickly clarifies. "Animals, personal objects, monetary items. But there were notes. Theories. About larger sacrifices potentially yielding better results."

"People." Sterling blows out a heavy breath and starts pacing again.

He says the word so casually, but the hardness of his features and the haunted glint in his eyes convey the truth. We've both killed out of necessity. To defend ourselves and those we love. And Sterling murdered people when he was corrupted and physically incapable of disobeying King Xenon's orders.

King Mihel said his guards found a so-called prophet who talked about using human sacrifices, and now we have confirmation that it's happening. They kill innocents, and for what? A chance at regaining magic? To appease gods they're not even sure are angry?

Pure madness.

Rafe nods, dust falling from his messy hair. "That was the suggestion. Nothing to indicate they've crossed that line yet, but the theoretical framework exists."

I set my glass on a side table before my shaking hands betray me.

"That's not all." Agnar folds his hands over his stomach. "It seems like the Tír Ríogans are preparing for battle. Or a siege."

Sterling whirls around. "Explain."

"We found massive storage facilities." Agnar unclasps his hands and scrubs a hand across his jaw. "Recently constructed or expanded. They're stockpiling everything. Food, medicine, raw materials."

"Could be normal precautions." The hope in my voice sounds hollow even to my own ears. "After what happened with Narc, prudent kingdoms would—"

"It's not normal precautions." Rafe earns a sharp look from Sterling for interrupting me. "I'm a guild master, Lark. I know supply chains. These aren't the stores of a kingdom preparing for a harsh winter or potential famine. These are the preparations of a nation expecting to be completely cut off."

"Or planning to cut themselves off." Sterling moves to stand behind my chair.

"There's more." Agnar averts his gaze, as if he's reluctant to disclose something. Which is very much unlike him. "They're strengthening their border fortifications. Not just maintaining them but actively reinforcing them. New watchtowers. Extended walls. Additional garrisons. They've been building self-sufficiency into their systems for months."

Sterling remains silent, but tension radiates from him. When he finally speaks, his voice is measured. "They're not just readying themselves for a world without magic. They're readying themselves for a world without allies."

I flinch. "They trusted us." Agnar and I even risked our lives to warn them of corrupted Aclarians attacking their border.

Sterling's hand settles on my shoulder. "And now they're preparing for a world where they can't."

Determination floods the hollow spaces inside me, washing away my exhaustion. Tirene's allies don't trust Tirene anymore. They're prepping for isolation or war. And while I've been trying to be the perfect diplomatic queen, reciting carefully memorized speeches and following protocol to the letter, the world has been fracturing around me.

"Okay, so we fix it." I tilt my head back to meet Sterling in the eye. "If they're scared of magical aggression, we show them magical cooperation. If they're bracing for isolation, we demonstrate the benefits of alliance. If they're listening to the Devoted because the Devoted speak to their fears, we address those concerns directly."

Sterling's expression remains neutral, but I catch the flicker in his eyes. Pride mixed with worry. "That won't be easy. Not when they're actively preparing against us."

"I'm not saying it will be easy. I'm saying it's necessary." Rising, I walk to the window. In the distance, the sun catches on the damaged dome of the Divine Commons. A cracked symbol of unity. A metaphor too obvious to ignore. "We'll start with rebuilding the Divine Commons. Not just with magic, but with labor from the kingdoms." I turn back to face them. "Rafe, can your guild mobilize craftspeople?"

He straightens, forehead crinkled in surprise. "Of course."

"And Agnar, I need you to work with our military contacts. Find the reasonable, moderate voices in their ranks. The ones who remember fighting alongside Tirene against Xenon."

Agnar nods, some of his usual confidence returning to his stance. "Consider it done."

Sterling watches me, his expression softening just enough for me to notice. "And what will you do?"

I consider the question. What would the perfect queen do in this situation? The answer comes with surprising clarity.

"I'm going to listen. Not just to dignitaries and nobles, but to ordinary people. The ones who lost magic and don't know how to live without it. The ones who are terrified enough to find comfort in Devoted rhetoric." Feeling the phantom weight of my crown, I square my shoulders. "And then I'm going to show them that Tirene stands with them, not against them. That we'll face this new world together."

CHAPTER FIFTEEN
LARK

In the days following the events at the Divine Commons and the flight home, time loses meaning as I focus on my queenly duties. I devote as much of it as I can to my citizens, listening to pleas and requests.

Each sunrise brings a new test, a fresh opportunity to fail.

Except failure isn't an option.

So I push harder, stretch myself thinner, and ignore the hollow sensation behind my ribs where certainty should live.

The Bricklayer's Guild conclave meets once a month in the room known as the Guild Hall in the palace. Rafe insists it needs to be someplace secure and localized, which makes it easy for me to answer their request to attend.

When I enter, twenty-seven men and women rise as one, their expressions shifting from boredom to awe so quickly it would be comical if it didn't knot my stomach.

The room, a salon much like the one where Sterling's mother used to store sweet treats for her children, is as practical as it is grand. With two long wooden tables in the center and an assortment of sofas and chairs along the walls, the lofty space could easily fit twice as many people.

For the next two hours, I listen to impassioned speeches about the demands placed on guild members, the historical context of their service obligations, and increasingly detailed descriptions of mortar compositions.

"What say you, Your Highness?" The guild leader's bright green eyes bore into mine, and the unamused expression on the stern redheaded woman's face confirms I spaced out for a minute.

I clear my throat, scribbling a meaningless note on my parchment like I've been deep in thought about the guild's contribution to the capital in the hope that Constance Cochran buys it.

Expectant eyes settle on me.

I haven't prepared for this. As the queen, I should know exactly what to say. How to say it.

Instead, I'm about to wing it.

"Well, Constance, I think the contribution of the Bricklayer's Guild to Tirene's security cannot be overstated." I begin cobbling together what I remember from historical accounts. "Your ancestors helped create not just our walls, but our very kingdom."

Somehow, I find words that light up their faces with pride. I grant a partial easement, enough to honor their request without compromising security. By the time I leave, they're practically glowing with loyalty, Constance Cochran included.

Miracles do happen.

The next day brings trade negotiations with merchants from the Eastern Provinces. I stay up until dawn reviewing grain prices and tax structures only to have my carefully prepped arguments dismissed with a casual, "That's not how King Jasper handled these matters."

I muster up a tight smile for the haughty merchant. "Perhaps it's time for new approaches."

But inside, doubt gnaws. What if the old ways were better? What if I'm too ignorant, too foreign still, to lead properly?

In the evening, I cancel my dinner to read more about Eastern trade relations. I ignore the way my stomach growls in protest.

The day after brings a military inspection. I stand straight-backed beside Agnar as we review the troops. The soldiers' eyes briefly flick to me. Worried about being led by a woman? Believing the rumors that I destroyed magic? Concerned we will be attacked simply because I am their queen?

"They respect you." Agnar bumps me with his elbow.

I give a small shake of my head. "They tolerate me."

His crude noise almost tempts me to smile. "No, truly. They would die for you. Every last one of them."

"That's exactly what I'm trying to prevent." The words come out sharper than intended.

Agnar's eyebrows rise, but he says nothing more.

Back in my chambers, I trade my formal gown for a comfortable pale yellow tunic and breeches. Then I head to my private sitting room and wave a flame into existence in the fireplace so I can read in comfort.

Accounts of battles from centuries past. Strategies for deploying troops against navy, air, and land troops. Prayers and countermeasures. The insights from generals whose names have been lost to the ages.

I fall asleep at the table and dream of Sterling with empty black eyes and blood on his hands.

The pattern continues, day after day. Council meetings where I speak with authority I don't feel. Public appearances where I smile until my face aches. Late nights poring over books until the words dance before my eyes.

It's still not enough.

I sit in my public sitting room, surrounded by towers of books and scrolls unrolled across every surface. Astrid, ever my dedicated assistant, is busy penning replies from my notes. I'm deep into *A History of the Five-Fold Wars* when the door opens.

I don't glance up. In just a few more pages, I might find something useful about countering divine influence.

"You're trying too hard to be something you're not."

Sterling's voice cuts through my concentration. My head jerks up, and I find him leaning against the doorframe with his arms crossed. His mouth is set in a hard line.

"You mean a queen?" The fear that's been my constant companion flares. "You think I can't be a good queen?"

He pushes away from the door as he gestures to the disarray around me. "You don't need to be this kind of queen."

I survey the mess I've created in my attempt to prep. "What kind of queen should I be? The kind who doesn't know her kingdom's history? Who can't quote precedent when the council challenges her decisions? Who doesn't understand the first thing about—"

"The kind who knows her own mind." Sterling moves closer, cautious not to disturb any of my carefully arranged piles. "The kind who trusts her instincts. The kind who brought peace to all kingdoms not through dusty old laws, but through courage and kindness."

I turn back to my book. "That's a pretty story. But pretty stories don't run kingdoms."

"Lark." His voice takes on that alluring timbre that still causes my heart to skip, even after everything we've been through. "You're burying your head in history books, but we need to learn what's happening with the gods in the here and now."

I tap the heavy tome before me, refusing to look up. "There was strategy about dealing with the gods in the *Five-Fold Wars*. I'm sure I'll get to it...soon."

Sterling paces the room, careful to avoid stepping on scrolls. "I hope so. Because I'm fairly certain our issues aren't going to be solved by fretting over what everyone thinks. Not when you can change their perception through action."

That gets my attention. There's something in his voice that triggers a memory.

I offer a tired smile. "You sound like your mother."

His expression softens. "Good."

"She told me something like that once, and it stuck with me. 'A leader's first responsibility is to define reality.'" The Dowager Queen might have been flighty, but she had moments of startling clarity. Remembering that conversation with Alannah about what it meant to be a queen, to truly lead people, brings tears to my eyes. "I wish she were still here to guide us."

"So do I. And that sounds just like her." Sterling runs a hand through his glossy hair, a rare gesture of uncertainty that snags my attention more than his words.

Before I can question him further, Astrid opens the door and offers a quick bow. "Your Highness, you have a visitor."

I'm about to say I'm too busy when a small figure darts past. A little girl with blond hair and bright blue eyes. Rose. The tiny ball of fire hovering above her shoulder casts dancing shadows across her freckled face.

"Queen Lark!" She skids to a stop, eyes wide with excitement. "And Prince Knox! I found you both!"

Sterling raises an eyebrow at the guard peeking inside, who has the decency to appear sheepish.

"Hey there, Rose. You know you don't have to use fancy titles with us." I set my book aside, ready to suggest we take a break from research to entertain the child, when she suddenly becomes serious.

"I know. But Mama says it's the polite thing to do." She

peers up at her flame familiar, then back to us. "The flame wants to show you something."

The familiar flickers as if in agreement.

Sterling and I exchange a glance, and for the first time in days, I feel a spark of something other than exhaustion. Curiosity.

CHAPTER SIXTEEN
LARK

"Your flame wants to show us something?" I glance at Sterling, the curious confusion on his face mirroring my own.

Rose cups her small hands beneath the flame, cradling the air like it's something precious.

The familiar responds, dropping lower and spreading wider until it's a floating pool of fire hovering above her palms. Light paints her face in shades of amber and gold, her eyes reflecting twin flames.

Not ordinary fire. Not anymore.

The edges ripple, then still, creating a fiery basin that hangs in the air. Within its depths, shadows begin to waltz, light begins to swirl, and images—actual images—form in the heart of the flame.

"A scrying flame," I breathe, unable to mask my awe. Such things have been written of in the histories, but no one alive knows how to do them.

Sterling hovers closer, skepticism written in the tight lines around his eyes. "Impossible. Fire can't—"

"Apparently, it can." I motion toward the floating basin of flame where shapes are already becoming clearer. It's like looking through a window into somewhere else. "Rose, how long have you been able to do this?"

She shrugs, her childish nonchalance at odds with the miraculous thing happening above her hands. "I'm not doing anything. But Kin has never done this before." Her eyes widen, and her voice drops to an astonished whisper. "It's excited. It wants to help."

Sterling arches his eyebrow. "Kin?"

Rose rolls her eyes in that particular way only children can perfect. The look that conveys she thinks adults are hopelessly slow. "That's its name."

"The flame told you its name?" I attempt to stay calm and collected.

"Like kinfolk. You know, family." She gestures with her chin toward the flame since her hands are still occupied. "And 'kindle,' like a flame does." Her tone, with such matter-of-fact certainty, makes me wonder how many other conversations she's had with her familiar that no one knew about.

As if responding to its name, the flame expands even more. It's nearly a foot across now. The images within gain clarity. I glimpse what looks like a doorway but...wrong somehow. Not built. Torn. A passage hewn into something that bleeds silvery light. The vision pulses rhythmically, like a receding heartbeat. Around the ragged edges, shadowy shapes emerge. Sharp, pointed objects that might be knife tips. Or mountain peaks. Or teeth. I can't really tell.

A chill runs down my spine.

"If this is a vision, I'm stumped."

An expectant sigh parts Rose's lips.

Sterling's gaze never strays from the flame. "We need Bastian. Now."

At his command, Astrid dashes to the door, relaying the order. I lean closer, studying the silvery light that spills from the tear. It doesn't behave like normal light. It bends in ways that hurt my eyes to follow, flowing rather than shining. It's more like water.

Bright water? Could this place be in a lake or ocean?

We wait in silence broken only by Rose's occasional whispers to her familiar that are too quiet for me to hear. The flame continues its display, the vision cycling through subtle variations. The tear widens, then narrows, the silvery light pulsing brighter, then dimmer.

Bastian arrives in a flurry of motion, his tall frame filling the doorway. "What's the emergency? The page said—" He gasps when he sees the floating fire. "Gods above."

"Or below. That's what we're trying to figure out." Sterling gestures for him to come closer. "Look at what's in the flame."

My brother gazes into the fiery basin with an expression I've seen before. Somewhere between reverence, scholarly excitement, and blissful love. "There are accounts in the old annals..."

He starts pulling books from my shelves while muttering under his breath, his fingertips skimming across spines until he finds what he's seeking. He flips through pages frantically, ignoring the rest of us.

Sterling catches my eye, the corner of his mouth quirking. "Lark had better get reading her Five-Fold War annals faster."

I elbow him in the ribs but can't stop the smile that stretches my lips. It's the first time in weeks I've felt anything like my old self.

Bastian, oblivious to our exchange, continues his harried search. "The light...the way it ripples...just like the accounts... glowing water." His fingers fly across pages yellowed with age.

"What accounts?" Hearing my own thoughts has my patience evaporating. This is just too exciting.

Startled, Bastian meets my gaze as if he'd forgotten we were here. "There are stories. Legends, really." He returns to rifling through pages, his movements careful despite his obvious enthusiasm. "About physical pathways to the godly realm. Most scholars dismiss them as metaphor, but…"

He holds up an ancient text, pointing to an illustration with a trembling finger. The painting in the book matches what we see in Rose's flame with uncanny precision. A jagged tear with mountainous edges and silvery light spilling from within.

My breath hitches. "A portal. An actual portal to the gods."

The words hang in the air, heavy with possibility. A portal to the godly realm. A way to reach them directly, to demand answers instead of waiting for cryptic signs and portents. My mind spins with the implications.

"Where can we find it?" The practical part of my brain's already planning logistics. This could solve all our problems.

Bastian points to words beneath the illustration. "Volox. That's the old name for the continent Tír Ríoga is on. Before it broke up into several smaller kingdoms. And there's only one mountain range. Though it's a long one."

"I told you Kin wanted to help." Rose is matter-of-fact and not at all surprised by this earth-shattering revelation. Her flame familiar, having delivered the message, returns to its normal size and shape and dances above Rose's shoulder.

"Some ancient texts mention actual pathways to the divine realm. A physical way to step into their domain. Most considered it blasphemy to even suggest such a possibility, but there are accounts…" Bastian flips to another page to show us a different illustration. "Pilgrims who claimed to have found such passages, who returned changed. Either blessed or cursed by the encounter."

Stunned energy zips through the room like a current. A portal to the gods. A way to reach the beings who have remained so frustratingly silent while our world tilts further into chaos. A chance to demand answers about the unusual occurrences in Tirene and beyond, about the strange events at the Divine Commons, about why everything is going sideways in the mortal world.

Sterling catches my eye, and a slow grin spreads across his face. "If the gods won't come to us—"

"We go to them." My grin matches his.

His expression shifts, his gaze darting over his shoulder.

"What?" My tension returns.

"It just felt like someone was watching me." Then he shakes his head with a dismissive gesture. "It's nothing." His posture straightens, radiating defiance. If someone is watching, he clearly doesn't care. "Time for an adventure."

The word breaks whatever lingering hesitation grips us. Excitement takes over, propelling us into action. I hurry to my wardrobe, pulling out my travel pack while Sterling rummages through a chest for maps.

"We'll need thick clothes," I call over my shoulder. "The Desolate Lands are known for their barbed plants and fierce animals."

"And weapons," Sterling adds. "Gods or not, we don't know what else might be living near this portal."

We talk over each other, discussing routes and supplies, our voices overlapping in our enthusiasm.

I track a path on the paper. "We'll fly north—"

"Then cut northwest, toward the Desolate Lands." Sterling's finger follows the sigils for the mountains.

I push books aside so I can spread a map across my desk. "We may have to hit the Withered Undulations."

Bastian joins the planning frenzy, finger tracing lines on the map. "The Withered Undulations are treacherous. Especially the western edges. There are trenches there that go down hundreds of feet, some filled with poisonous gas from old volcanic activity."

Sterling nods, writing out a list of necessary gear. "Rope and winches. Some of those trenches run deep."

Rose perches on a table, swinging her legs and watching us with bright interest. Her flame familiar darts around the room, seeming to catch our excitement.

Bastian points to the image in the ancient text again. "The illustration definitely shows mountainous terrain, although it's likely to be underground. At least partially. So look for mountains...maybe with extensive roots."

I mentally catalogue what we know. "If we don't find anything in the West, we'll head for the Eastlands." An unexpected but welcome laugh bubbles up through me. "Maybe I can find out what happened to my wedding flowers."

I look up to find Sterling crouched, motionless before his pack. A strange stillness has come over him. I follow his gaze to Bastian, whose face has gone carefully blank.

They both scrutinize me with serious expressions.

"What?" I demand, alarm rising.

"You can't both leave the kingdom at the same time again." Bastian's voice is low and measured. "Not when so many blame us for their magic weakening. Not when the other kingdoms are discussing war."

The words slam me in the gut.

Of course. It's so obvious, I can't believe I didn't see it immediately. Tirene can't be without both her rulers for long, especially not now. Not with such cunning, dangerous strangeness at play. Not when enemies might be spying on us.

One of us must stay behind.

My zest deflates all at once. "Dammit. You're right."

Who will stay behind to govern the kingdom while the others search for a way to confront the gods?

Chapter Seventeen
Lark

Bastian leaves our room, sealing us off from the chaos of the palace and its endless demands. I fidget with the edge of my sleeve, my thoughts forming and dissolving in quick succession. Sterling's shoulders drop a fraction as he runs a hand through his dark hair.

We need to discuss who's going to find this portal, but neither of us wants to start the conversation that will separate us. While I want to go, I can't turn my back on all my duties. Duties that Sterling doesn't technically face yet.

The silence between us stretches, not uncomfortable but growing thicker with each unbroken moment.

When I journeyed to the Lost City and Hidden Valley, he stayed behind. He dealt with councilors, war preparations, and securing the borders. But I went because Nyc reached out to me, told me where to go, what to do. That was my responsibility. Not his.

This time...

Sterling crosses to the window, his gait unhurried yet purposeful. The light glinting off his profile sharpens his already strong features. My heart stutters in my chest, as it always does when I allow myself to simply gaze at him.

Our eyes meet. "You should go." We both laugh as we talk over each other.

"Well," I move toward him, "that didn't work out as planned."

"No." Sterling's mouth quirks into his private half-smile that weakens my knees now more than ever. "But it does highlight our problem."

I squeeze his fingers, feeling the callouses that mark him as a soldier rather than just a prince. "I should stay. I'm the actual coronated queen. The kingdom needs a ruler here, and that's me. When you were officially in charge, you stayed back and let me go."

His brow furrows. "The kingdom needs its strongest fire wielder and only dragoncaller to find this portal. That's you."

"I've read all about the Five-Fold Wars. Surely that will come in handy should we encounter any troubles here at home." The words sound right, but something inside me twists in discomfort.

Since my first day at Flighthaven, I've always been the one rushing headlong into danger, leading the charge into adventure. The thought of remaining behind, of pacing these marble halls and waiting for reports while Sterling faces unknown dangers, chafes like an ill-fitting gown.

Cursed responsibilities. Mother always said they were a shackle willingly applied on behalf of those we love.

Sterling doesn't miss my internal conflict. The gold flecks in his brown eyes flicker like hearth-fire as he searches my face. "You don't want to stay."

It's not a question. He knows.

I sigh and turn away, drifting toward the small table where a pitcher of water sits. "What I want doesn't matter. What matters is what's best for Tirene."

"And what's best for Tirene is for its strongest leader to follow this vision from the gods." Sterling trails behind me, his reflection appearing in the mirror beside mine. "The dragons like you, Lark. They respond to you in ways they never have to anyone else. Hells, with your dragonbond, you can read each other's emotions. That will make the journey much easier."

"The dragons like you too." I smile to hide the pang in my chest.

I'm just...afraid. Afraid of what might happen to him if he goes. Afraid of what might happen to me if I'm left alone to rule without him. Afraid of what I might mess up without him here to help me.

All the details I missed while setting judgments that first day in court as Tirene's ruler still haunt me.

"It's not the same." Sterling wanders closer until I can feel the heat of him against my back. "And the gods...they've reached out to you before. They kept me asleep and unaware while they were showing you visions."

At the time it had been so scary, so intense, it never crossed my mind it might be something someone would want to happen. Even though I did feel special—chosen by them—the prophecy of my death always intermingled with those visitations.

I turn to face him, my hands coming up to rest on his chest. "That doesn't mean—"

"It means something." His voice is firm now, with no hint of emotion. "You know it does."

I let my forehead fall against his chest and inhale his familiar, delicious scent. His arms encircle me, pulling me closer, and I feel the steady beat of his heart against my cheek. "I don't want to be apart from you. To not be the one covering your back."

He strokes my hair, which is sweet, even if it musses the

elegant half-up, half-down style Rhiann labored over this morning. "I know. But we've faced worse, haven't we?"

A soft knock interrupts us.

We don't spring apart. Not in our private chambers. But I do lift my head from Sterling's chest as the door opens.

Agnar's broad form fills the frame. He advances a step and falters, his emotions flitting across his face. Pain, loss, and a whisper of longing are quickly shuttered away behind his usual mask of calm competence.

When I catch that brief glimpse of raw emotion, my heart aches for him.

"Sorry." He's already retreating. "I can come back later."

"No." I pull away from Sterling. "Come in, Agnar. What is it?"

He hesitates, his blue eyes darting between us. "Just wanted to report that the packs are ready for tomorrow. Whenever you decide who's going."

This is so unlike the Agnar I know, who would normally jump at the opportunity to crack a crass remark in a situation like this.

Sterling hasn't looked away from Agnar's face. "What's wrong, my friend?"

"Nothing." The word comes too quickly, too defensively. He issues a hollow laugh and turns as if to leave.

Sterling steps away from me, his hand reaching out to clasp Agnar's shoulder. "We've known each other for a long time. Don't lie to me now."

Agnar's shoulders slump, and his throat works on a swallow. "It's nothing. Really."

"Sit." Sterling gestures to the chairs by the hearth. It's not an order, not quite, but there's enough of the crown prince in his voice that Agnar complies by sinking into one of the cushioned seats.

I take the chair opposite him, while Sterling sits between us, leaning forward with his elbows on his knees. The three of us form a small triangle, intimate and closed off from the rest of the world.

I keep my voice soft and gentle. "Talk to us."

Agnar shifts in obvious discomfort, his large hands fumbling with the edge of his tunic. "It's stupid. I shouldn't have…it's just…" He heaves a deep breath. "You're both so good together. And don't take this the wrong way, because no one is happier for you guys than I am, but sometimes I'm a little envious of what you two have. Even with everything stacked against you, you beat the odds."

The wistfulness in his voice surprises me. My heart softens. "Cliché as this may sound, you'll find someone when the time is right. You're a wonderful man with an amazing heart. Plus, I've seen how women ogle you when you're training."

A flush creeps up Agnar's neck and disappears into his hairline. "Think it's the scars? They do lend me a sort of rugged charm, don't they?" He tries to laugh again, but it's even weaker than before.

Sterling leans back in his chair. "Miara is pretty. Why haven't you ever gotten serious with her?"

"Oh, she's pretty." Agnar grimaces. "Also not the brightest woman in all the land."

I chuckle despite myself. He's not wrong. After the truth about eyril got out, she stopped drinking all teas and any other dark liquids. Even ones she prepared herself.

She's not the only one who's shown interest in Agnar though. "Elowyn likes you a lot. She's always watching you."

"Only when she's drunk on dragon's blood." Agnar hides his face in his hands, groaning.

I shrug while thinking of the fortified liqueur distilled from the fruit of the same name. It's potent enough that a few cups have even the most reserved nobles dancing on tables.

The fruit itself is so sweet most people won't eat it, but dragons and winemakers love it.

I pat Agnar's arm. "That doesn't mean her interest isn't genuine. Dragon's blood just gives her the courage to show it."

"Exactly. Don't knock a little liquid courage. Lark was half drunk the first time she—"

Knowing what Sterling's about to say, I cut him off with a warning look. As much as Sterling loves to remind me of the night I snuck into his instructor's quarters at Flighthaven following a drinking game with my friends and threw myself at him, I doubt that's what Agnar needs to hear.

"But liquid courage isn't real courage." Agnar straightens, running a hand through his coppery hair. "And who wants a woman who has to rely on alcohol in order to have a relationship beyond that first kiss?"

Sterling nods in silent agreement. "What about Brynn? She's smart and capable."

"And devoted to her studies." Agnar shakes his head. "She barely knows I exist, and what she does notice doesn't impress her."

I remember the fiery redhead who recently became a royal guard. "Serilda? She's a skilled fighter."

Agnar's already frowning. "Pretty sure she's got her eye on Helene."

We continue like this, where Sterling and I name eligible women and Agnar finds reasons why each wouldn't work. It would be annoying if his arguments weren't so sound that I agreed with them. With every name, his shoulders tense even more, until finally he raises a hand to stop us.

"I don't want pretty and party." His eyes flick between us. "I'm ready for something more."

"You want what we have." I almost feel bad admitting that truth. "I know."

Agnar peers down at his hands. "Someone who sees me.

Not just the soldier, not just my sarcasm. But all of me. Is that too much to ask?"

Sterling leans forward to grip Agnar's forearm. "It's not too much. And you'll find it. But rushing into it with the wrong person won't get you there faster."

"The right person is out there." I start reflecting on all the women I've met since coming to Tirene. "And when you meet her, you'll know."

Agnar glances up at me, a small smile touching his lips. "How did you know? With him?" He dips his chin toward Sterling.

I ponder those first few encounters, the tension and the anger and the unexpected pull I felt toward him even then. "I didn't, not right away. It was...complicated."

Sterling's laugh is low and warm. "That about sums it up. Let's just say we had a love-hate relationship for a while there." He squeezes my hand, and I squeeze back. "But I always respected you and admired the way you kept fighting for what you wanted. No matter the consequences."

A comfortable silence falls between us, and I realize with a start how far we've all come. From enemies and strangers to this. A queen, her prince, and their most trusted friend sitting together in the fading light, discussing love and future possibilities.

Agnar clears his throat. "Kind of thinking you two have missed your calling because I'll be honest, I feel a thousand times better than when I walked into this room. And right now, I'm ready for this adventure I'm about to go on. With one of you. Which one will it be?"

Sterling and I exchange a glance. In that brief look, I see everything I need to know. His determination, his silent plea to let him protect me and our kingdom, his unwillingness to risk losing me again.

I dig my nails into my palms and release them. "Sterling

goes." I remain steady despite the flutter of anxiety in my chest. "Tomorrow. First light."

Agnar nods, accepting the command of his queen and friend without question, though his eyes harbor a thousand questions about how we came to this choice.

Sterling leans over and presses a soft kiss to my temple. Tomorrow, at first light, he'll leave me behind. But tonight, we still have each other. And somehow, that will have to be enough.

~

Lark

The door closes behind Agnar with a soft click that seems to echo in the sudden silence of our chambers.

Sterling's eyes find mine from across the room. Their dark and questioning in the fading light. I've made my decision. He will leave tomorrow at dawn. I feel the distance between us— just a few steps but somehow vast—and I long to close it.

"Are you sure?" Sterling's voice is a low rumble. "About me going instead of you?"

I cross over to him, breaching that small yet infinite gap. My hands find their way to his face, tracing the strong line of his jaw, feeling the slight stubble that scratches pleasantly against my palms. "Yes. You're the right choice. The kingdom needs me here." I swallow around the lump in my throat. "But I will miss you. Every hour. Every minute. In every room you're not in with me."

Something shifts in Sterling's eyes, darkening them more. His hands tighten on my waist. A smile spreads across his face, not the polite one he shows to the court, but a different one altogether.

Hungry. Like he wants to devour me.

My breath arrests as my pulse speeds up.

"Well then. Sounds like I need to give you something to remember me by." He takes my hand and tugs me toward our bed.

I follow willingly, heat burning in my core and spreading outward to my fingertips and toes. It never ceases to amaze me how quickly my body responds to him, like a flower angling toward the sun. "And what exactly did you have in mind, Your Highness?"

Sterling's smile becomes predatory as he stops at the edge of the bed. He pulls me against him until we're pressed together, his hardness evident against my stomach. "I think you know exactly what I have in mind, Your Majesty."

Nimble fingers work the fastenings of my dress. I step back just enough to grant him better access and watch his face as he unwraps me like a precious gift. The yearning in his eyes feeds my own desire, stoking the fire that's always smoldering between us.

When the bodice of my dress loosens, I ease the fabric down over my shoulders in a deliberately slow fashion. Sterling's breath hitches as he tracks the fabric's descent.

The gown pools at my feet, leaving me in my winter chemise. "A memorable goodbye. Something to keep you warm during those long, lonely nights you're gone." When I pull at the ties, the garment slides free, baring my breasts to Sterling's heated gaze. "A reminder of why you should return home. Quickly."

His throat bobs before his eyes turn molten with his desire. His hands find my waist and slide up to cup my breasts, thumbs brushing over my nipples and hardening them into stiff peaks.

"You," he growls, "are the most beautiful temptation I've ever faced. The only one I've never been able to resist."

A soft laugh slips through my lips as my hands drift to his shirt. "Good thing, since you seem to resist so poorly."

Sterling offers me that wild, open grin he only reveals in our most private moments. "I'd be a fool to resist at all. And yes, I was a fool back when I was still trying to."

He steps back, yanking his shirt over his head in one fluid motion. The firelight plays across the planes of his chest, highlighting scars both old and new. A map of battles he fought and survived.

I reach out to trace a particularly jagged one that runs along his ribs, a reminder of how close I've come to losing him. "Promise you'll come back to me."

Sterling catches my hand, bringing it to his lips to press a kiss to my palm. "Always. Not even the gods themselves could keep me from you."

I believe him. I must.

Though a small part of me hopes the gods don't take his words as a challenge.

His hands fly to the front of his breeches, unfastening them quickly. "I'm more than happy to go a night without sleep, no matter how early we need to leave."

As he straightens, fully naked now, I drink in the sight of him. All hard angles and powerful muscles that he's earned through years of training.

My soldier. My prince. My very heart.

A delicious heat spreads through my entire body at the sight of his erect cock.

Our bodies collide with a familiar urgency. His ravenous, demanding mouth finds mine as his hands roam over my bare skin, igniting trails of fire wherever they touch.

I curl into him, greedy for more contact, more of him, more of everything he has to give.

Sterling walks me backward until my legs hit the edge of the bed, and he follows me down as I fall onto the mattress.

He grips his erection and lines himself up. "Brace yourself, love."

The next instant, he drives into me, blasting all coherent thoughts from my head. I cry out at the sheer pleasure of him filling me, of his warm, solid body on top of mine. I clench around him, eliciting his low growl.

My nails rake down his back, my fingers glorying in the muscles shifting and bunching beneath his skin as he plunges inside me. With each thrust, the pleasure builds, tightening the coil in my low belly.

Our bodies settle into a perfect rhythm. We understand this dance well, knowing where to touch, how to move, what drives the other wild with need. Yet somehow, each time always feels new and thrilling.

His lips trace a path down my neck, lingering at the sensitive spot just below my ear in a way that has me gasping. I thread my fingers through his silky dark hair, holding him close as his mouth continues its journey southward to my breasts. When his tongue circles my nipple before drawing it into the heat of his mouth, I arch off the bed with a moan that would scandalize the court.

His answering growl is positively feral, vibrating against my skin while his hand slides down between my legs. He finds where we're joined and gently bites my nipple. His fingers stroke and circle, increasing the tension inside me until I writhe beneath him, desperate for release.

I squeeze my eyes shut. "Sterling, yes. Fuck me. Just like that."

"Such a filthy mouth." His lips press a lingering kiss to mine. "Look at me. I want to watch those beautiful eyes when you come on my cock."

I force my eyes open, meeting his gaze as his fingers continue to move. They find that bundle of nerves that shoots electric shocks of pleasure through my entire body. He tracks every pulse, every jerk.

The pressure compounds until finally it breaks, crashing over me in waves that leave me gasping his name into the charged air between us.

Moments later, Sterling follows me over the edge, his rhythm faltering as he buries his face in my neck.

A groan rips from deep in his chest. I hold him tight as he comes inside me, our bodies trembling together in the aftermath of our passion.

We lie tangled together, sweat cooling on our skin, hearts gradually slowing their frantic pace.

His breath tickles my neck as he presses more soft, lingering kisses to my skin. "I will come back to you. Nothing will keep me away for long."

I tighten my arms around him as if I could physically prevent tomorrow's dawn from separating us. "I know." I do my best to ignore the fear still lurking in the corners of my heart. "I know you will."

Sterling rolls to his side, bringing me with him so we're facing each other, our legs still intertwined. He traces lazy patterns on my hip as we stare at each other in the dimming light, memorizing features we already know by heart. "We should sleep. Dawn will come too soon."

I shake my head and scoot closer. "Not just yet. Sleep can wait a little longer."

His smile is downright sinful as his cock hardens against my belly. "As you wish, Your Majesty."

Chapter Eighteen
Lark

The fire paddock awakens to the soft blush of dawn. Sunlight expands across the sand and crushed stone, illuminating the dust motes swirling in the chilly morning air. Steam rises from the dragons' scales as they finish their meals and stretch, prepping for a long flight.

Today is not just another sunrise. This is the day Sterling leaves to seek answers from the gods.

Around me, some of the people I love most in this world prepare for their journey. Agnar fidgets with his gear, laughter bubbling just beneath the surface of his stern facade, while Leesa offers him an affectionate eye roll.

My eyes drift back to Sterling, and my heart clenches as I watch him methodically tie the final straps of his armor.

He looks like a knight readying himself for battle. And in a sense, he is. This is a war for our future, and the thought rattles me.

He comes closer, his dark gaze boring into mine as if attempting to hold my spirit in place with willpower alone. "Your Majesty."

I know he means to distract me with that formal title, but

my attempt at a smile falters under the weight of my worry. "Stay safe."

That's all I can manage before a knot of emotion clogs my throat and moisture fills my eyes.

He pulls me to him, squeezing me like he's grasping me for dear life. "I'll come back, love. We all will. If anything, you might enjoy getting me out of your hair for a while."

He trails kisses along my neck, my jaw, and the corner of my mouth.

The knot in my throat grows to the size of a boulder, and I can't even manage a snarky reply.

Sterling must catch the heartache in my eyes because he lowers his head, his lips a breath away from mine. "Hey, none of that. I'm too damn pretty for anything to happen to me. Besides, if death came for me, I'd look him right in the eye and tell him to fuck off. Not a damn thing in this world or any other will keep me from you. I'd find a way to break out of all three hells to return to my rightful place at your side." His lips graze my temple. "My queen. You are my everything."

The boulder crumbles, and the dam bursts. Tears stream down my face only to be wiped away by gentle thumbs.

Then his mouth is on mine.

Our kiss is hungry. Raw. Desperate. He cups my cheeks, tilting my head back until he finds the perfect angle. His tongue tangles with mine, and his teeth nip my lower lip. A groan slips from him, the guttural sound echoing my own intense longing.

Much too soon, he pulls back, pressing one last kiss to my swollen lips.

Chest heaving and heart hammering, I swallow down the next wave of emotion that threatens to drown me. "I love you."

He skims his knuckles down my cheek. "And I love you.

Madly. With every fiber of my being. Too much to let anyone or anything keep us apart for long."

My heart drops as he turns around and walks away. The others follow.

My sister. My friend. They join Bastian, who is already standing next to Nailah. Though he isn't going with them, he's here to help load the dragons with what they'll need for the journey. That, and to send off my sister.

My stomach cramps at the thought of them braving the dangers ahead. What if they don't come back? What if I never see them again?

Tanwen extends his foreleg, prompting Sterling to mount. Then the green dragon gives me a knowing look. A very human one. He's claiming responsibility for Sterling. The two have shared a bond for a long time, and that fact brings me comfort.

Tanwen, Kaida, and Nailah won't let anything happen to their riders. I project my emotions to the dragons, conveying both my gratitude and concern.

A collective blanket of reassurance washes over me. As if they're saying, "We'll be safe, Mother. Stop worrying."

With a roar that echoes across the palace grounds, Kaida launches into the sky, his dark scales shimmering beneath the waking sun. My pulse stutters as the other dragons follow suit, their powerful wings beating the air.

For a moment, I'm suspended in time, wishing desperately to carve through the heavens with them. To seek answers from the gods and help protect the people I love.

As I watch them disappear into the horizon, a familiar sense of worry sinks its claws into my heart, clenching tight.

Bastian wraps an arm around my shoulders, anxiety flickering in his own eyes. "They're strong. They'll figure it out. And they'll all come back to us unharmed. Have faith, Lark."

I know his words are just as much for himself as they are for me.

I try to straighten my shoulders. They left, and I'm expected to sit on the throne and serve the kingdom with my imitation of a queen.

I know I need to ready myself to tackle the duties awaiting me, but I'm struck numb by the hollow ache of absence. The void in my heart.

And I don't see any of that changing until they all return, safe and sound.

~

Lark

The tables in my private sitting room are an ocean of scrolls, papers, reports of alliances, and mundane wedding details that can't hold my attention. The sun is high in the sky, flooding the space with warm light. I should feel invigorated. Instead, a thousand unattended tasks weigh down on my shoulders like a lead blanket.

For five days, I've thrown myself into my duties. Anything to distract myself from the glaring absences in my life.

Words blur together, weaving into a tapestry of scribbles I have no desire to decipher. I rub my temples and will my mind to focus.

Just as I do, a burst of bright energy barges into the room, accompanied by the flicker of a flame sprite.

"Lark! Lark!" Rose bubbles with excitement, her small frame frenetic. "You have to see what Knox is doing."

I blink, attempting to draw myself back to the present. The guards have given up on trying to keep Rose out, and I can't say that I mind. No matter how busy I am, spending time with the little girl always lightens my heart.

"What?" With my curiosity piqued, I push aside the burdens of leadership.

She scampers across the room. "Kin can show you. We've been practicing." Rose plops down cross-legged on the chair.

It's hard not to smile at her enthusiasm. "Show me."

For a second, I consider if spying on Sterling this way is okay.

Then my concern for his safety—for everyone's safety—snuffs out any lingering doubts. Five days have passed without an update from them. There's no way I can say no to Rose's offer.

With a delighted clap, Rose encourages Kin to expand.

The flame swirls and coils before shaping into a pool of shimmering light. Inside the magical window, vivid images flicker with the fire.

My lungs flatten and reinflate as the view swoops down and centers on Sterling. He's grappling with the rough terrain alongside Tanwen as they climb a mountain slope.

The scene transfixes me as he clings to the dragon's scaly neck, his face set with grim determination.

"Look at them!" Rose cheers with awe. "Isn't it amazing?"

"Yes. Amazing."

And terrifying.

The scene shifts to reveal Leesa using the sword imbued with my magic to chop away sinister plants writhing toward them.

Crafting a weapon infused with both my phoenix fire and regular fire element was Bastian's idea. Thanks to his forethought, the bladesmith—along with a little assistance from me—began the finicky process of fashioning the magical sword a few months ago.

My heart races at the sight of my sister working by Sterling's side.

That's when I realize what's happening in the scrying pool

isn't current. The magic's showing me events that have already transpired.

The scene shifts again, this time revealing Agnar holding a rockslide at bay, his imposing figure steady as he channels earth magic to keep his companions safe. The juxtaposition of their strength fuels my pride, yet a gnawing dread unfurls in my gut.

Up next is Sterling again. He kneels at the edge of a high cliff while trailing his hand through a waterfall that flows upward. Sparkling droplets hang in the air. His face is intense with focus, brows knitted. I can practically feel the wonder radiating off him.

Rose claps her hands in delight. "He's really good!"

Though my chest still tightens with anxiety, I can't help but admire the way he moves. His bravery.

"He's certainly taking plenty of risks." I frown on the last word as my chest twinges with both trepidation and longing.

Rose hops down from her chair. "Look, he's about to do something wild again! It's because he hangs out with Uncle Agnar so much. That's what my Mama says. Uncle Agnar is always doing big things. Watch!"

The flames flicker, and my eyes are glued to the scrying pool as Sterling leaps into action once more, nearly putting himself in danger for the fourth time within the short span of our viewing.

"Be careful!" Rose squeals, nearly jumping with glee as he effortlessly dodges another threat. My heart thunders in my ears, torn between pride and an overwhelming sense of dread. "Do you think he'll be okay?"

I want to reassure her, but the answer sticks in my throat like bitter ash. "He'd better be, or he's going to be in so much trouble."

Rose giggles and squirms. "You can get the dragons to pick him upside down and use his head as a mop!"

Despite my apprehension, that visual elicits a snicker. "Now there's an idea."

We watch as he navigates through the forests and heads toward the cloud-covered mountain peaks. Rose views his adventures with bright eyes and the innocent, unyielding belief that everything will work out. I wish I could embody even a fraction of her faith.

Hesitating, I nod to the flame. As Kin flickers back, I gently remind myself to cherish this. Such magic was unheard of before. Whether this is something new, or something old and reborn again, it fills me with dual fascination and hesitation.

What would the other kingdoms think if they knew we weren't merely retaining our powers while theirs falter, but utilizing a new ability to peek in on them at any time, past or present?

What would happen to Rose?

My stomach twists. I don't intend to find out.

❧

Lark

The next evening, the air is crisp and clear, providing a welcome reprieve from the tangled web of palace duties as I land in the middle of the training fields.

This is the only time I allow myself to detach from the demands of the throne. Especially since no one is watching. Of course, the guards are around, but they know better than to get too close and reveal their presence while I unwind for the day. No cheers. No calls from soldiers. No attendants hurrying me along.

This is where I shed the layers of royal expectation and

become something else. Where I can be myself, where the fire within me truly burns.

I step through the gate of one of the rings.

The soft glow of the moon bathes the arena in silver light and dances along my short sword when I free the weapon from its sheath.

I begin to move, fluid and fierce, testing out the techniques I've practiced both alone and with a partner. A silent choreography of stepping and turning. Advancing, retreating.

The sword glides through the air, slicing invisible foes. Each swing sends a surge of power through my veins.

Flame and steel.

With the crackling energy intensifying, I push myself even harder, driven by a desire to surpass what my title demands. The perfect queen seems a distant ideal as I embrace the fighter within myself, flowing through techniques that weave fire and steel into a deadly dance.

Too long. It's been too damn long since I've trained with a physical weapon.

I ignore the fatigue creeping into my muscles. Instead, I focus on the freedom of movement, the strength rising in my core, on breaking the chains of expectation and worry.

From the corner of my eye, I catch a glimpse of Rafe as he observes from outside the ring, his arms crossed in a casual yet assessing manner. His intense gaze dares me to be better, to evolve into the leader I've always envisioned yet haven't fully embraced, and I try my best to meet that challenge.

"Impressive." His expression possesses a hint of something I can't quite place. Approval? "You've made remarkable progress."

A swell of warmth ignites in my chest, grounding me in this moment. "I need to be more than just a crown. I need to be able to protect those I care about."

"That's the spirit of a true leader." He nods, a flicker of admiration illuminating his features. "You're not just a queen, Lark. You're a warrior. Embrace it. Follow your heart. That's the only reason we're all still ourselves and not puppets being controlled by a god."

As I strike against the air once more, I vow to embrace my duality.

I am not merely a queen. I am also a fighter, a protector.

With that knowledge burns a fierce determination. I won't allow the world to dictate who I am any longer.

CHAPTER NINETEEN
LARK

I jolt awake with my heart in my throat, momentarily confused by the bright sunlight pouring through the windows. The realization that I've overslept—again—hits me like a bucket of cold water.

The sheets twist around my legs like hungry vines as I scramble up, my mind already cataloguing the meetings I've missed, the reports I haven't read, and the people I've disappointed.

Sterling would never have missed the morning report. But Sterling isn't here, and I'm the one wearing the crown.

My head pounds with the remnants of not enough sleep and too many hours bent over ancient tomes. Royal decrees and historical precedents swarm behind my eyelids, a jumble of should haves and could bes that I'd been trying to memorize until the candles burned down to nubs.

A knock at the door has me spinning in place, one arm thrust through my robe sleeve, the other flailing for balance. "Your Majesty?"

"Just a minute!" My voice comes out higher than I intend,

betraying my panic. I cinch the robe tight around my waist. Telling myself I'm ready for anything, I lift my chin. "Come in."

Rhiann Barda steps inside and gestures behind her to communicate that someone else is waiting. Bastian appears in the doorway, his face creased with concern.

"Bastian, I know I'm late. I'll be at the meeting as soon as —" I gesture to Rhiann, who is hurrying to my wardrobe to retrieve today's outfit, which she's already hung and prepared.

Rhiann has assisted me since I first came to Tirene, and I've never been more grateful for her help than today.

"Lark, reports are coming in from across the kingdom." My brother's words clip my apology short. "The morning briefing has...evolved."

My stomach sinks. "How bad?"

"Bad enough that I came searching for you." He steps inside, closing the door behind him. "Merchants from the Western Provinces are refusing to travel. Something about bridge tolls being collected by..." Bastian hesitates, as if checking the words before they leave his mouth, "stars."

Rhiann's hairbrush stills in my hair, and I blink at him. "Stars?"

Ever the proper Lady of the Bedchamber, Rhiann snaps out of her momentary shock and sets herself to getting me presentable.

"Lights, they're saying. Descending from the sky and forming barriers across bridges." His fingers twist together. "Anyone who tries to cross without payment is...well, they say the stars burn through their wagons."

We all jump when there's another knock on the door.

With what we've just learned, I think we're only expecting things to get worse.

"That'll be your breakfast." Rhiann finishes tying my hair

back as Bastian opens the door for the maid, who's holding a tray of tea and a single piece of toast. "I assumed you'd be heading off, so we'll send you the rest to wherever you need."

I nod, still trying to process this strange information. Stars attacking merchants? What would a proper queen do with this news? What would Sterling do?

Before I can formulate a response, the door bursts open again. Bastian's hand drops to his sword as I instinctively snatch my own weapon from the table beside my bed.

A guard rushes in, her armor askew as if thrown on hastily. She stares at Bastian's hand and my glower before bowing. "Your Majesty, I apologize for the unannounced intrusion into your bedchamber, but refugees are streaming in from Greenmeadow. Dryads have emerged from their reclusive haunts to attack the village."

My hold on my sheathed sword loosens with shock. "Dryads don't attack." Just saying the two words in the same sentence is enough to spin my head in dizzying circles.

"These ones do." The guard's face goes a shade paler, a stark contrast with the bright red hair peeking out from under her helmet. "Three people have died already, and dozens are injured. The village elder is waiting in your receiving hall."

Two crises before breakfast. No Sterling to offer his military expertise. And not a single idea of what to do bubbling up in my allegedly royal brain.

I take a deep breath. "I'll join him shortly. Rhiann, you know where I'll be. Bastian, please assemble the council."

With my scant breakfast now forgotten, Rhiann focuses on getting me dressed. It's a simple gown since I have no time for the formal regalia. No time for anything other than facing whatever fresh hells await me downstairs.

I arrive at the place we use as a receiving room, a long, narrow space perfect for processing lengthy lines of people in record time. The people enter on the far side and wait their turn to reach me at the desk on this side. Once finished, they'll be escorted out.

There are no fancy decorations in such rooms, not anymore. I don't care about showing off luxuries, or paintings, or expensive rugs.

Under my reign, there are no distractions and no hiding places. Nothing to make the proceedings last longer.

Guards stand at their posts near the walls, keeping an eye on everyone. The space buzzes with urgency. Nobles, guards, and messengers cluster in tight groups, their voices overlapping like competing instruments in a badly conducted orchestra.

They quiet when I enter and bow hastily, faces heavy with expectation. The village elder from Greenmeadow, one of the largest farming villages on the eastern side of Tirene, stands at the front. He removes a sun-faded hat to reveal a smooth bald head. Soil clings to his weathered boots, his clothes stained with what might be blood or sap. Or maybe both. Considering it's not yet ten in the morning, he must have left at dawn in order to arrive when he did.

Meaning the attack happened at or before sunrise.

"Your Majesty." The relief in his voice clenches my stomach.

These people think I can help them. They have faith in their queen.

I just hope I don't let them down.

Before he can speak further, a woman in merchant's garb strides forward. "Western roads are closed to us, Your Majesty. The star toll has tripled in the past day. We cannot afford—"

"The dryads have burned three homes already." The elder pushes forward, glaring at the merchant. "People are dead. Not just running out of money. We need soldiers, archers—"

"Your Majesty!" A thin nobleman I recognize from the Coastal Provinces waves a sealed parchment. "The crops in Millvale were blighted overnight. They've completely rotted in the fields."

"The well in Southmark runs with black water." Another woman clutches her arms, as if to keep them from shaking. Her nails dig into her simple homespun cloth. "Three children have fallen ill already."

"Sacred birds are attacking kids in the temple gardens—"

"The doorways at the Temple of Althy no longer lead to the inside as they appear. People have plummeted hundreds of feet into the sea. The ones already inside tried to leave and were also found in the waters."

This last report rips through the clamor, silencing the room.

A nobleman strides forward as the people around him rear back. His fingers worry the embroidery on his fine silk sleeve. "I funded that temple myself, Your Majesty. Solid stone, blessed by three priests. Now the doorways...they just...open to air. Above the cliffs. Two acolytes dead already."

My head spins at the bizarre occurrences all being spewed forth at once. "Wait a minute. Are the acolytes children? If they're old enough, why didn't they just open their wings and fly?"

"We don't know." The nobleman looks like he might vomit. "They just fell to their deaths, screaming the whole way down. A few people flew out to catch them, and their wings disappeared."

Now *I* want to vomit.

If we can't trust our wings...can't trust our steps...can't trust our temples, even, then what can we trust?

Horrified mutters join the snapping of expanding and retracting wings. Everyone's checking themselves. Even the guards. Though those few at least appear guilty about their actions.

I raise my hand, and to my surprise, the room goes quiet. Wings freeze, some up, some down. Every eye regards me.

Now is not the time to show uncertainty. I can't run off with weapons and magic like I did when facing Narc. I am a queen, and my kingdom is disintegrating in ways I can't comprehend. "Let me think."

What would Sterling do? No. What would any good leader do?

A few of the council members wander in, with Bastian at their backs. Their arrival gives me an idea.

"Dalya," I nod to the coastal nobleman, "send a platoon from the military. This man will show you where. Two squads will help you close off the temple completely. No one enters until we understand what's happening. The other two will search the ocean for any survivors. Take war alicorns, just in case. They know how to get under falling riders."

Dalya doesn't bat an eye at the sudden order. Simply bows her magenta head, collects the nobleman, and ushers him to the door.

I turn to the merchant woman. "Tell me about these star tolls. How many bridges? When did it start?"

She describes the phenomenon as light descending at sunset, hovering above bridges, and burning through the carts and clothing of those who try to pass without payment.

"What kind of payment?"

Her honey brown eyes grow hazy, as if she's recalling all the details. "Sometimes coins, sometimes food. And even blood."

I reach out with my mind, searching for the dragons. Kaida's consciousness brushes my mind, and through a series of emotions and mental images, I convey my request to him.

"Go to the fire paddock and tell the dragontenders that I

said Kaida is to follow you home. He's already eager to help your people carry your goods so that you don't need to use the bridges. Those will be closed off until the situation is sorted. No one is going to tax the people of Tirene without my leave."

The woman gapes at me, then jumps back as Kaida's golden eye peers through a window. I can feel his mischief building as he debates licking the glass for even more attention.

People shuffle away. It's one thing to love dragons and know they live at the palace. It's something else entirely to have a head the size of a horse fog up the glass panes right next to you.

"Never mind. He's already here and ready to go." I project my gratitude to Kaida through our bond, and I swear he winks at me. "And he knows what he needs to do. You just have to lead the way."

My mind catalogues and separates each crisis into components of frightened merchants, displaced villagers, environmental anomalies, and supernatural disturbances.

I find Rafe and Helene Mortimer standing near the back of the room. "Rafe, Helene, I need you to assemble a team of scientist-priests to investigate the Temple of Aletheia. Gather whatever resources you need."

Rafe bows and steps out. Helene opens her mouth to speak before clamping it shut as if she realizes how busy I am. The Aclarian noble simply nods and takes her leave.

This politeness is a far cry from when my former classmate and I first met at Flighthaven. The raven-haired, fair-skinned young woman was the bane of my existence in those days. Though I wouldn't exactly slap the friendship label on our relationship, we've come a long way.

Next, I gesture for Duke Bron.

He comes forward, clean-shaven chin lifted, blond hair windblown. "How can I assist, my queen?"

"Open the Eastern Garrison for housing Greenmeadow refugees. Take grain from the military stores to feed them while we sort this out." I peruse the room but fail to spot any of the healers. "Someone fetch Healer Luci and bring her to me. With her understanding of herbology and connection with the temples, I'm sure she can find someone well-versed in dryads who can help us understand why this happened."

The doors open, and Rhiann walks in carrying a tray.

My throat is parched, and I realize I haven't even had a sip of water since I woke up. "You." I nod at the thin nobleman and his sealed parchment. "Come join me at the table. And bring me the captain of the palace regiment." It's time to mobilize the military.

Rhiann hurries over, every step a smooth glide that doesn't even rattle the spoon on the saucer.

A guard steps forward to pull my chair back for me. With a grateful smile, I sit.

Rhiann speaks in a low voice while setting the tray down. "Astrid will be here shortly. Along with your papers from last night. Pages have been brought and are waiting outside to carry any orders." She finishes placing my breakfast beside me, lifts the cloth from the tray, and lays a sheaf of papers in front of me, as well as pens, ink, wax, and my seal.

"Thank you, Rhiann. Go ahead and send the first one in."

"Of course, Your Majesty." She dips into a curtsy and steps away.

I lift the cup with one hand and reach for the parchment with the other, continuing through each crisis methodically.

Military patrols for the dryad-infested regions. Water purification experts to Southmark, along with earth users and plenty of water-wielding soldiers. Earth elementals specializing in plants and fire users to assess the blighted crops.

With each order, my voice grows steadier. Each page is required to report back with any additional information so we can change plans as needed. I don't know if these are the right decisions, but they are decisions. And sometimes that's what people need most. Someone willing to act when the world is crumbling.

After I've taken all the complaints for the day, the room empties quickly. People hurry off to fulfill my orders. Sipping my cold and over steeped last cup of tea, I catch a glimpse of myself in a polished shield mounted on the wall.

Brown hair hangs slightly disheveled over wide hazel eyes and a stubborn chin.

I'm looking the part, if not feeling it.

An unbidden thought creeps in that Sterling is probably flying over mountains right now, discovering ancient secrets, and fighting tangible enemies. Not trapped in...this nightmare.

Ashamed, I push the thought away.

Sterling was exactly who we needed on this journey. And managing a kingdom in crisis is my duty. Tirene needs a queen, not another adventurer.

"Not bad for someone who claims she doesn't know how to rule." Bastian walks in, interrupting my thoughts.

Before I can respond, Helene appears in the doorway, Rafe at her shoulder.

They were supposed to be gathering scientist-priests. There's no way they could have finished that already, let alone gotten answers from them. "What is it?"

Helene glances at Rafe, who appears unusually subdued. "We just learned that a number of the most renowned scientist-priests have gone missing."

"Missing?" How could such a large group of people go missing? "Since when?"

"Over the past month." Rafe doesn't glance away or hide the anger simmering in his caramel-colored eyes. "One by one.

Thinking they were isolated incidents, the temple authorities kept it quiet."

I massage my forehead, trying to ease the building ache. "And they were not?"

Helene tightens her lips. "There are rumors of Devoted involvement."

Staring at the wall behind them, I attempt to process this new information. Is this genuinely ridiculous, or is this just a normal day in the life of a royal? Fanatics who wear star-marks on their hands and preach about the supremacy of Zeru. And now we have stars collecting tolls on bridges. Missing priests. Temples with doors that lead to nowhere.

I'm struggling so hard to be the perfect queen while the world dissolves into chaos around me.

Perhaps that's exactly what a queen does. When the kingdom is falling apart, she holds it together. Any way she can.

I inhale another sip of tea, the cold liquid soothing me. "Find out if that's true. If the Devoted have moved from being a religious nuisance to a national security threat. I want to know where those scientist-priests are and what connection, if any, exists between these incidents."

Once they're gone, I start to sag. Then I catch myself. Guards still line the walls. Pages sit just out of sight, waiting for Astrid to call them again.

"Bastian, care to take a walk with me?" He's at my side before I can finish pushing back the heavy chair I've been sitting in for the last few hours. "I need some air."

And to stretch my body before my legs go numb.

"With my favorite sister?" He gives an exaggerated bow. "Always."

Once we're in the hallway, and the guards are trailing behind us, I blow out my breath. "I'm making all this up as I go."

His mouth quirks up at one corner. "That's called ruling."

He startles a small laugh out of me. "Is it always like this?"

"Going from my knowledge of court life," he gives me that big brother look he's perfected over the last several months, the one that says he's older, wiser, and more experienced, "sometimes it's worse."

Fantastic.

CHAPTER TWENTY
LARK

My neck aches from hours of hunching over reports. The candles have burned low, casting flickering shadows across endless pages about sewer systems and tax collection. The unglamorous backbone of ruling that no bard ever sings about. My head throbs with numbers and complaints and the constant pressure of trying to be so damned regal.

I reach for my tea, which went cold hours ago, when the world around me warps like heated glass.

Shit.

I've really gone too far this time. Mother always said if I drank too much tea—

The vision hits without warning.

No gentle lead-in, no courteous tap on the shoulder of my consciousness, no confusing blend with where I already am. Just a violent yank into somewhere—something—else.

My study dissolves.

The neat stack of reports, the polished desk, the comfortable chair.

All gone in an instant.

Images flood my mind. Not clear and precise like Mar's

visions were during my coronation. Those warned about what would happen if I failed in my quest to burn Narc's bones.

These...I can't decipher. They're fractured. Twisted. Smeared.

What am I seeing?

The images are bent and splattered, as if ridden through by muddy hooves. Every time I attempt to focus on crucial details, it's like looking at words penned with water. The truth might be there, buried under all the obscurity.

I know one way to enhance my ability to see.

With a shrug, I unfurl my wings. They sprout from my back, sweeping up unseen. My vision sharpens, informing me that my eyes have turned golden.

I see a temple.

No. Several temples. Layered over each other. Narc's, Ziva's, Zeru's, Aletheia's, Cyphero's, Valk's. Crystalline growths smother their stone walls and pulse with inner light.

Clear crystals spread like ivy, consuming archways, statues, altars. They grow in straight lines but jut out in crazy angles.

Then the crystals curl. Melt instead of fracture. Bleed away like watercolors in the rain.

The scene shifts.

People kneel in prayer, hands clasped, lips moving. Suddenly, their bodies flatten. They become two-dimensional, paper-thin silhouettes against a backdrop I can't quite identify. Their bodies wave like shrouds in the wind. They're not dead. Their prayers continue.

But the people are...changed.

Wrong.

Their mouths still move, but now they pray with the frantic urgency of innocent people facing the gallows.

What are they saying? Who are they praying to?

I strain to hear their words, but the sound is muffled, as if I'm underwater.

The vision changes again.

Three figures hover around a pool. Their features blur like faces viewed through a waterfall, but their posture suggests importance.

Power. Arrogance, even. Divinity?

They each watch the water, never looking away. Their attention is absolute. One reaches toward the pool, trailing their fingers through whatever they see there.

I squint, struggling to spot what has their attention.

The water ripples, yet the reflection remains clear.

Sterling.

My heart stutters, and my mouth goes dry.

He stands alone in a chamber of ancient stone. Water rises around him and has already reached his knees. His face appears calm but determined as he studies an inscription on the wall. He doesn't see the rising water. Doesn't notice how it swirls with unnatural purpose, or how it creeps up his thighs with hungry intent.

Not just rising...but *climbing* him.

I try to call out, to warn him, but my voice doesn't exist here. I'm just a helpless spectator. The water creeps up to his waist. His eyebrows knit together, his focus still on the writing rather than his element overtaking him.

Then the vision crumples.

As brutally as it started, the scene's torn from my eyes by an unseen hand.

I come back to myself with a gasp, hands gripping the edge of my desk so hard my knuckles have gone white. My body shakes with tremors I can't control. Feathers slide over feathers, shivering and weak. Sweat plasters my hair to my temples, and my throat is raw, though I don't recall screaming out loud.

My eyes burn. Tears run down like sea water. I bow my

head, and the tears drip onto the table. I squeeze my eyes shut, wanting to unsee everything I've just witnessed.

For several long minutes, all I can do is breathe.

I'm in my study. I'm safe. Sterling's element is water. There's no way he could drown.

When my heart stops attempting to hammer its way out of my ribs, I force myself to focus. To analyze what just happened. Without a doubt, that was not Mar's doing. Even after only one vision, I know the touch of her presence. This wasn't it.

The crystalline clarity at the edges, the faint sense of apology for the truth she brings. How bright it all was...

Aletheia.

The Goddess of Light and Truth.

As soon as the thought swells up in my mind, I know it's true. But why such a obscure message? It's as if someone else deliberately interfered with the vision. The smears...the tears... the blurring...

If someone can distort divine messages...

The implications chill me to the bone. Gods have rules. Limitations. They can't interfere directly in mortal affairs, so they send visions, omens, and even avatars.

But those communications are sacred. Inviolable.

Or at least, they're supposed to be.

Someone or something has found a way to tamper with them. Something is very, very wrong with the divine order of things. If gods can't speak clearly to mortals, if their messages are being intercepted and distorted...

Who would dare to stand against the gods? Who would defy them so blatantly?

Chapter Twenty-One
Lark

The morning sun catches on the shiny silver coins as I pass them from my palm to weathered hands. I'm supposed to be distributing food, blankets, medicine, and other essentials.

But I've tucked away some of my personal allowance too.

The palace treasurer would have an apoplexy if he found out, but what Felix doesn't know won't hurt him. And what good is being queen if I can't slip a few extra coins to those whose cheeks have gone hollow with hunger?

Besides, no one's watching too closely. I'm sure of it.

An elderly woman's fingers tremble as they close around the provisions I've handed her. "Your Majesty is too generous."

"It's my pleasure." I squeeze her shoulder gently. "Hopefully this will help get you through the winter."

Behind me, several of the guards distribute larger packages. Sacks of grain, bundles of firewood, carefully wrapped vials of medicine. I've ordered them to spread out so we can cover more ground.

Efficiency, I'd claimed. In truth, I just want to be able to breathe without their hovering. Even Elijah, who's only recently joined Windmyre's royal guards, watches me with an intensity that prickles my skin.

Despite the early hour, the street teems with life. Merchants hawk their wares from makeshift stalls. The smell of fresh bread battles with the less pleasant scents of a waking city. Children dart between adults, their laughter a counterpoint to the serious business of survival.

This part of Tirene doesn't see royalty often. The cobblestones are uneven beneath my boots, the buildings lean into each other like drunken friends, and the gutters...well, I'm careful where I step.

I reach into my satchel for another bundle as a young mother approaches, a baby strapped to her chest and a toddler clinging to her faded skirts.

"My Queen." She attempts a shallow bow, cautious not to disturb the sleeping infant. "We're honored."

"Please. You don't need to do that." I wave away the formality. "How old?" I nod toward the baby, who has more hair than I've ever seen on an infant.

"Three months, Your Majesty. Her name is Scarlet."

"A beautiful name. And your children are precious." I add another blanket to her bundle. "Babies need extra warmth in the winter."

My gaze drifts up to the rooftops, where out of season greenery pushes through gaps in the tiles. Even in the most unlikely places, life finds a way.

I'm so lost in thought that I don't notice the figure until it's nearly upon me. A shadow slides into my peripheral vision. When I spin around, I find myself face-to-face with a person in dark robes.

My heart stutters before I force it to steady. Dark robes aren't that unusual. It's what peeks from beneath them that has me on edge. Constellation marks trail up the figure's wrist, disappearing underneath billowing sleeves.

The Devoted.

I glance around for my guards, but they're exactly where I wanted them. Several paces behind, distributing goods to a cluster of families. Elijah's back is to me as he passes a sack of grain to an elderly man. In a handful of months, he's gone from entitled aristocrat to a palace guard handing out charity to refugees.

"Your Majesty." Though a hood obscures their features, the rough timbre of the Devoted's voice sounds masculine. "What a blessing to find you among the people."

The Devoted aren't technically outlawed, but they've been linked to enough disturbances that their presence jangles my nerves. I'm particularly incensed over the one involving the missing scientist-priests.

I incline my head, keeping my posture open but alert. "I try to be where I'm needed."

He steps closer, just inside the boundary of propriety. The intimidation tactic won't work on me. "Indeed. I wonder if I might trouble you with a question. About the...changes we're all experiencing."

I immediately know what he means, but I force him to spell it out. "Changes?"

"The magic, Your Majesty." His voice drops, becoming conspiratorial. "The way it's fading. Like the gods themselves are abandoning us."

"The court mages are investigating. We have our best minds working to figure out what's happening." In other words, royal bullshit for, *We're clueless.*

While they claim to honor the whole pantheon, the Devoted worship Zeru above all other deities. This man seems genuinely interested in my response.

His head tilts just so, his body language conveying openness.

But something's off.

The way he leans a little too close. The way his gaze never strays from mine, not even for a blink. He's waiting for something. An opportunity. With his trimmed, clean nails, I suspect his hands have never seen hard work. They're folded but loose. Ready. For what?

He takes another step, and an herbal aroma I can't quite put my finger on wafts off of him. "But you feel it, too, don't you? You, with your fire magic. Rumor is you're the strongest in generations. Surely you've noticed the diminishment."

My shoulders tense. How does he know about my magic's strength? It's not exactly a state secret, but it's not common knowledge either.

Has he seen me use my power? Did he lurk in the shadows when I practiced merging with Sterling? "Magic has always had its ebbs and flows throughout history. This could be a natural cycle."

"Natural?" He smiles, and his hood shifts to reveal a shock of white hair and the palest, most unnerving blue eyes I've ever encountered. "Is it natural when prayers go unanswered? When the faithful call to the gods and hear only silence? Don't worry." His voice drops, and his tone becomes more menacing. "You're not alone. You're never alone. The stars watch you, my queen. And count your every breath."

My skin crawls.

But I've dealt with worse than this silk-voiced, pampered zealot.

Hells, I'd rather confront him than a ballroom full of tipsy nobles any day of the week.

I straighten to my full height.

"Careful." I don't raise my voice, but I do sharpen it. Several townspeople swivel around to watch. "That sounded like a threat against your queen. And my dragons don't like it when I feel threatened. Nor do I."

The Devoted's smile doesn't waver. "Queens rise and fall.

The gods are eternal. And I speak only truth. As Aletheia would want."

After last night's mangled vision, his casual mention of the Goddess of Light and Truth lands wrong. "You don't speak for the gods."

"No?" He tilts his head, the fluid motion reminiscent of a snake. "Then why do they grant us power? Why do they—"

"You prey on people." I inch closer, the heat of my anger warming my skin. "Why? Why do you do that?"

His smile falters, though his eyes remain alight with malice.

Just for a second, a flash of something raw and hateful shines beneath the pious veneer.

"Those who destroy magic must pay the price." His hand reaches under his cloak, but I'm faster.

One hand catches his wrist while the other goes to his throat. Not squeezing. Just there...and uncomfortably hot.

To remind him of who holds the power here.

One flex of my magic, and I could incinerate him. Truthfully, I don't even have to touch him to do that, but the gesture's surely gotten his attention. "I wouldn't if I were you."

People are definitely gawking now.

Good.

Let them witness how their queen won't be intimidated. Even if my heart's racing like a trapped hummingbird. Though I have no desire to burn a citizen alive.

His eyes widen, and his hand goes slack by his sides.

"Problem?" Bastian appears, his presence solid and reassuring. He doesn't draw his weapon, but his hand rests on the hilt. "I would be more than happy to take him off your hands. Or I can remove *his* hands instead, if he doesn't stop reaching for whatever is under his cloak."

The Devoted man's eyes flick between us. His lip curls like he's disgusted just to be in our presence.

Or maybe it has something to do with the fact that I'm still holding him by the throat.

"No." I release the Devoted, taking silent satisfaction in the way he flinches. "No problem. And it's going to stay that way. Wouldn't you agree?"

"Of course, Your Majesty." The man holds my gaze for a heartbeat before disappearing into the crowd.

Bastian releases a low whistle.

I raise an eyebrow. "Care to enlighten me on what that means?"

His lips twitch, and his eyes sparkle. "For a minute there, I thought I was going to have to intervene."

"Oh, please. I had him."

"Wasn't you I was worried about. How would we explain away Tirene's queen burning one of the Devoted to a crisp?" Bastian tsks. "Not exactly the best way to win friends and influence people."

I shoot him a glare, mentally congratulating myself for resisting the urge to make a very unqueenlike gesture. "Shut up, Bastian."

He winks before motioning to a nearby guard.

Within seconds, the guards begin clearing the area of onlookers, their voices firm but not alarming as they direct civilians away from the scene. Most people move on, though some linger, either curious or concerned.

Elijah positions himself at my right, brows scrunched as I recount the near incident with the Devoted. "Should we find him?"

Chewing my lip, I consider what I want. The Devoted threatened me. Or at least, it felt like one. Which is good enough when it's directed at a monarch. But arresting a member of the Devoted, even an inauspicious one, could spark exactly the kind of unrest they seem to crave.

In fact, that might be his real purpose here. "No, but once you do find him, follow him. Discreetly. Tell me where he goes, who he talks to."

After I give a description of the man, Elijah and two other guards peel off, disappearing down an alley.

"Time to return to the palace, I think." Bastian eyes the rest of the crowd. "We've distributed all the provisions."

I'm tempted to argue, not wanting to come across as cowardly, but the encounter has left me feeling exposed. I reluctantly nod.

The trek back passes in a blur of cobblestones and unsettled glances. Bastian keeps close. He doesn't speak until we're safely inside the palace walls, away from curious ears. "What exactly happened back there?"

"A power play." I'm not sure if I'm angry or frightened, and the uncertainty has me twitchy. "He was fishing for information about the decline of magic, but there was something, I don't know, *wrong* about him."

"Wrong how?"

I haven't told anyone about the distorted message from Althy, but the man seemed to know. How? Are the Devoted so strong they can interfere with the gods' communications?

I struggle to articulate what I mean without going into detail about my recent vision. "Like he knew things he shouldn't."

Bastian's expression tightens, but he doesn't press. "The Devoted have been growing bolder. This isn't the first report of them approaching people in positions of influence."

When we reach my chambers, I sink into a chair, exhausted despite the early hour.

Bastian stalks over to the side table where a teapot sits

warming over a small brazier. "Fusion Root Vine Tea? It might help."

In addition to hastening a magical merge, the tea is known for its hydrating and soothing properties. Queen Alannah started cultivating the plant in her garden over a decade ago, allowing its power to strengthen with age.

But as I open my mouth to accept the beverage, I change my mind.

No tea.

No hiding in my chambers.

I need something stronger than leaves steeped in water. "Dragons." I stand abruptly, already excited. "I'm going to visit the dragons."

Bastian raises an eyebrow but doesn't argue. He knows me well enough to recognize when I've set my mind to something. "I'll come with you."

I nod, already feeling more centered at the thought of the fire paddock, of scaled wings and ancient eyes. If anyone can make sense of what just happened, of what's going on with magic across the kingdoms, it's the creatures who've lived with it longest.

Besides, no one would dare threaten me when I'm standing next to a dragon.

CHAPTER TWENTY-TWO
LARK

The late afternoon sun beats down on the fire paddock, sending shimmers of heat dancing across crushed stone and sand. I shield my eyes, scanning the enclosure for Dame and Chirean, but the nesting pair is nowhere in sight. Not unusual. They have eggs to protect, and though I'm still not certain when their young will hatch, I know the time is getting near.

I understand the instinct. Even royal duties can't compete with the promise of new life.

Something feels different today though. Expectancy charges the air, prickling my skin beneath my riding leathers.

Ryu nudges my shoulder with his snout, nearly knocking me sideways. As the largest and oldest of Tirene's dragons, he's usually also the calmest.

Unless he's hunting.

Today, he's restless, shifting his weight from one clawed foot to the other, his clubbed tail sweeping arcs through the paddock's crushed stone.

I run my hand along the smooth scales of his neck. "What's got you so fidgety?"

He doesn't use words—dragons rarely do—but his emotions brush my mind.

Anticipation, excitement, urgency.

Images flash between us as well. The open sky, clouds, the rushing wind. He wants to fly, and not just a casual patrol around the palace grounds.

In the corner of the paddock, Mygist regards us with hooded golden eyes. His midnight scales absorb the sunlight, granting him the appearance of a shadow given mass and form. The dark frill around his neck twitches when our eyes meet, but he makes no attempt to join us.

I gesture to Ryu. "You're insistent on taking me somewhere."

Bastian frowns, pushing off from the wall and striding toward us. His boots leave neat imprints in the sand. "Not alone, I hope. The Aclarian ambassador is still in the city, and we've received reports of suspicious movement along the Eastern border."

I sigh, itching to climb the massive dragon's extended foreleg. "I'm not going to hide in the palace forever, Bastian."

From anyone else, being told I shouldn't go somewhere alone would irk me. Though I've only known my brother for less than a year, I understand that his protective streak is born of love, not the need to control me.

"It's not hiding. It's using caution." While he keeps his tone light, I recognize the worry beneath it. The scene in town is probably still haunting him. "Let me come with you. Mygist and I could use the exercise."

As if hearing his name, Mygist releases a low rumble from across the paddock. The feeling that washes over me is clear.

I interpret the dragon's emotions as, *Absolutely fucking not.*

Ryu echoes the sentiment, more firmly.

This offer is for me alone.

"The dragons disagree." I scale Ryu's foreleg, the maneuver lasting a matter of seconds. Much faster than the first few times I did this. "They want me to go solo."

Bastian's frown deepens into a scowl. "Very reassuring, Lark."

Okay, maybe big brother is being just a teeny bit overprotective.

"I won't be alone." I climb onto Ryu's back, settling into the familiar spot at the base of his neck. "I'm safer with the dragons than I am anywhere else. You know it's true."

"All right." Recognizing the futility of arguing, he raises his hands in surrender and steps back. "Just be careful. Knox would have my head if anything happened to you."

My chest flutters with warmth at the mention of the crown prince. "I should be back before dinner." I then lean forward to whisper to Ryu. "Ready when you are."

Needing no further encouragement, the dragon launches skyward with a powerful thrust of his legs, wings unfurling with a snap that echoes through the paddock. My stomach drops as we rise. The palace shrinks beneath us faster than it ever does under the might of my own wings.

The wind whips my loose hair into a frenzy, and I feel my wings stirring beneath my skin, aching to join the dragon's flight. To soar alongside him. I resist the urge. Ryu wanted to carry me to our destination, so I'll follow his lead.

We soar higher, the landscape of Tirene spreading below us like an expertly crafted tapestry. The palace with its sprawling wings and royal gardens, the city with its bustling streets, the forests and fields beyond.

My kingdom. My responsibility.

Ryu banks sharply northeast, in the direction of the mountains. I recognize our destination long before we reach it.

A sheer cliff face with a narrow ledge that's barely wide enough for a dragon to land. Dame showed me this place months ago. The cave has a hot spring inside that's perfect for incubating eggs, regardless of the season.

Worry and hope bubble up inside me. Ryu keeps his mind blank, but I still catch traces of his smugness about keeping this a secret from me.

He lands with surprising delicacy, folding his wings tight against his body.

Dismounting is tricky in this place, and my boots scuff against the rocky ledge as I find purchase.

"Why did you bring me here?"

But Ryu's already launching himself back into the sky, disappearing around the curve of the mountain.

"Great." I confront the dark maw of the cave. "Very helpful."

Concern knots my stomach. Has something happened to Dame? To the eggs? I duck into the cavern, blinking as my eyes adjust to the dimness. I could light a fire, but that might startle the soon-to-be parents. Since I'm clueless about what I might find, I tread as carefully and quietly as possible.

The passage slopes downward, widening as it goes, the rough walls bearing marks of Dame's claws where she's expanded the space. The air grows warmer and moister, carrying the mineral scent of the hot spring.

I hear it before I see it.

Beneath the gentle steam of spring water, there's... humming. A melody. Haunting and beautiful, it resonates in my bones, more felt than heard.

Someone's inside this cave with me. Someone other than the dragons.

My heart races with trepidation, and I find myself rushing toward the eggs. If something's happened to them, if someone's harmed them in any way—

I refuse to finish that thought.

Rounding the final bend, I stop short. The cave opens

into a chamber large enough for the two dragons that currently keep vigil at the edge of a steaming pool of water. Dame stands beside the spring, her reddish-brown scales gleaming in the strange, diffused light that seems to have no source. Her pale yellow underwings quiver with anticipation as she watches over the pair of floating eggs.

But Dame's not the one humming.

Near the water, a small figure with blond hair and a spattering of freckles across her nose sits cross-legged in a nest of straw.

Rose Lockwood.

My heart stops, then beats double-time, and I release a breath. The eggs are safe. No one has harmed them. As for Rose? I don't have the slightest clue how she got here, but I'm relieved that she appears unscathed.

Now's not the time to question her about her antics.

Absorbed in her song, the little girl doesn't notice me at first. The flame familiar hovering above her shoulder casts flickering shadows across her face. The sprite flares in rhythm with her melody, growing brighter and dimmer like a heartbeat.

I've never heard the song before. Then again, I grew up in Aclaris, so I've missed out on a lot of my native Tirenese culture.

Chirean stands guard at the far side of the chamber, his orange scales burnished to copper in the weird light. Both dragons exude calm, as if entranced by Rose's humming.

Following their lead, I do my best to emulate their apparent serenity. I move closer, careful not to disturb the scene. The eggs pulse in their watery cocoon, as if responding to the melody. I've never heard, read about, nor witnessed dragons reacting to music before.

"That's pretty." When Rose pauses for a breath, I scoot closer. "Where did you learn it?"

She glances up, not at all surprised to see me. Her blue eyes shine with a wisdom far beyond her years. "Kin taught me. It's old. From before."

"Before what?" I settle down beside her. Chirean and Dame don't seem to notice, their gazes still locked on the pool.

Please, Ziva, Goddess of Fire, let this be a good thing. Protect this new generation of your favored creatures.

"Lots of things." Rose shrugs and resumes humming. Her flame sprite dances more energetically.

The song cloaks me like a warm blanket, soothing away the tension I hadn't realized I was carrying. Sweat drips down my skin, but not in an uncomfortable way. More like...a cleansing.

Fear, confusion, worry, and the constant pressure of responsibility all recede, leaving only this moment, this cave, this miracle about to unfold.

The first egg rocks gently, then more insistently.

Tiny cracks appear on the surface.

A hairline fracture spreads like ice breaking on a pond. Both parents crane their necks forward.

The wait is unbearable. I hold my breath, anticipation sending a rush of restless energy through my body.

A small but perfect claw pushes through. Yellow with the faintest hint of orange. That's followed by a red snout glistening with moisture.

Dame croons a welcome, her entire body vibrating with maternal pride. She lowers her massive head, delicately helping the hatchling free itself from the remnants of its shell. With infinite gentleness, she lifts the baby from the water, purring as she sets the newborn creature on the warm stones beside the pool.

Chirean grinds his claws into the stone, turning rocks into powder as Dame licks their firstborn clean.

There's a tightness in my throat and a pressure behind my

eyes. Tears leak out unbidden before streaming down my face. Rose reaches out, giving my hand a quick, gentle squeeze.

This...this is goodness. This is purity. This cuts through every scarred, calloused layer I've built around my heart.

Moments later, the second egg cracks, throwing ripples across the water.

The pool fills with mirk as the other hatchling breaks free of the shell and swims to the surface unaided. Dame plucks the brilliant silvery baby up and settles her onto the powdered rock their father continues to create. Her brother waddles over, tiny claws sliding over her soft scales as he tries to climb her.

The air fills with tiny chirps and the sound of Dame's contented rumbling.

I inch closer, barely breathing, projecting tentative thoughts toward Dame and asking for permission through the tiniest opening in my dampening.

A flutter of agreement brushes my mind, followed by a second, then a third and a fourth. The whole family. Golden baby eyes blink up at me, confusion and amazement wafting up from them at this strange being, this human who can communicate with them.

The first one is already dry and exploring his surroundings on wobbly legs. His scales are a perfect blend of Dame's and Chirean's coloring, with hints of gold along his spine. The female is still wet. She's a brilliant shimmering silver, unlike any dragon I've ever laid eyes on before.

Except for Cailleach. The ancient dragon in the Hidden Valley. The only dragon ever to converse with me in full sentences.

Rose meets my gaze, eyes brimming with childlike wonder. "They're perfect."

Unable to form words, all I can do is smile.

Another round of tears hit my lips, and the salt mixes with

the mineral tang of the cave air. My heart feels too large for my chest, swollen with a fierce, almost painful love. It's mine. And Dame's. And Chirean's. All of our shared emotions, building upon the others.

These tiny creatures, so exquisite, so vulnerable.

How can the world be worthy of them? How can I?

The second hatchling, dried now by Dame's careful attention, stumbles toward me. Her spear-shaped tail drags after her sheep-sized body. The silver dragon chirps, bumping her head against my outstretched hand. Her shiny scales are warm and soft, not yet hardened by time and elements.

Something inside me cracks open like those eggs. All my carefully constructed barriers, my queenly composure. They crumble away, leaving only raw truth.

"I don't know if I can do this." I stroke the hatchling's head with a single finger. "How will reading books and attending meetings save anyone? How is being the perfect queen going to protect them?"

The hatchling chirps again, pressing against my palm with surprising strength.

"The world needs protection." My voice hitches. "Books and diplomatic niceties matter, but I feel wasted on them. What good are they when everything is breaking open?"

No one answers.

Rose is once again caught up in her song. The dragons are enraptured by their children. The hatchlings are too busy trying to figure out their legs and wings.

I sigh, knowing I will do anything to safeguard these precious lives.

Dame moves closer, her massive body curving around her babies and, by extension, around me. There's comfort in her posture, but something else too. A readiness. A coiled tension.

She understands protection. She understands that sometimes love means fighting.

Chirean joins us, adding his warmth to our circle. The dragons chuff and flutter, and the hatchlings tumble about, exploring their new world with boundless curiosity.

Rose continues to hum, the melody shifting subtly and becoming something more resolute.

I don't want comfort. I don't want to be soothed. I want to fight back.

These hatchlings deserve a better world than the one they've just entered. They deserve a world where they can grow and thrive without the shadow of war hanging over them.

A world where Rose can sing her songs in sunlight rather than hidden caves.

The silver hatchling climbs halfway into my lap, tiny claws pricking through my clothes. She peers up at me with guileless eyes.

My heart clenches with the gravity of my responsibility to these newborns. "Somehow, I'm going to make it better. For all of you. I promise."

Chapter Twenty-Three
Lark

Dawn's light spills through the high windows of the palace, bathing the grand hallway in a soft golden hue and illuminating the hopeless state of my clothing after spending the night in the hatching cavern. I took Rose to her mother hours ago, then I flew back to the cave to continue admiring the newborns and the bond between the babies and their parents before returning to the capital.

Dame and Chirean remained behind, ready to feed their hungry brood. I don't know how long it will be before we see them at the palace again with their hatchlings in tow.

Though my bed beckons, I'm too energized to sleep. My heart races with the knowledge of what I've witnessed, and I replay the events of this miraculous night in my head over and over again.

The moment I round the corner toward the royal wing, I stop dead in my tracks.

Sterling stands in the dim light at the end of the hall.

For a heartbeat, time stops.

Gold-flecked eyes, stormy with fatigue and something deeper, meet mine, and the world narrows until it's just the two of us. I drink in the sight of him, cataloguing every line of his face, the scruff on his jaw, the new scar on his forearm. He's dressed in all black and strapped with enough weapons to supply a small army. His glossy black hair is loose and wild, hitting just past his shoulders.

My body launches forward without thought.

I race toward him, my boots pounding the floor.

Sterling's mouth is on mine in a matter of seconds.

He kisses me—no, *devours* me—like he's starving. His hands tangle in my hair, pulling me closer until there's no space between us. I wrap my arms around his back, reveling in his familiar warmth. He smells of wind, leather, and spice, and the grounding scent ignites something fierce and comforting inside me.

Home.

The frenzied kiss grows gentle, lazy. We take our time tasting each other. Exploring. Relearning what we already know.

Minutes later, he pulls back far enough to study my face. "You look like you just battled a dragon and lost. What happened?"

A laugh bubbles up and spills free. "Well, it did involve a dragon, but there was no battle. I'm happy to see you, too, by the way."

A grin splits across his face. "Oh, that kiss? That was only the beginning of me telling you just how glad I am to be back with you. Once you've visited the others and I've had a hot meal, I plan to whisk you away to bed and not let you leave until I've given you at least a dozen orgasms."

My cheeks flush and my toes curl at his promise, leaving me a little breathless. "I'm going to hold you to that."

He kisses me again, long and slow, then lowers his forehead to mine. "I'd be disappointed if you didn't. Now tell me about whatever happened that involved a dragon."

"Dame's eggs hatched." I launch into the story, ending with, "Newborn dragons are messy eaters. And did you know they don't have full control of their tails yet? They just trip over the swinging safety hazards. It looks so painful and adorable at the same time."

"That's amazing. I can't wait to see them." His brow furrows when he catches something else in my expression. "What else happened while I was gone?"

I shake my head, my throat thickening. I don't want to think about all the other crap. Focusing on the dragons is way more fulfilling. "Later. You first. How did it go?"

Sterling shrugs, but the nonchalant gesture fails to hide the burdens he carries. "We didn't find what we were looking for. Just—"

Familiar voices approach, laughter and chatter rolling down the hall like a welcome wave. When I spy Leesa and Agnar at the end of the corridor, relief floods me. Their presence acts like a balm, soothing the frayed edges of my anxiety.

Agnar spots me and straightens. A grin spreads across his face. "Agnar Kerrin reporting for debriefing, Your Majesty."

Leesa's eyes are wide and bright, and I'm pretty sure she's biting the inside of her cheek.

Which doesn't explain the muffled giggle coming from their direction. Nor the wriggling lump under Agnar's coat. Or why Kin's hovering over Agnar's head.

I play along. "Agnar, I'm so glad to see you. Though you seem to be suffering from a strange form of humpback."

Agnar shrugs his shoulders, and the bouncy act produces even more girlish giggles from behind his back. "Ah, yes. It's a family affliction, you understand. Tends to flare up after I've been away for a while."

When he lifts his arm, the lump under his coat scrambles. A familiar leg pops out before digging into his side in an attempt to climb back up into hiding. A set of hands is suddenly visible at his collar as well.

By this time, I've reached them. I pat him on the oddly head-shaped lump just below his neck. "Yet despite your travels, you show up smelling like roses."

"I don't smell! Mama made me take a bath!" Rose's voice is muffled by her uncle's coat but indignant enough to make us all fight to keep our composure. Except Agnar, who just continues smiling with innocent eyes.

Sterling chokes down a laugh. "Well, we all appreciate this new rosy disposition of yours. Let's get some breakfast. Then we need to talk."

≈

Lark

Unfortunately, all the jokes and levity are left at the door. The air feels thick in my private sitting room as Sterling, Agnar, and Leesa recount the strange things they ran into during their journey.

Abandoned villages stretch across my mind. Children "dedicated" to temples like sacrificial lambs. Fourteen ships off the coast of Tirene lured to their doom by harpies. Temples filled with blank-faced worshippers, like the corrupted, but without black eyes. People who, when questioned, vowed that they chose their fate without regret.

As they speak, every fact bleeds into another, each detail worse than the last. The collective horror of their discoveries cocoon us like a thick, suffocating shroud that demands to be torn apart.

My heart sinks, and I'm sure of the answer before I even voice my question. "And the portal?" I glance over at Rose, who's happily swinging her legs at a table on the far side of the room. She's eating a cream pastry, unaware of the "adult talk" happening over here.

Honestly, I don't know how her mother keeps up with the little girl. Though, now that they've moved into the palace, Quinn no doubt enjoys some quiet moments to herself when Rose is hanging out with me, Sterling, or Agnar.

Sterling shakes his head, the shadow on his face deepening. "Gone. Hidden. Maybe never existed. While we located places resembling what we saw in the scrying and book illustrations, we never actually found it. But the worst part was what we *did* find."

A chill runs through me, and the room grows still.

Rafe and Helene arrived during these disclosures, joining the circle silently. Their presence heightens the tension because I'm still waiting on their discoveries about the missing scientist-priests. With every new piece of information, faces grow grimmer. Bastian slipped in last and took a seat beside Leesa on one of the couches. He's since pulled her into his lap.

With anyone else, I'd be willing to bet they missed the last five minutes of the conversation. But I have no doubt that between stealing kisses when he thought no one was looking and whispering into Leesa's ear, Bastian's processed every word.

"It's not just the other kingdoms we have to worry about." Helene clenches her hands tight in her lap. I know she has to be worried for her own family back in Aclaris. "If this corruption spreads, it could reach our borders and devour us whole. We need a plan, and we need it fast."

"Something is wrong with the elemental balance." Rafe toys with his breakfast, using his air magic to push a sausage around on his plate. "This is all the gods' work."

Sterling's brow creases as he stares into the hearth in contemplation. "If we could find the portal, we could demand

205

answers. We could..." His voice trails off, the possibilities weighed down by harsh reality.

Agnar catches my eye, his expression shifting from camaraderie to urgent concern. "Lark, Sterling's being watched. He felt it the whole time. The presence is getting stronger."

The tension uncoils around my heart, pulling my breath short. I recall my garbled vision of three figures staring into a pool. Of gazing down at Sterling surrounded by water. Sterling didn't mention anything like that happening.

Questions race through my mind, like fire raging through the underbrush. Thinking of that distorted vision reminds me of something else I saw. Or thought I remembered seeing. "Rose, can you come here, please?"

The little girl perks up, scrambling down from her chair to race over to me. The others shift to let her through. She licks pastry cream off of her lips and brushes her hands on her dress.

"Do you think we could see Kin scry again? The first one you showed us of the portal." At my request, Rose's flame familiar flickers and flutters at her shoulder, its soft glow illuminating her blond hair.

When Rose nods and smiles, the flame-image shimmers to life with images of mountains, caves, and mist.

There.

Something I hadn't noticed the first time.

I point to a blurred section. "There's something odd there. It's as if some illusory, gauzy film floats overtop, hiding what's beneath."

It reminds me of the spots in my shattered, twisted vision that I couldn't see until I enhanced my eyesight. The area where something attempted to cover up the message intended for me.

With that in mind, I unfurl my wings to improve my vision.

Around me, others follow suit. Rose stares open-mouthed at us, her face tinged with jealousy.

Agnar's eyes brighten with understanding. "It's like the earth magic I use to make a cave entrance look like solid rock when it's just a thin veneer of sandstone."

The room's a little crowded with everyone's wings out, but we shift around so we can all see what we missed before.

Sterling bends over the flame, his focus sharpening. "I recognize that cave. It was in the Withered Undulations. That's where the portal lies. We can go straight back to it."

Maybe my mangled vision wasn't a failure after all. The gods certainly speak in strange ways.

CHAPTER TWENTY-FOUR
LARK

After an afternoon of meeting with the council, planning, and packing, Sterling and I are finally alone together. His eyes smolder with a molten gleam as they track me across our bedchamber, though I absorb other details as well...the way his shoulders sag, how his fingers fidget with the edge of his sleeve. A habit he'd vehemently deny.

Too much time has passed since we've been alone together. I've spent too many days with only the memory of his voice to keep me company. Now he's here and I find myself suddenly tongue-tied, unsure of how to bridge the gap that absence carved between us.

"What happened while I was gone?" He attempts to sound casual, but I don't miss the underlying strain.

"Later," I say as I cross the room. I don't want our reunion tainted by plots and politics.

He reaches for me as if on instinct, hands settling on my hips when I step between his knees. The familiar warmth of his touch seeps through the fabric of my breeches, and a jolt of awareness shoots through me.

I've missed this. I've missed *us*.

He draws me down onto his lap, and I go willingly, straddling his legs.

"First, a bath." After spending the night in a cave, there's no way I'm going to make love with Sterling until I'm clean.

His throaty laughter rumbles through me as he lifts his arm, sniffs his armpit, and scrunches his nose in an exaggerated manner that pulls a chuckle out of me too. "That bad? Bathing in rivers isn't the same as bathing here, but—"

"No, you smell like home." I cup his cheek with my palm and gently stroke the stubble. "But as much as I want you, I think we'll both feel better if we washed up first."

The hard lines of his face melt into something softer. "You just want to get me naked." His hands slide up my back. "And I'm okay with that."

"And wet. And lathered up."

I press a quick kiss to his lips before standing. He accepts the hand I offer, allowing me to lead him into the adjoining bathing chamber.

The room has become one of my favorites in the palace. A high-ceilinged space with warm stone floors and an enormous tub fed by hot springs that run deep beneath Tirene. Steam rises from the surface of the water, curling upward in lazy tendrils. I busy myself with the jars of fragrant herbs on a nearby shelf, selecting dried lavender and mint.

Sterling stands behind me, close enough that I can feel his warmth, but not touching. I'm acutely aware of him observing me as I sprinkle the herbs into the water and release their scent into the steam. "I missed this."

I pivot to face him, my fingers slipping to his shirt fastenings. "The bath?"

"You." He allows me to undress him. "Just...you."

I work in silence, sliding the fabric from his shoulders. New scars ravage his skin alongside the old ones I know by heart. My gut clenches as my fingertips trace one on his ribs that's still pink with healing.

"It's nothing. A careless moment." His body still carries the lean muscles of a soldier, but the fatigue shows in the slope of his shoulders, in the subtle hollows beneath his cheekbones. Whatever he found on his journey has taken a toll.

For now, I opt not to press him and instead continue undressing him until he stands naked before me. As always, the sight of him steals my breath, and my lower belly dips.

No one could argue that Knox Sterling Barda isn't a magnificent specimen of a man.

He steps into the tub with a grateful sigh, sinking down until the water reaches his chest. I gather soap and a cloth and kneel at the edge of the tub. We've shared the intimacy of me washing him before, this simple act of care.

He catches my hand, thumb stroking my knuckles in a gentle caress. "Tell me something sweet. Something from home."

So I share stories while I bathe him. I talk about the daily ongoings of the palace in his absence as the cool night wind sings through the umberheart trees.

I work the cloth down his arm. "The Bricklayer's Guild had their quarterly meeting."

Sterling grunts, signaling his mild irritation. "Let me guess. They're trying to get out of the Eastern District repairs again."

"They tried." I offer a sly smile. "I reminded them of their contractual obligations."

"Good decision." His eyelids slide to half-mast as my fingers trail through his silky locks. "They'll respect you more for it."

I tell him more about the two newborn dragons. How the hatchlings stumbled on wobbly legs, their wings still damp and clinging to their sides and their big eyes blinking.

Sterling's wet hands capture my wrists mid-sentence. "Join me."

When I glimpse the vulnerability shining in his eyes—a softness he only reveals to me—I know I can't refuse.

I undress wordlessly, my skin growing hot beneath his intense stare. The moment I slip into the water beside him, he tugs me close, yanking my back against his chest so his arms can encircle me.

"Now it's your turn." I settle against his water-slicked skin. "Tell me something wonderful."

With his lips press to my temple, his voice rumbles through me as he begins to speak. He talks of a coastline where the sand shimmers like crushed diamonds, of caves with walls that glow blue in the darkness. He describes birds with wings spanning twice my height that soar above mountains so tall their peaks disappear into clouds.

I close my eyes, letting his words paint pictures in my mind.

His hands sketch erotic patterns on my skin. "I wish you could have seen it all. But at least we're going together tomorrow. After this last trip, I refuse to go on a journey like that without you ever again."

"Promise?" I twist in his embrace to meet his eyes, causing the water to lap gently around us.

Instead of answering, he kisses me, slowly and deliberately. He cradles my face as if I might break. I taste his longing, his relief at being home. When we part, his forehead rests against mine, and our breath mingles in the space between us.

"I promise." His hands slip down my sides, tracing the contours of my body as if recommitting the curves to memory. "Being without you is pure torture. Every day is long, boring, dreadful, and bland. Like my senses are dulled and the world is just a terrible place."

"Tedious. Joyless. Gray." My own hands wander, finding

the places where he's most sensitive. The hollow of his throat, the inside of his wrist. The spot just below his ear that makes him shiver whenever I stroke or kiss it.

Abruptly, he gathers me into his arms and lifts me. As he stands, water cascades from our bodies, and I wrap my legs around his waist. My pulse begins to accelerate as he carries me to the padded stone bench against the wall.

He lays me down with a gentleness that causes my heart to ache, his eyes never straying from mine. "I thought of you every minute of every day. Every night spent without you. You even filled my dreams."

I pull him down to me, needing to experience the delicious sensation of his weight on my body. "Show me."

Sterling takes his time, as if we have all the hours in the world at our disposal. His lips skim a leisurely path from my mouth to my neck, across my collarbone, between my breasts. Every touch is reverent, calculated, and draws small whimpers from me that echo in the steam-filled chamber.

We touch each other with the synchronicity of lovers who know each other's bodies intimately. There's no hurry, no desperation. Just the slow, heavy pleasure of reconnection.

With our eyes closed, our bodies slide together without hesitation. Lips to chests. Hands to thighs. My ankles around his waist in a position that feels as second-nature as breathing. My nails trail down his scalp.

His hands find mine, and our fingers interlock as he positions himself above me. "Look at me."

I do, holding his heated gaze as he enters me with exquisite tenderness. While he joins us together as one, I watch the play of emotions on his face. Pleasure, yes. But also relief, love.

Home.

I lift my hips to meet him, and we set into a rhythm as ancient as the stone beneath us.

The world narrows to just us while his body and mine

move together in the dim light and damp heat. The harsh rasp of our breathing grows more ragged as we climb toward release, as his hand slips between us and strokes the center of my desire.

When I shatter, it's with his name on my lips. My fingers press into his shoulders hard enough to leave marks. Moments later, he follows, burying his face in the curve of my neck while a tremor racks his powerful body.

That felt like a homecoming. Emphasis on coming.

I giggle at the thought, then wrap my body tighter around him, holding him close and deep within me. I never want to let him go again.

His skin is chilled, so I call my flames to the surface. He groans and melts on top of me. "You're the best...everything."

"Not the best pillow though." I rotate my shoulders, trying to get comfortable now that we're not lost in our lovemaking.

"I'd have to disagree." Sterling sits up, but I cling to him, forcing him to lift me as well. He grips my thighs as he carries me to our bed. "Let's get a little more comfortable. I promised you twelve orgasms, and I'm nothing if not a man of my word."

Sometime later, exhaustion finally overtakes us.

We drift off tangled together, skin to skin, and for the first time since he left, I sleep without nightmares.

~

Lark

Morning arrives too soon, and we quickly find ourselves surrounded by packs and travel accessories. Servants shuffle in and out of our chamber, bringing supplies and removing items deemed unnecessary.

Sterling and I eat standing up, snatching bites between instructions and preparations. Agnar, still appearing weary from his last journey, materializes with maps and spreads them across a table already cluttered with equipment.

He points to a spot on one of the maps. "We need to leave by midday if we want to reach the foothills before dark."

Sterling swallows a mouthful of a savory pastry. "We'll make better time than before since we know exactly where we're going and don't need to stop to investigate along the way."

I pick at my food while my mind races ahead to the journey before us. This time, I'll be going too. Seeing what they found, what they missed.

Keeping Sterling within reach.

The thought instills me with equal parts excitement and dread. "We need to decide who will govern in our absence. The kingdom needs a steward."

Sterling frowns, considering. "It can't be one of the council members. Too much risk of favoritism."

"It needs to be someone who understands what's happening." I set my food down. "Someone who knows the situation...who we can trust absolutely."

We trade a glance, still silently weighing options when Agnar bends to grab the last pack from the floor. "Bastian, of course."

The simplicity strikes me immediately.

He's right. Bastian is the obvious choice.

Through his research, he possesses intimate knowledge about what we're confronting. He's also the queen's half-brother, which grants him legitimacy without giving him a claim to the throne. And I'd be willing to bet that he knows the laws of Tirene better than either Sterling or I do.

"That's perfect." Relief floods through me. "Bastian would be an excellent steward."

Sterling nods his agreement. "He has the breeding, the knowledge, and the loyalty. And the council won't intimidate him."

I call over Astrid, who's been hovering nearby with her portable writing desk. "Please draft the paperwork for Bastian to serve as our royal steward in our absence. I want us all to sign it before we leave."

She bows and hurries away, leaving us to continue our preparations.

Sterling adjusts the strap of a pack. "Hope Leesa's ready to be a surrogate queen."

I smile at the thought of my sister in that role. She'd be good at it, actually. But a twinge of guilt lurks beneath the humor. I know exactly how Bastian will feel about getting left behind again. Though he'll understand the importance of his role and the trust we're placing in him, he'll also experience the sting of exclusion in the same way I did when Sterling left without me.

Some separations are necessary, I remind myself. Some burdens must be carried alone. Yet, as I watch Sterling check his weapons one last time, relief swells in my chest when I remind myself that this time, we'll face the unknown together.

CHAPTER TWENTY-FIVE
LARK

The mountains in the heart of the Withered Undulations tower above us like sleeping giants, their peaks lost in wisps of cloud that curl around them with a lover-like embrace. Ancient forest stretches in every direction, hiding ruins that books claim exist but can only be found through hunting.

Just like this damn portal we've searched for since departing the palace yesterday.

With each passing hour, Sterling's shoulders grow more rigid, and I catch the twitch in his jaw that means he's grinding his teeth again.

We all have our wings out, using the enhanced vision that comes with them. We're utilizing every advantage we have.

And still, nothing.

"We've walked the entire perimeter of this cave twice." Sterling drags a hand through his dark hair for perhaps the twentieth time today. His fingers leave furrows resembling a freshly plowed field. "Our notes on the map said—"

"It said 'vicinity of the northern peak.'" I share his frustration, the emotion a low-grade fever in my blood. "That covers a lot of ground."

Agnar slaps a palm against the stone wall. The hollow clang echoes deeper into the cave. "Excellent progress, wouldn't you say? At this rate, we'll find it by next winter. Maybe the one after."

I shoot him a look that he pretends not to see while his blue eyes scan the ceiling like the answers might be written there. His sheathed sword bumps against his leg as he shifts his weight in the nervous habit of a man who'd rather be taking action than standing around.

I press my palm against the cool stone wall, seeking... something.

Anything.

My fire magic tingles beneath my skin, but I hold it back. Magic responds to magic. That's what the old texts say.

Then I see it.

A shimmer in the rock face, like the air above a bonfire but more subtle.

"Wait." I gesture straight ahead. "Look."

Sterling and Agnar both pivot. Sterling's brow furrows, but Agnar's eyes widen ever so slightly. "What is that?"

I gravitate closer. "The rock...it's moving."

As I approach, the gleam intensifies, spreading like ripples in a pond.

Sterling's fingers close around my arm in gentle warning, but I slip from his grasp, lured forward by an inexplicable urge.

Magic recognizes magic...and something inside me recognizes this.

Before our eyes, the rock melts away like dispersing mist rather than crumbling stone, revealing a crystalline archway that wasn't there a moment ago. These are the same kind of crystals that cover the temples.

Anticipation builds as the three of us exchange glances. No words necessary.

Finally. We've found the way through.

I flex my fingers and summon a small flame, letting the blaze dance across my palm before shaping it into an orb that hovers just above my open hand. The fire casts warm light that pushes back the darkness and creates strange shifting shadows on the cave walls.

The crystals catch and split the flickering light into dazzling colors I've never witnessed before. Shades that shouldn't exist and have no name.

A shiver quakes my body as I step through the archway. "Stay close."

Beyond the entrance, a high, narrow passageway lined with massive crystal formations awaits. Ancient. Impossibly old. They jut out from the walls like giant beehives, translucent and seemingly filled with old honey, the amber fluid trapped in geometric prisons.

My flame illuminates the formations in unsettling ways, refracting and reflecting until finding the light's origin becomes impossible.

The effect is beautiful but wrong, like tumors formed of jewels.

As I stare at them, my stomach begins to writhe.

"Anyone else feel that?" Agnar's voice is strangely muffled.

I don't need to ask what he means. The crystals vibrate in intermittent waves that cause my ears to pop repeatedly. A metallic tang clings to the air.

Sterling says something, but his words echo and distort until they're incomprehensible. When Agnar replies, his voice is swallowed entirely, as if the air itself is eating the sound.

If Sterling's hand weren't still on my arm, I'd be terrified of losing them both.

As we venture farther down the passage, the temperature fluctuates.

One moment, my breath clouds before me, and my fingers numb with cold despite my flame. The next, sweat trickles down my spine, and I battle the urge to extinguish my fire because of the unbearable heat.

Agnar wipes his palm on his shirt before gripping his sword hilt again, knuckles white. Sterling prowls forward with careful precision, each step measured while he constantly scans our surroundings.

The farther we go, the stranger things become.

On my next step, the ground tilts at an impossible angle. I gasp, bracing to slide down it like a child's playground slope, but nothing happens. My feet remain planted as if the ground were still level, though my mind screams otherwise.

"Don't look down."

Though I can hear him clearly again, Sterling's advice comes too late.

I peek at the ground, and my stomach lurches with vertigo.

Ahead of us, gravity seems to reverse in patches. Loose stones float upward in spinning, cylindrical sections like inverted underwater whirlpools.

Agnar extends a tentative hand into one of these phenomena. Immediately, an invisible force pulls his arm upward. He yanks it back. "I don't like this."

I shudder. "The feeling's mutual."

We press on because we have no choice and dodge what we can. The passage narrows even more, and I inch through it only to find myself lunging forward and covering twenty paces in a single stride.

Sterling cradles my elbow to steady me. "Careful. The distances aren't what they seem."

"You think?" My next step barely moves me at all, as if space itself is fan-pleated, expanding and contracting at random.

To my left, a crack appears in the floor, widening into a chasm that didn't exist seconds ago.

I jerk back, heart hammering.

The crevice seals itself just as quickly, leaving no trace behind. "It's like the laws of nature are fighting among themselves."

Sterling cocks his head to the side, as if listening to something only he can hear. His eyes carry that distant haze they get when he's working with his magic. "The water. I can feel it everywhere."

He extends his fingers, and tiny droplets of moisture appear from nowhere, coalescing into a thin stream. The water flows ahead of us along the tunnel, bending and curving to avoid invisible obstacles.

The unease dripping through me shifts into a languid trickle of fear.

I squeeze his hand. "What's happening?"

"The water shows the safe path." His eyes stay fixed on the liquid's movement. "Where it travels freely, we can walk. We shouldn't step where it distorts or breaks."

I eye the stream with suspicion. "Because that's not weird or anything."

After Sterling nudges me, we follow the elemental guidance, growing more confident as we progress without issue.

Then the booms begin.

The first one, a low, resonant sound that rumbles through the passage like distant thunder, catches us off guard. We stop short, hands on our weapons. Another boom shakes the ground. Then another.

Followed by...silence.

Sterling sways into the wall. Afraid he might fall, I grab his arm.

"Sterling?"

"The water here..." Radiance imbues his face, and his eyes

brighten. "It's everywhere. In the air, the crystals, the stone. It's like..."

Agnar tilts his head as if listening before kneeling and pressing his ear to the ground. "Like what?"

"Like I've been reading single words my whole life, and suddenly I can see entire libraries." Sterling extends his hand again, and this time the moisture droplets prance around his fingers in complex patterns. "The water wants to be shaped. It's alive."

My neck tingles. I've never heard him speak of his power this way. Sterling is always practical about his abilities, using them efficiently, strategically.

This level of reverence is new...along with the idea of an element *wanting* something. My fire has never shared any desires with me. Unless...what am I missing?

The passage begins to climb, steeply at first, and then more gradually. The air changes, carrying a new, fresh quality. Ambient light appears, though I can't identify the source. My flame seems dimmer now, less necessary, but I maintain the fire out of habit. And to stay vigilant.

We venture up the spiraling path. The crystal formations grow larger and more complex. Some pulse with internal light in time with the distant booms that continue intermittently.

Without warning, the narrow passage ends.

Beyond it, we find...absolute nothingness.

No floor, no walls, no ceiling. Just open, swirling space filled with glowing pinpoint stars that swirl in anomalous patterns. The void twirls and eddies like a whirlpool of light and shadow.

Beyond the nothingness lies a vast, verdant meadow.

Lush grass ripples in a breeze. Wildflowers, surrounded by trees with silver bark and golden leaves, explode in brilliant colors. Sunlight bathes everything, but how? How can the sun reach deep inside a mountain?

Crystal forms the "sky" above the meadow, refracting colorful prisms. Stars wheel through this bright "sky" in slow, deliberate constellations.

A fragrant breeze caresses my face, carrying the scent of autumn leaves, crisp air after a storm, sunbaked grass, and something that reminds me of the pure air of a cold winter night.

"Well," Agnar stares, eyes wide, "that's properly godly, isn't it?"

Another boom—this one louder and closer—echoes. The noise is followed by deep sonorous voices angrily arguing in a language I don't recognize.

With each boom, the glimmering formations on the walls pulse like heartbeats. Goose bumps erupt over my skin.

I'm starting to feel as if we marched right into the stomach of an enormous crystal beast.

Agnar grips his sword hilt. "Not liking those booms."

"Same." Those noises are concerning, but what can we do? Retreat? Everything in me screams *yes*, to haul ass out of this unnatural place. But we came here for a reason.

We need this passage.

I gesture to the whirling, sparkling mist of nothingness before us. "How do we get across that?"

The void might be ten paces across, or it might be fathomless. Distances are meaningless here.

A reply emanates from the air itself. "You don't."

The voice surrounding us comes from everywhere and nowhere.

Before I can freak out about that, a figure emerges from the void as if walking through an invisible door. His armor twinkles like liquid starlight. Weapons gleam in both his hands, but they shift shapes even as I watch. A sword morphs into a spear before changing into an axe, followed by an object I have no name for.

Energy swirls around him. Magic beyond my experience. Not elemental like mine or Sterling's, but something wilder. Ancient.

"You should not be here." The command in his voice hums through my bones. "You do not belong."

His hands wrap around the shifting hilts of his weapons. Oh. Shit.

CHAPTER TWENTY-SIX
STERLING

What the hell is this...person? Some sort of guardian of the cosmos? A protector for the portal? The sheer energy twisting around him beckons me. Calls to my magic.

As if my power recognizes this being.

The armor he wears is fluid, like starlight captured in mercury. It flows across his form with tidal precision. The weapons appear to be extensions of the man himself, pulsing with the same galactic heartbeat.

An otherworldly chill seeps into my gut. "We're only here to find answers. Not to disturb anything or anyone."

Stalking forward, I position myself between Lark and whoever the fuck this is.

Not that I doubt her abilities for a second.

She's just too damn precious to risk.

The armored figure regards us through void-like eyes that reflect vortices of cosmic light. "Who are you to demand answers of the gods?"

His voice carries harmonics that vibrate my teeth in my skull.

Behind me, I sense Lark's tension. The slight shift in her

stance tells me she's ready to fight. Agnar is a solid presence on my other side, his breathing controlled but audible in the cavern's strange acoustics.

I hold the figure's gaze, bristling at his condescending tone. "Not to demand, but to petition."

He glides closer, oozing power. The charged air bows around him, reality itself bending in deference to his presence.

The hairs on my arms rise, responding to the creature's energy as if I'm standing too close to a lightning storm.

Pebbles on the ground roll and slide toward him.

"He's not lying. We only seek answers from the gods." Lark's hand rests on my back, and it's all I can do to keep my eyes fixed ahead. "And...who exactly are you?"

Suddenly, he buries his blade in the soil and leans over to use the pommel as an armrest. "I am the Guardian of the Gods. I am their weapon. And you are trespassing."

That last word feels like a wall ready to tumble over and crush our very existence.

Irritation prickles my skin.

We may not know the depth of who we're facing, but I refuse to cower.

"We tried other ways to contact the deities. They only replied with vague and confusing messages." Shrugging, I gesture to our surroundings, determined to ignore his intimidation tactics. "Which is why we risked our lives to come here. We need to know what they want."

The Guardian tilts his head, a gesture almost human save for the unnatural smoothness of the motion. "And when the gods didn't respond, why did you not consider that your answer?"

I don't need to glance at Lark to sense the fury rolling off her.

To be honest, I'm shocked she hasn't already snapped at the arrogant prick. "Because there are bizarre god-related disturbances in our realm. And we need to understand what's happening."

The Guardian's chilling laugh reminds me of ice cracking across a frozen lake. "Your realm? How charmingly territorial."

With each word, the temperature drops.

This being doesn't just control the environment. He *is* the environment.

My water magic responds, preparing for defense.

"People are dying." I glance over my shoulder to find Lark's chin raised in a familiar, stubborn tilt. "Sacred places are corrupted. Land is shifting. That is our territory. According to the God of Lost Things, one must obtain the permission of the landowner before fundamental changes can be made."

She's right. We needed to trick Xenon into giving us permission before we could cleanse the soil of Narc's corruption.

The tension in the chamber rises.

"Ah yes, the Tirenese queen." The Guardian's armor flickers like fire as he shifts his attention to Lark. "Your recent victory over Narc has given you an inflated sense of importance. That law is for humans, not gods. You know nothing about what is unfolding."

"No shit. That's why we're here." Agnar sweeps his arm out, gesturing to whatever the hells it is we're standing in. "To learn about what's 'unfolding.'"

Though part of me wants to shut Agnar up for taunting a powerful being that could blast us into next week if he wanted to, another wants to congratulate him for giving the Guardian shit.

Arrogant fuck.

The Guardian considers Agnar for a heartbeat, and then dismisses him with a flick of his fingers.

I hurry to reclaim the conversation. "Enlighten us. What exactly is transpiring?"

The entity inches closer, his armor shimmering in patterns that hurt my eyes when I stare directly. The magic surrounding him brushes my senses like hoarfrost freezing through my skin.

"You mortals. So eager to insert yourselves into matters beyond your comprehension." His gaze settles on me, holding my attention for a second too long. A spark of recognition flares in his eyes that I don't understand. "If you're so fed up with the gods, stop giving them so much power, and they won't have so much power."

"Please answer our questions." The strain in Lark's voice indicates she's clinging to politeness by a thread. "You have our word that our intentions are honorable."

A beat passes. "Very well. You have three questions. I suggest you use them wisely."

"And we get three answers?"

Lark reaches over me and slaps a hand over Agnar's mouth as soon as the query tumbles from his lips.

The Guardian's eyes narrow ever so slightly, but otherwise, he ignores Agnar, dismissing him as though he's spoken to the air itself.

I glare at my impulsive friend. So help me, if that counted as a question—

Another boom rocks the cavern, vibrating through my boots and rattling my spine. The noise has gotten closer, more forceful.

Something's happening on the other side of that portal. Something important.

I flex my fingers and widen my stance. Here goes nothing. "What is that sound?"

The Guardian's expression remains bland, as though he has little interest in this conversation. "Echoes. Negotiations."

"Now see, that's not an answer." Agnar crosses his arms over his chest as I turn to toss another glare at him. Lark's hand shoots out, ready to cover his mouth again if necessary.

"You want to know? You only think you want to know." This time, the Guardian smiles. The act is beautiful in a terrible way, like watching an avalanche begin its descent. "It is war."

The ensuing silence brims with trepidation.

In my mind, the pieces click into place, connecting disparate facts like a battle map coming into focus.

A divine war.

Of course.

The corrupted temples, the garbled messages, the strange attacks. All of it makes sense now. Not messages...a war.

Lark edges around me until she's standing by my side. "A war between the gods." Her eyes dart around the cave, as if she believes deities lurk in the shadows.

The Guardian's gaze slides to her. "The kind that corrupts temples, shifts lands, and draws sailors to harpy-infested shores."

So he does realize what's been happening. Even though he's standing at the door to the gods' realm. What else does he know about our struggles, our plans?

"The kind that garbles messages from other gods?" Lark presses.

"Is that your second question?"

"Shit. No, sorry." Lark's hand tightens on her sword as she bites her lower lip.

The Guardian detects the motion, and his own lips curve in mild amusement. "That puny weapon will be of no use in the godly realm, mortal. Certainly not in a divine war."

Tension rolls through my body. Now the bastard's toying with us.

Lark's eyes meet mine in silent communication. I incline

my chin in the slightest nod, acknowledging her restraint. We both glance at Agnar. He gives the tiniest shake of his head, though I swear he mumbles something under his breath.

"I meant no offense or threat. I was simply shaken by the thought of a civil war among the gods." Lark's careful not to ask a question. "That they're fighting at all seems odd. Fighting among themselves is unheard of."

The Guardian tilts his head, neither confirming nor denying. "You should be glad they fight among themselves here. If they did so in your realm, you'd be razed to the ground before you even realized what was happening." His voice holds no malice, only cold certainty. "Some mortals understand that. Your Devoted have chosen sides early. Wise of them."

"Not my Devoted." Lark's diplomacy slips from her grasp.

"They are mortal. That means they are yours. You are all the same." He taps a finger on the hilt of one of his weapons, the casual gesture an unmistakable threat.

I debate our remaining questions cautiously. We need specifics. What's happening, who's involved, and most importantly, how this affects our realm.

I inhale a measured breath. "Who is fighting in this war?"

"Second question." He taps two fingers on his hilt. "The fight is between those who understand the rightful hierarchy and those who are too afraid to seize that truth."

Rightful hierarchy.

I store the phrase away to unpack later. An ideological war about the proper order of things. About power. About who reigns over who.

The oldest conflict in the world, divine or mortal.

The God of the Heavens himself is being challenged. By whom? And what does that have to do with the Devoted? They're clearly on Zeru's side. But do they realize their allegiance pits them against other gods?

Lark remains rigid beside me, some of the same questions

no doubt racing through her mind. But neither of us can voice our thoughts for fear of letting a question slip.

I snap my gaze to Agnar to forestall whatever action he might be considering. For all his steadfastness, the man possesses a tongue sharper than any damn blade I've ever wielded.

He holds his palms up and shrugs, as if to say, "What did I do?" But the tightness around his mouth confirms he's biting back some retort.

The Guardian watches our silent exchange with detached curiosity, like a scientist-priest trying to divine the hidden meaning of spiderwebs.

Then his star-infused gaze slides from Agnar to me. "Why do you hang around with those of lesser station?"

Surprise catches me off-balance. He aimed the question at me specifically, as though the others aren't worth addressing. His phrasing strikes me as familiar, formal yet also casual in a way that doesn't fit a celestial power.

Before I can formulate a response, Agnar bristles. "Because some of us understand loyalty isn't just a word to throw around."

The Guardian's attention whips to Agnar. The temperature plummets so suddenly that frost forms on my eyelashes. "Careful, earth wielder. Some remember when mortals knew their place."

I fling my arm in front of Agnar's chest, physically restraining him even as Lark clamps a hand over his mouth.

The three of us share a look. The weight of our situation presses down on us like a physical force.

One question left.

My brow wrinkles

When mortals knew...

Does that mean he's not a god, but also not a mortal? What else exists?

I study the Guardian more carefully. The armor that flows like water but shines like stars. The weapons that seem more extension than tool. The eyes that harbor cosmic depths yet flash with recognizable emotions.

"Are you mortal?"

The best question? Maybe not. But I need to learn who we're dealing with.

For the first time, the Guardian seems affected. The starlight armor darkens like storm clouds passing over a celestial body. His beautiful, precisely sculpted features harden, crystallizing into something less divine and more... human. His hand tightens on his weapon.

"No. As I said, I am the Guardian." An element enters his voice that wasn't there before. Regret, maybe?

I continue to prod him. "Yes, so you've said. But what does that mean?"

His face closes like a fortress gate. "You've asked your three questions. Get out. Never return through the portal again. To return here is to tempt death."

"That isn't—"

Cyclone winds strike from nowhere, ripping the words from my throat and shoving us backward. We tumble down the passageway, scrambling for purchase on slippery walls.

My hand finds Lark's arm and clutches tight as winds propel us through space that shouldn't exist.

Down, down, down the long climb.

Back into blackness.

When we drop in a tangled heap somewhere in the middle of the passageway, the winds cease. Lark presses against me, her familiar warmth a comfort in the absolute darkness that follows the starlight.

Behind us, Agnar grunts. "What the fuck?"

I can't see his face, but I can imagine the expression. Somewhere between outrage and bewilderment. The image matches the storm in my own mind as I try to process what in the three hells just happened.

"What the fuck?" is exactly right.

≈

The Chronimūrti

The three Gods of Time hover within the ancient stone chamber. Their ethereal forms glide above the dim light that envelops them.

Silence pulses with a rhythm both familiar and foreign, as if the chamber itself resonates through reality. The air is heavy with ancient magic.

Chronir stares into water. His gleaming robes flow like liquid silver, echoing the infinite knowledge of the ages. "Mortals at the portal. That hasn't happened in—"

"Three thousand four hundred and twelve years." Chronoth leans over the pool.

Chronir edges closer, drawn in by the shimmering reflection of possibilities. "But they failed."

"They always do." Chronoth's gaze sharpens as he regards the mortal realm through the darkened veil and notes the fervent desperation that seems to fuel their attempts.

Chronira watches in silence as she shakes her head. The possibilities waver, thin, and fade as their time of emergence passes.

"Hurry," she utters in a whisper too soft even for her siblings to hear.

The gentle waves ripple across the dimmed light, foreshadowing a looming conflict that's outcome is slowly being etched in stone.

Chapter Twenty-Seven
Lark

The council chamber resembles my mind right now. Cluttered, chaotic, and stretched far beyond its intended purpose. Maps crawl across tables like invasive vines, reports stack in precarious towers, and the air hangs heavy with too many hours of debate. Elijah's account of the Devoted man who confronted me is mixed in as well.

The man was long gone, and so far, they haven't been able to locate him.

I press my fingertips against my temples, where a headache throbs in time with my heartbeat. For four days, including this morning, Bastian took care of everything, but I still need to read through the documents detailing his decisions.

He's currently finishing up today's report. I'm sifting through the papers while Sterling informs the council of what happened during our excursion.

We hoped the journey to find the portal would provide answers. Instead, we returned with even more questions and the terrifying knowledge that the gods themselves are at war.

And now the councilors sit around the table, struck dumb by the news.

Breann and Fenton appear to be praying, which seems a little risky given what we learned.

"Lark, need another cup of tea?" Rafe hovers at my elbow, uncharacteristic concern pinching his handsome features. "Or some extra light so you don't strain your eyes?"

On any other day, I'd tease him about mothering me. But now is not the time.

"Thank you, but no." My voice sounds distant even to my own ears. "Maybe a shot of whiskey in the tea for Knox?"

Nira pushes her cup forward, silently requesting the same.

Sterling hasn't stopped pacing since he started relaying his story of our journey. He stalks around with the restrained energy of a caged predator, reminding me of the cave cats at the Divine Commons. The water in every glass and pitcher ripples with his passing, tiny wavelets climbing the sides before receding.

His sensitive magic is a sure sign of distress.

Dalya says nothing as her fierce gaze follows the sway of water.

Bron opens his mouth only to snap it shut like he's thought better of speaking.

In a chair across from me, Agnar rests his head in his hands, his broad shoulders hunched forward and his coppery hair escaping its tie to frame his battle-scarred face. Dark circles shadow his blue eyes, mirroring my own exhaustion. "Maybe we should stick to Tirene. Things work better here. And it's small enough we can handle everything that happens within our borders."

The same solution Tír Ríoga settled on. Their response does possess a certain practical sense. Global isolation. Just stay within their borders, protect their own lands and people, and let everyone else deal with the divine war the best they can.

But how does that solve anything? The fallout from a celestial war will affect every kingdom.

"We're Tirenese. Not clams who hide in the sand every time the tide goes out." I meet the gaze of each council member, ensuring they're paying attention.

Sterling stops pacing long enough to raise an eyebrow at me.

"Segregating ourselves will only limit our knowledge, resources, and ability to respond to the crisis. I believe our strength lies in our numbers and our willingness to work together. It's the only way we can hope to survive whatever the gods throw at us." I tap my fingertips on the world map. "What would other nations say if we tried to explain what we saw and learned?"

Sterling plants his hands on the table opposite me. "What do we actually know? A gods' war. But who's fighting against whom? Why?" He pushes upright to resume his previous movement. "How do we protect our people from being collateral damage in a divine war?"

Dalya shifts her sharp gaze from the water to the map. "And that's exactly why we can't seclude ourselves. The pattern only emerges if we can see enough of the board. Let's lay out what we know for certain."

I pull a fresh sheet of parchment toward me. Might as well add to my stack. "First, the gods are at war with each other."

Agnar straightens in his chair. "Second, the odd events are fallout from that war." He counts off on his fingers. "The sacred springs boiling in the Eastern Provinces."

Nira sips her fresh cup of whiskey-laced tea, her shiny brown hair spilling over her shoulder. "The flock of sheep that grew two extra heads each. The night sky appearing in daylight over the Western Marsh."

"The Devoted have chosen a side." Sterling plops into a chair across from me with a generous pour of whiskey in his tea.

Fenton steeples his fingers under his chin. "Except we don't know whose side, or even what the sides are."

"Clearly, they're on Zeru's side. Or that's what their tattoos would indicate." Rafe rubs the knuckles of one hand while staring off into the distance.

"But surely there's more than just the Devoted on Zeru's side. That's the most troubling part. We don't even know who's fighting whom." I write each point in hurried script.

Nira sets her cup down, sliding it away from a haphazard stack of papers. "Which gods would align with Zeru?"

A thought strikes me that I'm glad we don't know.

Because if we did...

If we knew which gods stood against each other, we might be forced to choose. And what if Nyc and Ziva are on separate sides? Who would I align myself with?

"I wouldn't know how to choose."

Sterling's dark eyes find mine. "Choose what?"

I realize that I've spoken out loud. Swallowing hard, I do my best to ignore the terrifying implications. "If we knew which gods were fighting which, we'd have to pick a side, wouldn't we? The kingdom would have to ally with some deities over others."

Horror blooms across the face of every council member.

"No." Sterling's voice is firm. "Our allegiance is to Tirene and her people. Not to gods who've decided to use our world as their battlefield."

Agnar scratches his chin, where stubble has formed after days without proper grooming. "Noble sentiment, but practically speaking, the temples would force the issue. The high priests would never allow the crown to remain neutral. Citizens can abstain, but the queen must choose. Not picking a side is the same as aligning us against them all."

Even worse.

I rub my eyes, fighting frustration and fatigue.

236

What if Rivlan, God of Water, stands against Ziva? Sterling and I aren't the only ones who would need to pick a side. If the elemental gods insist their magic users side with them, it would tear families and friends apart. No matter the kingdom.

My headache throbs.

"Let's focus on what we can control. Immediate actions." I draw a line under our list of facts and begin a new section. "First, establish and maintain perimeters at sacred sites. Every temple, shrine, and holy spring needs additional guards. Not to impede anyone from coming and going, but to be on hand for when emergencies happen. With couriers ready to send word."

"Teach magic merging." Agnar shrugs as if it's obvious, but his suggestion gets blank stares from the councilors. "What? Queen Alannah taught dampening to all the guards and servants during the drachen attacks. That was picked up by the nobles, the craftsmen, and then their families. It's how we got away with as few casualties as we did. If I'd taught my sister..."

He slams his cup to his mouth as if trying to drown out the next words.

My heart squeezes when I realize what he cut off.

He believes that if he taught his sister to dampen, she wouldn't have been corrupted, Rose wouldn't have been taken, and his brother-in-law wouldn't have died a gruesome death.

While I doubt any of that is true, I know how quickly the mind can settle all the blame on one's own shoulders.

"I like that. It's a good idea." Dalya plants her fist on the table. "Teach magic merging. Though it won't do much good to those outside Tirene, it will at least strengthen the magic of our kingdom."

"In that case..." Rafe starts rummaging through the piles

of papers he always brings to these meetings. "We need to cultivate the Fusion Root Vine. The tea made from it helps people merge smoothly. We'll grow as many of them as possible."

"Rafe." I dip my chin at him, and his eyes snap up to meet mine. "You've merged with us. Work with Bastian to write down detailed instructions on how to do so. Once you agree on the wording, start making as many copies as possible."

Sterling, catching on, addresses Fenton. "Your herbalists are top-notch. Do they have Fusion Root Vines in their gardens?"

"I'm sure they do. Everything started growing better after Narc and his drachen were defeated." Fenton straightens his wiry frame. "I'll have them take stock of the plants and get an inventory. Would you like me to coordinate with the palace herbalists to..."

"Yes. But I want you to take charge of it. Find out how many plants we have access to and how quickly they can be propagated." Sterling writes a quick letter and pushes it to me. "Anyone who has an herbalist or a garden of their own, please check yours immediately."

Several chairs scrape across the floor as most of the council members stand.

Scanning the message, I find it gives Fenton authority to query and work with all herbalists, including those employed by other nobles. The letter only requires the queen's signature to be valid. "Report back as soon as you can. The faster we get this moving, the sooner everyone will be able to protect themselves."

Agnar rises, grabbing the stack of papers Rafe has been collecting. "I'll help write up instructions."

"We also need to prepare for refugees." Sterling gestures to my list. "When strange things happen, people flee. Every major city should establish protocols for housing and feeding sudden influxes of displaced people."

I watch him while chewing on my cheek. Something's off. Something beyond the obvious stress of our situation. I've experienced Sterling worried, angry, and even frightened, but this is different. His movements, usually economical and controlled, contain a jittery quality I've never witnessed before.

I sigh and create a mental reminder to revisit that concern later. For now, we have solid ideas and a host of orders to distribute.

For the next few hours, council members come and go, reporting the good news of a growing number of Fusion Root Vines. The royal scribes busy themselves with drafting copies of the map, adding all the markers and jotting down notes to explain the overlapping lines of interference.

As we continue to plot the instances on the map, the pattern I thought I saw starts to emerge more clearly. The affected areas form direct lines between temples, as well as around them. As soon as that pattern takes shape, sometime after the moon sets, Sterling and I begin writing letters to the rulers of the other kingdoms.

Even Meridia.

Eventually, sunlight streams through the tall windows, painting golden paths across the scattered papers on the table. With my quill scratching across the parchment, I draft yet another missive to a neighboring nation. Sterling sits at the far side of the room, his face a mask of concentration as he works on his own diplomatic correspondence.

Agnar sprawls in a plush chair near the fireplace, one leg thrown over the armrest in a decidedly un-military posture. He's supposed to be writing instructions, but so far, his assistance mainly consists of occasionally calling for more supplies and ordering couriers and pages around.

"My brain is nearly mush now. How's this?" Sterling holds up his latest draft. "'In these troubled times, the mortal kingdoms must stand together—'"

"Boring!" Agnar lobs his apple core toward the bin. The remains hit the rim and bounce onto the floor. "Add something about how we could all die excruciating deaths if we don't unite."

I smirk. That might be just the kind of wording required to get the point across to the pompous Kamorians.

Sterling lowers the parchment, his expression flat. "I'm not writing that."

"Fine. How about this? 'The gods are at war, and we're their chew toys.'"

Sterling's quill hovers mid-air, and I note the debate in his eyes. "That's...not terrible."

Agnar preens and folds his hands behind his head. "I have my moments."

I push my chair back, working out arms stiffened from hours of writing. "What about this? 'Strange forces threaten all our lands. What befalls one kingdom today will reach another tomorrow. Only through unity and shared knowledge can we hope to weather the coming storm.'"

Both men gawk at me.

Sterling's lips part, and he gazes at me like he's seeing me for the first time. "That's—"

"Perfect." Agnar slow claps. "Ominous enough to get their attention without sounding like we've lost our minds."

Sterling nods, his eyes brimming with a warmth that eases some of my concern from the previous night. "You've always had a way with words, Your Majesty."

"Well, one of us needs to." Despite our dire circumstances, a smile tugs at my lips. "It can't all be curses and threats."

Agnar snorts while stretching his long legs. "Remember when our biggest problem was Sterling kidnapping you?"

Sterling scowls at his closest friend. "I did not kidnap her—"

"You absolutely did!" I point my quill at him. "You literally snatched me from the Flighthaven trial and carried me through the air to a different kingdom."

"That was a strategic extraction during wartime." Sterling's lips twitch with suppressed amusement. "And if I recall correctly, you nearly killed me with the sword I gifted you afterward."

"As any reasonable person would do when abducted." I pet the sword at my hip.

Agnar watches our banter with a wide grin. "The question is, was she worth it?"

Sterling narrows his eyes and studies me. His gaze travels over me in a way that floods my cheeks with heat. "I'm still debating."

I huff and toss a balled-up piece of parchment at him, which he easily dodges with a chuckle. The sound lightens the mood, pushing back the shadows of worry.

Our laughter feels good. It's a reminder that beneath the titles and responsibilities, we're still human. But beneath this light moment, unease lingers, because we all know it won't last. The humor in Sterling's eyes dims too quickly, and Agnar's smile fades from his haunted blue eyes.

Outside the windows, clouds gather on the horizon, dark and heavy with the promise of rain. I can't help but wonder if they're natural or yet another sign of the divine conflict raging above our heads.

How long before the war in the heavens fully descends upon us? And when that happens, do we have any hope of surviving?

I expel the air from my lungs and return to my letters.

No point in borrowing problems from tomorrow.

Not when tomorrow may never even come.

Chapter Twenty-Eight

Sterling

I jerk awake, my heart pounding against my ribs like a war drum. The air in our bedchamber feels different. Wrong. Heavier and charged with invisible pressure that prickles my skin.

Next to me, Lark's breathing remains soft and steady, her face half buried in the pillow and her dark hair spilling across the sheets. I slide from the bed without disturbing the mattress, a skill honed through years of military training. Despite my toes sinking into the thick rug, a chill racks my body.

The cold isn't what raises the hairs on my arms.

There's something else here. Or *someone*.

Spying.

Or maybe recent events overstimulated my imagination.

Moonlight streams through the window, casting our bedchamber in silvery shadow. I glide silently toward the basin by the window while straining to hear any sound out of place. Lark shifts in her sleep, murmuring something indistinct.

Water gleams in the basin, still and dark as a midnight lake. I lean forward, cupping my hands to splash my face, hoping to wash away the lingering sense of dread. Before I can touch it, the water rises to meet my fingers.

I freeze, noting how the liquid defies gravity to form a perfect sphere that hovers above the basin.

Not my doing.

"Your magic grows stronger by the day, Knox."

The voice emerges from behind me, fluid and deep, like water rushing over polished stones.

I spin, reaching for my magic as I confront the threat head-on.

The space between me and the bed ripples and gradually takes shape.

Not quite a man. His edges blur, his form shifting like sunlight through waves.

Rivlan.

The elemental God of Water. What the blazes is he doing here?

Muscles tensing, I study him as he studies me. Seconds pass before I recall that I'm completely naked.

Not ideal to meet a god with my dick out, but oh well. "You've been watching me."

Rivlan's form solidifies slightly, though the bedposts still show through the translucent blue of his torso. "I have."

"Why?" I keep my voice neutral, but my pulse quickens.

Close personal attention from a god isn't exactly typical. Close, personal attention from a god during a divine war? The reason can't be good.

"Why do you think?" His question trickles through the air.

"Oh, I don't know." My voice hardens. "Perhaps because of your godly war?"

The atmosphere grows thicker, like the moment before a thunderstorm breaks.

Rivlan materializes more fully. His features sharpen,

revealing eyes like deep ocean currents and skin that appears to flow across his body rather than remain still.

All the statues of him seem to be accurate. He possesses the chiseled, perfect features of a priceless sculpture. High cheekbones. Strong chin. Dark, well-shaped eyebrows the same color as his hair.

"Ah, yes. The Guardian." Amusement flickers across his liquid features. "Of course he would open up to you. Well, he simply preempted my telling you."

Irritation courses through me, and my words come out clipped. "He was light on the details."

"Let me illuminate them." Rivlan drifts across the room. "There is indeed a war among the gods. Two factions. One I call 'the traditionalists,' led by Zeru."

I listen carefully, analyzing each word, each nuance. Gods are notoriously selective with the truth.

"They believe gods should rule absolutely. That we are inherently better than mortals, and mortals are growing too powerful." His form darkens. "Lark's destruction of Narc rather proved their point."

"Our destruction of Narc," I correct, steel in my voice. Lark will not be isolated or targeted. If they need a scapegoat, I'll take the blame. "We had to work together to craft a power strong enough to destroy the god's corpse. And it still took everything we had."

Rivlan smiles. Or at least, I think he does. His mouth doesn't move in the way a human's would. Instead, his lips pull straight back, reminding me of a shark. "However you categorize it, the action sparked their fear. They want to reassert their divine dominance. They would rather break the world than share it." His essence becomes almost opaque. "My faction believes differently. Gods must evolve with mortals or become irrelevant."

I take a minute to process his words.

Two factions.

Traditionalists who want to dominate mortals, and... what? Progressives? Reformers? Whatever they call themselves, my skepticism runs deep. Gods are gods, after all.

Power corrupts, and they've claimed power longer than a mortal mind can comprehend. "And you just let it all happen? Left mortals to fend for ourselves?"

The temperature drops a few degrees. "You do not understand the situation. Or the gods."

I cross my arms, unmoved by his display of power. "So explain."

"We have fought back. We tried to communicate." Rivlan's form expands, filling more of the space between us. "Cyphero, aided by my waters, placed stains on Viridian's temple. Warnings. Directions."

"That was you?" I raise an eyebrow and snort a derisive laugh. "Maybe you should work on your skills. They weren't exactly clear."

The temperature plummets again. "Zeru's gods twisted the messages. Used their Devoted to spread fear instead of truth."

"I think it worked." I remember the panic after the temple incident, how the rumors spread like wildfire through Tirene. "The Devoted have been more active than ever."

"The God of Lost Things returned hundreds of missing items to mortals, accompanied by truths."

I shake my head in disbelief. "And that backfired spectacularly. Now people toss heirlooms into wells hoping to get godly dispatches back. Theft has run rampant. There's a thriving black market for lost-then-stolen items."

Rivlan's form bubbles with what might be frustration. "They corrupt our every attempt at communication and twist the meaning. They use their Devoted, but they also make

direct attacks on communications between us and mortals."
He pauses, studying me. "Did Lark not tell you?"

My spine stiffens as I glance at her sleeping form. "Tell me what?"

Uneasiness stirs in my chest. Has Lark been keeping secrets? The thought cuts deeper than I care to admit.

"Aletheia, the Goddess of Truth, tried sending Lark visions...warnings. But they were...contaminated. Degraded into confusing nightmares."

White-hot anger flashes through me.

At Rivlan, at the gods who targeted Lark, at myself for not noticing the extent of her distress. She's been having nightmares, waking in cold sweats, but she's never elaborated. And I haven't pushed. "So you gave up?"

Rivlan's hardened presence becomes icy. "We did not give up. We changed tactics." His voice gets lower. "Why do you think I'm here now, talking to you?"

I cross my arms, advancing a step toward him. "Why are you here?"

A beat of heavy silence fills the room.

"Because you could be a guardian, Knox. You could turn the tide."

My head jerks. I have no fucking clue what being a guardian means, but the mere mention still turns my blood to ice. "What's a guardian?"

Though I feign disinterest, I recall *the Guardian* from the portal. Remember the massive power radiating from him.

"A guardian stands between worlds." Rivlan expands to encompass more of the room. "Mortal and divine. Given power by the gods but not bound by their limitations. Enhanced abilities, both magical and physical, far beyond what you've already mastered. With enough practice, you could protect on a scale no mortal has ever imagined."

My pulse quickens. The same way the Guardian protects the portal between worlds? I could become that strong?

The real question is, would I want that much strength?

I try to picture everything I could do for Tirene, for all the kingdoms. The potential spins my head so much that I need to brace myself. I've survived a hundred soul-bashing things in my life. Lost so many people. Done so many horrible things. We may laugh now, but deep in my heart, I still feel like shit for what I put Lark through.

If I had been stronger back then...

With such power, I could protect Tirene from any threat. Ensure Lark never faces danger alone again.

I rein in my growing excitement. "And how would I achieve such exalted status? Let me guess, there's only one small catch, right?"

"Just one." Rivlan's smile is almost gentle. "I would teach you. In return, you would need to be my champion."

I scoff. One little catch, my ass.

Fucking gods. "Meaning?"

"It means you fight. For me. Against a champion for Zeru's gods." Rivlan's form wavers as he shrugs.

Or maybe he hiccupped. Hard to tell.

There's no way to keep the shock off my face. "Give me one good reason why I should oppose the God of the Heavens."

Rivlan's form eddies with what might be frustration or amusement. "Zeru wants to turn mortals into cowed beings afraid of their own shadows and begging for scraps of divine favor. Far worse than they are doing now." His voice becomes stronger. "But an ancient covenant provides the means to avert such a thing. It only requires willing champions. Overall, it is a peaceful solution."

The Devoted? Zeru wants to transform all humans into the Devoted?

Holy shit.

Rivlan pauses, his watery gaze fixed on me. "You can be that solution."

Utter shock floods through me.

"Why me?" The question slips out before I can stop it.

"This is why I've been watching you. Testing you." Rivlan drifts closer. "You're already powerful. But trained to use guardian abilities? You would be unbeatable."

The possibilities tug at me like an invisible current.

Power. Protection for those I love. An end to the chaos threatening my kingdom. Threatening every kingdom.

The allure is seductive.

Still, I've witnessed enough of the way gods work to know better.

There's always a greater price. Consequences beyond what's initially revealed. Agreeing now would be premature. Yet refusal might prove catastrophic.

I need time to consider, to investigate, to plan.

I move away from the water basin. "No offense, but I don't think I want to get in the middle of a gods' war."

Rivlan's focus stays riveted to me. "Clearly, you don't understand what's been happening. You are already in the middle of the war. All mortals are. But especially the Tirenese whom you hope to rule. Now you must decide what to do about it."

Fuck. "Sounds interesting. Tell you what. I'll think about it."

Rivlan studies me for another long moment before dissolving into mist, leaving only the lingering scent of rain.

I stand motionless in the center of the chamber, the weight of his offer pressing down on me like the ocean's depths.

Guardian. Champion. A war among gods with mortals as pawns. Or worse. And me, supposedly the means to end it all.

The implications are staggering. And beneath all that lies the unwelcome thrill of possibility. The power Rivlan described would change everything. Would change *me*.

The bed hasn't moved, but I know the rhythm of Lark's breathing too well. The current pattern is too measured, too careful.

The little faker. I have no idea how she managed to stay awake when Nyc, Hallr, and Orin sent me into some kind of charmed sleep when they visited her, but she did. Maybe each god independently decides whether or not they care about an audience.

I stalk toward her. "You can stop pretending to be asleep now, love."

CHAPTER TWENTY-NINE
LARK

The Council Tower radiates tension as Sterling reveals the encounter with Rivlan to Agnar, Bastian, Leesa, and the council members. I fidget with the sleeve of my tunic, trying to focus on Sterling's words rather than the way my stomach twists into knots.

A god has chosen my fiancé.

A god has offered him power beyond our wildest imaginations.

I should feel proud, relieved even. And a huge part of me is. At the same time, I'm drowning in a conglomeration of disparate emotions.

Sterling stands by our circular table, fingers splayed across a detailed map of Tirene. Flickering candlelight catches the angles of his face and grants him a more regal appearance than usual. More distant.

"Champion and guardian." His eyes meet mine before scanning the room. "That's what he said."

The division is already visible in their postures and expressions.

Dalya's eyes alight with eagerness. "With a king holding such powers, no one would dare even threaten us."

Fenton strokes his chin, his fingers rasping over morning stubble. "This could be a sign to the rest of the world that we are favored by the gods."

Agnar scoffs from his position at Sterling's right side, arms crossed over his broad chest. "Not gods. God. What of the others? Don't forget what we heard at the portal. Those bone-shaking booms. No offense to your would-be patron, Knox, but I've seen enough celestial intervention to last several lifetimes."

My mind drifts to my own experiences with Nyc, Orin, and Hallr.

That alliance helped us defeat Narc.

But at what cost? The gods have always sought their own agendas, played their own games that spanned millennia while we mortals lived and died in the blink of their immortal eyes.

Then again, we didn't get much of a choice. Narc tried to strip us of our free will and turn us into puppets dancing on divine strings. And none of the other gods stepped in to stop him.

They left that little task to us. To me. To defend ourselves against a rogue god.

"I see your reasoning." Rafe's eyebrows knit together. "But just think about it. A guardian's power could give us the edge we need. With godlike abilities, we could strengthen our defenses beyond anything Aclaris or any other kingdom could breach."

My fingers find the ledge of the table, and I trace the worn wood. "The gods help themselves first. I hate to say it, but I'm afraid any benefit to us is...incidental."

Leesa toys with a loose strand of dark golden blond hair, her features etched with concern as she regards me with a cocked head.

My adopted sister knows me too well. No doubt she can see the turmoil beneath my careful words.

Bastian clears his throat, drawing our attention. He sits surrounded by ancient tomes, his fingers stained with ink from hours of research. The resemblance between us—the same hazel eyes and dark brown hair—seems more pronounced when he's focused like this.

"There's something you should know." He flips open a particularly weathered book with reverent hands. "In all of history, there have been fewer than fifty documented guardians. And right now, only one's known to be active. *The* Guardian himself."

"That's one more reason for me not to accept Rivlan's offer." Sterling's features harden. "I don't want to risk becoming something like him."

I nod in agreement. That's when I realize I understand very little about a guardian's purpose. "Bastian, what exactly does being a guardian entail?"

He runs a finger down a yellowed page. "The texts describe enhanced magical abilities that are significantly stronger than what the person could naturally wield." He glimpses up at Sterling. "You'd likely find your abilities amplified beyond anything we've witnessed before."

My stomach clenches at the thought of that much power. Of the potential consequences. Of the gravity of becoming so godlike.

"There are also accounts of divine senses. The ability to perceive things hidden from mortal eyes. Incredible physical strength and endurance. Enhanced healing. And," Bastian hesitates, shooting me an uneasy glance, "a significantly longer lifespan."

The room stills, every breath magnified in the sudden silence. My heart drops as the implications stab me in the heart.

Sterling would outlive me.

"Define 'significantly longer.'" Sterling voices my fear.

Bastian grimaces, shifting in discomfort. "Ahh, I'm not sure. I'm thinking centuries. Possibly longer."

My jaw drops open.

Hundreds of years? Gods. That means he'd watch me age and die. Our children age and die. Their children.

Sterling's gaze finds mine from across the room, and understanding passes between us. The emotions playing over his handsome face echo my own. Shock. Sorrow. Determination.

We both saw the Guardian. Despite his otherworldliness, he resembled a man in his prime.

My throat constricts, eyes burning with unshed tears. I open my mouth to speak, but no words come out.

Sterling pushes to his feet, the chair scraping against the stone floor. His shoulders are rigid, his jaw set in that stubborn way I've come to know so well. "That makes the decision a no-brainer."

I gather my courage. "Knox—"

"No. Absolutely fucking not. I'm not spending centuries without you." His voice cracks a little, and something inside me breaks with it. "I won't live while the people I love die. I've already done that too many times."

The room erupts into arguing.

"That's exactly why you should do it!" Rafe slaps a hand on the table. "Centuries of protection for our kingdom. Think of what that means for future generations."

"Are you out of your mind?" Agnar shoots Rafe a *what-the-fuck* look. "At what cost? His humanity? His soul? We saw what the Guardian has become. Not quite mortal, not quite god. Something in between. And there's no one else like him. A depressing way to exist, if you ask me."

"But the power you'd gain could do incredible good,

Knox." Nira's calm but firm statement rises above the others. "We must consider the bigger picture."

"The bigger picture?" A vein throbs in Sterling's temple. "Like the 'bigger picture' that led us into war with Aclaris? The 'bigger picture' that nearly cost Lark her life? I'm tired of 'bigger pictures' painted by gods who view us as pawns."

"No offense, dear," Duchess Breann pats Nira's hand, "but you haven't lived long enough to know how time and loss can harden someone's heart. I agree with Prince Knox. This is not a path he should walk alone."

I stay silent, my mind a battlefield of conflicting emotions. Though relief washes over me at Sterling's refusal. Selfish, perhaps, but honest. I don't want him to suffer centuries alone. Or imagine him tormented while I, along with our children, wither away from old age.

Guilt simmers beneath that relief.

Am I the sole reason he's declining such power? Power that could protect our kingdom? Our people? The world?

As the arguments swirl around us, I try to catch Sterling's eye again, but he deliberately avoids me, focused instead on the maps spread before him.

A phantom hand squeezes my heart. Is he angry with me? Does he think I want him to accept Rivlan's offer? Or can he read the worry on my face?

"Enough!" Sterling pounds both fists on the table. "This is my decision and not up for debate. We're wasting time. Divine offer or not, we have more immediate concerns. Tirene cannot become collateral damage in this divine war. We need to revert to our previous plan because this one is not. Fucking. Acceptable!"

The bickering ceases. The room's attention snaps to the prince.

I seize the opportunity to gather my composure and rise to my feet. "Knox is right. Whatever games the gods are playing, our priority is protecting our people." I stand close enough to Sterling that our arms brush. "We've survived invasions, assassinations, and a rogue god. We'll survive this too. Through our own strength, not through divine power with doubtful motives."

Sterling finally glances at me, his eyes bright with gratitude. "My queen speaks wisely. Listen to her."

"Well then," Agnar rubs his temples, as if the conversation has given him a headache, "what's our plan?"

I spread my hands over the map and trace the borders of Tirene. "We prepare. We fortify our magical defenses. We teach magic merging. We continue to patch up the holes the gods leave as they battle. We stay vigilant."

"And Rivlan's offer?"

Ugh. Leave it to Rafe not to let the subject drop.

"It remains just that." Sterling meets the guild master's gaze, his tone brooking no argument. "An offer. Not an acceptance."

Rafe swishes his hand. "For now."

While Sterling dips his proud head, the stubborn set of his shoulders conveys that his mind is made up. "Yes. For now."

Bastian begins gathering his books. "I'll continue researching guardians and champions. There may be alternative ways to gain some of the benefits without all of the...complications."

I nod, grateful for his practical approach. "Thank you, Bastian."

As the council starts to disperse, breaking into smaller groups to discuss specific defensive strategies, Sterling's hand finds mine on the table and squeezes.

"I didn't mean to put you in that position," I whisper.

"You didn't, love." Sterling drops a gentle kiss on my forehead. "Rivlan did."

I study the strong line of his jaw and determined set of his mouth. "Are you sure about this?"

He faces me fully, and the intensity in his gold-flecked eyes steals my breath. "I've never been more sure of anything in my life, Lark. Some powers aren't worth the price."

I want to argue, to insist that he shouldn't base his decision solely on me, but the words die in my throat. Because a selfish part of me, that part that wants to keep him for the mortal span of years we have together, is grateful.

Somehow, we're going to figure this out. "Okay. It's settled. We'll find another way. Together."

CHAPTER THIRTY
LARK

My fingers tingle with excess magic as I press my palm against another stone block, channeling heat through my skin until the rock glows orange-red at the edges. The sweat trickling down my neck follows the curve of my spine as I fuse the ancient stone to the shrine wall on the outskirts of Tirene's capital.

The sacred space hums with power.

Sterling's water magic spirals with Agnar's steady earth energy while my fire fuses the elements together. My muscles ache, but there's satisfaction in restoration, in healing something broken before it's lost forever.

The tiny woodland shrine doesn't look like much. A simple stone structure nestled between ancient drakewood trees, it's older than the palace itself. A place where our ancestors once prayed for good harvests and healthy children.

Sterling works with his characteristic focus. His brow furrows as he coaxes water from the air, freezing it into mortar that binds the stones together more securely than any human-made cement.

His motions are precise, economical. No wasted energy.

My pulse gives a familiar flutter as I observe him.

"You two ready for the next one?" Agnar's cheerful query breaks my reverie. He uses his earth magic to heft a stone block that's too heavy for three normal men to carry.

I wipe sweat from my forehead with my sleeve. "Always the overachiever."

Agnar grins, the light catching on the thin white scar across his cheek. "Just keeping pace with your fire, Your Majesty."

Movement at the tree line captures my attention.

Not the casual stroll of forest creatures, but rather, the stumbling gait of someone in distress.

A woman staggers into the clearing, her simple village dress torn at the hem, her face streaked with mud and wild panic. Behind her, others follow. A man carrying a child. An elderly couple supporting each other. More villagers wobble into the sanctuary of the shrine's clearing.

I gather my fire just below the surface, readying myself for a threat. Sterling and Agnar drop what they're doing, their hands flying to their weapons as they settle into defensive postures. Around us, guards lift swords and draw arrows, watching for whoever or whatever is chasing so many people.

I come forward when the woman reaches for me. "What's happened?"

Leaves and twigs tangle in her hair. Scratches cover her face.

"The grove." She clutches my arm in desperation, her eyes wide with terror. "It's alive. Expanding. Swallowed half our village already." Her nails dig deeper into my skin as she leans closer. "It's eating people. Snatching them from the sky. We had to flee."

A chill sinks into my flesh. Another side effect of the gods' civil war. Though this new calamity sounds especially vicious.

Once is strange.

Twice may or may not be a coincidence.

But three times? That's a conspiracy.

The question is, why?

And are these attacks only targeted at the Tirenese?

"Which grove?"

She points northwest with a shaking hand, toward the direction of the woods that border the village of Lydonia. "The old one. With the sacred trees."

Against the darkening afternoon sky, an unnatural green glow pulses like a heartbeat on the horizon. "Sterling."

He's already at my side, his body a wall of steady strength. "I see it. We'll send word to the capital and call for reinforcements."

Agnar pulls a message tube from his belt, scribbles a quick note, and whistles. A royal guard emerges from the tree line to take the message before soaring away. With the way the world is going, we always have at least a few guards close by.

"Come on." I swallow the lump of apprehension in my throat. "These people need help."

We reach the edge of Lydonia in minutes, Sterling and I flying ahead, Agnar following with a contingent of guards.

What greets us isn't destruction in the usual sense.

No fire. No broken buildings. No screaming livestock. Not even traces of blood.

Instead, the landscape itself appears to be...shifting.

We land on the outskirts of the village, out of reach of the sacred grove. The once expansive group of ancient trees revered for centuries now flashes with sickly green light.

My jaw drops when a tree at the edge yanks its roots from the ground. In an eerily humanlike motion, the tree lurches six paces forward, branches creaking like old bones as it settles into the soil again.

Right on top of a winged corpse.

I rub my chest. That's what I get for thinking no one was hurt.

"Gods." I clamp my lips closed as soon as the word leaves my mouth. At this point, calling the gods' attention upon myself seems more likely to harm than help.

The trees groan as they move, their roots tearing through soil like fingers through soft dough. Branches reach for the village walls with deliberate, insidious intent. The unnaturalness fills me with dread.

Villagers scream and scatter as another tree uproots itself and crushes a small shed beneath its massive trunk. Water gushes from the earth in abnormal fountains, threatening to wash away what's left of the village.

Sterling raises his hands to direct his power. "I've got the water."

Agnar lands with a heavy thud behind us. "We've got the earth." He and two of the guards march forward, arms moving in tangent as they push back the encroaching trees.

Fire sparks at my fingertips. "I've got the trees." A firebreak across the advancing line should stop this assault.

"Don't!" Agnar grabs my wrist, blue eyes wide with more than just fear. "They're sacred trees. Who knows what burning them might trigger? Don't forget what happened with the dryads."

Dammit. He's right.

These aren't ordinary trees. Even notwithstanding their new ability to walk.

And eat.

I shudder at the visual.

They're ancient, connected to the magic of the land itself. Destroying them could worsen an already shitty situation. Leaves already smolder among the branches. Proof the villagers tried to fight back before giving up and fleeing.

Agnar drops to one knee, pressing his palms to the

ground. Earth rises in response, forming barriers to redirect the flood waters Sterling's struggling to contain. But even as the wall takes shape, the soil beneath Agnar shifts and warps.

The hill we landed on stretches and moves as if being worked by invisible hands.

Instinctively, we all jump and hover just above the ground.

Branches snap out. A leafy appendage grapples a guard who doesn't get out of the way fast enough. His screams rend the air, then abruptly stop when his neck snaps. The branches release him, and his body smacks the earth.

A wave of nausea crashes over me. I gulp in air, wishing I could burn the image of the lifeless guard from my memory.

Then the tree grapples another unsuspecting guard.

Fucking magical trees.

Just because I can't destroy them doesn't mean I can't stop them.

I pour flameless heat into the curve of the branch holding the guard.

Steam rises and wood creaks as it dries. Sap runs thick and slow. Not one to be caught unaware twice, the guard, a young woman who looks barely old enough to serve, retracts her wings. Without the extra appendages, the curve of the branch no longer holds her, and she slips loose.

At least this one survived.

"Sterling, freeze the sap! Agnar, funnel the water. Fire users, dry the soil so it hardens." The orders tumble from my lips as I swoop forward to catch the woman.

The falling guard is no slouch. As soon as she's free, her wings snap out to slow her fall. "Yes, Your Majesty!"

She spins and directs her magic to the hillside, helping to stabilize it while bending her knees to soften her landing.

Oh. She's impressive.

"Ha!" Agnar pivots to face a different direction. "You

always come up with the most innovative uses for magic, Lark. Full of surprises!"

I can't help but smile at that. Fire doesn't need flame to be effective. Dirt can be dust just as much as boulders.

Above us, a dragon's roar splits the sky. All heads snap up.

Several of the great beasts loop overhead. Their scales reflect the abnormal green glow. When I release the mental dampening that keeps me from being overwhelmed by their emotions all the time, I sense their unease. Nailah, her orange and yellow hues blending with the sun, circles high. Kaida hovers below her like a living shadow.

The rest seem to be wild dragons, drawn here by their own curiosity.

Dragons don't fear much, but something about this phenomenon disturbs them deeply.

Then again, they might also instinctively fret that the trees are larger predators.

Great. If the dragons feel too threatened, they'll burn down the grove without hesitation.

A redhaired guard flies down on a tan, sweat-dampened alicorn. "Your Majesties!" Her voice cracks with urgency. "The Shrine of Dawn—"

"Not now," Sterling grits out, muscles straining as he wrestles with casting a freezing rain over the sacred grove.

"It's moving." The guard gestures wildly behind her. "Taking the entire hillside with it. People are trapped inside!"

I shift toward Sterling, and our eyes meet in shared horror. The Shrine of Dawn is far away, on the Eastern border. If the same phenomenon is happening there...

"Go." Sweat drips down Agnar's face as he raises another earth barrier, his voice filled with grim determination. "I've got this."

Before we can move, two more guards arrive.

The first one, a male guard with spiked blond hair,

approaches. "The Temple of Mercy is sinking into the ground. The priests are evacuating, but many elderly devotees are refusing to leave."

"Border villages are fighting over suddenly shifting landmarks." The other guard, a middle-aged man with ebony skin, pauses to take a breath. "The river that marks the boundary with Aclaris and Kamor has changed course three times since dawn."

Yet another guard comes flying in low, her pale wings extended to slow her descent. "Kamor's troops are mobilizing along the Western Front."

The messages blur together, each crisis more impossible than the last.

The sacred grove continues its inexorable expansion. Hungry trees advance on the screaming villagers. Even with our combined abilities, we're barely containing one disaster while others multiply around us.

I grab Sterling's arm and pull him up Agnar's hill for a better view.

My stomach plummets. From here, the scope of the chaos becomes clear.

In the distance, three more sacred sites glow with aberrant light across the kingdom. The Shrine of Dawn to the east, the Temple of Mercy to the south, and what looks like the ancient burial mounds to the north.

Beyond them, plumes of dust mark the villages fighting over shifting borders. On the horizon, storm clouds gather at an anomalous speed, swirling in patterns that appear intentional rather than random.

Sterling stands beside me, his breathing ragged. "We can't be everywhere."

"We have to do something." But we both know it's a lost cause. Whatever is happening is too big, too widespread for us to contain. My chest tightens. My people are suffering, and I can't protect them.

Three sharp blasts of a blaring horn cut through the chaos.

Sterling straightens, recognizing the signal before I do. "Reinforcements."

Royal guards descend from the skies on the backs of alicorns, their armor glinting in the strange light.

Behind them comes Rafe, his guild master insignia visible even from a distance, leading a contingent whose practical clothing marks them as craftspeople rather than soldiers. "I'll help where I can with air but thought earth users would be useful here, so I gathered the ones I know."

Bastian follows, descending on Ryu.

The mighty dragon's blue scales glimmer as he lands. Ryu's head swerves toward the moving trees, and he bugles a challenge.

The trees nearest to us still.

"I got your message. Take these!" Bastian drops down two leather buckets before reaching for the straps carrying even more. "Redthorne berries." He jumps from Ryu, cupping his wings to pad his fall. "From the royal reserves. Blend the crushed berries with water and pour the alloy on the roots of the trees."

My brother's a freaking genius.

Redthorne, with its spiny branches and crimson blossoms, is a plant of protection. Known for its fibrous wood, the leaves are associated with overcoming obstacles and warding off evil. Farmers sometimes plant it at the edge of fields to keep the soil stable, and the berries are used in religious rites to guard against malevolent forces.

The guards fan out at Bastian's direction, dumping the mixture where the roots meet soil.

The effect is immediate.

Trees stop moving, held in place with frozen sap and hard-packed earth. The sickly glow dims. Beneath us, the ground's rippling settles.

Rafe touches down, his tall frame vibrating with barely contained energy. He tucks his dark brown wings against his back. "I have news."

Sterling's face glowers. "I will shoot you with a fucking arrow."

I fling out my palm. "No. More. News." Every muscle in my body aches with exhaustion.

Rafe's expression remains grim, but there's something else. A hint of...vengeance? "You're going to want to hear this. It's not completely bad."

He gestures, and two Tirenese soldiers drag forward a pair of figures in dark cloaks. Their hands are bound, and when they glance up, I note the star-marks crawling up their wrists that disappear.

Devoted.

"My informants spotted them chanting at the edge of the grove right before the trees started moving. Then kept an eye on them until we could arrive and arrest them." Satisfaction radiates from Rafe. "Seems someone might know exactly what's happening to our sacred sites."

For the first time since the chaos began, a tiny spark of hope ignites within me.

Not much. Just enough to fan the embers of determination still burning in my chest. One enemy we can see is better than a thousand we can't. And we have two of them.

Rafe shoves the two Devoted forward, allowing their robes to drag through the mud.

Even with blood trickling from the man's split lip, my skin crawls when they smile. Like they know something we don't. Their sparkling constellation marks serve as a subtle reminder of their devotion to Zeru.

My teeth clench. I'd like nothing more than to sear those marks right off their skin.

All around us, royal guards form a protective perimeter, their faces somber beneath their helmets. Farther down the slope, Agnar directs a group of earth elementals who continue to stabilize the area, their hands pressed to the ground as they channel magic into the soil. The earth still trembles occasionally beneath my feet, aftershocks from whatever the Devoted have done.

Sterling towers over the male prisoner, his presence commanding and cold. I recognize the stance well. Legs slightly apart, shoulders squared, chin lifted just enough to stare down his nose. He's assessing the situation.

And looking as intimidating as hells.

I take my place beside him, and our shoulders nearly touch. Even in this moment of tension, I find comfort in his proximity. "Start talking."

The male Devoted tilts his head up. A thin red line trickles from his split lip and disappears into the scruff of his beard. His head is shaved bare, including his eyebrows. When he smiles, he reveals red-stained teeth. "About what, Your Majesty?"

My jaw tightens. "What were you doing here?"

A muscle in Sterling's neck tenses. The only indication he's as pissed as I am. Inside my chest, fire magic throbs in time with my heartbeat, begging for release.

Should I brand the word *Traitor* on both their foreheads?

"We're here to watch you flounder." The Devoted man settles into the churned mud like it's a throne. He possesses the soft hands of a nobleman. Or perhaps an accountant.

My own fingers curl into fists at my sides, nails digging into my palms. The pain helps center me and keeps the fire inside where it belongs.

For now.

Rafe lurches forward, radiating impatience. "Where are the scientist-priests?"

The Devoted woman lifts her brown gaze, her eyes unnervingly vacant. "Who?"

Yeah, time for a branding.

Sterling must sense the direction of my thoughts because his shoulder brushes mine in a subtle reminder to maintain my cool.

The male Devoted's smile widens as he watches our exchange. "Or...maybe you'd rather know what happened in Kamor's central square this morning?" His voice drops to a conspiratorial whisper. "What about in Tír Ríoga's temple district?"

An icy finger trails down my spine.

His female companion picks up the thread, her previously vacant eyes now alight with unhinged fervor. "Meridia's central plains? The outreaches of the Northern Volox?"

Sterling shifts beside me. "What the fuck are you talking about?" His voice remains level, but I catch the undertone of worry.

"While you've been here playing with trees," Baldy's gaze sweeps across the grove and damaged village, "magic has become possible again. It will soon be returned to the world."

The words hang in the air like suspended droplets of water. No one speaks. Even the earth users assisting Agnar pause in their work, their heads swiveling toward us. My mind struggles to comprehend what he's suggesting.

"The Devoted have demonstrated true magic in their own kingdoms. Just as we did here." The glee in his voice churns my stomach. "Simultaneously. Water, fire, earth, and air. All elements bent to our will regardless of the user's heritage."

Stunned silence blankets us.

I share a glance with Sterling, whose eyes have darkened

with concern. Rafe curses under his breath, flexing his fingers as if he wants to summon a gale to blow these fanatics away.

"You're lying," I finally manage, but even to my own ears, my voice lacks conviction.

The woman laughs, the high-pitched tinkling reminiscent of shattering glass. "Are we? Ask your scouts. While you've been containing our little distraction here, we've been changing the world."

Realization dawns in Sterling's eyes. "This was just a diversion."

Baldy's expression gentles, like that of a proud teacher when his slow student finally grasps a concept. "The first move in a very long game, Your Majesties."

Holy. Shit.

If what they're saying is true—if the Devoted somehow coordinated magical demonstrations across every kingdom simultaneously—we're facing something far more organized and dangerous than we ever imagined.

These religious zealots outplayed us before we even knew the game had begun.

Chapter Thirty-One
Sterling

Behind me, Lark's anger boils with the heat of a volcano. Her patience with these fanatics wears dangerously thin. Moments ago, her hands were nearly as hot as branding irons.

My boots sink into the sodden earth as I stare down at the woman kneeling before us.

She has brown hair, brown eyes, and chafed cheeks. Her expression bears the serene arrogance that all Devoted seem to cultivate. Mud streaks her face in the spot where one of our guards was less than gentle, but she doesn't appear to notice or care.

The male Devoted kneels a few feet away, similarly bound but with a split lip that glistens with fresh blood. His pale eyes track our every movement.

I've experienced that look before. Cataloguing weaknesses to report on later.

The eyes of a prisoner merely biding their time.

"Our faith has been rewarded." The woman attempts to gain her feet while pitching her voice loud enough to carry. "Magic will return to all the world, not just your selfish kingdom!"

Your?

This woman is Tirenese too. But she clearly only identifies with her faith now.

Lark shifts her weight, twigs snapping beneath her boots. I can picture her expression. The tight jaw and blazing eyes.

Ready to spit nails.

She advances until we're shoulder to shoulder, close enough that I can smell the smoke that still clings to her hair. "I'm getting really damn tired of the narrative that Tirene somehow wants to hoard magic from the world. We've never wanted that."

Visible tension shows in Lark's hands. The slight curl of her fingers indicates that she's resisting the urge to call forth her fire. The accusation of selfishness cuts deep for Lark and pisses me off. She's devoted her entire reign to healing, rebuilding, and protecting.

She was willing to sacrifice herself to save the world, for fuck's sake.

"Haven't you?" The woman lunges forward again, but Rafe drags her back. "Your borders remain closed. Your magical knowledge locked away. Your scientist-priests refuse to share their discoveries—"

"We've spent the last few days doing the exact opposite of that." Lark crosses her arms over her chest. "Rafe, these prisoners are useless. They know nothing."

The male Devoted's harsh laugh is akin to stones grinding together. "We know war is coming again, regardless. But this time, you won't be the only ones with power."

Lark pushes into his space. "No shit. Everyone knows that. We sent out decrees warning about it."

Watching Lark—this fearless, incredible woman—refuse to back down stirs something primal inside me.

Rafe edges around us to confront the Devoted himself.

Mud cakes his boots to mid-calf, but somehow his guild robes remain pristine. "Where are the scientist-priests?"

The man's expression shutters closed. A vein in his temple pulses. "I wouldn't know."

"I told you." Lark releases an exaggerated sigh. "We're wasting our time."

The female Devoted sneers and makes an obscene gesture with her bound hands. "And that just proves how wrong you are. By now, thousands have witnessed our power. They're flocking to our temples, begging to learn."

I don't miss the specific phrasing. "Our power." Not the gods' power, as they usually claim. An interesting slip.

Heavy footsteps announce Bastian's arrival. He emerges from the tree line, hazel eyes grave beneath furrowed brows. "That part is the truth, at least. There have been reports of magical displays in every kingdom while you were here, fighting the grove."

My stomach tightens.

Lark rolls her eyes.

Suddenly, I understand what she's doing. Without asking a single question, she's using their pride in their cause to provoke them.

A brilliant strategy. *She's* brilliant. Fanatics love preaching about their ideals.

"See!" A swift and triumphant smile touches the female Devoted's mouth before she masks it.

"You planned this?" I gesture around us. "The grove, the moving temples. It was a distraction, wasn't it?" I glance at Lark.

She shakes her head and starts to turn away.

"Think of it as a test." The man throws himself forward, only to be grabbed by the guards. "One you failed spectacularly. Did you truly believe you could breach the gods' realm without consequences? The stars saw your presumption."

Agnar moves to stand in front of the male prisoner and narrows his eyes. "So did the big guy we talked to. We weren't sneaking. We walked right up to the door and knocked. Also, I'm pretty sure his name wasn't Stars." He strokes the hilt of his sword, the action leisurely but unmistakable in intent. "Want me to take him out back and see if he's got any useful information in that annoying as fuck brain of his?"

Lark smooths a wisp of hair that hangs loose from her braid. "Agnar, we're already out back. There's nowhere else to take them from here."

He shrugs, mouth quirking into a dangerous half-smile. "Guess that means I don't have to worry about their screams bothering anyone."

The man's throat bobs, and some of his bravado cracks. That pulse in his temple speeds up. Good. Fear often loosens tongues faster than pain ever could.

Lark crouches to meet the woman at eye level. "What's the point? We're just wasting our breath. They won't know what happened to the scientist-priests. They're just lackeys meant to slow us down."

"Oh, we know what happened to them. Everything they deserved. Heretics, questioning the gods' methods."

The woman's expression grows cunning. Something in her dark eyes shifts.

I tense. Here we go. This is what she's been building toward.

"You should hurry back to your palace, my queen. Other kingdoms wonder why Tirene ignores their pleas." She leans forward until her face is inches from Lark's. "How long before they decide they don't need you anymore?"

Bastian stiffens. If this was the male who'd threatened Lark, her brother would be flat on the ground already.

I would have knocked the fucker out myself.

The air between them shimmers with heat.

Lark doesn't flinch, but I can see the tiny flames in her cupped palm. "You still don't get it. We're not keeping anything from the other kingdoms. The only ones controlling the flow of magic are the ones you claim to serve."

That confuses the woman, who glances at her partner.

He scowls, split lip widening. "It's too late for your lies. The stars are watching, and they're hungry."

"So are the trees." Lark straightens, peering over her shoulder at the pacified grove. "Feed one of them to the trees and take the other one back to the palace dungeons to save for a later meal. They're the ones who upset the sacred grove. It's only fair for them to appease it."

The woman's eyes widen until the whites show. She jumps toward the man, but neither says anything.

Four guards grab the prisoners and haul them to their feet.

As they drag the two Devoted members away, the woman twists in their grip to call to us. "Wait! You can't do this."

"Of course I can't." Lark shrugs, her face passive, her tone measured. "The last time I killed traitors it took them a while to burn to death. According to you, I don't have that kind of time. That's why I'm delegating this task to my soldiers."

Rafe goes a little green around the gills. He'd witnessed the fires, heard the traitors' cries. But they didn't meet their fates until after they managed to kill Lark's grandfather and my mother.

I focus on the worry creasing Bastian's brow. "Is it true? Have messages arrived from other kingdoms?"

Bastian nods, features set in grim lines. "Many. Urgent ones. The kingdoms are in chaos. While some are celebrating what they think is magic's return, others are suspicious. Kamor is threatening to sever all diplomatic ties. Claims we're not responding because we're hoarding magical knowledge."

My jaw tightens. A perfect strategy. Draw us away from the palace during a critical moment, leaving no one with authority to answer the inevitable diplomatic storm.

Lark's face flushes with frustration. "It's been less than a day! Do they think we sit around just waiting for someone to talk to?"

Her hands, pinned by her sides, clench and unclench. Small sparks flicker and extinguish between her fingers.

I recognize the desire to scream etched across her features, along with the effort required for her to stifle that urge. The crown weighs heavier in moments like these. "They're moving faster than we anticipated. Coordinated attacks, magical displays in multiple kingdoms simultaneously, and diplomatic sabotage."

She nods, her expression tight. "They've been planning this for months...maybe longer."

"And we still don't know what 'this' is."

Dread sits like cold eel pie in my stomach, slick and writhing. The corrupted grove is contained, but the other horrors unleashed by the Devoted are just beginning to multiply.

CHAPTER THIRTY-TWO
LARK

"The Northern border has three more acres of twisted trees since last week." I push a report across the small table in our sitting room. It's just me, Sterling, a copy of the big map from the council chamber, and a whole stack of ever-growing reports. "That's twice the rate of the previous month."

Sterling nods, tracking the inked border that keeps shifting and advancing. "And the Devoted?" He scribbles a note on the bottom corner.

"Getting bolder." I flip to another report, attempting to ignore the ache growing behind my eyes. "It's only been a day since they made their worldwide declaration. They've started public displays of elemental magic at their gatherings. Nothing spectacular, but enough to draw crowds. Enough to make promises they can't possibly fulfill about returning magic to their followers."

Sterling grunts.

We've been at this all day, and I'm pretty sure he slept poorly last night. He woke with bags under his eyes, and the reports started rolling in before Rhiann even finished helping us get ready for the small court Bastian holds for emergency cases only. The council is off ensuring our orders are being implemented properly. Leesa, Helene, and Elijah are working with Agnar and Rafe to test magic merging with Tirenese and non-Tirenese people. The stonemasons have changed their priority from repairing walls to building grow houses for the Fusion Root Vine plants we've started collecting.

Sterling sets his quill down. "We could station more guards near—"

The air in the room thickens and condenses like gathering storm clouds.

His head snaps up, and he reaches for his sword. The weapon isn't on his hip because we haven't yet managed to leave our chambers today. His sword, along with mine, remain in our bedroom.

As a haze forms in the air, the temperature drops, dew forms, and the hairs on my arms rise.

Sterling stills. I open my connection to the dragons, feeling the instant snap of the mental cord. If we need aid, I want to be ready.

The air continues to coalesce into the shimmering, near-transparent figure of Rivlan. Water glows from within his figure, through eyes that somehow reveal a depth of knowledge beyond mortal comprehension. He's not in his fully human form.

I frown with discontent. Why is the god who offered to make Sterling a champion appearing in our rooms? Maybe the danger hasn't passed.

Sterling, on the other hand, tosses the papers onto the table and rubs his eyes. "Let me guess. You've been watching."

"I have." Rivlan's watery features shift and flow, but his voice contains an element I'd never expect. Fear. "The expanding grove. The Devoted's calculated displays of magic. Everything. You handled the situation well, but things will worsen. The gods mark their territory like animals now, and they care nothing for the mortals caught between. What are you and Lark," he nods to me, "to do in such times, when a viable solution is beyond your means?"

I catch Sterling's shoulders subtly relaxing. It's as if he's relieved to hear someone else spell out what neither of us will admit. We're plugging holes in a dam when the gods have offered us a permanent solution.

Still, discomfort prickles my spine.

"And you know a better way?" Sterling keeps his face neutral and his tone casual. As if he's speaking with a council member instead of an honest to goodness god.

"I can give you a way to end this." Rivlan's essence, a cool mist that whispers across my skin, consumes the room. "These attacks are symptoms. The gods are at war. The mortal realm is their battleground."

I lift my chin, refusing to let his presence intimidate me. "Forgive my confusion, but how does a fighting match end this?"

Rivlan's liquid eyes focus on me. "The Champions Match is an ancient tradition, bound by covenant. When gods reach an impasse that threatens to spill into war, we may invoke that covenant."

A sinking feeling in my gut informs me that I already know where this leads.

"What covenant?"

He drifts closer, leaving no wet footprints on the plush rug. "The most sacred of agreements between gods. Created after the Five-Fold Wars."

Between one step and the next, his form solidifies.

Weird, and a little creepy. I refuse to even attempt to wrap my mind around the amount of power the gods have and what they can do.

His features sharpen. Even the hair on his head

materializes, the locks hanging thick over his shoulders and cascading down his back like a cape.

Sterling arches a brow at me.

"I haven't gotten to any covenants yet." Since becoming queen, I've been reading a book about the Five-Fold Wars and studying our kingdom's history, but embarrassing gaps remain in my knowledge. I haven't had enough time to learn everything yet.

Not like I've been busy dealing with crisis after crisis or anything.

Rivlan's smile is a disconcerting sight on his fluid features. His skin has adopted an almost human appearance, though he still moves with an alien grace. "The covenant allows us to settle our differences through champions rather than unleashing our full powers upon the mortal world."

Sterling's gaze skims over me before returning to Rivlan. While his expression reveals nothing, his fingers stop drumming on the table. "And you want me to be your champion."

"Yes." Rivlan's eyes are deep pools. "A god in the conflict must name a willing champion. These champions face each other in combat to determine which god's vision prevails."

My stomach clenches. "To the death?"

"Well, of course. If one isn't willing to die for their god's cause, they're not worth the amount of training it requires to mold them into champions." Rivlan smooths the sleek black coat that has formed along his body. "The stakes must be absolute for the covenant to bind. But understand what this means. One death instead of thousands. Millions, even."

Sterling's fingers flex. "And if I win?"

"Zeru and his faction must abandon their plans to dominate mortals. They must accept a more balanced relationship between gods and humanity." Rivlan's voice grows passionate, his nearly solid form gushing with intensity.

"No more manipulation, no more treating humans as pawns. As objects of possession."

"And if he loses?" If he dies...

I shove down the fear bubbling up inside me. Ignoring mind-numbing terror every time Sterling's life is endangered should be almost routine by this point.

Rivlan pins me with his steely gaze. "The gods would rule more directly, demanding increasing devotion with dire consequences for anyone who displeases them." He lifts his chin and pauses for dramatic effect. "Any of the gods."

The words punch the air from my lungs.

I fight to keep my expression neutral, to breathe normally, to not leap across the table and scream at this god for even daring to suggest such an idea.

The gods often ask for conflicting things, which is why their temples are kept so far apart in some cases. You cannot live in the darkness of Nyc while also maintaining Ziva's flames.

Rivlan studies Sterling again, and I can't help but notice their similarities. Both are tall. Both wear their silky hair to their shoulders. Both possess long, muscular torsos. "But he won't lose. His potential is extraordinary. With proper training, he'll be unbeatable."

Sterling and I exchange glances.

I give a slight head shake, trying to convey my doubt without words. There's more to this. There must be. The gods never present simple solutions. I'm one-thousand-percent positive I don't want Sterling to accept this mission.

It's too risky, and we can't trust any of the gods.

Not to mention, imagining Sterling losing me along with generations of his family to old age guts me. Living lifetime after lifetime without me or the people he loves.

But even as that thought manifests, I feel a twinge. A twinge I don't want to acknowledge.

Guilt.

Am I holding him back from his life's purpose?

Rivlan observes our silent communication as if he has no stake in Sterling's decision one way or the other. "How's the wedding planning going?"

A startled laugh escapes me. "What?"

On a list of one hundred things I never expected a god to utter, that's got to be in the top five.

Rivlan glides over to the fireplace. "Get any good gifts?"

Sterling rises to his feet, covered in a rainbow display. "Why?"

I stand, too, confused by this sudden shift in conversation.

The god holds his hands to the fire, seeming to enjoy the heat. "The diamond waterfall was from me."

"You sent us a wedding gift?" I'd completely forgotten about the strange present. With everything that's happened since, resolving that mystery fell to the bottom of the priority list.

"Indeed. It's more than mere decoration. My gift can provide magic to humans in all kingdoms."

Hope flares in my chest. The solution to our problem has been locked up in the gift room all along? "But why? Why give us a way to restore magic?"

Rivlan's essence shimmers when he shrugs. "If he is my champion, I will teach you." He gestures to encompass the maps on our table and the reports of growing unrest. "Unless you prefer watching your world rip itself apart? I do not want that. You do not want that. And it does not need to be that way."

Indecision freezes me on the spot.

The solution is right here, if only Sterling reaches out and grasps it. My ribcage tightens, strangling my lungs. I feel as though my mind, soul, and heart are all battling each other.

Sterling takes a hesitant step toward Rivlan. "When would I need to fight?"

No. Absolutely not.

He can't be seriously considering this.

My first reaction is purely emotional, but rational reasoning soon prevails. If I were the one being offered this chance, I would seize it.

I know I would.

"That's the beauty. It's up to you, Knox." Rivlan glides away from the fire, and the prisms slide to the wall before disappearing. "The first named champion selects when and where the match occurs. A provision to motivate the gods to pursue this route versus war. While the Guardian is a, well, a guardian, he has not yet been named a champion in this war. The only condition is that the match must occur within a year and a day of the naming."

Sterling remains quiet, his eyes distant and considering. He won't meet my gaze. Won't even glance in my direction. My emotions have tangled themselves into a giant knot, and I no longer have any clue how I feel.

Shock. Pain. Eagerness. Hope. Grief. Panic. Love. A giant whirlpool that robs me of my voice.

"You've felt it, haven't you, Knox?" Rivlan circles Sterling like a shark. "The water responding differently as of late?"

Sterling's attention fixes on the water pitcher on our table. "Every time I use it, it changes. Stronger, but...yes, stranger too."

"And it will get stronger still." Rivlan leans over Sterling to speak directly in his ear. "I vow to you, Knox, your power has been waiting for this moment. Your true potential, dormant until now, awaits. We can tap into that magic. Amplify it tenfold, and then another ten. You're more powerful than you know, and I can help you improve."

For several long moments, Sterling doesn't move. "Why me?"

"Because you understand power isn't just strength. It must serve a purpose." Rivlan's smile gives him an oddly human appearance. "You want to protect your people, regardless of rank or birthing station. Yet you also reach out to help your neighbors. I want to protect all people from this war."

Sterling studies him. "By making me fight in it?"

"By providing you with the opportunity to end it. You've been fighting in it since it started. With far less power than what I offer you." Rivlan's form softens. "And Knox...there is no 'me making you.' It is all yours. Your choice. Your power."

Indecision wars in Sterling's eyes.

This isn't a competition.

This is about saving our people...and about Sterling achieving his destiny without the woman he loves trying to stop him. I would have felt betrayed if he'd stood in my way. I loved him more because he never tried.

How can I stand in his way now, if this is what he needs to do?

With uncertainty churning in my gut, I paste on a reassuring smile and give the subtlest of nods.

Sterling, eyes still on me, directs his question to Rivlan. "When do we start?"

"When you formally accept."

Sterling lifts his chin. "I agree to become the guardian and your champion."

The air stills, as if everything around us is suddenly listening.

The stars are watching.

I shiver. Despite his stoic pose, goose bumps erupt on Sterling's arms. The candles flicker before burning brighter. I swear the water in the pitcher on our table rises up and reaches for Sterling.

Rivlan nods, visibly relieved. "Then your training starts tomorrow. We'll worry about setting the date later. After we've had a chance to assess your abilities. Until then, things will start calming down in your world."

Sterling's smile feels like the first in a long time. I understand why. He can stop a war between the gods and properly return magic to the world. That's all that should matter, right?

After the God of Water leaves, dissolving like mist at summer's dawn, the quiet between us lingers. In the center of our chamber, we hold each other, his arms wrapped tight around me, my face buried in his chest. His heartbeat drums a steady thrum in my ear.

"We'll figure it out," Sterling murmurs into my hair.

I nod, not trusting myself to speak. We both know which "it" he means. Not the gods. Not the war.

The years. The endless years ahead that we might not get to share.

I hold him tighter, memorizing the feel of him, the scent of him, the solid presence of him in my arms. In case this is all we get.

CHAPTER THIRTY-THREE
STERLING

Water surrounds me in perfect circles, parting as if I stand in the eye of a storm. The surface trembles, reflecting the light in fragments that prance across my skin.

After a long night of losing myself in Lark and managing far too little sleep, I barely finished my breakfast with her this morning before Rivlan appeared.

With just a wave of his arm, he brought me here.

Godly training ground, he'd called it. A place that exists somewhere between realms.

He probably just named it that to feel important.

As far as the eye can see, crystal clear water stretches toward the horizon. The glassy surface mirrors a sky of sorts, the faint glowing blue interspersed with fluffy clouds in a mimicry of the real world.

I flex my fingers, feeling the water respond not just to my touch, but to my thoughts as well. My intentions tremble beneath my skin like an anxious alicorn. The water rises, not in the familiar wavering columns I typically create, but in massive, perfectly formed pillars that shoot upward with breathtaking speed.

With just a bit of focus, I shape them with my mind. There's no need to gesture as they bend and twist, forming archways that curl together and towers that stretch high.

The water doesn't merely obey. It anticipates.

Normally, I coax water to my will. But now...the element feels like an extension of my soul. I can sense every molecule, every ripple. The entire body of water vibrates in harmony with my heartbeat.

None of this should be possible.

The thought cuts through my mind, breaking my concentration. Cracks appear in the liquid architecture before me, spreading like spider webs across the magnificent structure.

Too late, I try to hold it together, to reinforce the failing points.

The entire creation collapses with a thunderous splash, and water rains down around me. Pacing in a tight circle, I drag in air that fills my lungs but does nothing to cool the frustration flooding through me. My legs move in swift, angry strides that leave wet footprints on the strange ethereal ground.

"Fuck."

This is both simpler and harder than anything I've ever done. The power is so easy to handle, so long as my focus doesn't waver. Once that happens, everything goes to shit.

I wipe spray from my face.

Rivlan approaches, cups a hand around the back of my neck, and tugs me closer so our heads are bent together. "You're a cocky bastard."

Despite my frustration, a reluctant grin tugs at my mouth. "And you're observant."

"Point proven." His fluid features shift into a fierce frown. "Do not be cocky. Be confident." His fingers tighten on my neck, and I psyche myself up for a god's version of a pep talk.

"Cocky craves power. Confidence understands that power is already there. Use it. Be calm. Be confident. Accept who you are now."

He releases me and steps back. My forehead is dry. The water rejoined Rivlan, leaving not even a trace of moisture behind.

I sigh and rub the back of my neck. Confidence has never been a problem. Then again, I've never trained with a god before.

Rivlan's form gains definition as he straightens. Muscles crafted from currents run under translucent skin. His color changes with his direction and even his mood. He wears a garment resembling a long vest that reaches past his knees and loose pants that bag around tightly cuffed ankles. His feet are bare.

He twirls his pointer finger. "Again. Stop thinking like a mortal. Don't ask the water to obey. Know that it has no choice and already is."

I snort. "Kind of difficult when I *am* a mortal."

Or at least, I was.

Honestly, that part's freaky as fuck. I don't feel any different than I did yesterday.

Holding my hands up, I check for any changes. I wiggle my toes in my boots but can't feel anything between them.

"Are you seriously examining yourself as if you might change colors? You're trying too hard. Just be yourself, and the rest will come naturally." With a scoff, the water deity turns away, the dark strands of his hair flinging over his shoulder.

Irritation swells at his assessment, but I nod, considering his words. "Okay."

Maybe he's right. Maybe I've been approaching this all wrong, thinking like a soldier giving orders and expecting resistance.

That's not how my relationship with water works. Not

anymore. Water isn't my subordinate but a part of me. My arms move without conscious commands. Water magic should now function the same way.

I close my eyes to center myself.

The sensation hits differently this time. It's an acknowledgement of what already exists rather than a gathering of power. My breath slows. My pulse steadies. I open my eyes and stretch out my power.

The water rises again. Only this time, the action is effortless.

Structures emerge from the surface. Towers, bridges, and archways interlock in patterns that I envision with my mind. The liquid bends and defies gravity yet holds its form with perfect stability.

Light refracts through the structures, casting rainbows across my skin and the strange ground beneath my feet.

Pride surges through me.

Just yesterday, I couldn't even imagine this level of control. This level of power.

"Better." Rivlan's voice is measured. Bored, even. But I don't miss the smile that tilts the corners of his lips.

Exhilaration courses through my veins, my blood pumping hot and fast. With barely a thought, a wisp of an idea, I draw the water upward and outward, shaping the fluid with greater detail and precision.

A perfect replica of Tirene's palace rises before us, rendered in water so clear it might be crystal. Every tower stands at the correct height. Every archway curves with architectural accuracy. I add the fire paddock, the wide walkways of the main halls, and even the balconies that serve as perches for the winged citizens.

The West Tower's always been my favorite.

I add a tiny water figure to one of the balconies. Lark, with her wings outstretched. My chest aches with sudden longing.

I'd give anything to have her here with me, sharing in this experience.

Rivlan's expression shifts from approval to exasperation. "Are you planning to defeat Zeru's champion with architectural models?" He waves a hand dismissively through my creation, causing ripples to distort the scene. "Focus, Knox! And stop showing off. This isn't a game." He pauses, eyeing the disturbed water. "Also...the West Tower was leaning a bit."

I laugh and sweep up the tunic I discarded earlier, using the material to wipe my face. "Do you know who Zeru's champion is?"

"The logical choice is the Guardian, though you shouldn't necessarily expect Zeru to do what's logical." Rivlan considers me, his ocean-deep eyes unreadable. "It could be anyone. A powerful magic wielder, no doubt. You need to be ready for everything."

That little piece of news prompts me to physically stagger back. Once I regain my balance, I drag my palm down my face. There's a chance I might face off with the Guardian? If that's the case, I'm fucked.

If Rivlan notices my shock, he ignores it. "Anyway, you're progressing faster than I anticipated. Perhaps it's time to introduce you to the others."

Others?

He gestures toward the edges of the training ground, where several radiant beings materialize like condensation forming on a cold glass.

Gods from his faction?

Alarm tenses my muscles, and I ready for attack.

A feminine figure approaches first, her form cloaked in swirling air currents that twist her features into a shifting mask. She says nothing, not even her name.

With a sudden, sharp movement, a tornado spirals toward me without warning.

Battle instincts kick in. Whether this is a goddess or a likeness of one conjured by Rivlan, I'm not about to let her kick my ass.

I spin in a full circle, drawing water up around me. Instead of creating a shield, I shape the water into a funnel that meets the tornado head-on.

The collision vibrates up my arms. I hold steady, reshaping the combined energies into a massive waterspout that I redirect toward my assailant.

Clearly pleased by my counterattack, the divine creature laughs, the sound reminiscent of wind chimes in a storm. She disperses the waterspout with a flick of her wrist, absorbing her wind and allowing the water to fall without that added momentum. Her eyes, bright white like flashes of lightning, regard me with new respect.

Before I can react, the ground trembles.

An earthen figure crafted from packed soil and stone emerges to my right, its face humanoid. With a gesture that reminds me of a catapult release, this new opponent hurls shards of stone at me from all directions.

I drop to one knee, throwing both hands outward.

Water pours into a dome that catches each projectile mid-flight. The stones hang suspended in the liquid barrier and slowly soak up the water as the dome starts to collapse from the weight.

With a mere thought, I freeze the entire structure into a crystalline shield, imprisoning the projectiles in a steady sheet of ice.

"Not bad." The creature's voice rumbles like a raging river.

"Oh, you like that? I'm just getting started." With a sharp gesture, the frozen shield explodes outward, shooting the stone shards, each now encased in a spike of ice, back with doubled force.

The earthen creature raises a wall of stone to block them, but a few still drive into his form. He nods with grudging approval.

The air creature doesn't move, allowing the frozen pieces to penetrate her form.

But I know there's also water in her air. Even within her divine body, I can feel it responding to me.

Instead of passing straight through, the ice projectiles expand. The crystals in her body grow, holding her rigidly in place.

She bares her teeth in a snarl. Surging lightning finds and disperses the crystals, which she then thrusts toward me.

Each challenge comes faster than the last, barely giving me time to recover.

More opponents appear without warning.

A new attacker, with skin like flexible metal, hurls balls of fire that sizzle and steam as they collide with my magic. A shadowy creature tries to blind me, forcing me to sense the water through touch rather than sight.

They might be fast, but I'm one step ahead.

I dive into a whirlpool of my own creation, disappearing beneath the surface. The water welcomes me, embraces me, becomes me. I can see through the magic, feel through it, exist as part of it. Then I erupt from its center, water-dragons coiling around my arms, their liquid maws open in silent roars.

A wall of fire stretches across the training ground, but I walk through the flames, untouched within my protective water sphere. I emerge on the other side with steam rising from my shoulders but not a mark on me.

Exhilarating, dizzying power gushes through my veins.

Is this what being a guardian means?

Above me, someone creates a miniature avalanche. A massive mound of snow and ice crashes toward me.

Instead of creating a new barrier, I extend my hands and concentrate on the moisture within the avalanche itself. With a single sharp gesture, I freeze the entire mass into a thin, solid sheet of ice. The structure hovers in mid-air, the force of the avalanche arrested.

"Enough!" Rivlan calls, and the others retreat to the edges of the training ground.

I let the ice sheet dissolve back into water that splashes at my feet. My body aches, and my muscles burn, but I welcome the discomfort. Pain means I'm powerful and alive. I utter a silent vow to do whatever it takes to win the match.

For Lark. For Tirene. For humanity.

I accept a cup of water that Rivlan conjures—an irony that doesn't escape me—and down half of it.

"Your progress is remarkable." Rivlan studies me with those unreadable eyes. "At this rate, you'll be ready for the Champions Match well before the deadline."

"Good." When I finish the water, the cup disappears from my hand. "We can start spreading the news about the match in Tirene."

The god hesitates, his form rippling like disturbed water. "Let us keep it quiet for now. The date and the fact that you are training."

I pause midway through wiping sweat from my face. "Why?"

"The announcement will bring...attention. Expectations. Distractions." Rivlan's form shivers, briefly losing cohesion before solidifying again. "Better to continue your training in peace, without the added pressure."

Tactically, his words possess a certain logic. Keep my progress hidden from Zeru and his faction. Let them underestimate me and remain unprepared for my growing power.

"Fine." Magic flows through my veins like never before, accompanied by an uncomfortable realization.

I've entered a game with rules I don't fully understand, where other players have been moving pieces for millennia.

While I may be gaining strength, I'm still basically mortal, surrounded by gods with their own agendas.

And though I refuse to let it show, that knowledge fucking terrifies me.

CHAPTER THIRTY-FOUR
LARK

I slam my quill down, and black ink splatters across the latest trade agreement from the Southern Provinces. The tiny droplets blur the carefully penned words like tears. My eyes burn from hours of reading, but it's not the physical strain that instills me with the overpowering urge to scream.

It's the endless parade of decisions, each one more consequential than the last. All piling onto my shoulders like stones.

"Are you going to throw that one too?" Rose sits cross-legged in the corner of my private sitting room, her flame familiar Kin dancing above her small hands as she claps in a rhythmic pattern. The little sprite flares brighter with every clap, illuminating Rose's face.

I fake a scowl. "Don't be cheeky."

The little girl became my unexpected companion today, and I'm pretty sure her presence is the only thing stopping me from setting this entire stack of paperwork ablaze.

"You threw four already." She issues the matter-of-fact statement with her attention still on Kin. "I counted."

I huff. Of course she did.

"Are you sure?" I absorb the mess of scattered papers comprised of petitions, treaties, inventories, and appeals from nobles seeking advantage in the new regime.

Rose's blond curls bounce when she nods. "Four. And you used that word that Mama says I'm not allowed to say."

I press my lips together to hide my smile. "I'm so sorry. Please accept my humble apology, Lady Rose."

She giggles at the formal title, her small shoulders shaking. "I'm not a lady."

"Oh, but you are." I'm grateful for the momentary distraction. "Anyone who sits so patiently while a queen has a tantrum must surely be a lady of the highest caliber."

This time she laughs outright, the uninhibited, joyous sound so free of burden that my chest aches. When did I last laugh like that? Probably before my coronation. Maybe even before I acknowledged my feelings for Sterling and discovered the fear that accompanies such a love.

Sterling.

My fingers tighten around the trade agreement, crinkling the parchment. This morning at dawn, Rivlan woke us up by popping into our bedchamber and announcing that Sterling's training would begin immediately.

I barely had time to register what was happening before they vanished. With a grunt of frustration, I fling the trade agreement onto the floor to join its brethren.

Without batting an eye, Rose continues her clapping game as Kin spins above her hands. "Five."

"Yep." A heavy sigh slips loose from my lips. "Five."

At least I didn't curse this time. Small victories.

I push back from the desk I asked the servants to bring me earlier, back when I aspired to finally make headway on the mountain of state business. I stand and pace to the fireplace, seeking warmth for my chilled, stiff fingers.

I stare into the depths of the flickering flames, willing

them to provide answers. What's happening to my love right now? Is he in pain? Danger? Is Rivlan reshaping him into someone who won't need me anymore?

I stifle a groan and berate myself over that last selfish thought.

Sterling deserves whatever gifts the gods bestow upon him. After everything he's survived, he's earned all the blessings. Still, the fear gnaws at me.

What if his new purpose steals him away from me? What if he transforms into something I can't follow?

Rose giggles again. "You're making the fire do something funny."

I blink at the rising flames. The fire's responding to my distress. I force the blaze back down to size with a subtle nudge of my mind. "Sorry. I was thinking too hard."

"Mama says thinking too hard gives you wrinkles." Rose bobs her head like a sage priestess instead of a six-year-old.

I chuckle despite myself. "Your mother is very wise."

"She also says—"

Whatever other nugget of wisdom Rose's mother shared is lost as the door to my chambers crashes open with enough force to ricochet off the wall. I spin around, instinctively reaching for my short sword.

Sterling stands in the doorway, his chest heaving as if he just returned from a ten-mile run. His wet hair clings to his forehead and neck, and water drips from his soaked clothes.

But his eyes are what halt my breath. Bright and wild, they gleam with an almost feverish glow.

My heart lurches as I rush toward him while scanning his body for injuries. He doesn't appear hurt though. He looks... changed. "Sterling!"

"Lark." His velvety baritone rumbles my name like a prayer.

His entire body vibrates, practically humming with

energy. Water droplets fall from his hair toward the floor, but they never hit the rugs. Instead, the liquid hovers for a moment before rising back up to him, as if he's become a lodestone for the element.

"What happened?"

He tunnels a hand through his hair, arcing water droplets that hang suspended for a heartbeat before sinking into his skin. The gesture is quintessential Sterling, except tinged with something otherworldly.

"It was..." He pauses, likely searching for language to describe events too alien for human words. I experienced the same issue when trying to articulate the dragons' emotions.

I find myself observing that simple action. I love the way his eyebrows pull together when he thinks. I love how his lower lip curls slightly inward when he's concerned. I love him entirely. Completely.

The man he was yesterday.

The man currently standing before me. He's still Sterling, only more so. The air around him bends and shimmers.

"Incredible." His shoulders relax. "The water responds differently to me now. Like it knows what I want before I do."

Rose peeks up from her game, Kin forgotten as she regards Sterling with undisguised curiosity. "Did you fight?"

Sterling laughs, the sound lighter than I've heard in weeks. It's the laugh of the carefree young man he could have been before war and responsibility and loss aged him beyond his years. "Not exactly. More like I pushed away boundaries that were never there."

He gestures with his hand, and the water from the pitcher on my desk rises up, defying gravity. The liquid twists and shapes itself into a miniature dragon, no larger than a cat, with delicate wings and a sinuous body. The water-dragon glides through the air with such lifelike movements, I can hardly believe it's crafted from liquid.

"I made one of these but as big as the room." Sterling watches my face for a reaction.

Rose gasps in delight and jumps to her feet, chasing the water-dragon as it swoops around the chamber. "It's beautiful!" She reaches for it.

The dragon playfully darts away from her before disappearing into the wall on the far side of the room, leaving no trace of water behind.

Rose spins back toward Sterling, her cheeks flushed with excitement. "How did you do that? Where did it go? Can you make it come back?"

Sterling's eyes find mine over Rose's head, and I note the almost manic energy vibrating through him, barely contained beneath his skin. "I made an ice formation as high as a mountain. Rivlan says no one has managed that in centuries."

"Show off," I tease, smiling.

Despite my fears and worries, the tightness in my chest eases. Lightens. I adore seeing him like this, nonchalant and almost boyish. After all the heartbreak he's endured, all the royal pressures, he deserves moments of pure joy.

Rose bounces on her toes, and her flame sprite mimics her actions. "Do the dragon thing again!"

Sterling obliges by drawing water once more from the pitcher. This beast is larger, more detailed. The water-dragon swoops low over Rose's head, and her giddy squeal rings out as she pursues it around the furniture.

"Careful with my papers!" I clasp my cheeks in my hands as Rose nearly tramples the scattered documents.

"Sorry." His eyes shine with leftover adrenaline and the thrill of discovery. "Rivlan says I'm progressing faster than he expected. That my potential..." He trails off, noticing something in my expression. "What?"

"Nothing." I wave off his concern and force another smile. His own smile fades, the euphoria dimming from his eyes.

The water-dragon spews a tiny flame of steam at Rose and leads her in another direction, keeping her occupied as he moves closer to me. "But?"

"But nothing. Truly." I stroke his cheek and find his skin warmer than usual. "You're...glowing."

"Rivlan says that's normal." Sterling leans into my touch. "Part of becoming a guardian. Renewed vigor and health." His eyes search mine. "I wish you could feel it, Lark. The power, yes, but more than that. The purpose."

My chest tightens again, an uncomfortable pressure building behind my ribs. Not fear exactly. Not fear for him. But...if Sterling's discovered his purpose, where does that leave us?

The water-dragon dissipates into mist that vanishes before it hits the floor. Rose yawns, the excitement of the chase catching up with her.

I focus on her, grateful for the distraction. "Time for bed, little one. Your mother will be here soon to collect you, and I don't want her thinking we've worn you out."

Even as she rubs her eyes with small fists, Rose pouts. "But I'm not tired."

"Of course not." I work to hide my amusement, not wanting to rile her up even more. "But maybe you could rest your eyes for a few minutes? Just until your mother arrives."

She considers this compromise with the seriousness only a child can muster for such negotiations. "Okay, just until then."

Rose settles onto the small settee in the corner and curls up with a cushion. Within seconds, her eyelids droop and Kin's warm glow dims.

Once she's asleep, Sterling pulls me close, his arms encircling my waist. "You're worried."

Power crackles beneath his skin like lightning. "I'm not—"

He strokes my hair. "You are. But this is good, Lark. This is what I'm meant to be. I can sense it."

I nod against his chest, not trusting myself to speak. Because what terrifies me more than him being wrong is the worry that he might be right. That he truly is meant to be an entity greater than just a man. More. A being different than my king, my husband, my love.

Something too magnificent and wonderous for the likes of me.

Pressing closer to him, I inhale the familiar scent of leather, soap, and spice, along with the newer fragrance of fresh rain and open skies that clings to him. His heart thumps a steady rhythm beneath my ear, the same rhythm that's lulled me to sleep on countless nights.

While that bit of normalcy reassures me, I also sense a subtle current running beneath his skin like a hidden river.

I can't help but wonder if one day that current will grow stronger than the man, washing away the Sterling I love and leaving only the Champion of Water behind.

CHAPTER THIRTY-FIVE
LARK

The Council Tower feels even larger today. Only five of us currently inhabit the room, including Leesa. She sits quietly in the corner, thumbing through a leather-bound tome.

Our circular table dominates the center of the space, the polished wood reflecting the morning light that streams through the eastern windows. Fires crackle in the twin hearths, warding off the chill. Scattered papers and maps serve as reminders of yesterday's meetings and today's agenda.

Sterling lounges in a chair on the other side of the table, his brow furrowed in concentration as he reads a letter. His long, elegant fingers tap a silent rhythm against the paper. Normally, Rivlan would have whisked him away by now for more training, but today the god is absent.

A rare gift I intend to savor.

A week has passed since Rivlan began Sterling's training, and my fiancé has changed. That subtly healthy glow he attained after his first session became permanent, and a preternatural steadiness now guides his motions. Strength radiates from him like heat from a sun-warmed stone.

I love him this way, confident and whole, even while loathing the reason behind the alterations.

Rafe has positioned himself near the windows, his tall figure silhouetted in the sunlight. Agnar slouches in a chair to my right, his boots propped on the table. I shoot him a dark look, gesturing at the stacks of papers he's mangling together.

He grins, unrepentant, but drops his feet to the floor. "These stone-dry reports suck every drop of moisture from my body." Agnar grabs his flask, but when he tries to lift it, nothing happens. "What the...?"

Slowly, water rises from the container without splashing or spilling, instead forming a perfect shimmering sphere that hovers just beyond Agnar's grasp.

I sneak a peek at Sterling, whose eyes remain fixed on his papers. The corner of his mouth twitches.

Agnar heaves a loud sigh and reaches for the floating orb. "Really? Is this necessary?"

The sphere drifts higher, away from his fingertips. Cursing, Agnar leaps and misses. A snicker escapes me.

There's something endlessly entertaining about two grown men, one a fierce soldier, the other the soon-to-be king, behaving like boys at the breakfast table.

"Very mature." Agnar crosses his arms. "What are you, twelve?"

Sterling maintains his facade of studious indifference.

The ball of liquid bursts into tiny droplets, each one catching the sunlight. The golden sparks rearrange themselves, spelling out a single word in mid-air.

Y-E-S

I laugh outright. Even Rafe's perpetual scowl cracks, and a reluctant smile tugs at one corner of his mouth.

Agnar thrusts his hands up in defeat. "Fine. Enjoy your immature parlor tricks. Just remember this when we practice earth barriers later." His volume lowers to a threatening whisper. "I make no promises about how soft the landing will be."

The droplets swirl together, creating a tiny detailed figure who bows apologetically before dissolving and splashing back into Agnar's flask.

Not a drop hits the table.

Agnar rolls his eyes. "Show off." He shoots the flask a suspicious glance before taking a long drink, but his expression holds more affection than annoyance.

Sterling winks at me, causing my heart to perform that same stupid flippy thing he always evokes. My cheeks warm.

Queens shouldn't blush over winks, but here we are.

The door opens. Glancing up from her book, Leesa slides into a seat closer to me while the remaining council members file inside. Bron and Dalya are deep in conversation, blond head pressed close to magenta. Fenton Wick follows, Nina trailing behind him and laughing over something he's said.

Duchess Breann is the last one to arrive. She ushers in two servants with trays full of tea and wine.

Rafe clears his throat. "Your Majesty, Your Highness, members of the council. I have something unusual to report." He pauses for effect. "Nothing. Nothing at all has happened."

A confused silence settles over the room.

My ears thrum in the sudden quiet. "Meaning?"

"Meaning, no disasters. No emergencies. No weird magical occurrences." Rafe ticks items off on his fingers. "No shifting geography. No temple attacks. No harpies luring sailors to their doom. No animated statues rampaging through villages. No hungry trees." His expression appears bewildered. "Nothing. It's been completely, utterly peaceful."

The statement's significance begins to sink in.

For months, we've catapulted from one catastrophe to another, the magical disturbances growing more frequent and dangerous. Lately, I've been double-checking with all the couriers, worrying we've missed reports of some awful new horror.

Nira toys with the silky sleeve of her stylish teal gown. "I have to admit that this sudden calm almost feels suspicious."

"I know. I felt the same way. But it's real. Nothing has happened." Rafe's shoulders drop about an inch. This is the most relaxed I've ever seen him. A corner of his mouth lifts.

Agnar gasps dramatically, clutching a hand to his chest. "Did you...just smile? During a meeting, no less? Clearly the apocalypse is nigh."

The creases around Rafe's eyes deepen. "Don't ruin the moment."

Sterling leans forward, resting his forearms on the table. "This is exactly what Rivlan promised. According to the covenant, once a champion is named, all parties are bound to settle their dispute through the Champions Match. The fighting stops. That's why there's no more," he waves a hand, "weird stuff happening."

"Well, that's great." Agnar's voice drips with fake enthusiasm. "So the future of the entire world rests on how well you fight your opponent in a magical death match. Gee, I feel so much better now."

My stomach clenches at the words "death match." I've tried not to obsess over what the Champions Match will entail, but the reality of the looming event sits like a stone in my gut.

Sterling might die.

The thought sours the few sips of wine in my stomach.

Dalya drums her fingers on the table. "Any word on who you'll be fighting?"

I set my cup down. "We've been compiling information on the most powerful warriors across the kingdoms."

Breann tops off her cup of tea and holds up the pot to ask if anyone needs a refill with a grandmotherly smile on her face.

"The logical opponent would be a strong magic user. Though with magic still mostly stripped away from all but us here in Tirene, the opponent's patron god would probably need to restore their power."

Fenton studies the map. "Tír Ríoga has some formidable warriors."

"The Devoted have been gathering powerful individuals too." Rafe's customary scowl returns with a vengeance. "They could have recruited someone we don't know about."

Agnar shifts uncomfortably in his seat. "What about the Guardian?"

The festive mood evaporates like morning dew under a harsh sun. Sterling's expression remains unchanged, but tension creeps into the set of his shoulders.

My heart stutters over the memory of that towering figure.

"He's a guardian, too, right? I mean, he calls himself *the Guardian*." Agnar glowers at the table. "Half-god, half-mortal, utterly loyal to Zeru. Deadly with every weapon known to mankind. Been training for centuries. Blah blah blah. It would make sense for him to serve as Zeru's champion. Rivlan even told you he'd be the logical choice."

Dalya releases a low whistle. "If that's the case, then you need to train harder."

"She's right." I wring my hands together while addressing Sterling. "I know you train every day with a god, but..."

Sterling reaches across the table, unlocking my hands so he can link his fingers with mine. "You offering to train with me?"

Before I can answer, a courier enters with a sealed message. "From Tír Ríoga, Your Majesty. Their response to your diplomatic inquiry. You asked for it to be sent to you immediately."

I break the seal and scan the contents. My heart sinks with each line. "Tír Ríoga is forming an alliance with Kamor. They say Tirene is not invited to join." I pass the missive to Sterling, who reads the correspondence with a deepening frown.

Dalya remains stone-faced but shoots a glance at Fenton, who simply closes his eyes and shakes his head.

Agnar attempts to read over Sterling's shoulder. "Have they been infiltrated by the Devoted?"

Sterling holds the letter up to give Agnar easier access. "They've somehow come to the conclusion that we destroyed magic deliberately to make them dependent on Tirene for resources. They're pulling away from us politically and economically."

Rafe gasps as if suffering an apoplexy before scribbling furious notes. This is not good news for the guilds he heads.

"Why don't we just tell them the truth?" Agnar thumps Sterling on the shoulder. "Let them know that you plan on returning magic to the world after the Champions Match. That should shut them up."

Bron leans forward, his eyes bright and eager. "Yes! And then—"

Sterling shakes his head. "Rivlan wants to keep the match private. At least for now."

"Why?" I still don't understand the need for secrecy. "Shouldn't people have hope?"

"He says he doesn't want me distracted, especially with the fame it would bring." Sterling throws the letter on the table, resentment thick in his every action.

Leesa snatches up the message and glares. "When will be the right time?"

Sterling shrugs. "I assume once the other champion is named."

Agnar rubs his jaw. "In the meantime, the other kingdoms continue to believe Tirene stole their magic on purpose."

The council room fills with overlapping voices. Suggestions and counter-suggestions fly across the table.

Sterling remains quiet, studying the others with a thoughtful expression until they run out of steam. "Then let's prove them wrong."

The room falls silent, and all eyes turn to him.

Bron sighs. The young duke appears weary and much older than his twentysomething years. "How?"

Silent communication passes between Sterling and me before Sterling replies. "By saving them anyway."

The simplicity of his statement strikes me like a punch in the gut. Of course. We don't need their trust or their alliance. We just need to do what's right.

Pride swells in my chest. This is why I love him. Not merely for his admittedly impressive physique, or his quiet confidence, or the way his eyes soften when they meet mine, but for moments like these, when his moral compass points true north despite aggravating and potentially dire circumstances.

"Knox is right." I sit up straighter, the phantom weight of the crown heavy on my head. "If Tír Ríoga and Kamor don't want to be our allies, fine. But our actions still affect them, so we'll help them whether they like it or not."

Agnar grins. "I do enjoy a plan that involves being aggressively helpful."

"And if they still hate us after we save them?" Rafe asks.

I shrug with more lightness than I've experienced in days. "Then at least our consciences will be clear."

Sterling catches my eye again and winks. Not a flirtatious gesture for once, but a conspiratorial one, signaling that, whatever comes next, we're in this together.

Chapter Thirty-Six

Lark

The Impassable Desert isn't just hot. This place is a slap in the face from the sun itself.

Sand stretches in every direction, rippling like water under the relentless heat. Even with my fire affinity, sweat beads on my forehead and other body parts. Above us, dragons circle in lazy loops, their shadows brief respites from the glare. After enduring the chillier temperatures in the capital, they love luxuriating in this heat, the sun, and all the sand they can bathe in.

The desert plays no seasonal favorites, scorching any creatures foolish enough to breach its borders year-round. Even in the middle of winter.

Sterling clutches his already half-empty water flask in one hand. "You know," he wipes his brow with the back of his hand, "when I asked you to train with me this morning, I wasn't expecting something quite so challenging." Despite his complaint, his brown, gold-flecked eyes sparkle with humor. "Water magic. In one of the hottest, driest places in the world. Very thoughtful of you, love."

A devious cackle bubbles up my throat. "Consider this

payback for all those brutal training sessions you put me through when I first got my wings." I stretch my shoulders. "You forced me to fly until my muscles screamed, remember? Threw weighted balls at me to catch while I struggled to hold my position in the air. Not to mention those dawn sessions at Flighthaven when you behaved like a total ass."

His eyes widen. "That was different. All necessary training."

"And this isn't? You know what we're up against." I raise an eyebrow. "The gods chose you as a champion, Sterling. You think they plan to make it easy?"

He sighs, conceding the point with a nod. "Fair enough."

I just smile and take three steps back. Without warning, I summon fire from deep within, feeling it jet through my veins like liquid gold. "Hope you're ready."

A massive fireball erupts from my palms and spirals toward Sterling with deadly intent.

He laughs while creating a water shield that transforms my flames to steam with a satisfying hiss.

"That all you've got?" He's a blur of muscle and magic.

I track him while hurling smaller and faster fireballs that scorch patches of sand.

Sterling dodges most of them and counters others, his water magic leaving brief shimmers of moisture that the desert instantly devours.

"Lower your shield edge!" I shout as one of his shields becomes a little wonky. "You're leaving your left side exposed."

He adjusts mid-movement as seamlessly and fluidly as the element he commands. "Better?"

The dragons, apparently bored with just observing, decide to join the fun. Tanwen launches a stream of dragonfire—hotter and more vibrant than my own magic—directly at Sterling's back.

Horror grips me. I open my mouth to warn him, already knowing I'll be too late.

Somehow sensing the attack, Sterling drops and rolls, allowing the flames to pass safely overhead. "Trying to kill me, love?"

Smirking, he leaps to his feet.

I toss up my hands, palms out. "Don't look at me. That was Tanwen. Apparently, he thinks you're not training hard enough."

I glare up at the dragon, opening our connection to blast him with my disapproval.

Tanwen replies with a burst of amusement before attempting to soothe my stress. Clearly, the dragon had confidence in Sterling's ability to dodge his attack.

"There went a few years off my life," I mumble as I prepare my next assault.

For nearly an hour, we dance across the desert.

I fling flames. The dragons occasionally assist and add their own flair with dragonfire, tails, and even gusts of gritty wind.

Hmm, not a bad idea. The next time Sterling pivots to focus on Kaida's dive, I widen my stance and unfurl my wings, beating them back and forth. While the sand swirls and spins, I heat the grains until they start to glow and then fling them at Sterling's unprotected flank.

He keeps pace with everything, his layered ice sheets chilling and trapping my fiery sand.

His power is incredible.

Finally, with my lungs burning almost as much as my magic, I call for a break. "Enough! I surrender to your superior endurance."

Sterling collapses onto the blanket we brought, chest heaving. "About damn time. I was actually starting to worry I might keel over." Tanwen swoops overhead, blasting him with a snort strong enough to stir the sand. "I surrender, Tanwen!"

I flop down beside him. "You were amazing." The dragons take to the skies again and drift lazily on the updrafts.

"Thanks." He passes me a water flask, and our fingers brush. Even that innocent contact ignites a spark between us. "So what about you? Want to try some of my training routines?"

I gulp several mouthfuls of water, considering. "The ones you were doing last week with Rivlan?"

"Yes. The training might benefit you since your magic classes were cut short at Flighthaven. In the beginning, Rivlan's lessons were less about using the magic and more about getting in tune with my element. If that makes sense. It's a lot easier than what we were just doing." He stands and extends a hand. "Come on. Your turn to suffer."

I let him pull me up. To my surprise, he only lifts me into a sitting position.

He settles on the blanket beside me, putting enough distance between us so we won't accidentally touch. "First, I want you to sit there with your eyes closed. Relax. Without calling on your power, try to feel the magic. Notice where it lives in your body."

I fill my lungs and close my eyes, understanding exactly what he means. "There's two spots, actually."

Surprise laces his tone. "Two?"

"Well, yeah." I shift on the blanket, surprised I never explained this to him. "My elemental fire and the phoenix fire. The phoenix fire is," I focus on the portion that thrums like a second pulse, "somewhere just below my own heart. The other fire sort of sits behind my belly button."

"Can you merge the two?" Awe colors his words. "And keep the result inside you?"

I used both types of fire at the same time while fighting Narc, but merge them?

"Well..." I reach inside, coaxing the two magics to join.

They twine easily, offering no resistance. Swirling, combining, but not actually mixing, each flame holds a distinct place. Gold, red, and a brilliant white shine behind my eyelids.

"Like that. Yes. Now instead of calling the flames up, allow them to rise to the surface."

My nose wrinkles. What does he mean, *like that*? The fire is still inside my body. Can he see something anyway? Or sense something?

His husky voice soothes like a warm breeze after playing in the snow.

Heat surges to my skin. "Okay."

"This might sound strange, but try to picture your magic as part of you rather than a separate entity living beneath your skin. Accept that the magic shifts with a thought, the same way you unconsciously move your arm or leg."

I flash back to the cave where Narc's bones rested. Under duress, I didn't need to focus on pulling my magic along with me. I just did it. I was holding Rose when I destroyed Narc and all the drachen. I imagined what I wanted, and then it happened.

"Holy shit."

When I register the amazement in Sterling's voice, my eyes fly open.

Red, yellow, white, and orange swirl as my flames engulf me. I have to admit, it's pretty damn cool. On the far side, Sterling gapes.

A tiny lick of flame stretches out and taps his tongue.

He sputters, slapping at the fire while jerking back. "Wha-wha...?" His dry tongue prevents him from finishing the word.

"Oops. I didn't expect it to move so fast!" I collapse to my knees, howling. "You should have seen your face."

I'm cracking up so hard that I'm gasping for air and my stomach's burning. I can't remember the last time I laughed this much.

Around me, the fire wiggles, matching my joy.

Just as Sterling claimed, the training is glorious rather than strenuous. I feel as if I've grown into my full body. Like I'm finally completely...*me* in a way I never knew could happen. Then again, this is only the first lesson. The exercises surely get tougher.

Sterling stops batting at his dry tongue to glare at me with faux anger. "Oh, you think that's funny, do you?"

Rain starts prickling my fiery skin, the drops so light that they tickle.

"Sterling!" When I attempt to swat them away, the drops grow colder, barely above freezing. Rolling over, I do my best to dodge them. My flames ripple in an effort to sizzle and evaporate the droplets.

Sterling gets on his knees and pursues me, refusing to let me escape. Our laughter and yelling ring out.

Then a new sensation washes over me.

Suddenly, Sterling's magic fills me, too, like a cool rush of water alongside the burning heat of flame. Our eyes lock from across the swirling vortex of steam and sparks, and I know he feels it as well.

With our heightened emotions, we opened up to each other and synchronized. Our magics merged without requiring us to do anything.

The rush intoxicates me, the surging power beyond anything I've ever experienced. With our fire and water in perfect harmony, we feel more like a single entity than two separate magic users or bodies.

The sensation reminds me of when we shared the dream state together.

Sterling appears equally shaken. "What was that?"

"I don't know." I search for a way to describe what just happened. "But it felt—"

"Right." He grins. "And good."

I nod, unable to find better words. The experience awakened something in me, a rush nearly smothered by the pressures of acting as queen.

"I've missed this." I stare across the vast, harsh beauty of the desert. "Being part of the action instead of just twiddling my thumbs and watching others."

"You've always been more than someone who watches events unfold from afar. Always will be." Sterling's fingers find mine in the sand and squeeze gently. "But what's this about watching me? Were you scrying on me?"

The truth flows through our merge. So does the sexual thrill. The heat simmering between us now has nothing to do with the desert sun.

I remain silent, unwilling to verbally admit that Kin helped Rose and me spy on Sterling when he trained with Rivlan.

Sterling's eyes darken as they hold mine. A new tension permeates the air. "You were!" He tsks.

I sip from my water flask, wetting my dry throat while feigning nonchalance. "I was curious about your training methods. That's all."

"Curious, hmm, Duchess?" The gold flecks in his irises turn molten. "You like watching me, do you?"

Blood rises to my cheeks. "Maybe."

He edges closer. "I like watching you too." His heated gaze travels down my body, unhurried and appreciative. "Take off your clothes."

The command is so direct, so Sterling, that I laugh even as desire coils in my belly. "Here? In the open desert?"

He gestures to the expansive emptiness around us. "The dragons are hunting. No one else is around." His fingers tug at the laces of my training shirt. "Unless you're feeling shy?"

I cover his hands with mine. "Hardly. I just wasn't planning on getting sand in...unfortunate places."

"The blanket's plenty big. But if you'd rather do more training—"

"No." I drop my hands from his so he can work on the laces. "No more training. I want you."

Less than ten seconds later, Sterling yanks my shirt off. He strips his own off next, with the rest of our clothing quickly following suit.

The sight of all that naked, sweat-glistened skin encasing muscles sculpted from years of training temporarily collapses my lungs.

I trace a faint scar on his chest. "I've missed you. Just the two of us, training together, spending time together. Life has been chaotic lately."

"Chaotic is an understatement." He brushes a windswept strand of hair from my face. "But do me a favor?"

"Anything."

"Forget about everything outside of us, right here and right now." He hooks two fingers under my chin, tilting it up so my eyes are on his. "Can you do that for me?"

"Yes." I barely breathe the word before his lips crash onto mine.

I don't care that we're in the middle of a desert, or that our days might be numbered, or that thousands of responsibilities vie for attention once we return to the palace. In this moment, only the feel of Sterling's arms around me and the sensation of his tongue stroking mine matters. The delicious sensation of bare flesh touching bare flesh. He groans and kisses me senseless, stoking a stream of desire and need within me.

He pulls me down beside him so that our bodies touch along with our magic and minds. The contrast of his coolness against my heated skin sends delicious shivers prancing down my spine.

"I've wanted you all day," Sterling murmurs against my neck, his lips tracing a path that has me arching against him.

"Watching you throw fire, commanding the dragons...the fierce, focused way you react. It drives me wild."

"Mmm." Coherent thought slips away as his hand finds exactly the right spot and slips between my thighs. "In a good way?"

"In the best way." His caresses tease me...light where I want pressure, slow when I crave quick.

I retaliate by using my knowledge of his body, nibbling the sensitive spot below his ear and scraping my nails over his scalp. Stroking the delicate flesh at the crease of his thigh.

We've played this game before, each trying to distract the other first. By now, we understand our respective desires, but the chilled fingers rippling over my center of need is new, startling a low moan from me.

Today, I forfeit the game, surrendering myself to his skillful touch and the heat of his mouth. He waits until I'm writhing before finally slipping inside me. Our bodies join with practiced ease, like two halves coming together to form a whole.

I need to bite my lip to keep from crying out. "Sterling."

"I love watching your face when I fuck you." Strain crackles Sterling's voice. "The way you can't hide anything you're feeling. And now it's indescribable, how I can experience everything you experience too. How much you love the way I fill you up, and how right we feel together."

He shares every sensation, just as I share his, all of them bundled together, joining, tangling, strengthening. The overwhelming feelings are too much for me to put into words.

Instead, I tug him closer as we move in time on the blanket, the desert around us forgotten.

Twisting my hips, I surprise him by pushing him over so I can straddle his hips.

He wants to watch? I'll give him a good view of more than just my face.

"Yes, love. Just like that." Sterling's eyes roll up in his head as I rock my hips. His hands encircle my thighs, lifting me up and then yanking me down so that his erection slides inside me.

"Agreed." I tremble, taking a moment to savor the sensation. Rotating my hips, I revel in the fullness, in the way his hard flesh presses into my softness. How his breathing becomes ragged each time I lift and lower myself. The way the angle provides delicious pressure to my sensitive bundle of nerves.

At this rate, neither one of us will last long. I already feel the tension mounting, leading me closer to the cliff. Still, I hang on as long as I can to this little sliver of paradise. I never want this glorious handful of moments to end.

He plunges into me as I ride him, bucking his hips up to meet me while his hands release my thighs to splay around my waist. As I fight the building pleasure, a whimper escapes me.

Sterling shudders beneath me, changing the pace from steady to frenzied. "Come with me, love."

That soft command is all it takes.

I come apart, falling over the edge as my body shakes with my release.

Our magic rises with our pleasure. Sparks literally fly where our skin touches, a miniature storm of fire and water that cocoons us in a haze of steam and light. Sterling groans through his own climax before collapsing beside me. We both pant, dazed and replete while our magical connection slowly fades.

He leans over and strokes my face, planting lazy, drugging kisses against my mouth.

Seconds, or minutes, or maybe half an hour passes before we speak.

I reach blindly for the water flask. "Gotta do more of this."

Sterling's laugh vibrates into me where our bodies still

touch. "You'll get no argument from me. Every minute of every day would never be enough."

For a while, we lie here, the repressive heat becoming more bearable as the sun begins its descent.

I trace idle patterns on Sterling's chest, pondering the power I felt during our training. "You're really something, you know that? Not many people can stand up to a dragon, let alone more than one. Your magic has always been incredibly strong, but now? It's unprecedented."

"I've noticed the change. Suddenly, more magic is available to me. More water too. I feel like I can take on anything and anyone." A quiver runs through him. "Except for the Guardian. Though Zeru's faction could always name a new champion, the same way Rivlan did with me."

The memory of our encounter with the Guardian and the way he so easily threw us out of the portal hangs between us.

I snuggle closer to Sterling, as if I can somehow shield him with my body. "Well, like I said, you've gotten stronger. And you won't be alone."

"Won't I?" His eyes find mine, questioning. "If this is truly to be a Champions Match—"

"I don't care what the gods decree. I'm not letting you face this alone."

At first, he looks like he might argue. Then his expression softens, and he plants a kiss on my forehead. "Always the rebel queen."

"Always." A chill runs through me despite the desert heat.

The odds feel impossibly stacked against us. Then again, they always have been.

CHAPTER THIRTY-SEVEN
STERLING

A thick layer of mist shrouds the palace training grounds this morning, which I use to my advantage. With a twist of my wrist, the moisture responds, coalescing into a shield formed of half mist, half liquid.

Agnar's stone shards shatter against my barrier like glass, and droplets scatter across the field. I discovered this trick while merging with Lark and have since learned to implement it on my own.

Reactive magic.

Until disturbed, the magic looks like nothing, and it requires no extra effort from me in order to become deadly. My fingers tingle with the cold, the familiar numbness that arrives whenever I push my elemental abilities this far.

Witnessing Agnar's frustrated grimace is well worth the discomfort.

"You call that a water shield?" His blue eyes gleam. He summons more earth from the ground beneath us, fashioning soil into lethal spikes with nothing but a flick of his fingers. "I've seen better protection from a leaky roof."

I maintain the barrier with little strain. The water

molecules hum with energy, ready to shift with a thought. "At least my element doesn't require me to grunt like a constipated bear every time I use it."

I lift a sphere of water from the nearby barrels with ease. The liquid hangs suspended in the air, glinting in the morning light like crystal.

Agnar narrows his eyes. "Like this, you mean?"

He stomps his foot hard enough that vibrations travel up my legs. "The grunting is part of the technique. Creates intimidation."

The ground rumbles and pitches to the left. I stumble and lose my concentration just enough that my water sphere splatters to the ground.

A laugh escapes me. "Is that what you tell yourself to feel better? No wonder Blair always said you had the subtlety of a landslide."

The mention of Blair dims Agnar's smile. Though months have passed since his death, the loss still hurts like hells.

Needing to lighten the mood before the heaviness takes over, I flick my fingers, splashing a gentle spray of water across his face.

"Hey!" He sputters and pushes his coppery hair out of his eyes. "That's fighting dirty."

"Never pretended to fight any other way." I roll my shoulders and gather more water. The element spirals around my forearms, hardening to ice where it touches my skin while remaining supple on the outside. Perfect for deflecting attacks.

Agnar nods, and his expression grows more serious. "You really think you can take Zeru's champion? These gods don't play fair."

"I don't need fair." I craft the water into a series of ice daggers. "I just need to win."

"Okay, but if I were you—"

I still as something shifts the air around us.

Something divine.

The water rings around Agnar's head shiver and disperse without my command. The earth beneath our feet stills, as if holding its breath.

The familiar prickling sensation of being watched by a being greater than myself crawls over my scalp. Though I've experienced the sensation before in Rivlan's presence, this feels heavier. More oppressive.

Agnar's lip quivers, his attention fixed on a point beyond my shoulder. "Sterling..."

I pivot slowly, already knowing what I'll find.

The air shimmers, and reality folds open in smoldering sparks of light as the God of the Heavens comes forth. The radiance from his crown of stars materializes first.

I wondered if this asshole planned on making an appearance.

Blazing with starlight, Zeru's form burns too brightly to stare at directly. Gazing at him is the equivalent of peering into the sun. Divine power radiates from him.

My stomach clenches, reacting to the energy.

"Awww, fuck." Agnar tosses his blade to the ground in a gesture that's half respectful, half resignation.

I remain standing, my water still circling my arms, though the element now trembles against my will. The god's presence interferes with magic. Particularly mine, it seems. No doubt a deliberate move.

Zeru's gaze—like the sun at its highest peak—settles on me.

It's not like the spring sun that dapples through the leaves, painting those below the canopy in warmth, or even the hot summer sun that roasts those clad in leather and metal armor.

No, this is the type of radiation that blisters human skin. Direct and unrelenting rays that wither feathers and evaporate every last bit of moisture from your throat.

Centuries of divine judgment bolster that power.

Fuck. Why is he here? This can't be good.

My chest tightens with apprehension, but I remain calm and resolute. No matter the purpose of Zeru's visit, no amount of intimidation will prevent me from standing as Rivlan's champion. I've already sealed my commitment to the God of Water.

I straighten my back, allowing the water around my arms to dissipate. No point in pretending I can command the element effectively in his presence.

But I'll be damned if I bow to him.

Zeru glides forward, his celestial form rippling. The air around him glimmers, distorting the ground's boundaries as if the world itself bends to accommodate his presence. That veil fades just enough for me to discern his features. Golden hair, brilliant smile, and gold eyes, all reflecting the light that emanates from his skin.

His expression is carefully composed into something resembling fatherly concern, his brow furrowed. The effect is akin to tying a bow around a wolf's neck. No attempts at masking can hide the animal's underlying predatory nature.

"Prince Knox." My formal name chimes in his otherworldly voice. "I understand your reservations. Truly, I do. You and your queen are in a difficult position."

My skin hums with irritation, but I say nothing. Zeru isn't here for an explanation. Gods don't visit mortals to understand. In their arrogance, they believe they already know everything about us.

Agnar inches closer to me, his shoulders tense.

"Tirene has suffered greatly in recent years. War. Betrayal. The transition of power twice in so few years." Zeru's fingers trail starlight as he gestures. "And now you align yourself with Rivlan's interests." His tone shifts to admonishing. "You're being foolish by tying yourself to his side of this conflict."

I work to keep my face neutral, careful not to show my disdain.

The god's responding smile doesn't reach his eyes. "Something you should know. Rivlan usually chooses the underdog. The ones with little chance of surviving."

So I'm the fucking underdog? Does that mean he's already chosen a champion, or is he blowing smoke out of his ass to scare me? "Was there a reason for your visit, or did you come here just to hear yourself talk?"

"Careful. You would do well to remember who you speak to. But I'll let that little comment slide just this once." Zeru's eyes adopt a menacing gleam as he motions to the field, where puddles from our training still remain. "I've been watching you. Your power has grown. Your command of magic is impressive."

His compliment attempts to flatter me and gain my compliance, but the divine attention leaves me cold.

Zeru tilts his head to one side as if deliberating something. Then he offers a condescending smirk. "I can make things right. Secure your future and Tirene's. You only need to switch sides. Fight as my champion instead."

Ah.

The true purpose of his visit.

Question is, why in the three hells do two different gods want me as their champion?

I dip into a shallow bow, skirting the line between respectful and mocking. "I'm sorry, but I've already given my word to Rivlan."

"Words can be easily broken in light of my offer." Zeru waves a glowing hand as if my vow is of no importance. "You'd gain substantial benefits by aligning with me. I always show gratitude to those who help me."

Contempt prickles my spine, but I bite my tongue. As

much as I dislike this arrogant dickhead, I know better than to piss him off.

"My gratitude," Zeru struts closer, the light from his crown and skin blinding me, "could mean prosperity for Tirene. Protection from drought. Favorable winds for your ships." His voice drops lower. "Even assistance with those rebellious Northern Provinces that still resist Queen Lark's rule."

The offer is tempting. Or would be if I didn't see straight through his manipulation.

I'm familiar enough with the gods to know their gifts always come with hidden costs. Not to mention betraying Rivlan would mean putting my magic at risk. Rivlan is water. Angering the god of my element wouldn't be wise.

When I still don't respond, Zeru's expression sours.

The false warmth vanishes, replaced by a cold calculation that suits him better. "You should consider carefully before declining my generosity. Everyone who has opposed me, gods included, has ended up regretting it. My displeasure is a heavy burden to bear."

An odd satisfaction zings through me at the threat. At least we're finally speaking plainly. "As generous as your offer is, I made my choice when Rivlan approached us. To change it now would be dishonorable. I must stand by my decision."

"As do I." Agnar speaks from by my side, his voice unwavering despite the sweat beading on his brow.

Zeru's face contorts with fury, all pretense abandoned. His gaze scorches me, and I feel like my skin should be crisping and flaking off. When he raises his hand, the air crackles with power.

I tense, preparing for an attack, but instead, he directs his rage at the ground. A section of the field, at least twenty paces across, simply vanishes. Not destroyed, not blown apart.

Erased.

A perfect hemisphere carved from the earth, creating a gaping crater with no sign of the rock, plants, or soil that were once there.

Well. That's alarming.

Agnar, thankfully, holds still. Not even a twitch. Frozen is better than reactive at this point.

"The fight will be fierce." Zeru's tone slides into icy calm, as if he's barely containing his rage. "I suggest you prepare yourself better than this display I saw today." His knowing gaze lingers on me.

Then his form shimmers and collapses in on itself, leaving nothing but the faint scent of ozone behind.

Agnar whistles. "That went well. Can't wait to see who he chooses as your opponent."

He reaches out with his earth magic, drawing rock and soil from the surrounding land to begin filling the hole Zeru created.

As I watch the dirt flow into place, unease churns in my gut. "He'll probably choose the Guardian simply out of spite."

Chapter Thirty-Eight
Lark

Agnar's voice burns like acid as he relays what happened with Sterling during training. His vivid blue eyes, often crinkled at the corners with easy humor, appear flat and hard as he recounts Zeru's visit. Each word carves new lines of fury into my heart.

The god's threats linger in the air of my sitting room like acrid smoke that taints everything and seeps into the fabric of the cushions and weave of the rugs. I dig my fingernails into my palms, the sharp pain a welcome distraction from the storm building inside me.

"And he destroyed the middle of that training field." Agnar shifts his weight, his posture stiff. "Then, poof! He disappeared. Like the laws of space meant nothing."

"Because they don't. Not to them." I think back to all the times gods popped in and out of my life at will. "Neither do basic manners."

Agnar's coppery hair falls across his forehead when he nods. "He claims the gods are displeased with how things are progressing." He clears his throat, clearly uncomfortable. "He said if you continue, there would be consequences. Not just for you and Sterling, but for all of Tirene."

The fire magic inside me swells in response to my anger, boiling my blood until I'm certain steam must be rising from my skin. "Prick gods. Playing with our lives like we're game pieces on a board isn't enough for them. They've gotta be creepy and pushy about it too."

Agnar waits without flinching while I rant. He's experienced this version of me before, the one with barely contained fury and magic thrumming at my fingertips.

"I need to find Rafe and Helene." I gnaw on my lower lip. "See what they've discovered about those scientist-priests."

Agnar nods, relief loosening his shoulders. "Last I heard, they were meeting with Leesa and Bastian. Not sure where."

"I'll find them." I head toward the door before pausing. "Thank you, Agnar. For telling me everything. For not... softening the news."

A ghost of his usual grin flickers across his face. "Wouldn't dream of it, Lark. You'd see right through me anyway. Besides, watching you lose your shit is oddly satisfying."

I snort. "So glad I could entertain you."

On that note, I leave him and stride through the corridors with purpose. Servants and couriers flatten themselves against walls as I pass, no doubt noting the angry flames flickering along my skin. My magic has started reacting to my thoughts and emotions.

Cursed gods. Damn all of them with their riddles and threats and manipulations. Haven't humans suffered enough at their hands? Haven't we sacrificed enough already? Haven't I given enough? My birth parents, my childhood, my adoptive mother and biological grandfather. Olive, Nick, Blair, as well as other friends, and very nearly Sterling...

The memory of Sterling, his mind controlled by Narc's

magic, triggers another irate wave of blistering heat. I spent my entire life as a pawn, shuffled between kingdoms, lied to about my true heritage, nearly murdered more than once. And now that I finally have some measure of control, enough power to steer my own fate, the gods want to threaten me into submission?

Not fucking likely.

I check the usual meeting rooms first—the council chamber, the war room, the archives—but find no sign of Rafe or Helene, let alone my sister or Bastian. With each empty space, frustration mounts. Where in the blazes are they?

It's pure chance that I glimpse light spilling from beneath the door of a rarely used chamber in the eastern wing. Slowing my steps, I listen as I approach. Raised voices filter through the heavy oak. Rafe's distinctive bark, followed by Helene's caustic tones. My sister's higher pitch slices through them both.

I shove the door open without knocking, using more force than necessary and sending it crashing against the wall.

Four heads swivel toward me, the expressions ranging from surprise to guilt. The group is gathered around a table littered with maps, ancient-looking scrolls, and architectural drawings. Rafe leans over the table with his hands braced on the wood. Helene faces him with her arms crossed and her mouth twisted in disdain. Leesa and Bastian stand by Helene, my sister's hand clutching Bastian's forearm as if restraining him.

Silence falls over the room like a blanket. I arch an eyebrow. "Well, isn't this cozy?"

Rafe straightens, brushing nonexistent lint from his sleeve. "Your Majesty, ahh, Lark. I apologize. We were just—"

"Arguing? I gathered that." I enter the room and let the door swing shut behind me. "I could hear you from down the corridor."

Helene sniffs, her dark eyes cold. "More like discussing our differing professional opinions." When my eyebrows lift even higher, she tacks on, "in loud voices," with a grumpy huff.

"I see." I stride over and scan the documents spread across the table. Most appear to be maps of the city's temple district. "Where are you at in your investigation of the missing scientist-priests?"

The four of them exchange glances, a silent communication passing between them that snaps my teeth together. I'm so tired of secrets. Tired of half-truths and careful omissions.

"We've made progress." Rafe kneads the back of his neck. "We think we found where their own investigations might have taken place."

My eyes narrow. "And you're just now telling me?"

Bastian shifts toward me, his hazel eyes earnest. "We only confirmed it this morning, Lark. We were debating the best approach to the location before bringing the information to you."

I cross my arms. "What's the location?"

Rafe taps a spot on one of the maps. "A crypt. Under Cyphero's temple."

The chill running through me momentarily cools my anger. Cyphero, God of Hidden Knowledge. Notoriously enigmatic about his allegiances. "You think the scientist-priests were working in a crypt? Under a god's temple?"

"We know they were. We have testimony from three separate sources, plus these." Helene pushes forward a stack of parchments covered in cramped writing. "Records of supplies being delivered there over the past season. Equipment consistent with magical experimentation."

I scan the list. Crystal rods, silver wire, specialized herbs, inks crafted from rare minerals. "What were they trying to do?"

Leesa clears her throat, drawing my attention. Her wavy hair is pulled back in a simple knot, her brown eyes troubled. "That's what we were discussing when you arrived. We can't be certain what they were researching, but," she glances at Bastian, who nods encouragingly, "we believe it has something to do with the boundary between the mortal realm and the gods' realm."

"We don't know if Cyphero sanctioned this research or not." Bastian rubs his eyes. "We can't figure out if he's a good god or a bad god in all this."

A harsh laugh scrapes my throat. Just hearing the words "a good god or a bad god" spoken aloud pitches my stomach. "Maybe they're all bad. I mean, if we follow the gods, but the gods themselves don't follow their own teachings, are any of them truly 'good'?"

The room falls silent.

Even Rafe, never one to mince words, remains quiet and shifts his weight from one foot to the other.

"They're all-powerful." Bastian breaks the quiet, his voice gentle but firm. "And complicated. And we can't risk showing favoritism to one and pissing off the others."

I rest my palms on the table, staring at each of them in turn. "We can't risk not going either."

More glances are traded, along with more silent communication.

"Now?" Rafe's eyebrows disappear into his hairline.

"Yes, now." I straighten to my full height. Zeru's surprise appearance worries me. We may not have as much time as we thought, so everything needs to happen faster. "Unless you have a more pressing engagement, Rafe?"

He has the grace to look abashed. "No, of course not. But perhaps we should call for Knox first. His magic might be useful if there are...traps."

"He's sleeping." I slash my hand through the air, cutting

off that line of thinking. "He's been training with Rivlan for days, pushing his magic to new limits. He staggered to bed this morning, barely conscious."

An image of Sterling, his bronze skin ashen with exhaustion, his usually alert eyes dulled, flashes in my mind. He's been working so hard, trying to master new techniques under Rivlan's demanding tutelage. I refuse to wake him for this or anything else unless absolutely necessary.

Helene assesses me coolly. "All the more reason to wait. If the crown prince is depleted, and you rush into danger without him—"

"Surely the five of us can figure out what a mysterious religious cult is up to on our own?" The question rushes out of me, dripping with sarcasm.

Bastian and Leesa trade another look, this one laden with meaning I can't quite decipher.

My brother sighs, his posture slumping. "Fine. But Leesa stays."

I blink, my gaze shifting between them. "Why?"

Leesa steps forward, her hands clasped together in front of her. For the first time, I notice a subtle new roundness to her stomach, accentuated by the way she's cupping her belly.

A thrill runs up my arms, and I wait for the announcement with bated breath.

"I'm..." She pauses to inflate her lungs. "I'm pregnant."

The words transform the atmosphere. The tension in the room dissipates.

"Pregnant?" I need to check that I heard her correctly.

She nods, a small smile playing at her lips despite the seriousness of our discussion. "About three months along. We only just confirmed it last week."

Bastian moves closer to her, his hand coming to rest protectively at the small of her back.

A feeling so complex I can barely name its components cracks open inside me. Bright joy as clear as morning sunlight. Fragile but persistent hope.

And beneath it all, a current of dread.

A baby.

New life in the middle of all this chaos and danger. A child who will be my niece or nephew, who will bear the legacy of our complicated family, our magic, our royal blood.

A child whose safety might be threatened by this looming war with the gods.

I push away the fear and focus on the excitement. "I can't believe it! I'm going to be an aunt! You're going to be a mom!" Squealing, I embrace Leesa, holding her tight for several long moments before releasing her and repeating the gesture with Bastian. "Congratulations, I'm so happy for you both."

When I pull back, my eyes are damp, but my resolve has only strengthened. This only solidifies my determination to figure everything out. To understand what the gods want, the reasons behind the scientist-priests' actions, and the threat dangling over us all.

Leesa shakes her finger in my face. "Pregnancy doesn't automatically turn me into a porcelain princess."

I grab the appendage and yank it down. "But pregnancy does mean that you shouldn't take any unnecessary risks when there are others who can instead. If I had to stay home to deal with royalty crap, you can stay home to grow a baby. The rest of us can go as soon as possible. We don't have the luxury of time."

Rafe and Helene appear disgruntled but begin gathering the most important maps and documents. Bastian presses a soft kiss to Leesa's lips and murmurs something in her ear.

She nods while focusing on me, worry and pride mingling in her gaze. "Be careful. All of you."

With effort, I manage a smile. "Aren't I always?"

Her bark of laughter follows us as we head out to seek an ancient crypt located beneath the temple of a god who may or may not be our enemy, in search of secrets that could either save or damn us all.

Basically, just another day as Queen of Tirene.

Chapter Thirty-Nine
Lark

Fire crawls up my arm like a possessive lover, eager and hot against my skin. The narrow streets of Dern press in around us in a maze of worn stone and whispered fears. We all wear plain cloaks to blend in and keep the night's chill at bay. This city is almost as old as Tirene's capital yet, despite its proximity, not nearly as well-built or maintained.

We landed in the market, the only area large enough to accommodate the dragons. Unfortunately, the place we're heading to is nowhere close to the open, well-traveled routes of Tirene's third-largest city. The location is closer to the river, where the sewers drain and the leather is cured.

And where criminals lurk behind every shadow, if I'm to believe my brother. Erring on the side of caution, I cup a small flame in my palm as we weave through the twilight.

Bastian walks a half step ahead, his form tense beneath his cloak, while Helene's gait remains loose and her expression carefully blank. She wears the perfect diplomat's mask even in this decidedly undiplomatic excursion.

"Stay close." Bastian's directive barely carries over the

distant noises of night markets and taverns. "The temple district narrows ahead."

Agnar nods as he scans our surroundings, one hand resting on the hilt of his sword. Since Leesa stayed back, I picked him up on the way out of town. Rafe trails me, managing to scowl and look alert at the same time. The streets twist and fold in on themselves, designed to confuse visitors and protect the sanctity of Cyphero's domain. Only those who learn the secret ways can find his temples.

My fire flares without conscious thought. The flame doubles in size, morphing our shadows into grotesque elongated shapes against the weathered walls.

"Careful with that," Helene hisses. "Unless you're trying to announce our arrival to the entire district."

I close my fingers a bit, willing the flame to shrink. The magic resists for half a heartbeat before grudgingly complying. "Sorry."

My mind races. The fire shouldn't push against my will like a living creature with its own desires.

With a start, I remember what Sterling told me weeks ago.

That his water answers differently now. Quicker. As if the element anticipates what he needs before Sterling does.

At the time, I nodded without really comprehending. Now, with my own element practically purring beneath my skin, I finally understand. This is what happens when you're more in tune with your element. You develop not just more control, but a partnership with your magic.

"Here." Bastian stops before an unassuming stone building. No grand columns or ornate statues mark Cyphero's temple, just clean lines and perfect proportions. A temple devoted to precision and knowledge. "The entrance to the crypt should be inside, hidden beneath the main altar."

When Rafe tests the door, it swings open without

resistance. "Unlocked." His eyebrows draw together. "Probably not a good sign."

Great. Just what I hoped to hear.

As we slip inside, I encourage my flame to reach higher to illuminate the modest interior. Unlike the lush, fragrant temples of other gods, Cyphero's sanctuary is austere. Measurement tools hang on the walls instead of tapestries, and a simple stone table etched with mathematical formulas instead of prayers comprises the altar.

Bastian blinks a few times as if orienting himself. "The entrance should be—"

"Right there." Agnar stalks ahead, pushing the altar aside with a scrape of stone to reveal a narrow staircase descending into darkness.

The stairs are worn smooth from centuries of footsteps, moss growing in the cracks between stones. I take the lead, my flame casting an unsteady light as we proceed. With each step, the air grows cooler and damper, carrying the scent of old paper along with a sharper odor. Chemicals, perhaps.

"So, this sect of the scientist-priests." Bastian's voice echoes in the narrow passage. "They've been the kingdom's thinkers for generations. Measuring stars, charting weather patterns, creating medicines. But in recent months, they've become afraid. Some have gone into hiding. Others simply disappeared."

"Why?" I take cautious steps on the slippery surface. "What frightened them?"

Bastian shrugs. "That's what we're here to find out."

"Let's hope information is all we encounter," Rafe's ominous statement prickles my skin.

The stairway finally opens into a large circular chamber. Half laboratory, half shrine in appearance. My magic illuminates worktables covered with delicate instruments, shelves of books and scrolls, and in the center, a smaller altar to Cyphero.

But the room is in chaos, the air coated with a faint copper odor.

Papers scattered across the floor crunch beneath our boots. Chairs lie overturned, shelves hang broken from walls, and dark stains mark the stone floor in irregular patterns.

"Blood." Agnar kneels to examine one of the stains. "It's not fresh."

Well, I guess that explains the copper.

No ever-lights illuminate the space, so I swallow hard and use my fire to light wall sconces and candles. The flames leap to their new homes, almost too eagerly, and bathe the crypt in dancing light that does nothing to dispel the heaviness in the air.

Anger and worry trickle down my spine. What the hells happened here? Who would disrupt Cyphero's temple like this? "Spread out. Search for anything that might tell us what they discovered. And why it potentially got them killed."

We disperse through the room, our shadows flickering across the walls as we cautiously navigate the debris.

Helene crouches to pick up a shattered crystal lens. "Someone didn't want their research found."

Rafe heads to a workbench where intricate measuring devices remain mostly untouched. His fingers brush over a brass instrument with delicate gears. "So methodical. They documented everything."

I find myself drawn to a shelf of bound journals, their leather covers worn from frequent handling. Opening one at random, I find page after page of meticulous notes written in a cramped, precise hand. "I've got something."

The others step over broken furniture and equipment to gather around.

The journal contains systematic observations of prayer

responses throughout the kingdom. Pages full of data, tables, measurements, and conclusions that clench my stomach.

I start reading aloud. "Prayers are being answered more frequently. Worshippers leave temples feeling drained yet compelled to return. The prayer-response cycles are intensifying."

Bastian flips open another journal. "They were tracking patterns across different gods. Look. Some prayers seem to build fear and desperation while others focus on hope and faith. But in either case..."

"Mortals have ramped up their devotion," Rafe finishes, skimming over Bastian's shoulder. "More prayers, more offerings, more connections to the gods."

Helene scrunches her nose in disgust. "More power flowing to those ancient fucks."

I can't help but agree, which is a horrible thought. As I flip through more pages, my unease grows. The later entries become more frantic, the handwriting less precise. Charts show spikes in divine activity that correlate with increased prayer gatherings.

Two pages stick together. Once I manage to separate them, I turn to the next one and freeze. Reddish brown stains—probably the cause of the stickiness—discolor the paper.

Blood.

Ignoring the dread squirming in my gut, I read the final entries. They're rushed. Desperate.

"Look at these." Helene points to a series of sketches pinned to a wall on the other side of the room.

I move closer, and my blood chills. The drawings show crystalline formations. Beautiful, intricate, and vaguely grotesque. I know these formations too well.

"According to the notes here, these are growing in temples everywhere." Helene stalks closer to the wall, and I cast extra light to help her read. "The scientist-priests were studying them."

Bastian leans in, his mouth set in a grim line. "Like the ones from the fountain. And at the Divine Commons."

Agnar catches my eye. "And the portal."

"Exactly." My fingers start to tingle, and I realize my fire is responding to my fear by heating the air around us.

"The scientist-priests learned the formations seem to appear during intense prayer gatherings." Rafe flips through more journal pages. "They tracked the patterns. More prayers equals more crystals. That could either mean more people praying, prayers being more intense, or prayers happening more often. They charted it out."

I gravitate to a table where diagrams display what look to be energy measurements. Lines surge and fall but trend steadily upward. "What were they measuring?"

"They believe the crystals were connected to divine power somehow." Helene shuffles through papers. She pauses, squinting at a page heavily stained with blood. "Their last entry is partially obscured. 'The gods aren't helping us.' I can't make out the rest. 'Heeding'? 'Seeing'?"

We all crowd around, but blood has damaged too much of the text. So much blood that the page is glued to the back cover, rendering the final words of the scientist-priests a mystery.

Bastian frowns at a small box containing crystal cuttings before lifting one carefully. The object glints in the light like frost on a window. "These remind me of ice chips that never melt. But what exactly is being frozen?"

Agnar shrugs. "Things could be trapped inside it. The same way salt will grow around other minerals, which changes the color and flavor."

Discontent mounts as we ponder the possible implications. Gods gaining power from mortal prayers, crystalline formations appearing at sites of worship, scientist-priests murdered for their discoveries...

Still, the true meaning remains just out of reach, like a word on the tip of the tongue. "We need to get these journals back to the palace. Maybe Knox can—"

"No." Agnar slams the box of crystals closed. "He's got the Champions Match to prepare for. His focus needs to remain there."

"But this could be connected to everything else." I gesture toward the mess. "The religious cult, the attacks, all of it. The Devoted wanted this hidden. To keep from us whatever the scientist-priests discovered."

At the mention of the Devoted, we all instinctively study the signs of violence around us.

Helene gestures to the bloodstains. "You think the Devoted did this?"

"The missing scientist-priests, the destroyed research..." I nibble on my lip. "Who else would want to silence people questioning the nature of divine power?"

"Definitely the Devoted." Rafe nods, his voice hard. "Without a doubt."

"Let's pack everything up. Maybe once we get the papers cleaned, we can figure out what got them killed." I search for bags, baskets, and anything else we can use. "And maybe find others of their order to give this stuff to."

We gather what journals and papers we can, stuffing them into bags and cloak pockets. The crypt feels colder, or maybe that's just the chill of revelation settling into my bones.

As we climb back up the stairs, the weight of knowledge presses down on us, and each step becomes more laborious than the last. So much carnage left behind, and no one to blame for it.

No one to make pay.

Outside, the frigid night air slaps me in the face, and I

huddle into my cloak. I would expand my wings to raise my body temperature and help chase away the cold, but our group forms a tight cluster. I don't want to risk smacking someone in the face, especially not while carrying important items. The darkness enveloping the empty street feels watchful, aware. And not in a divine way either. In a very mortal, very dangerous way.

"We need to move against the Devoted now." Rafe grinds his teeth, constantly glancing over his shoulder. "Before they silence anyone else."

"With what evidence?" A shivering Helene hunches into her cloak. "Bloodied journals and crystal formations that have existed in temples for centuries?"

"You saw the remnants of what happened in there." Agnar gestures back toward the temple. "People were killed for what they knew."

"Or what they thought they knew." Helene hesitates, waiting for Bastian to tell us which way to go. "These are theories, not facts. The scientist-priests could be wrong."

Bastian points down an alley. "Multiple temples, multiple gods, and the same patterns. That's not coincidence."

I shake my head, still trying to piece the puzzle together. The scientist-priests came from every temple. Why kill them when at least some must have served Zeru or his allies? "We need to be careful about—"

"Careful?" Rafe scoffs. "While more people disappear? While the Devoted grow stronger?"

Okie dokie then. Good to know Rafe's gotten over his reluctance to speak freely around me. Oh wait, my bad. That was never an issue.

"And what about Knox?" Agnar tightens his grip on the three worn leather satchels he carries. "Does he need this distraction? Or do we wait until after the Champions Match?"

"If the gods are using us," Bastian directs us to the right, "using our prayers to fuel something—"

"We don't know that!" Helene pivots on him, her heavy cloak flapping. "The crystals could be a natural phenomenon of divine presence. They've been documented for centuries."

"Not like this." While not as well-read on the topic as my brother, I have seen references to them before. Specifically in times of great troubles. "They're not just growing. They're spreading to more areas outside of the temples."

"So, what's your plan, Your Majesty?" Helene's eyes challenge me as she over-emphasizes my title. "What brilliant solution does our queen propose?"

The entire group regards me with an expectant air. Even with their faces shadowed in the dim light I can recognize their fear. Reading about these problems in reports is one thing, but it's something else entirely to creep through cramped alleys while carrying bags full of journals soaked in the blood of the scientist-priests we all hoped would provide us with answers.

The fire in my palm flickers faster to match my accelerating heartbeat. "We don't act rashly. Let's return to the palace and study what we've found. We don't tell Knox yet because he needs to focus. After the match, we bring our findings to the council."

No one seems entirely satisfied, but they also don't argue.

We weave our way to where we left our dragons, the tension between us thick as a blade. The flight back is silent, each of us lost in our own thoughts as we soar above the city. The palace glows against winter's early sunrise, its spires reaching up like fingers trying to touch the stars.

When we land in the central courtyard, the dragons settle with soft huffs and rustling wings.

I thank Nailah, stroking her scaly nose before she lumbers away to join the others in the paddock. The weight of the journals in my bag feels heavier than it should.

Before I can even take three steps toward the palace, the air before me glistens and warps.

I stop short, my heart leaping into my throat. Dropping the bag, I reach under my cloak, ready to draw my short sword. Behind me, the others chatter, but their words sound like gibberish.

The space in front of me splits open like a wound in reality.

This is how Agnar described Zeru's visitation.

My hand clenches with the urge to grab my sword hilt even though I know that action would prove useless at best against a god and insulting at worst.

Or viewed as a challenge.

To avoid temptation, I curl my fingers into a fist. Light pours through the slit in the air. But it's not the radiant white glow Agnar recounted. This blaze is red, orange, and yellow.

Ziva steps through the crack.

My lungs flatten as I gaze at the goddess. She's fire in human form, her body a constantly shifting flame contained in the rough shape of a woman. Charcoal black eyes settle on me.

"Hello, mortal queen." Her voice crackles. "We need to talk."

Power shivers over my skin while I stand frozen, the Goddess of Fire burning before me like a living torch.

As I gape at her radiant image, all I can think is that our troubles have only just begun.

CHAPTER FORTY
LARK

My goddess. Ziva. The deity whose fire magic runs through my veins.

I stagger back, fingers curling into my palms and cupping the flames that try to jump out beyond my control. Behind me, the dragons bugle. Not just one or two. All of them. Together. In harmony.

No, not just bugling. I hear crooning mixed in too.

They're singing. Worshipping the goddess who views them as her favored beasts. I guess the adoration goes both ways.

My knees wobble, my body yearning to bend, to bow. How many nights did I pray to Ziva as a child, begging for help with my magic? For the ability to control it. For the skill to tap into the power that my mother feared and tried to extinguish with alchemy.

Back then, I was a child. Now, I'm a queen. And I cannot behave as though the monarchy is choosing sides.

Especially not with everyone in the courtyard watching. Figures appear in the windows, too, their attention drawn by the dragons' song. But no one can ignore Ziva's fiery glow as she stands at the edge of the courtyard.

"My goddess." I incline my head, the best compromise I can muster up on the spot.

Ziva sweeps toward me, her feet hovering just above the ground. With every step, her flames bank lower, revealing the coppery skin underneath. "Lark. You've faced so many challenges lately." Her brilliant glow casts my skin in shades of amber and gold. "All the madness you've battled, all the confusion and conflict, the tensions between your mortal kingdoms. I've seen it all."

Seen it all, yet never once reached out to help. Not even during my childhood.

Anger flares through me, but my flames remain stable. I keep them contained, controlled by the willpower I worked so hard to cultivate. Fire is just as much the element of life as destruction. Flames can provide necessary warmth or destroy.

The heat blazing from Ziva's fire is just short of charring. Enough that every nerve in my body screams, "Stay back! Danger!"

The goddess stretches, her feet unmoving while her body somehow curves around me. If she wanted to prove how inhuman she was, she couldn't have picked a better way. Her presence toasts my skin, my bones, even my blood. I feel suddenly exposed, as though she can see through flesh to the truth beneath.

"I've always been proud to call you one of mine. Your fire burns true, even in darkness."

The warmth of her presence and praise undulates through me, around me, inside me. Swells in my chest and fills me with pride, belonging, and purpose. All things I craved as a child, things I didn't realize I still hungered for.

A chill skates over my skin when Ziva returns to her spot near the rift in the sky. She presents me with her back as she cranes her neck to stare up at the palace. Flame red hair floats behind her, lifted by the updraft created from her own heat. "You know the gods are at war."

A hesitation flickers beneath her words. An unnamed shadow. Pride mingled with...what? Regret? Fear?

Whatever it is, my skin tingles with alarm. "I do," I respond warily.

"That's why I need you, Lark."

Oh gods.

I stamp out the prayer before it can continue. "For what?"

The graphs and the blood-spattered drawings of those crystals flit through my mind like a hazy warning. I hope with everything inside me that my instincts are wrong and she's not about to ask what I think she is.

She shifts to the side, waving her hand and highlighting the air with her glowing hair. "Be our champion."

So much for hope.

The words hang between us, terrible in their simplicity. We gaze at each other while a hysterical laugh races up my throat, along with the burn of stomach acid.

No. Absolutely not.

I bury my fingers in my hair and yank. This cannot be happening. Surely, even the gods would never be so cruel, would they?

But with dread settling into my bones and ice filling my veins, I fear I already know the answer.

My mind rebels. Fragments. All I can do is stare, slack-jawed.

"This is nothing new for you. You protect things." Ziva reaches for me but stops short of touching, her blood-red nails creating sparks. "You protect your people, your kingdom, the dragons. All excellent things you should be proud of. Now I'm offering you a chance to protect the entire world."

In a daze, I find myself seeking the face and body beneath

the aura of heat. Her features are sharp, almost catlike. Narrow, upturned nose, thin upper lip, slightly pointed ears, sharp cheekbones, pointy chin.

Maybe this is all a nightmare. Maybe I'll wake up and realize I never met the Goddess of Fire. Everything will be okay because no one asked me to face off with the love of my life in a battle to the death.

Except, by now I know better.

I close my eyes, inhaling through my nose to stop myself from hyperventilating. I open them again with frantic denial still racing through my mind. "Knox." His name is a talisman I cling to against the horror unfolding before me. "Are you aware that Knox, my betrothed, is the other champion?"

"I am aware of who serves my soft-hearted, wayward brother." Her black eyes peer over the rift before her body finishes traversing it. Flames waltz above her head.

Her fluid movements mesmerize me, threatening to disrupt my train of thought. "One of the champions will die. Will be killed by the other."

"Death is merely another state of existing. This battle is about the very nature of existence. The fight will determine whether, and how, mortals serve gods." Her voice rises, crackling like embers. "This is about maintaining, or restoring, the order that worked well for the protection of mortals for so long. Recent events have bumped the relationship between humans and gods out of balance. You can restore that balance."

Whether we serve the gods? What does that mean? Does a possible future exist where we don't have to? If so, who's fighting for that?

All questions I dare not ask. Especially not with that gaping rift behind her. The stars are always watching, and right now, the realm of the gods has an open view to this discussion.

The goddess leans closer, her warmth a caress that both lures me in and urges me to bolt. "If you agree to be our champion, to fight for Zeru's faction in order to protect the way of life you've always known, you would be richly rewarded."

Dread sucker punches me in the gut.

"No." I somehow grate out the refusal through my dry mouth and throat.

Ziva's expression changes into something less benevolent. Less human. "That's very bad news. For all those living, including the dragon hatchlings you love so dearly. I don't see how they can survive what's coming unless you help me."

I stumble backward as if kicked by an alicorn. My heart pounds so hard I can feel my pulse throbbing in my fingertips. My temples. The Goddess of Fire just threatened the newborns. While the dragons continue to sing for her.

Ziva advances on me, invading my personal space.

Her heat no longer feels comforting. It scorches, sucking up the moisture from my eyes and cracking my lips. "And your own thread in life's tapestry may become unexpectedly short. Along with everyone who lives in this delicate stone palace." Her black eyes flicker over my shoulder in the direction of the fire paddock where my group probably still waits.

"Why are you doing this?" My heart wrenches in agony. I've always admired Ziva. I've prayed to her, told myself she was the flame and life of the world. My learning how to control my magic was a tribute to her. And now...

If I don't agree to fight for her, to face Sterling in a death match, she'll end the lives of everyone else I love?

My desperate mind grasps at straws. There must be an alternative. Another way. I could talk Sterling down. I could take his place and agree to throw the fight.

Something. Anything.

But Ziva is already taking her leave, her amber light sliding into the opening in the air.

She disappears until all that remains are spots in my vision, the acrid smell of smoke…and the pain of my heart shattering into a million pieces.

∾

Lark

I drop onto the stony rim of the courtyard fountain, my legs suddenly unable to hold my weight. She threatened the dragons. She threatened me. And everyone else too.

Why?

"Be our champion."

The words stab at me, sharp as knives in my skull. Harsher than Ziva's flames against my skin.

The cold stone seeps through my clothes, but I barely notice. My thoughts spiral in tight, panicked circles. Is this some sort of twisted divine punishment? Did I do something to bring this on myself? Did the others who live within this "delicate stone palace"?

Only a goddess would consider a marble palace delicate.

Staring at the gleaming arches, my mind paints terrible pictures. I know what my fires can do to this place. But Ziva's?

The marble would melt. The wood would incinerate. The air would fill with noxious gases. Anyone who managed to survive those horrors would need to stumble over molten floors to escape. Feathers would wither to ash.

Little Rose's sweet smiling face flashes behind my eyes.

I suck in several deep breaths before pushing to my feet. There must be a way out of this. A solution that hasn't yet occurred to me because I'm too worked up. Maybe someone else could—

The courtyard is empty.

I've no idea when the others left or what they heard. Even the dragons have disappeared from the paddock. I'm alone in the darkness.

I have no time for self-pity or recriminations. Not while the gods are moving their pieces across the board, pitting Sterling and me against each other to save the world. I need to get to him and tell him what's happening.

There's only one thing I know with bone-deep certainty. I will never hold him back or plot against him.

But the whole world might pay the price.

With stumbling steps, I finally reach our chambers. Sterling waits in our sitting room, eating an apple and flipping through a book.

When he notices me, his mouth curves into a wide smile. "There you are. I heard you were out of the palace, but..." He trails off, his face falling when he gets a good look at me. "What happened?"

I open my mouth, but nothing comes out. All the things I wanted to share about the crypt and strange artifacts we found there fade in the wake of Ziva's visit.

"What is it?" He straightens and pulls me into his lap. "Are you hurt?"

My throat closes up, trapping my reply behind a wall of grief and fear.

"Lark." Sterling brushes my hair back to peer up at my face. "Talk to me."

I crumble, cradling his arm to my chest like a lifeline. His other is tangled in my dry, windblown hair. "Ziva just came to me in the courtyard."

He stills, his eyes adopting a steely glint. "What did she want?" His hand stops for a moment before continuing to stroke my hair.

"She..." I clear my throat, my mouth dry as sand. "She's

aligned herself with Zeru. She's asked me to be their champion."

The silence between us is so complete I can hear the rush of blood in my ears. Sterling's hand falls away from my hair. His face, his expressive, beautiful face, drains of color. Anger, shock, and resentment twist his lips. Pain, confusion, and doubt pinch his eyes.

"The champion that you will fight against. To the death. Not the Guardian. They want me now." The words spill out in a desperate rush.

The shock, which has carried me this far, starts to dissipate. I begin to tremble as I desperately try to hold him closer.

This can't be real. I can't believe I have to say this. I never even saw it coming.

He cradles my face, beseeching me with his eyes. Begging me to tell him that I'm lying, teasing him. Anything other than speaking the truth.

I wish I could.

But I'm not even capable of making up a lie as cruel as the gods' proposal.

"Fuck." He leans his forehead against mine, sucking in a sharp breath. "What happens if you refuse?"

I shake my head, a boulder-sized lump forming in my throat. "Everything will be lost. The gods will lash out to punish me. You, me, the dragons. Ziva said the palace is delicate. It was a threat. She'll kill everyone here. Agnar, Rose, Bastian, Leesa, her baby." My breath catches on that last part. Bile scalds my throat.

He goes completely still. "Baby?"

In the rush of today's events, I forgot he didn't know about my sister's news. "She's pregnant. She and Bastian are going to have a child. And Ziva is going to kill everyone I care about unless I agree to be their champion."

The utter despair in his eyes mirrors my own. We're trapped, cornered like animals with no escape.

The sudden urge to move sends me bolting from his lap. I pace, dragging my hands over my cheeks to dry the tears. "I don't even know why they want me. You're stronger. Faster. You've been training and fighting and wielding magic for years."

My pacing leads me to the end of the room, right next to the fireplace. With disgust, I snuff out the flames keeping the space warm. Then I spin around.

Something changes in Sterling's face. His grief vanishes in an instant. He rises so quickly, the chair tips over. The hollow expression disappears from his eyes, leaving them focused. Determined. Angry.

No, not angry. Enraged.

In mere seconds, I stand before him. His arms encircle me, and I lift my lips to meet his. Our kiss is fierce at first, a desperate crashing of mouths. A claiming.

His lips become slick with moisture.

I jerk back to stare at him.

Water beads on his face. Not sweat.

Armor. He's subconsciously putting on his armor, the same way I wrap myself in fire.

Lifting my gaze from his mouth to his eyes, I see why. Not because he's scared. No. Murderous determination glints in his eyes. He's thought of something.

"Sterling?" I grab for him, but he's already pivoting on his heel and marching toward the bedchamber. "Where are you going? What are you going to do?"

He doesn't acknowledge or even seem to hear me.

Frantic to know his thoughts, I follow.

But his longer stride carries him faster, and he reaches the door to the patio just as I make it to the bedchamber. His wings unfurl, and he launches skyward, vanishing into the darkness.

CHAPTER FORTY-ONE
STERLING

I toe the edge of the Storm Cliffs on the westernmost side of Tirene, where the ground ends in a ragged drop straight down to monstrous rocks. Below me, nothing exists beyond sky and the ocean's relentless assault on the land. The sea, a dark roiling mass observed by the distant light of the stars, rages, its power calling to me. Salt spray bites at my face.

As the water churns, the waves begin rising higher and higher, crashing against the cliff face with unnatural force.

Reaching for me. Responding to the frenzied anguish boiling inside me like a toxic stew.

I've gained all this power, and for what? So I can enter a death match with the woman who owns my soul?

I tip my head back to the heavens. "Fuck every last one of you!"

When yelling doesn't help, I drop down, grab a rock, and chuck it into the water with all my might.

I hate letting those assholes box us into a corner, hate the pain their bullshit has already caused Lark. In-ex-fucking-scusable. We need to find a way out of this mess, some sort of cosmic loophole, but what?

If Lark and I accept the gods' request and fight each other, we save humanity, but one of us dies at the other's hand.

If we don't fight and spare ourselves that horrific pain, we damn humanity to the gods' sadistic wrath.

Either way, we're royally fucked.

Despair mixes with fury, carving a hole in my chest. As my heart hammers and my breathing grows ragged, my fingertips fill with an icy chill and the waves continue to swell.

Balling my fists up, I once again scream my denial into the night. "I refuse to fight. I. Won't. Do it!"

"Such insolence from my champion. I expected gratitude for the power I've granted you."

Jerking in surprise, I pivot to find the air behind me shimmering. The salt spray takes form, condensing into a humanlike figure. Almost. Rivlan, God of Water, possesses no heart, no compassion, no honor. He claims none of the qualities mortals respect in others.

Except power.

My top lip curls into a sneer. "Gratitude? For making me your pawn in some empyreal chess match? For telling me I either kill the woman I love or condemn everyone else I love to death? Yeah, I'm overflowing with gratitude."

The sea erupts, a massive wave crashing against the cliff and sending spray thirty feet into the air. Rivlan's form glimmers with renewed intensity. "Watch how you speak to me. You may be drunk on your newfound power, but I assure you, yours does not compare to mine."

The raging beast inside me snarls in reply, egging me to accept the challenge. "I don't give a flying fuck who has more power. I'm not fighting the woman I love to the death. Find another champion or solution."

Ice crystals materialize in the air around us as the temperature plummets in response to my mood.

"You think either of us has a choice? You accepted the

mantle. You cannot refuse the fight. We are both in the same boat." Rivlan's resounding shout crashes like a river pounding rocks. "Don't for a second believe throwing this match will save you either. Once a champion accepts the challenge, they either win or die. The moment you surrender, you. Will. Die."

The waves grow monstrously huge, battering the cliff incessantly.

The impacts shake the earth beneath my feet, but I stand my ground. "I didn't agree to kill Lark. I agreed to be your champion. Big difference."

"There is no difference!" The god jets forward, his form expanding to loom over me like a tsunami. "The challenge has been issued. Champion against champion. To refuse is to forfeit, and forfeiting means you and everyone you love will pay the price."

A humorless laugh scrapes my throat. "So you threaten me? That's how gods maintain loyalty these days?" Another wave approaches, but I'm not in the godsdamned mood and shove the water back. Foam splatters the ground around my boots.

"Not a threat. A reality. Let me make something crystal clear." Rivlan's form morphs and shrinks, his skin rippling like a stream. "If you go back on our agreement, Tirene ceases to exist."

My heart assaults my ribs. "You can't do that."

"Can't I?" Rivlan circles me like a predator, and as with any predator, I keep a wary eye on his movements. "You know what your kingdom is built on?"

"Lies?" I spit out the word through gritted teeth.

"Funny." The god's hollow laugh rumbles like water in a cave. "An island surrounded by water."

My hands twitch impatiently. "Thank you for that informative geography lesson."

Rivan shoots me a warning glare. "I own water. I *am* water."

Cold terror stabs me. Not for myself, but for Lark. For Agnar. For Rose. For Leesa and Bastian and all the other innocents in my kingdom.

The soldier in me demands I destroy this threat, but the military also taught me when to retreat and strategize. Impulsively launching into an unwinnable battle does no one any good.

Wrestling my emotions under control, I straighten my posture and meet the god's eyes. "What are you saying?"

"If you do not fight as my champion, I will submerge your island nation into the sea so deep it won't even be recalled in the annals. It will be as if Tirene never existed."

This motherfucker. Only years of practice allow me to cling to the last shreds of my control. "Why would you do that?"

"Do you not understand?" Rivlan's volume increases as he shifts closer. "However grotesque you found Narc's plans, they are nothing compared to what some of the gods have in store for mortals."

A red haze fogs my vision. "Oh, I understand perfectly. But if you think I'll choose my kingdom, the world, over the woman I love, think again. You may believe I'm a good man who'll choose the higher moral ground, but screw that. I'll watch the kingdom sink to the depths of the ocean and the whole world burn to ash before I lift a single hand against Lark."

Not again. Never again.

"You're angry, and I don't blame you, but consider the consequences. The bigger picture." Sorrow flickers across Rivlan's face before vanishing. "Your hatchlings? All your dragons? Dead. Even the wild ones. Power? Another distraction. Trust me, Zeru will find a way to destroy every trace of mortal magic. The gods will steal everything from you, leaving humans worse than puppets."

His form steams as mist rises from the ocean.

A gigantic wave barrels for the cliff. I brace myself, spreading my legs and planting my boots on the wet stone. My wings flare instinctively for balance.

Rivlan drifts closer still, speaking in a low whisper that somehow carries over the roar of the sea. "Know this. They plan to turn all humans into their livestock. To kill, breed, sacrifice, and use as their whims dictate."

The image sickens my stomach and almost causes me to stagger.

My people reduced to cattle for celestial amusement. Lark, who fought so hard to be queen, stripped of her agency. Any children we create together born into divine slavery.

My fingertips boil with the force of gathering power. I curl them into fists at my sides.

"Do you truly not understand?" Rivlan presses. "Do you not remember what I said? Guardians aren't gods, but neither are they humans. A guardian ranks somewhere in-between. Why do you think you've gained such power?" He gestures at the sea below, which continues responding to my emotional state despite my lack of conscious direction. "You've used magic your whole life yet couldn't do half the things you can now. And you will only get better."

Halfway to a god? What in the three hells does that even mean?

Rivlan isn't finished. "Refuse, and everything you cherish, everything you love, will be lost. Lose, and it will be the same. You will simply not be here to listen to the cries of the dying. Do you truly care for humanity so little that you'd turn your back on them to save Lark?"

I peer out over the churning sea. The choice before me is no choice at all.

Either way, I lose what matters most. "The options you're offering are shit."

"Pretty much." Rivlan nods, and I detect a hint of sympathy in his voice. "I can only do so much. I cannot oppose the entire pantheon alone."

I pivot away from him, disgust roiling through me at the entire situation. At the gods who play with mortal lives, at my own powerlessness despite my newfound strength, at the impossible decision before me. "I fucking hate the gods."

I spin on my heel and begin stalking back toward the path that leads down from the cliffs.

"You're far from the only one," Rivlan calls after me. For the first time, his voice wavers with uncertainty. "But are you in?"

I pause without deigning to glance back. "I'm in."

The reply sears my gut like acid, but I force it out anyway. Because while no good options exist yet, the battle isn't over.

Any good commander knows there's always another option.

One that the enemy might not see coming until it's too late.

With a flap of my wings, I launch into the air, leaving Rivlan and the raging sea behind me. The waves begin to calm, responding to my new resolve.

I need to see Lark. Need to hold her. And then I need to figure out how to beat gods at their own game.

Because I'll be damned if I let them outmaneuver me and decide our fate.

CHAPTER FORTY-TWO
LARK

I trace meaningless patterns in the dust coating the patio railing, my fingertip crafting swirls that could be fire sigils or nothing at all. I've unfurled my wings to stave off the chill and draped them protectively over my shoulders. My feathers' burgundy streaks nearly match the wine in my cup.

The goblet sits untouched beside me. I should drink from it, numb myself, but even that simple action might be beyond my current capabilities.

Instead, I slump against the cold iron, letting the railing bear my weight as I peer out over Tirene. My kingdom, my responsibility, my home.

An almost imperceptible shift in the air signals that I'm no longer alone.

My body recognizes his presence before my mind does, and despite my rampant despair, my blood warms like embers catching fire after an influx of air.

Sterling's inherent grace and stealth carries him across the balcony without even disturbing the dust. His wings fold tightly against his back, the elegant silver feathers gleaming beneath the starlight.

He reaches my side, his posture a stark contrast to my own. With his back straight, his shoulders squared, and his hands clasped behind him, he gazes out over the same view I've been staring at without really seeing. The distance between us is both infinitesimal and vast.

"How can I fight you?" The raw, desperate question rips itself from my throat. "How can I choose between you and our kingdom? The goddess says if I refuse, Tirene burns. But if I fight you—" My voice breaks, the rest of the sentence impossible to utter.

If I fight you, one of us dies. If I fight you, I lose you or you lose me.

Sterling remains still, his breathing steady and controlled. "I met with Rivlan tonight. At the Storm Cliffs."

I straighten and face him fully for the first time. "And?"

Despite the threats, I cling to a sliver of hope that this is some sort of misunderstanding, or that the gods will take pity on our situation.

Sterling's gaze remains fixed on the horizon. That alone indicates the news isn't good. "He made the situation very clear. If I refuse to fight, he'll sink Tirene beneath the waves. If I fight and lose, at least some of our people might survive."

Akin to how Ziva threatened me. Either the pair of them coordinated, or smiting an entire kingdom is business as usual.

My hope extinguishes. "So we're trapped. Gods playing with our lives like children with toys." My fingers tremble against the stone railing, anger now mixing with my despair.

"No." Sterling's posture shifts, the muscles in his chest rippling. "No, we're not trapped. We're just not thinking creatively enough yet."

A hint of optimism rekindles in my chest. Not in the gods. Not in divine grace or mercy.

Any remaining hope in my body is due to Sterling. More

than anything else in the world, I believe in this man and what he's capable of. "What do you mean?"

"The gods have immense power, yes. But they're also predictable. Arrogant." He faces the view again, his profile sharp against the deepening twilight. "They expect blind obedience and fear. They're used to mortals cowering and accepting whatever fate is bestowed upon them simply because that's how we've always responded. Due to our faith in them, we've always followed their will."

His fingers flex at his sides with purpose, tiny ice crystals forming and melting in the air around them.

I wet my dry lips, almost afraid to ask. "What are you suggesting?"

Sterling's mouth curves into his calculating battle smile. "What if we give them exactly what they want...but on our terms?"

"How?"

His eyes come alive with ambition. "They want us to fight as champions. Fine. We'll fight."

My heart contracts as I try to piece together his intent. "Sterling—"

"We'll fight, but we'll control how we fight, where we fight, and what that fight means." He strolls closer to me. "We appear to comply. We train openly as champions and make it clear we're preparing for battle. But secretly, we find a way to undermine them."

My wings lift from their droop as I straighten. "And how exactly do we undermine gods?"

"By remembering what Rivlan told me tonight. I'm not just a champion, Lark." Sterling's demeanor grows more confident. "He called me a guardian. Like *the* Guardian from the portal. And reminded me that guardians are halfway between mortals and gods."

I blink, struggling to process this information. "What does that mean?"

"It means I have more power than they believe. And as a dragoncaller, you certainly have more than they expected, since they claim you destroying Narc set all this in motion." Sterling edges close enough that the cool aura of his magic mingles with the warmth of mine. "It means we're not just pawns. We're players."

My mind races. "So we pretend to play by their rules while actually—"

"Writing new ones." He tips up my chin. "What was it the God of Lost Things said to you?"

I immediately recall that conversation with Orin. "The gods love tricky things."

Sterling releases my chin and seizes my hand, bringing it to his mouth. "Wanna get tricky with me?" His lips warm my skin where they brush over my knuckles.

"Yes." I peer into his eyes and discover my hope reflected back at me. "I absolutely do."

The game has changed. The gods may have written the opener, but Sterling and I will write our own ending.

CHAPTER FORTY-THREE
STERLING

Barely restrained rage courses through me as Lark shares our discoveries with our small circle of allies. Agnar, Rafe, Leesa, and Bastian grow grimmer with every sentence. The breakfast splayed out in our sitting room sits mostly untouched, with fruit turning brown at the edges, pastries cooling in their baskets, and sausages abandoned in congealed puddles of grease.

No one retained much of an appetite after hearing that the gods arranged for us to fight each other to the death. Not that I can fault them for that.

The gods have manipulated us, giving with one hand while taking with the other. Despite how the priests try to spin things, that's what deities do.

Lark finishes speaking, and the silence that follows is thick enough to cut with a knife.

"Let me get this straight." A leather band holds Agnar's coppery hair back today, emphasizing the angles of his battle-scarred face. "The gods want you two to fight to the death as their champions, and if you refuse, Rivlan will sink Tirene beneath the sea? But if Lark refuses, the kingdom will burn?"

Another wave of fury rolls through me when I consider Agnar's words. "That's about the size of it."

From her seat beside Bastian, Leesa raises a hand to her throat as if trying not to vomit. "But that's...monstrous! They can't expect you to—"

"They're gods." Bastian grabs her hand and draws soothing circles with his thumb. "They can expect whatever they want."

With both his and Lark's jaws set at that same stubborn angle, the resemblance between them is especially pronounced.

Rafe props an elbow on his leg and rests his chin into his open palm. "So what you're saying is, we're fucked." His eyebrows push together in a single bristling line.

My gaze slides to Lark, and I draw hope from the sheer resolve in her beautiful profile. Instead of defeat, she hums with an air of almost palpable energy.

She's incredible.

"We're not fucked." Her steely determination prompts everyone to sit up straighter. "We're backed into a corner, yes, but that just means we need to get creative."

"So what's your game plan?" Agnar braces his forearms on the table. "How do we turn this death match into a victory?"

Rafe scoffs. "Let's start with what we have, which is a whole lot of nothing. No leverage, no power, and a divine war descending on us." He reaches for a pastry, breaking off a piece and popping it into his mouth with a defiant gesture. "We should just enjoy what we have now while we still can."

"How do you fight an enemy who's already won?" Leesa's soft but steady manner of speaking reminds me a lot of her sister. "Who holds all the cards?"

"Isn't that a given?" Agnar's eyes sweep over the group as if we're all missing something obvious. "You cheat."

He declares this without even a hint of uncertainty while spearing a sausage.

Lark bolts up, her focus trained on Agnar. "How? What do you have in mind?"

Agnar shrugs with a sheepish grin. "No clue. I just like the idea of cheating."

My head begins to throb, and I bite out a harsher response than intended. "Then why make a suggestion if it was just a shot in the dark?"

The *what the hells is your problem* glare Larks shoots me reminds me of our Flighthaven days.

"I'm morale. Keeping you guys going when things look bad." Agnar shakes the other half of his sausage at me, clearly unoffended. "Important job."

A huge part of me wants to rip Agnar a new one. Now's not the time for his asinine jokes. But something he said sticks with me. "Maybe it's not about cheating exactly. Maybe we need to change the rules of the game."

A subtle realignment occurs in the room, as if the air itself is changing its chemistry. I can see the shift embodied in their expressions. A glimmer of energy, of hope.

Rafe nods, straightening in his seat. "You divide their forces."

"Or their focus." There must be something we can exploit. "You make them look this way…" I gesture with my left hand.

"When they should be looking that way." Agnar points in the opposite direction.

Bastian brightens too. "Then you hit them hard."

"Precisely." A slow, evil smile curls Lark's lips. One that, given the situation, affects my dick a little too much for comfort. "From behind."

Leesa's hand drifts to her pregnant belly. "You make them think you're complying." Her eyes meet Lark's from across the table. "But you never, ever comply. If you're not allowed to go out the door, you go out the window. And never explain how the goat got in the storage room on the third floor."

That last bit throws me off, but Lark laughs. An inside joke between sisters, I suppose. Yet something still nags at me. A missing piece in our evaluation.

Rafe's eyes widen. "You use what they wanted to hide against them. I'll be right back."

We all stare, confusion evident on every face as he leaps to his feet and bolts from the room. The rest of us exchange puzzled glances.

Agnar frowns, pushing around an uneaten pastry on his plate. "What the hells was that about?"

Lark shrugs, just as bewildered as the rest of us. "Rafe has his...moments."

A few minutes later, Rafe returns, arms loaded with a stack of old, stained books.

"The Devoted," he drops the heavy tomes onto the table, "are acting according to Zeru's plan, right?"

Nods all around.

"So ask yourselves," Rafe brushes his hands on his tunic, "why did Zeru want to get rid of the scientist-priests? Even the ones from his own order?"

The question lingers for a moment before something clicks into place.

"Because they knew something." Bastian stands up to inspect the books. "Something he didn't want discovered."

Lark's lips part, and she snaps her fingers. "The crypt under Cyphero's temple."

A knock at the door interrupts us.

Agnar strides over to answer it, his hand resting casually on the pommel of his sword as befits his training. He opens the door to Helene, who's flanked by two scribes carrying more journals bound in leather and stained with a dark substance that might be blood. "I brought what you asked for, Councilor Bennett."

Agnar shifts aside so they can enter.

The scribes deposit their burdens on the table and leave without a word, dismissed by Helene's imperious nod.

She ventures farther into the room. "The journals of the murdered scientist-priests. We've been translating them."

Lark gestures to an empty chair. "Join us. Please."

Helene sinks into the seat, and one by one, we reach for the journals, spreading them open and scanning their bloodstained pages for anything useful.

Agnar squints at the cramped script. "Gods, this handwriting."

"Well," Lark flips a page, not bothering to look up, "they were scientists, not calligraphers."

I scan pages of diagrams, equations, and observations. The scientist-priests recorded changes in prayer-response patterns, documented the growth of crystalline formations, and noted fluctuations in magical energy during religious ceremonies.

"Look at this." Bastian points to a detailed illustration of what appears to be a crystal growth. "These formations that appeared in the temples grew in specific patterns based on the type of prayers offered."

A memory flashes through my mind. The diamond waterfall that Rivlan sent to us as a wedding gift. The cold emanating from the frozen structure.

Something about that visual bothers me, though I can't pinpoint why.

When Lark speaks, I almost believe she read my mind. She sits up and rolls her neck from side to side, her eyes distant. "The diamond waterfall gift. That thing was frozen and had to stay cold. Why? What does freezing do?"

We glance at each other in shared confusion.

"Holds things in place?" Leesa suggests.

Bastian gestures to the breakfast spread on the table. "Preserves food."

My head snaps up as the connection forms. "Preservation."

Lark frowns, tilting her head to stare at the books and journals. " What are these formations preserving? And for whom?"

Bastian shuffles through more of the scientist-priests' notes, using his finger to keep his place. "They grow during prayers and ceremonies."

Rafe's expression darkens. "When people are most devout."

Agnar frowns. "Most connected to the gods? They pulsed in the portal." He opens and closes his hands. "Like little heartbeats."

"Listen to this." Helene reads a passage aloud. "'The gods aren't helping us.'"

"We couldn't figure out the end of that part." Lark drums her fingers on the table before stopping abruptly. "Wait...what if that last line is something like 'they're feeding on us'?"

The reaction is immediate and visceral.

Everyone recoils as if the journals themselves are diseased, contaminated by the awful truth they contain...one even worse than the blood soaked into the pages. Leesa's olive skin pales, and her hand flies to her mouth while Agnar curses under his breath.

"That's what the Guardian said at the portal." Lark turns to me. "'If you're so fed up with the gods, stop giving them so much power.'"

"'And they won't have so much power.'" I remember the moment with perfect clarity. "It wasn't metaphorical."

"Fed. Up. The bastard even gave us a clue." Agnar shifts his shoulders. "If we're right about this, at least."

"The Devoted aren't just spreading fear." Leesa stares at

her sister. "They're creating intense emotions that lead to more prayers, more offerings—"

"More food for the gods." Disgust laces Bastian's tone.

Agnar whistles. "Imagine the flow of devotion at a Champions Match where each side's praying to their favorite's patron god. Or praying for a swift and merciful victory, or any of the other things humans pray for while loved ones fight, especially when lives depend on the outcome."

Another realization spears me as I mull over Rivlan's warning about humans being worse off than puppets with new perspective.

The elemental god came so close to divulging the truth to me—perhaps even wanted to—but in the end, he withheld crucial details.

A bitter sense of betrayal flays my chest. The intensity surprises me. Somewhere along the way, I started to trust Rivlan, began liking him on a personal level.

Meanwhile, the prick's been using me all along.

He may not be as manipulative as the other gods, but a spade's still a spade. "Rivlan wanted to keep the match quiet. He said it was to avoid distractions and attention."

Bastian considers this. "Maybe there was another reason. The only way that counsel makes sense is if Rivlan actually wanted to rein in the gods."

"Bullshit." Agnar folds his arms over his chest. "He's one of them."

"Think about it." Bastian continues to flip pages. "When people witness divine power, what do they do? They pray, they make offerings..."

I see where he's going with this. "And if they witness that divine presence in person, as they would at the match with the gods in attendance, imagine how many prayers would be offered. How much devotion could be harvested." The pieces fall into place. "Definitely explains why Rivlan wanted to limit witnesses."

"Which is exactly why we shouldn't." The expression of absolute disgust distorting Lark's features mirrors my own. "We need to push the gods to reveal who they truly are. I don't know what will happen, but in either case, everyone needs to see what these assholes are capable of. How predatory they can be." Her fierce, resolute eyes meet mine. "If people see how the gods obtain their energy, they might question feeding the deities their devotion."

Agnar pounds his fist on the table and hoots. "That's the answer! We starve those fuckers."

Damn, do I like the sound of that. "Exactly. Those asshole deities hit us with everything from floods to fires to crop destruction to tolls on bridges. They starve our people in order to get fat off our prayers. Drive us mad. Kill. The time's come to flip the script on them."

I examine the faces of our small council. Lark with her fiery determination, Leesa with her quiet strength, Bastian with his thoughtful resolve, Rafe with his calculating intensity, Helene with her reluctant alliance, and Agnar with his fighting spirit. For the first time since my conversation with Rivlan on the cliffs, I truly believe we have a chance.

The gods twisted our lives into a game, used our devotion as fuel, and forced us into positions where only sacrifice could save everything we hold dear.

But in this new version of the game, the gods are no longer the masters.

They're each merely another piece on the board.

Chapter Forty-Four
Lark

Dawn's pale, hesitant glow crawls through my sitting room windows like a thief. I've sat here for hours already, watching night retreat while trying to define the churning sensation in my gut.

Not fear exactly, but something close.

My fingers tap against the wooden table, tiny sparks following each impact. A rebellion is brewing, and since yesterday's revelation, my fire magic has started reacting to my emotions more strongly than ever, as if our new knowledge somehow amplified my power.

Or maybe that's just rage.

Pure, clarifying rage over being used as fodder for divine appetites.

The door opens, and Leesa enters, her face drawn with worry. Lately, she's struggled with morning nausea, though she tries to hide it. Pregnancy doesn't seem to care about celestial conspiracies or impending death matches.

"I was told you wanted to meet for breakfast again?" She drops a kiss on my cheek before settling into a chair near mine.

Her hand moves instinctively to her stomach, a protective gesture that squeezes my heart. "You look like you've been up for hours."

"Couldn't sleep." I offer her a weak smile. "Apparently, plotting treason against the heavens isn't conducive to rest. Who knew?" The teapot no longer steams, but the tea remains warm as I pour her a cup.

Bastian joins us shortly after, bringing with him a collection of the scientist-priests' journals. Judging by the messy hair, rumpled clothing, and sunken eyes, he spent his evening the same way I did. He nods to me and sets down his burden before immediately stationing himself behind Leesa to start massaging her shoulders.

I snort at the blissed-out expression on my sister's face and slide a second cup of tea over. "Any new insights?"

"Several." He pauses to yawn. "I've been cross-referencing the journals with older texts. This topic's been debated for years and frequently arises during times of calamity. Always linked with the growth of those crystals."

Agnar and Rafe arrive together, deep in conversation. Agnar's unbound waves cascade to his shoulders, giving him an almost feral look when combined with the dangerous brightness in his blue eyes. Rafe, by contrast, is meticulously put together, though the rigid set to his mouth betrays his anger.

"Your Majesty." Agnar greets me with a formal bow that transforms halfway through into a conspiratorial wink. "Ready to overthrow some assholes?" We've all agreed not to use the names of any of the gods so as not to draw attention to ourselves.

"Let's not get ahead of ourselves," Bastian cautions, though a smile plays at the corners of his mouth.

A maid enters with breakfast. Platters of fruit and berries, fresh bread, cold cuts of meat, cubes of cheese, and pitchers of juice. We fall silent as she arranges everything on the table, and I dismiss her with a sincere thanks.

"We need to be careful." I reach for a piece of bread more out of obligation than hunger. "Even mentioning our plans where anyone might overhear—"

"Could result in prayer." Bastian offers a glass of orange juice to Leesa before pouring one for himself. "A single prayer of concern from a loyal servant, and they might know exactly what we're plotting."

Helene sweeps in, her black braid twined perfectly around her head. As always, her snooty expression suggests she just smelled something unpleasant, but a new intensity gleams in her eyes.

I'm about to greet her when Sterling emerges from our bedchamber. My heart performs the usual flutter at the sight of him, but I cock my head when I take a closer look.

Today, something's different about his bearing, almost as if he vibrates with coiled energy, like a spring compressed to its limits. "Good, you're all here. We need to plan carefully. My 'sponsor' will be keeping tabs on me."

"And mine, too, most likely." I resist the urge to glance over my shoulder at the hearth, which remains unlit for the first time this season. "We need to give them exactly what they expect to see. And discuss the plans in ways that are less likely to draw their attention."

Another servant appears with a fresh pot of tea. We again pause our conversation, exchanging pleasantries about the weather until she leaves.

Once she vanishes, Sterling checks the corridor before closing the door. "This is how it's going to be. Everything we say in public must support the narrative that we're reluctantly accepting our roles as champions. In private," he gestures to our small group, "we plan our real strategy."

"Which is what, exactly?" Rafe grabs a piece of bread. "We

know they feed on devotion, but how does that knowledge help you avoid fighting each other to the death?"

I flatten my palms on the table. "We turn their weapons against them. The match will draw massive crowds, thousands of witnesses. What if, instead of fighting each other, we use that stage to reveal the truth?"

Bastian cuts an apple and slips the slice onto Leesa's plate. "The truth about their feeding on our devotion?"

"Yes." My heart warms as I watch him care for my sister. "But we can't just make accusations. We need proof. Evidence that people will believe."

Rafe rips the bread in half with more force than necessary. "Revealing the truth at the match will be too late. We need to prepare people beforehand."

"Seed the information." Agnar's eyes light up. "Make them start questioning things before they ever arrive as spectators."

"But subtly." Leesa nibbles on an apple peel, leaving the meat of the fruit untouched. "If the gods or the wrong people realize what we're doing..."

"They'll either sink or cinder Tirene." I use my knife to strip the peel from my own apple. Growing up in an all-female household, with mostly women visitors, I heard stories about strange and sudden cravings during pregnancy. If apple peel is what Leesa wants for breakfast, that's what she gets. "So we need to be strategic. Start rumors, not proclamations. Talk, not decree."

"And we need allies." Sterling's forehead crinkles with adorable confusion as I pass Leesa the peels. "Not just here in Tirene, but in every kingdom. People who will help spread the word without exposing the source."

"The Craftsmen's Guild." Rafe taps the emblem on his shirt. "We have members in every town and noble house. They can circulate information without raising suspicion."

Helene holds a grape up to her mouth. "I can use my Aclarian connections as well. After what happened at Flighthaven, there are those who already question the gods' benevolence."

As the afternoon wears on, our strategy takes shape. We map out key locations, identify potential allies, and debate the best phrasing to plant seeds of doubt without triggering divine attention. My legs ache from sitting for so long, but the discomfort is nothing compared to the growing sense of purpose in my chest.

"What about the actual fight?"

I stifle a groan. Leave it to Bastian to vocalize the question we've all been avoiding.

"We'll have seconds, maybe less, before they realize our betrayal." Sterling's gaze slides to me, his expression grim. "That's why the revelation needs to happen simultaneously. We need the crowd to see the truth at the exact moment we refuse to fight."

Agnar wipes his mouth with the back of his hand. "And then?"

No one has an answer. We've outlined how to expose the gods, but what comes after remains terrifyingly unclear. The threat of these powerful gods is real. Even if we sway the tide of public opinion against them, can we really stop them from destroying Tirene in retaliation? From obliterating other kingdoms?

The gravity of our course settles over the room like a thick fog. My fingers begin to tremble against the table's surface, so I quickly tuck them into my lap. I'm their queen, their leader in this impossible fight. I can't afford to show fear.

As if sensing the direction of my thoughts, Sterling gives my hand a reassuring squeeze under the table. "We won't be facing them alone. If we can turn enough people against them, if we significantly reduce the flow of devotion, their power will wane. Not immediately, but eventually."

"So we're really doing this?" Agnar is uncharacteristically subdued. "Taking on all of them?"

"Hopefully not all of them." Sterling glances up from the map. "Not if we manage to change the rules. Those arrogant bastards have sat at the top of the food chain for so long, I bet they've forgotten what it's like to go hungry. We simply need to remind them."

Agnar's battle-scarred features light up with a fierce joy that's almost frightening in its intensity. "Well, when you put it that way..."

The mood in the room shifts, fear ceding to determination. Our conspiracy against the heavens is set. We will transform the gods' greatest feast into their most public humiliation...or die trying.

I blow out a slow breath, clinging to calm while every tradition, every rule, every law I've ever lived under reminds me of how badly this could go. "Next steps. Knox, you send word that you've chosen the day and time of the match."

Sterling nods. "Two weeks from today, at the Storm Cliffs. Far enough away from the capital that if everything goes to shit, the palace and all the refugees housed here should be safe. Not to mention the hatchlings."

The expressions range from hope to resolve. "I'll accept the offer to serve as champion for the other faction. Ziva will be suspicious if I seem too eager, so I plan to play the reluctant but resigned queen, accepting my fate for the good of the kingdom."

"And while you two maintain that pretense and work on your training," Bastian gestures to the rest of the group, "we'll start propagating the truth. Carefully and strategically, but widely."

"The heralds should leave today." Rafe pushes back from

the table. "The sooner word spreads about the match, the bigger the crowd we can gather to witness it."

I rub the tingling sensation on the back of my neck. Well, I guess there's no going back now.

In two weeks' time, we'll either change the world forever... or lose everything.

CHAPTER FORTY-FIVE
THE GODS

Zeru paces, vibrating with anger and impatience. "She agreed?"

Nyc, Mar, and Hallr shift and shimmer in Zeru's realm, all of them inflated with power and ego.

Ziva clasps her hands behind her back. Even here, she burns brighter than the rest. "She agreed."

The others hum but remain silent.

"Good." Pleased, Zeru gives a clipped nod. "It is time. Time to broadcast the news. Time to make them fear. Time to make them pray."

The fire goddess shoots him a pointed look. "Tirene already knows. News spreads fast."

Zeru's attention snaps back. He studies Ziva, suspicion narrowing his eyes. "They're up to something."

"Probably." A beat passes, and Ziva's gaze slides to the others. "They are not fools."

As Zeru glares, his form expands. He dismisses her doubt and leaves her behind to speak to the other gods and begin their plans.

She watches their exchanges, defiance burning in her eyes.

"I will not harm the dragon hatchlings."

Zeru inclines his head. "Lark has agreed. You most likely won't need to hurt them."

Ziva glances at Nyc, who stays silent. "Still, I see no reason the mortal queen needs to be involved. It is—"

"It is necessary!" Zeru spins back around to face her, incandescent with rage. "She is required. Do you know how compromised Knox will be with Lark as his opponent? Theirs is a true love, not an infatuation or lust. That will make him incapable of fighting. It will leave him weak. He will die."

No one dares to move. Even Ziva's flames hold still.

His anger dissipates, losing focus. "And with him, our opposition. Lark is the perfect shield and spear in one. He will not harm her. But with her protective nature, she will have to attack in order to protect her dragons and the rest of her family. Her kingdom. It's the perfect match."

"Do you really think everything will play out this way?" The cool, soothing voice drifts from the darkness that surrounds Nyc. "Is winning all you care about?"

"What I care about is power." Zeru straightens, towering over them. Looking down on them. "Maintaining what is mine. What is ours by right. And they cannot stop us."

For a second, he pauses, as if doubting his own words.

Nyc opens her mouth to speak again but stops herself when Zeru waves a dismissive arm.

"Knox must die. As for Lark...?" He shrugs. "It makes no difference what happens to her after that."

 ～

Sterling

Agnar adopts a loose stance with his shoulders thrown back,

mocking me. "Come on, Sterling. Move faster. You've got fire magic to dodge too!"

He claps, and the world collapses. Lava jettisons upward, a red-hot fury that fizzles into steam and cooled stone when I push back with my own magic.

"This fast enough for you?" A laugh bubbles up from my throat as I launch into the sky, riding the steam thermals away from the danger of the training field we set up in the mountains that ring the Impassable Desert.

Agnar snorts. "I've seen better."

"Remember," Bastian ignores our bickering, "even merging with Agnar, we're still not as strong as Lark. You need to move faster and expect the unexpected. My sister is a tricky fighter."

Tricky fighter doesn't begin to do Lark justice. My queen is fucking magnificent.

Bastian dives from the sky with speed and grace. A flaming boulder appears behind him.

Dismissing my wings, I let myself plummet like a rock. Ten additional fire elementals follow my descent while launching flames at me.

Only, they can't hit what they can't see.

Shrouding myself in mist, I stretch the haze to the ground, solidifying it just enough near the bottom to provide a landing spot. Then I create steps that allow me to run across the sky, still hidden from view.

I pop out of the fog behind and a little below Bastian.

He hovers with the flaming boulder near the place where I initially dropped, waiting for a chance to strike.

With a single thought, I encase that smoldering chunk of rock in ice. The whole thing explodes from thermal shock, knocking Bastian out of the air.

One down.

Out of nowhere, Agnar appears behind me, jamming his heels hard on the backs of my knees.

Sneaky bastard found me.

His blows take me down, and I collapse on the floating steps. "If you pay attention, you can tell where the ice starts to form. I just used that to track you."

Good catch.

But I'm not going to let that dickhead best me just because he's helpful.

Grabbing my friend's hand, I jerk and bend at the waist to throw him. At the same time, I soak his wings with water.

He doesn't notice my next move until it's too late.

~

Lark

Sand scorches beneath my feet, the ocean a useless ally to the ten men and women attacking me. The heat, indifferent as the tide, licks my heels.

"Show me what you've got, Rafe!" I scream to be heard over the shrieks of wind coming off the Southern Sea. We chose this location to make it easier for my opponents and harder on me.

Overhead, a tornado and typhoon whirl and bounce off each other. Rafe, merged with a water elemental, hovers between the two.

Steam, ice, and water lash out at me, though not a drop penetrates the heat barrier I've built around me.

Their magic has created a pelting rain and rising river. They attack from all angles, fierce and relentless, but my flames burn bright and my heart even brighter.

We all refuse to surrender.

Sterling taught me well. I may be new to this way of

channeling power, but the method feels natural. The sand beneath my feet transforms to glass, which will soon become too slick if I'm not careful.

The very air begins to waver.

Their magic slams into the solid mass of my own, and Rafe yells for them to take another angle.

I'm more than ready as my fire expands.

Without warning, the ground buckles under my feet. The glass shatters. A hole forms, and for a hot second, I'm falling.

But not for long.

With a snap, my wings extend. The air buffets them, threatening to send me spiraling until I balance the surrounding heat to stop the air current.

As soon as I conquer that challenge, a sheet of solid soil races toward me.

I melt the ice, only to find a wall of hard-packed earth still barreling my way. My heart stops, then beats triple-time.

I succumb to a moment of panic before regaining control. Forget the magic...I'll stop the wielder instead.

I fly upward to gain a better view while the earth elemental pursues me.

There! I spy a strange lump in the land a good distance away from the water users and the beach.

With a sharp flex of my mind, smoke pours out of that hump in the ground. A woman quickly follows, slapping at her clothes as she rolls in the dirt.

There's more than one way to win a battle.

I get a few moments to bask in my success before another assault forces me back to work.

CHAPTER FORTY-SIX
LARK

The late afternoon sun slants through the windows of my private sitting room as I stiffly pace the length of the chamber, my muscles still sore from dealing with that dust storm Rafe set on me.

Our core group plotted treason against the heavens, and now we're recruiting outsiders. Necessary outsiders. The kind who can spread our message far and wide. But we need to proceed with caution. If word of our mission reaches the wrong ears, a single misplaced prayer could rain divine retribution down upon us all.

And I refuse to trust someone before I even meet them.

Sterling watches from his position by the window. His handsome face reveals nothing, especially to those who lack the experience to read his expressions. I catch the slight tension at the edges of his mouth, though, and the way he tracks my every movement.

"Helene has sound judgment. If she says this minstrel can help us, I believe her."

"I'm not questioning Helene's judgment." Not about this, at least. I stop to fiddle with the fruit arrangement on the sideboard, and sparks zip between my fingers. I must be too fired up from the training today because these little magical eruptions keep happening. "I'm questioning whether we can trust anyone outside this room with what we know."

Bastian glances up from the ancient texts spread across the table. "We can't do this alone, Lark. If we expect to turn people away from the gods, we need voices they already believe."

"And this Barnaby has the people's ear." Agnar leans against the wall with deceptive casualness, his clothes still damp from his morning sparring session with Sterling. "More importantly, he has no love for nobles or authority. Our opponents are the ultimate authority. He'll hate them on principle."

I send a wave of heat in his direction, drying and warming him. I'm about to respond when a sharp knock cuts through the room.

We all freeze.

"Enter." I straighten my posture into something more regal. Queen Lark now, not just Lark the scared shitless, desperate woman plotting against the gods.

Our combined stress eases when Helene sweeps in, her thick navy dress perfectly pressed and immaculate as usual. Her lips form that same perpetually crooked line of disinterest.

A man with a riot of loose brown curls atop his head, who's dressed in colors so vivid they seem to vibrate against the subdued elegance of the palace, trails behind her. He wears a crimson tunic embroidered with gold thread, azure leggings, and a cape of deep emerald that swirls with each movement. His steel gray eyes, deep-set and knowing, scan the room with quick assessment.

This must be Barnaby.

I've heard of him, of course. Everyone has. His songs are performed in every tavern across Tirene, and his pointed critiques of nobility have earned him as many enemies in high places as admirers among the common folk. Not a single trace of servility shows in his posture as he saunters into the chamber with the easy confidence of a man who believes himself equal to anyone, royal or not.

Based on this gives-no-fucks first impression, I like him.

"Your Majesty. Your Highness." Helene gestures to the wild peacock of a man. "May I present Barnaby Paloma."

The minstrel offers a bow that hovers at the border between respectful and mocking. "Queen Lark." Even in those two simple words, his melodious voice shines. "I hear you've asked for me specifically. I'm flattered. Or perhaps I should be concerned?"

"Barnaby's father was my father's minstrel." Helene's tone suggests this connection is reason enough for us to trust him.

"And I am no one's." He plucks idly at the small gittern hanging from his belt, producing a discordant note that somehow emphasizes his point. "I travel across the kingdoms and perform for no one but the people."

"There's no need for concern." Sterling smiles his court smile, the one he uses to put people at ease. "Please, come in, have a seat. We have an important matter to discuss with you."

I study him. Intelligence sparkles in those eyes, along with a healthy dose of skepticism.

Good. We need someone who questions everything.
Even us.

Especially us.

"Do you have children, Barnaby?" I cringe, worrying that I already managed to stick my foot in my mouth.

The minstrel's stance shifts. A barely perceptible tensing. His eyes narrow as they lock onto mine, searching for the threat behind my words. "I do. What of them?" Steel replaces the melody in his voice. "Did you invite me here just to threaten me?"

The change in demeanor draws Sterling forward, his affability gone. "No one is threatening anyone."

Oof. I probably should have phrased that better. "Just the opposite. Our discussion is for the sake of your children. For everyone's children. Not just those living in Tirene's capital. I want you to know that beforehand."

Barnaby considers me for a long moment with a slight furrow between his brows. "And why exactly am I here? Shouldn't the soon-to-be king focus on training for his upcoming Champions Match?"

Sterling gives me an imperceptible nod, encouraging me to continue. The minstrel catches the gesture, and his eyes narrow further.

"Good." Bastian ignores the tension radiating from Barnaby. "Word is spreading through the kingdoms."

"Whether through our efforts or the Devoted's. Either way, it works." Smiling grimly, Agnar shrugs. "Still feels weird to help them and their leader out, but the world has gotten really strange recently."

Barnaby's assessing gaze travels from face to face. "You people are exceptionally cryptic for a group that invited me here." The sharpness in his eyes belies his light tone as he addresses me. "So who is it? Who will your betrothed be fighting in this great spectacle? Some fearsome warrior from across the sea? A mighty sorcerer?"

A beat passes while familiar dread writhes in my gut. "Me."

That reply cracks his composed facade. He recoils, his eyebrows shooting up and his mouth gaping open. "You? Tirene's queen will fight the crown prince? Her own fiancé?" He glances between us, searching for the joke or political strategy that explains such madness.

My stomach twists. "Yes."

He shakes his head, and his expression hardens. "What game are you playing?"

"We're not the ones playing a game." Sterling presses a fist against the table. "The gods have pitted us against each other to rip apart the mortal world."

Barnaby releases a short, bitter laugh. "Right. The gods. Of course." He fiddles with his gittern again, as if debating whether to simply take his leave. "Why would the gods do such a thing?"

"Because they're at war." I gesture to Sterling and myself. "And they've chosen human champions to fight for them instead. And I must ask you to not refer to any of them by name, lest we risk drawing their attention to us. We have far too much of that already."

The minstrel's skepticism is palpable, his expression clearly questioning our sanity.

Bastian rises from his chair to approach the table with the ancient texts. He flips open a worn manuscript, its pages yellowed with age, the ink faded to a rusty brown. "The archives hold accounts of the last civil war among the gods. The descriptions match exactly what we're seeing. Corrupted sacred sites, rogue divine animals, transformed devotional objects, splintering reality."

Barnaby glances at the manuscript warily, as if he expects the book to attack. "And you expect me to believe this...why, exactly?"

Bastian ignores the question. "Do you know how that war ended?"

The minstrel's mouth curls. "Badly?"

"With a covenant." Sterling's voice holds the calm certainty of a man who's confronted unbelievable challenges and survived. "One that gave an off-ramp to divine war. Mortal champions fighting as the gods' proxies."

Barnaby's brows pull together, but I can see his mind

working to process everything. Which is good considering Helene explained how much he distrusts nobles, royals, and basically any authority figure. While I might be the queen and Sterling the prince, we're minor players when compared to the gods. A point in our favor.

"But the horror doesn't end here," I say. "It's the 'why' of their war that truly matters."

"So, why *are* they at war?" Seems that Barnaby's curiosity is beginning to override his suspicion.

Sterling's icy grin elicits a wary glance from Barnaby. "The gods need us more than we knew. Even more than we need them."

"For what?"

"Fuel." A few seconds pass before Agnar clarifies. "Food."

Barnaby's features twist in confusion. "Food? What are you talking about?"

I smooth a hand over my skirt and raise my chin. This next part sounds the most insane. "The gods harvest and feed on devotion. Our prayers are food to them."

His expression lends credence to my fear. This man believes we've lost our ever-loving minds.

"Have you ever noticed the crystalline formations in the temples? They've been growing and moving. Almost as if they're sentient." Bastian waits for Barnaby's nod. "The scientist-priests discovered that they grow during prayers, during moments of heightened devotion. They serve as storage devices, capturing and preserving the energy they use."

Barnaby appears unconvinced, but at least he hasn't stormed out yet. That's something. "And what role do the Devoted play in this?" He's connecting dots faster than I expected.

Agnar bares his teeth. "Now we're getting somewhere."

"The Devoted spread select news to foment specific reactions." Helene toys with the pendant on her thin gold necklace. "They disseminate false news, rumors, tales of doom and gloom, and—"

"And the only source of protection is fervent prayer to the gods." The muscles in Barnaby's jaw and neck work as he clenches his teeth. "I hate fanatics."

"Most reasonable people do." I motion to the rest of the group. "Which is why we need your help."

His eyebrows rise again. "My help? With what, exactly? Overthrowing the heavens?" Underneath the sarcasm that thickens his voice, I catch a spark of defiance.

"In a manner of speaking." Sterling rubs his jaw. "We need to undermine their power source. We need people to turn away from the gods."

Barnaby tilts his head. "Sort of like a mass prayer strike?"

I move closer to our visitor, my voice dropping to ensure no servants passing in the hall will overhear. "We need to convince people to ask questions. Lead them to doubt the gods themselves." I pause to ensure he understands the final, crucial piece. "And persuade them to come to the match."

Barnaby fingers the gittern's strings, his gaze distant as he plucks out a soft melody. I can almost see the trademark satire at work in his mind. "Always fancied being part of a revolution."

Agnar pumps his fist in the air. "Yes! Bring your friends. The gods hate that we have friends and loved ones."

"Well, they must really hate me then, because I have many friends. Minstrels, actors, storytellers." Barnaby's fingers prance across the strings. "People who earn their living by making others listen."

Hope flares in my chest. This could actually work. "We have ten days until the match. Ten days to turn as many people as possible away from the gods."

Barnaby nods, eyes calculating. "Ten days to start a revolution." He gestures at each of us. "I'll need details.

Specific incidents. Evidence I can point to that will incite questions."

"We have plenty. Backed by facts and trusted sources." Bastian points to the papers on the table. "The scientist-priests documented everything. Until the Devoted slaughtered them."

"And we'll need songs." Helene waves at his gittern. When we shift as one in her direction, she meets our surprise with her usual cool detachment. "What? Songs circulate faster than rumors, and they're remembered longer."

Barnaby grins. "I'm already composing." He plucks out a series of notes, humming softly under his breath. "A song about hungry gods and the mortals who feed them..."

I nod, impressed despite myself. "And the match itself. We need as many witnesses as possible."

"That won't be a problem." Barnaby waves me off. "A battle between Queen Lark and Prince Knox? Champions of the gods? Everyone will want to witness that unprecedented event." His expression gleams with anticipation. "Especially when rumor has it that there's more to the spectacle than meets the eye."

Bastian rubs his palms together. "If the gods realize what we're planning—"

"I understand the stakes." All traces of levity disappear from Barnaby's demeanor. "I have children, as Her Majesty so pointedly reminded me, and no desire to see them become livestock for divine appetites, despite how they sometimes test my patience."

Agnar snickers. "Oh, you'll fit in just fine."

"Then we're in agreement." Sterling extends his hand for the minstrel to shake. "You'll help us spread the word, lure people to the match, and inspire them to question their divine devotion."

Sterling's proffered hand elicits a subtle widening of

Barnaby's eyes before the minstrel clasps the prince's palm and shakes. "I'll do more than that. By the time I'm finished, the gods will wish they'd never heard of Barnaby the Minstrel."

As I watch them seal this pact, a rush of unidentifiable emotions floods my system. Maybe hope, or desperation, or madness.

Perhaps all three.

We're gambling everything on this plan. Our lives, our kingdom, our futures. But for the first time since learning of the gods' manipulations, I truly believe we have a fighting chance.

Ten days. Ten days to start a revolution that will shake the very heavens.

CHAPTER FORTY-SEVEN
LARK

Trying to ignore my exhaustion, I weave through the palace hallways to the Royal Archives. Between this morning's training session and too many late nights to count, I'm so tired that several minutes pass before I realize the weight dragging behind me is from my wings.

With a shrug, I banish them and reach for the handle of the heavy door that protects our kingdom's history and knowledge.

Illumination glows from every chandelier, as well as the scattered ever-lights. A page naps in the corner on a little stool.

At the first desk between the rows of bookcases, I find the subject of my search.

Bastian's hands tremble as he closes another ancient text, dust puffing from its pages in a tired cloud. Only a stub remains of the candle beside him, the wax pooling on the table like congealed blood.

Before I get a chance to speak, Leesa waves me over. "Earlier, Rose's flame familiar showed us something. In the section of the archives we hadn't reached yet."

I straighten, my fatigue momentarily forgotten. "Tell me it's good news."

She hesitates, pushing her dark golden blond waves behind her ears as she leans closer. "It's...interesting. But we're running out of time."

Leesa's gaze shifts to the far wall where we use charcoal to mark the days with harsh, vertical slashes. Seven days remain until the wedding ceremonies begin and the world pours into Tirene. The day after is the Champions Match.

Because nothing says honeymoon quite like squaring off with your new spouse in a fight to the death. "What did Rose's familiar show you?"

"Ancient binding protocol. The gods must follow certain rules when using champions." She pushes a thin yellowed scroll toward Bastian. "We're not sure what it means yet. Rose is with Knox, who's trying to make sense of it."

Bastian nods, pulling the scroll closer. "I'll add it to the pile of 'might save us, might not.'"

On any other occasion, Bastian's attempt to lighten a shitty situation would draw a laugh, but I can only muster a weak smile.

The door creaks open again, admitting Agnar. His coppery hair is wind-tossed and sweat-dampened, his battle-scarred face lined with exhaustion. Dust coats his boots and the lower half of his trousers, evidence of his day's work.

While Sterling and I spent the better part of the day training separately, Agnar helped to set up the arena for the match. We agreed on using the vast stretch of land on the West Coast near the Storm Cliffs, the most uninhabited section of Tirene. Nowhere near the palace or the dragons.

I squeeze his arm as he strolls by. "Everything went well?"

"It works, but I had to use every bit of my power." Agnar drops into a chair, his broad shoulders slumping. "The earth magic barriers will hold during the match, but if there's any sort of attack beforehand..."

He doesn't finish the sentence. He doesn't need to. We all understand what's at stake.

When the windows rattle, I spin to inspect them. For days, strange shifting clouds have slowly formed around Tirene. "Glad the weather didn't render your task impossible. Those clouds, or whatever they are, keep getting closer."

The oddities move with too much unnatural purpose to be real storm clouds and circle like cautious predators.

"Knox said to tell you he's training again. Against fire, wind, and earth." Rose issues the announcement from the doorway. Her blond hair reflects the fading light, and the flame sprite that accompanies her throbs with an anxious amber glow above her right shoulder. The child's blue eyes are far too serious for her young face. "The gods are watching."

"Thanks, Rosie." Agnar's expression softens. "Let them watch. You come give your uncle a hug."

The little girl races over and throws herself into his arms as her familiar casts dancing shadows on the marble floors. "Kin showed me things. In the old books. About rules."

Helene bursts in, her cheeks flushed with exertion. "Southern temples in Meridia just sent word. They're with us. Except for the lead priest. The Devoted got to him first."

Dammit.

"Thanks, Helene. Not as good as we hoped, but better than we expected." The temples going against the lead priest is yet another sign of the growing division in all the kingdoms.

"You realize, if this fails, we're not just risking ourselves." Bastian gestures at the room's occupants. "We're risking everyone who's helped us. The whole world."

I shrug, even that tiny movement almost too much for me to handle after hours of grueling training. "The whole world is already at risk."

Bastian grimaces. "It'll be worse for those involved in the planning."

So basically, everyone in this room and the people we recruited will be tortured by the gods if we fail.

Such an uplifting thought.

Leesa wraps her arms around Bastian from behind his chair and leans forward to kiss his temple. "That's why we won't fail."

Exactly. Because when the alternative is unthinkable, failure isn't an option.

CHAPTER FORTY-EIGHT
LARK

We researched until our eyes became bloodshot. Trained until we couldn't physically take anymore. The fighting ring is laid out, the stands ready to hold thousands. The news has spread, and trickles of people are already arriving. I'm so tired I don't even bother to light the candles or the hearth in the bedchamber as we enter.

All that's left to do now is get a good night's sleep before the diplomatic gauntlet we have to run tomorrow. We've changed our wedding to a small private ceremony where we'll be surrounded only by our close friends and loved ones.

I make a mental note to compensate Odessa well for the countless hours she spent planning. I couldn't tell whether the wedding coordinator was more relieved or disappointed when I told her about the shift in our agenda.

"Stop worrying, love. I can see your wheels spinning." Sterling's voice is husky. Deep. He knows what this voice of his does to me. "Dance with me."

The words almost undo me. My eyes sting. My breath catches. A startled sound escapes my lips. The last few days have been nothing but a slog.

Training. Planning. Researching. Eating just to survive.

Now, despite the fact that he's been working just as hard as I have, Sterling offers me joy.

How can he think of dancing at a time like this? We're standing on the edge of oblivion, one slip away from losing everything. My chest constricts, hot and tight. My mind races. We need to continue planning. Preparing. We need—

"Lark." Sterling's fingers brush mine. "Come here."

His touch ignites me, body and soul. It's warmth and hunger and every reckless impulse I've ever had.

I grab his hand as if I might drown without it. "I'm here."

The small distance between us disappears.

He pulls me to him, his lips brushing across the corner of my lips. "I love you."

My arms circle his neck while my heart pounds a frantic beat against his chest.

"Dance with me." With the way he's gazing at me, dark eyes boring into my soul, there's nothing I would deny him.

Though I think exhaustion just might kill me, dying in his arms doesn't sound so bad.

We move slowly at first, tentative as new lovers. The room spins around us. My fears and doubts spin with it. "Don't let me go."

"Never." He steps backward, dragging me with him. "Not even if the world burns."

"Or drowns." That hits way too close to home and shouldn't be funny but somehow, we both laugh. Laughter gives way to sensual kisses.

Sterling rears back, the smile on his face pure mischief. He knows how that boyish expression of his disarms me. "We'll be fine. Trust me."

"I do."

"Then close your eyes."

"I don't—" The words don't have the chance to leave my lips.

"Close them." He gives me no real choice by pressing a kiss against my eyelids.

I expect him to sweep me off my feet. Instead, the softest, gentlest chime surrounds us. I open my eyes just as Sterling wraps his arms around me.

Cold, silvery light that shimmers like ice fills the room.

Tiny droplets hang suspended in the air before falling slowly, beautifully, impossibly. Each one reflects us—two small figures caught in a vast and uncertain world—a thousand times over.

The droplets fall, glistening in the dim light. We're alone beneath their glowing cascade. Alone in the universe. Alone and together. Nothing else matters.

We begin to move, turning in slow circles. The motion is awkward at first, a jerky kind of swaying. But as we find our rhythm, my heart does a terrible thing. It dares to hope.

Then we dance.

We dance like this might be our last night of peace.

My lips tremble, straining against the weight of my own need. How can something so gorgeous hurt so much? "I don't want to lose you."

His grip tightens, drawing me closer. "You won't."

But he can't promise that. I can't promise that. We can't promise each other anything except this moment.

We're spinning now, fast and out of control. The air glistens with uncertainty. My dark fears twist and curl, looming in the periphery. I catch glimpses of them between the droplets, reflections of all the ways this could end. Reflections of what happens if we fail.

Reflections of who I am without him.

The tears I didn't know I had start to run freely, each one a fragment of longing, of fear, of love too big for me to hold.

Sterling wipes them away with his thumb, and warmth blooms in my chest.

I love this man more than life itself.

Our bodies move as one, the way they always have. But this time, there's an urgency that neither of us can ignore.

The water brightens his face. It's so fucking gorgeous that I can't breathe.

Without a thought, little flames dance with us through suspended water drops. A thousand reflections spin around and around and around, blurring into a single, shining truth.

I love him.

I love him, and I'm not strong enough to let him go.

Like music from another world, the droplets keep falling.

The fires continue to burn, beautiful and bold.

And my heart keeps breaking until it's not breaking anymore. Until it's so full that it can't be anything but whole.

The water and light surround us, the music of it all softer than the sound of my heart. We are wrapped in this glow, this cocoon of impossible love and unthinkable need. The droplets kiss our skin. We kiss each other.

We kiss like we'll never have the chance again.

We kiss like nothing else in the universe matters.

We kiss until I don't know where I end and he begins.

There's a thousand-pound weight on my chest, a bone-deep fatigue, and anxiety splitting me in two different directions. But I'm with Sterling, close and warm and for the moment, very much alive.

That's something I refuse to give up.

CHAPTER FORTY-NINE
LARK

The winter morning sun pours through my window like honey, bathing the palace in golden light that belies the chill in the air. Below, the courtyard vibrates with life, a stream of visitors flowing through the gates in colorful rivulets.

I press my palm against the cool glass while watching their arrival. Nobles and commoners alike, drawn by curiosity or duty or the simple human desire to witness something extraordinary.

First my wedding.

Then a masquerade ball.

And tomorrow, the Champions Match.

The thought of getting married—an impossibility made flesh—still catches in my throat sometimes. The girl I was, kidnapped and raised in an enemy kingdom, could never have imagined becoming queen, let alone marrying the man she loved. And now that dream hovers tantalizingly close, just beyond the nightmare we must first survive.

The reception line.

Maybe we should have scheduled the Champions Match first.

But Sterling and I both agreed, since there's a very real possibility one or both of us could die in the battle, that we would do so as husband and wife.

Morbid, but true.

Guards line the palace walls, their armor gleaming in the sunlight. From this height, they look like tiny precise figurines. The banners snap above them. Tirene's colors are vibrant against the cloudless sky, demanding allegiance from the wind itself.

How many of those guards will survive tomorrow? Will any of us?

"Your Majesty," Rhiann murmurs from behind me, her voice carefully neutral. "The gold thread or the silver for the final touches?"

I turn from the window, forcing myself back to the present moment. My gown for the ball lies draped across the bed, a cascade of midnight blue silk that shimmers with embedded magic. I trace the intricate embroidery at the collar, where stylized flames will glow when activated in a subtle display of my fire magic, designed to both impress and intimidate our guests.

"Gold."

At a nod from Rhiann, the seamstress begins the delicate work. Around her, the chamber bustles with quiet purpose. Servants arrange jewelry for tonight's feast, prepare the ornate mask I'll wear to the masquerade, and set up kits of makeup. None of them know that a war council's plans lurk beneath these wedding preparations.

Outside, a wild dragon I've never seen before soars overhead, its emerald scales catching the sunlight. Through the dragonbond, it sends down warm, content emotions. While the dragons don't understand weddings, they understand courtship flights. This is close enough to one that they all want to come witness it.

The crowd below gasps and gestures upward. Worry twinges within me for the hatchlings hidden safely away in the mountain cave with their parents.

If our plan fails tomorrow, they'll be among the first targets of divine vengeance.

We cannot fail. We will not fail.

The door opens, and Sterling strolls in, his formal attire doing nothing to hide the tension in his shoulders. His silvery wings are folded tightly against his back, but I can see the tension there, too, and the readiness for flight or fight. His gold-flecked brown eyes meet mine, and for a moment, we're back in each other's arms, dancing beneath a shower of water droplets, pretending the world might not end.

"The Aclarian delegation arrived an hour ago." Sterling points out the window to where they stand. "Fifty strong, including their new regent."

I nod, cataloguing this information with the rest.

We stand in silence, shoulders not quite touching, watching as more visitors stream through the gates. Representatives from every kingdom, drawn by curiosity, politics, and the invitation to witness the Champions Match. Every additional person is another soul to save, another witness to our rebellion against the gods. Another potential casualty.

Once again, the door opens. This time, Agnar enters.

I'm struck immediately by his uncharacteristic solemnity. His usual cheerful irreverence is absent, replaced by something grimmer and more focused. His coppery hair is tied back neatly, his ceremonial armor polished to a high shine. His piercing blue eyes hold none of their usual mischief.

"Against all odds, the Kamorian delegation has just arrived." He closes the door carefully behind him. "And the Devoted are gathering in the squares across the city."

The presence of the cultists, though no surprise,

complicates matters. They'll be watching us, reporting every action back to their divine master.

Out of instinct, I square my shoulders, and my wings respond to my tension by shifting against my clothing. While I can keep my face from displaying emotions, my wings are harder to tame. "We'll give them a show worth remembering."

The servants withdraw, leaving us alone. Agnar turns his back toward us and waits by the door. In this moment of privacy, Sterling's composure slips just a fraction.

He presses his forehead against mine, and our breath mingles in the space between us. "Are you ready, love?"

Am I ready to greet nobles who distrust us, to smile at visitors who've come to gawk, and to dance at a masquerade while plotting treason against the deities who could level our kingdom—our world—in a heartbeat? Am I ready to stand against the gods themselves, to risk everything and everyone I love on a desperate gamble?

Absolutely fucking not. But I will be. "To marry you, yes. Everything else, not in the slightest. But I'm doing it anyway."

"Same." Sterling's lips curve in the softest of smiles before he covers my mouth with his.

Desire coils low in my belly, and for a few seconds, I lose myself in him completely. The way his tongue sweeps in my mouth, teeth grazing my lower lip. The way one hand cradles the nape of my neck, the other tracing leisurely, sensual circles on my lower back. The way his eyes slide shut as he moans and deepens the kiss.

Way too soon, Sterling pulls back a few inches, dragging a breath through clenched teeth. "If we weren't obligated to greet our visitors, there is nothing, and I mean nothing, that would stop me from ripping that dress off of your exquisite body, laying you out on the nearest flat surface, and worshipping every inch of you. I'd start by sliding my tongue—"

By the door, Agnar clears his throat less than discreetly. "Hot as it is to listen to you two get down and dirty, Rhiann says it's time to go."

Sterling's responding growl earns him a laugh from Agnar.

"Okay, then." I head for the door, leaving Sterling to adjust the bulge in his pants. "Let's not keep them waiting."

~

Lark

The world might be ending, yet no one told the royal seamstress.

My gorgeous wedding gown is a miracle of engineering with layers and layers of diaphanous silk dyed in gradients. Pure white at the shoulders and sleeves flows into gold, orange, and then red at the hem, as if a bonfire rose from my ankles and set my bones ablaze. The cut is far more daring than I'd have tried in the past, but if the last year taught me anything, it's that fear is a wasted emotion unless you're running from actual monsters.

I spin in this small salon on the first floor of the palace, and the skirt sighs in a splash of shifting color. After we spent the better part of the morning welcoming our guests, I left my crown in my room. The wedding ceremony isn't about being a queen, only a woman in love.

Rhiann stands behind me, her professional expression forgotten. Today she's helping me not as Lady of the Bedchamber, but as Sterling's only living female family member. According to Tirene custom, the bride gets ready with the female members of both families. Between Sterling and me, we only have Rhiann and Leesa left.

The door creaks.

"Still alive in there?" Leesa pushes inside with a clatter of heels.

The sight of my sister almost undoes me. She's glowing. Radiant. Her olive skin and dark golden blond hair are somehow more luminous than usual, and she's holding—oh gods, please no—a bouquet that could double as a siege weapon. It takes both her arms to hold it up.

At the center, a Fusion Root Vine blooms, while the rest of the arrangement is a riot of blue and violet and those angry yellow bells that the gardener claims are native to our kingdom and nowhere else.

I stare in horror. "Is that just for me?"

"It was so worth it to carry all of these in together. Just to see you freak out like that." Leesa grins before dividing the bouquet into three sections, passing one to Rhiann before handing the largest bundle to me. "They're ready for us if you are."

I breathe a sigh of relief and thank my good fortune— because thanking the gods is at the bottom of my list these days—that I don't have to carry the entirety of the palace gardens in my bouquet.

I'm not ready, of course. But I smile anyway because Leesa is already sniffling, her pregnancy rendering her immune to logic or decorum. "Let's go before you get puffy."

"Damn these hormones." Leesa laughs and dabs her cheeks. "My baby sister is getting married. I just can't believe it. You look so grown up." She takes my arm and leads me toward the corridor, Rhiann following on my other side. "If you trip, I'll never let you live it down."

"Hey, it's your turn next. "I slide a good-natured glare her way. "And I hear payback's a bitch."

If my language offends Rhiann, she doesn't show it. She merely walks quietly beside us, flowers in hand.

Somewhere in the palace, an orchestra is tuning up, their

scales running in nervous spirals. It's ridiculous, how grand
this all is, considering the guest list fits onto a single page. I
almost regret that so few people will ever see this gown, but I
don't regret the rest. If I had to endure a thousand stares, I'd
never make it down the aisle or manage to speak our vows.

Two guards open the doors for us. One is Elijah, eyes wide
and posture stiff. Donovan is the other. The tawny-haired
guard flashes me a warm smile, a genuine gesture that helps
settle my nerves.

With Rhiann and Leesa, I head for the man who will
become my husband.

Agnar and Bastian, the men of our families, flank the path.
The hedges are alive with birds and bees, and about two dozen
chairs occupied mostly by council members line the central
aisle. With the political issues we're mired in, inviting foreign
dignitaries to the wedding ceremony itself is now out of the
question.

My big brother grins, but his eyes appear suspiciously
glassy. "You look radiant. I wish our father was here to see
you."

Or any of the other family members we've lost.

Agnar keeps shooting glances over his shoulder, where
Sterling waits next to the officiant.

My pulse spikes before steadying.

In the gardens, the cobblestone pathway is awash in
afternoon sun.

Sterling stands at the head of our makeshift aisle,
resplendent in layers of white and blue that make his wings
seem almost iridescent. The sight of him sends a shock of
electricity up my spine, and for a second, I'm worried I'll
actually start crying.

Until I see the way his eyes devour every inch of me, as if
he's already undressing me in his head.

My mind goes blank as we walk, save for three competing

sensations. The fragrant breeze, the weight of the bouquet in my hand, and the way Sterling's gaze holds mine all the way down the aisle like a lifeline.

The fountain comes into view, the familiar hedge behind it trimmed in the shape of two dragons.

When we reach the break in the pathway, Bastian pulls Leesa away. Agnar takes Rhiann. Everyone disappears until only Sterling and I are left standing by the fountain.

The officiant, a man with silver hair and a booming voice that could split granite, motions for us to halt. I grasp the hand Sterling offers me. This is the last time I'll hold his hand as his intended.

You sure about this? he mouths. It's not too late to back out.

I squeeze his hand, a knot lodging in my throat as I try to mouth back a response. *So sure.*

The ceremony is mercifully short. We tore out all mentions of the gods. Today of all days, I do not want them looking down on me. Not with blessings, or joy, or anything else.

Today is about Sterling and me.

But most of it's simple, and pure, and more honest than I ever imagined a wedding could be. Sterling speaks first, and he doesn't withhold anything. He trembles a little as he recites the ancient vows. To trust, love, and give me sanctuary in life.

Then it's my turn.

The words sound silly, almost childish, when I say them aloud. But he doesn't look away, not once. Not even when my voice breaks.

"You may kiss to seal your covenant." The master steps back, and before he can finish, Sterling's mouth is on mine, tender and urgent and impossibly sweet. His hand cradles the back of my neck, pulling me close enough that my wings threaten to burst free.

The small crowd erupts in applause, but I don't care. I'm dizzy, high on the contact, and when I open my eyes, my husband's staring at me with the kind of hunger that doesn't belong in a public garden. My cheeks go nuclear. He presses his forehead to mine, and in this moment, though all isn't right in the world, all is right in *our* world.

Rose appears out of nowhere, her arms encircling my waist, her hair shot through with flower petals and the persistent glow of Kin, who's temporarily doubled in size. She doesn't say a word, just peers up at me with wide happy eyes.

I catch Leesa watching us, her cheeks bright with tears. When I meet her gaze, she laughs and wipes her face. "You were always the brave one," she calls. "I just tagged along for the drama."

Sterling looks at me like I've hung a second sun in the sky just for him.

The ball is tonight. In a few hours, we'll have to play royalty again, parade in front of the court, and act as if nothing terrifies us anymore. But for now, there's a soft place to land, and a future with at least one person who will always be in my corner. I glance around at my friends and family and the dragons wheeling in the sky, and I wonder, for a heartbeat, if this is what peace really feels like.

Sterling's hand finds mine, and he squeezes gently. "Ready for the next hundred years?"

I nod, a little terrified, but mostly in love. "Ready as I'll ever be."

Chapter Fifty
Lark

Beneath my mask of gold filigree and flame-colored feathers, I watch the dancers twirl like exotic birds in flight. The masquerade fills our grand ballroom with swirling color and laughter that echoes against the vaulted ceiling.

Light glints off jewelry and sequined masks, off goblets of wine and the dewy skin of revelers who've danced too long without rest.

But everything is a beautiful, joyous lie.

This is our wedding reception, and we can't even dance after the inaugural number. We're stuck on the dais so the guests can come greet us and everyone can see.

Beneath this celebration, time ticks steadily toward tomorrow's confrontation.

My heart counts each second with painful precision.

Sterling stands beside me on the raised dais, resplendent in his pure white suit and simple silver mask.

Swan and phoenix. Two birds who mate for life. One of fire, the other of water.

The music swells, a complex melody played by musicians positioned in the gallery above. Beneath them, our guests dance, drink, and laugh. Nobles from distant kingdoms, merchants wealthy enough to purchase invitations, and representatives from every corner of our world.

Many wear the wings of Tirene's people as part of their costumes, a flattering mimicry that nonetheless causes my own wings to shift restlessly over my gown.

And then the air changes.

It's subtle at first.

A thick bending of light that makes flames in the wall sconces waver. The music continues, but the notes seem to hang longer in the air, stretched like taffy.

My skin prickles with warning.

Something is coming. Something not of this mortal realm.

"Lark." Sterling swivels his head, searching for the danger. My hand instinctively seeks his.

The air between us and the dancers ripples like heat over stone, and reality itself seems to fold inward, creating a space where no space should exist.

From that impossible fold, a figure trailing starlight like a cloak steps out, his perfect features arranged in an expression of amused contempt.

The Guardian.

Warden and protector of the realm of the gods. Not fully divine himself, but more than mortal. Someone who chose to serve the gods rather than humanity. His beautiful eyes hold the cold light of distant stars, and his golden hair seems to glow from within.

Around us, the ball continues, the dancers apparently oblivious to his arrival. A bubble of altered reality separates us from them. We can see the celebration, but the guests cannot see or hear what transpires on the dais.

"Clever." The Guardian's disdainful gaze drifts to me before immediately returning to Sterling, his dismissal obvious.

Dickhead. I summon a smirk. "We're very clever."

"Is that why you're fighting your lover to the death on the morrow?" His tone is full of mockery.

My body stiffens, wings pressing hard against my gown. Sterling strides forward, positioning himself between me and the divine messenger in a protective gesture that prompts the Guardian's lips to twitch with mirth.

"Or maybe you're not fighting him..." With a casual flick of his hand, he tears the fabric of reality. From the resulting rift, he pulls out a scroll that glimmers with the same starlight that clings to his form. "I intercepted your encoded messages to the Northern Kingdoms. They were hidden in trade manifests. Shall we discuss?"

My heart stutters, and I go still. My breath catches somewhere between my lungs and my lips until Sterling squeezes my hand. We sent those messages through our most trusted channels, and encoded them in ways that should have been impenetrable. No one outside our innermost circle should have known about them.

No one.

"Or perhaps," the Guardian shoves the first scroll aside and pulls out another, "we should talk about the supplies you've cached along the Western Ridge? The boats waiting in the cove?" With each revelation, my heart sinks even more. "The prayer strikes?"

All that we planned, every careful preparation, every contingency...he knows it all.

Everything.

Around us, the festivities continue in eerie silence, the dancers waltzing to music we can no longer hear, chortling at jokes we cannot share. Only a few feet of space and an unbridgeable gulf of knowledge separate us.

The Guardian's power, or another's?

He fixes his mocking glare on Sterling. "Such a waste of

potential." His voice drips with false regret. "By aligning with the gods as a guardian, you come closer to the divine." His perfect features contort with disgust. "Instead, you choose to debase yourself with these mortals."

His gaze flicks toward me, and I realize it's not because he thinks I'm unworthy of attention. It's because he doesn't want to risk engaging with me directly. He's wary. Despite everything, this emissary of the gods fears what I might do.

The realization sparks a small ember of hope in the frozen landscape of our compromised plans.

"You have until sunrise." He tucks the scrolls away again, hiding them in the rift. "Stop this foolishness, or I reveal everything to my masters. Zeru's reaction will make Rivlan's threats seem gentle by comparison." He turns as if to leave, then pauses, looking back over his shoulder at Sterling. "Do you know why they chose Lark as your opponent?"

I've never had a shiver get stuck halfway down my spine before. It's just as unsettling as the Guardian's words.

Sterling says nothing, his posture rigid with barely contained fury.

"Not because she could beat you." As expected, he answers his own question. "But because she's the only one you'll never beat. You'll never destroy her." His starlit eyes narrow. "You'll surrender. Ergo, Zeru's gods win."

As if we didn't already guess the reason. The gods really do think we're fools. Apparently, so does the Guardian.

His assessing gaze weighs me. "Though you're not without power. Dragons. Phoenix fire. You guard much." His smile twists. "The gods hate that."

"The gods hate a lot of things." Sterling finally speaks up, his voice steady despite the rage radiating from him.

The Guardian's expression sharpens. "You shouldn't worry about what they hate. You should worry about what they fear. Mortals using their brains...free will...magic." He practically spits out the last word. "The more magic mortals have, the less you need the gods. Honestly, Rivlan offering to return magic was counter to the gods' interests. You mortals might say he's a 'good guy.' As good as a god can be."

"And you?" Sterling raises an eyebrow, his voice lethally quiet. "Are you as good as a guardian can be?"

The Guardian's face hardens, and he snaps his gaze away as if the mere question scalds him. Without another word, he disappears through the portal he came in through.

The bubble of altered reality dissolves. Sound rushes back. Music, laughter, the clink of glasses, the rustle of fabric.

My gaze slides to Sterling, and in his eyes, I find the same cold, heavy understanding that's settling in my stomach. The Guardian is going to expose us—or worse, he's going to destroy us, our friends, our allies, and countless others—in the most devastating ways possible. The Champions Match is only hours away, and our carefully laid plans are unraveling before our very eyes.

"What do we do?" I whisper, though I already know the answer.

Sterling's hand grasps mine, our fingers intertwining with fierce pressure. "We stick with our plan. We fight. We reveal the truth about the gods. We break their hold on this world."

"Even if it's the last thing we do." Last time I died—or thought I did—I did so with quiet acceptance. Going out screaming and fighting sounds like a much better way. More... me.

He nods, his eyes meeting mine with an intensity that halts my breath. "Even then."

Around us, the ball continues, the dancers oblivious to the war being declared in their midst. Tomorrow, Sterling and I will face each other in the Champions Match, not as the pawns the gods intended, but as rebels determined to expose and end divine predation forever.

It's no longer meticulous strategy.

It's desperate defiance.

But maybe that's what we always needed. Not calculation, but the reckless courage to stand against gods with nothing but truth as our weapon.

The last night of the world as we know it stretches before us, filled with music and laughter and the quiet knowledge that by this time tomorrow, everything will have changed.

For better or worse, the age of gods feeding on mortal devotion is coming to an end.

CHAPTER FIFTY-ONE
LARK

The oval arena looms before me like the maw of some ancient beast, terrible in its grandeur in the morning sunlight. I peek through the flap in the military-style tent I've been using to prepare. The stands are already filling with people.

Nobles in their finery claim the better seats, and commoners pack into the higher tiers, all of them buzzing with anticipation for the promised spectacle.

Who the hells dresses up like that for a death match among royals? And these are the people we're fighting to save.

The air itself is different today, charged with something beyond mere excitement. My wings press painfully against my back, and I have to keep shaking them out. I flex my fingers, watching as small flames dance between them. My magic is stronger than it's ever been, probably fueled by fear and determination in equal measure.

This is it. The moment everything changes.

Yesterday may as well have been a fever dream. Sharing vows with Sterling without an altar or any prayers to the gods. The swirling dancers. The starlit intrusion of the Guardian, who left his cold threat hanging in the air between us.

Afterward, I barely slept. I spent all but a few of the remaining hours in frantic consultation with Sterling and the others, revising our already compromised plans and seeking a way forward through the ruins of our thorough preparations.

Grabbing a pitcher of water, I pour a steady stream of the liquid into a basin, watching as the surface ripples and settles. Sterling's element, not mine. He's in his own tent on the opposite side of the arena, prepping for what's to come. We'd have used the same tent, but we wanted to keep up our pretense for the gods.

I wonder if he's as scared as I am.

I splash water on my face, letting it drip down my neck and onto my battle leathers.

Outside, the crowd's murmurs swell into gasps and cries of wonder. I lift the flap of the tent again, peering out at what has caused such a reaction.

They've arrived.

Gods. Actual deities manifesting in physical form and visible to every mortal eye. Even knowing what I do about their true nature, the sight stops my breath.

They materialize in the special section reserved for them. An ostentatious display of cushioned seats beneath silk awnings to block the direct sun. Their forms shimmer and shift, as if reality itself cannot quite contain them.

Even I, who's met a few of them, find myself momentarily awed. What must the crowd feel, seeing their gods in the flesh? The wave of devotion rising from them is almost tangible.

Exactly what the gods wanted. Exactly what they came for.

And there, settling into the central seat with the casual arrogance of one who believes himself entitled to worship, is Zeru himself. He appears mostly human, though inhumanly perfect with his gold skin and eyes that hold the light of distant stars. His powerful divine essence occasionally breaks through. A flash of something too vast to comprehend, too intense to gaze upon directly.

Lesser deities sit on either side of him, each beautiful and frightening in their own way.

Among them is Ziva, my patron goddess, the deity who chose me as her faction's champion. Formed of living flame, her hair is a waving crown of red and gold embers, and her charcoal eyes burn with an internal fire that matches my own. But where the other gods' faces are alight with anticipation, hers is carefully blank, a mask that reveals nothing of her thoughts.

I find myself intensely curious about what she's thinking. Does she regret choosing me? Does she suspect what we're planning? Or is she simply playing her part in this divine charade, another predator waiting for the feast of devotion our battle will provide?

The crowd's reaction to the gods' manifestation is a study in human nature. Some fall to their knees, prayers spilling from their lips. Others stand transfixed, tears streaming down their faces at the beauty and terror before them. Many simply stare, open-mouthed, unable to process the reality of what they're seeing.

Some faces even look doubtful and wary...just not nearly as many as we'd hoped. Either Barnaby didn't play for enough people or his lyrics failed to elicit the desired response.

And through it all runs an undercurrent of excitement that borders on hysteria. The manic energy of people witnessing what they once thought impossible.

Perfect conditions for the gods to feed.

All that emotion, all that devotion, flows toward them like rivers to the sea.

There's also the constant hum of anticipation. They're waiting for us. Sterling and me, the champions, the entertainers in this divine spectacle.

They don't know they're about to witness not just a battle, but a rebellion. Not just a match, but a revelation that will shake the foundations of their faith.

My eyes slide shut, and I summon every scrap of courage I possess. I think of Sterling, of his steady presence beside me through every impossible situation we've faced. I think of my sister, who's been the dearest—and often only—friend I've had. I think of Bastian, the sibling I didn't know I needed and the best brother anyone could ask for. I think of Agnar, of the way he's stood by me without question, even during Sterling's corruption.

I think of little Rose, so young and full of life. I think of our friends, our allies, scattered throughout the arena in strategic positions, ready to play their parts in what's to come. I think of Tirene, my kingdom, and all the people who depend on me to protect them.

I think of the future that hangs in the balance. A world free from divine predation, where humans determine their own fate without gods feeding on their devotion like parasites.

When I open my eyes again, the fear is still present. I'd be a fool not to be afraid. But it's been pushed to the background, overtaken by determination. This is what Sterling and I have been working toward since we unveiled the truth. This is what all our planning, all our secret meetings, all our careful preparations have been leading to.

A deep, resonant gong cuts through the noise of the crowd.

My cue.

This is it. Ten minutes until the Champions Match begins. And with it, our rebellion against the heavens.

Chapter Fifty-Two
Sterling

The leather strap bites into my palm as I wrench it tight, securing the last piece of my armor. My hands should be cold with fear, but I only notice a strange numbness. Like my body already comprehends it's moving toward something far beyond normal.

Outside the tent's canvas walls, a wave of excitement swells. Thousands of eager people chatter, all here to watch me kill my wife or die trying.

Icy wrath flows through me, cold and relentless.

If the gods or anyone gathered here to view this shit show thinks I'll harm a hair on Lark's head for the "good of humanity," they're delusional. Over and over, she's chosen me, chosen to love me. She's accepted every part of me, good and bad. Forgiven me when anyone else would have left.

If any god so much as lays a finger on Lark, I'll destroy them. Every. Fucking. One.

She's the woman I love more than life itself. I need her more than the air I breathe and the water I wield.

She's mine.

A ripple disturbs the air beside me, like heat over stone. I don't have to glance up. I've been expecting this visit.

"Ready to make history, my champion?" Rivlan's voice carries the casual confidence of a being who's watched civilizations rise and fall like tides.

I continue adjusting my chest plate, testing its weight against my wings. "What do you think?"

"Touchy today, I see." The elemental god's form solidifies enough to cast a faint shadow across the tent floor. His appearance is more settled today, less fluid than usual. A calculated choice, I'm sure, to seem more relatable. More trustworthy.

I stay silent, because what is there to say? If Rivlan really thinks I'm about to fight my own wife, he's an idiot.

His attention shifts to the open flap of my tent, where sunlight cuts a bright rectangle into the dim interior. The noise of the crowd swells, rolling in like waves against a cliff. "Quite a mortal crowd gathering."

A song breaks out somewhere in the stands and is quickly taken up by hundreds of voices. A wedding song, ironically. For a new husband who is about to face his wife on the battlefield.

"Yes." I yank another leather strap tight enough to leave marks on my skin. The pain helps center me. "We invited them."

Rivlan spins toward me, his watery form losing cohesion before snapping back into human shape. "You...fool." The word spills from him like poison. "That only serves Zeru. We discussed this. Keeping the match contained. Limiting witnesses—"

"Why?" I finally look up, locking my gaze on him. "Why was that so important?"

Rivlan's form swirls, but he offers no reply.

The silence stretches between us, marked only by the

distant roars of the crowd as another dignitary is announced. I can almost see him calculating, weighing how much to reveal, how much to conceal.

I turn away to reach for the shield leaning against a wooden chest. It's beautifully crafted, inlaid with silver that matches my wings. A weapon created for spectacle as much as protection.

"Those diamonds you gave us as a wedding gift..." I run my fingers along the shield's edge, testing its sharpness. "They need to stay cold, don't they?"

A pause. Slight, but there.

"Of course." Rivlan's voice is smooth as polished stone. "All precious things require proper care."

"Proper preservation, you mean." I spin back around to face him. "Like frost on a window. Like crystals in a temple... or a portal." I wait a beat. "Like frozen devotion."

The temperature plummets.

Water droplets materialize in the air between us, suspended like perfect little beads of glass. Rivlan's expression shifts into something more inhuman. His smile stretches too far back on his face. A reminder that beneath his careful mimicry of mortal form lies something powerful and ancient.

"Clever. But that's why I chose you." He gestures dismissively. "What does it matter now? The die is cast. The decisions made."

"Let me spell it out for you, Rivlan. You may be a god, but I hold the dice." I set down the shield with deliberate care. "And I know everything. I know you harvest devotion. I know you stockpile it like winter preserves." I step closer, my magic responding to my rising anger, ice materializing beneath my feet with each step. "Tell me, do we taste different when we're fresh versus frozen?"

The god pales. "Don't be ridiculous—"

"Is that what I'm being?" I cut him off, my voice

dangerously quiet. "Because I've seen your crystals pulse. Seen them feed." The hanging water droplets between us begin to crystallize, reflecting our faces in countless miniature mirrors. "You didn't just want a champion. You wanted a guardian's devotion on tap. Premium vintage, is that it?"

Rivlan shivers like sunlight on water. Something flashes across his features. Frustration, perhaps. Or fear. "You need me. The other gods—"

"Are worse?" My laugh sounds harsh in the confined space. I point to where the stands are on the other side of the heavy canvas walls. "Maybe. But at least they didn't pretend to be my ally while planning to feed off my power."

"I gave you a gift!" Rivlan expands, filling more of the tent with his presence. The walls grow damp. "The gift of magic—"

"You gave me a larger storage container!" Water explodes from nearby vessels. The washing basin, the drinking pitcher, even the moisture in the air freezes into jagged patterns around us. The tent walls creak under the pressure of sudden ice. "Were you going to tell me? That if we used those diamonds in the future to restore magic, I'd be feeding you too?"

Rivlan draws himself up, dignity settling across his features like a familiar mask. "The diamonds have naught to do with devotion. They are clean. Crystals can be used to store many things." His voice softens, attempting to soothe. "And I gave them at great risk to myself."

The crowd outside roars again. Someone important has arrived. Lark? One of the gods? We're running out of time.

"How much risk?" My voice rises despite my efforts to control it. "Being killed? Killing someone you love? Fighting the woman you love to the death?" I invade his space, each question landing like a blow. "Was it that risky? The only risk you took was that I would reject your offer."

"You cannot see all things, Knox." Rivlan's voice takes on

the resonant quality of deep water, a reminder of his true nature. "And I am not bound to explain them to you."

I consider my next move carefully. The ice spreads farther across the ground, climbing the central support pole in delicate, translucent patterns.

My magic has never flowed so freely, never responded so instinctively to my emotions. "Exactly how much power does a guardian have?"

Rivlan blanches. Or whatever the equivalent is for a being made of water and divine essence. His form becomes less distinct, the edges blurring as if he's preparing to retreat.

This, I realize with sudden clarity, was always the risk the gods took.

Not that we would discover their feeding. Not that we would resent it. But that a mortal would actually seize the power they have access to through their connection to the divine.

I am that mortal Or close enough.

Moving to the weapon rack in the center of the tent, I lift a massive sword that glints in the dim light. It's ceremonial, meant for show rather than actual combat, but it emphasizes my point. The blade catches what little light filters through the pavilion walls, tossing it back in cold flashes.

"You're going to fight." It's not a question. Rivlan's form settles again, resignation evident in his posture. We both know the stakes haven't changed.

"Oh, I'm going to fight." The sword is light in my hand, as if my newfound understanding has altered the physical world itself. "But not as your champion. As Tirene's guardian. As Lark's husband. As myself."

Power thrums through my veins, not borrowed or gifted, but claimed. I see now what the gods have always feared, why they needed the devotion of mortals. They've forgotten what humans are capable of when not constrained by artificial limitations, by divine manipulation.

"The diamonds—" Rivlan begins, a note of urgency entering his voice.

"Can stay frozen." I turn away to gather my final pieces of armor. "Like all your carefully preserved power." I glance back over my shoulder, offering him a smile sharp enough to cut. "Better hurry. I hear there's a famine coming."

Rivlan's form flickers, indecision evident in his constantly shifting appearance. For a minute, I think he might attack me. Preserve his plans through force. But that would reveal too much too soon.

Instead, he begins to fade, his essence thinning until he's barely visible. "You play a dangerous game, Knox. The other gods will not be as forgiving as I have been."

"Forgiveness implies guilt." I buckle on my sword belt. "And I have nothing to feel guilty about."

His presence vanishes entirely, leaving only a lingering chill in the air. I stand alone in the pavilion, ice melting slowly around me as my emotions settle. The confrontation has left me strangely lighter, unburdened in a way I haven't been since I first learned the truth about the gods' feeding.

I gather my shield, placing it on my arm. The weight, balanced against the sword at my hip, is right. Outside, the noise of the crowd has reached a fevered pitch. They're ready for blood, for spectacle, for the divine drama they've been promised.

They want a fucking show?

We'll give them one.

CHAPTER FIFTY-THREE
LARK

Morning sunlight slices across the arena and beyond, casting a golden shimmer across Tirene's western shore. Thousands of voices wash over me, their expectation a vise clamped around my heart.

I'm on the west side of the stadium. Sterling's on the east, with water droplets already forming in the air around him.

Agnar and his team managed to lift and solidify a section of earth large enough to host a fighting ring almost the same size and shape as one of the training fields in the capital. Three dragons wide and at least four times as long.

Waves from the ocean crash in the distance, lapping and foaming against the jagged Storm Cliffs.

The roar of the crowd crashes into me like a tidal wave. It's a horrible replica of my first introduction to Chirean and Dame and my reunion with Leesa. Shoved into an arena where only a dragoncaller had a hope of surviving.

I'd give my left big toe to be facing dragons instead of gods right now.

The tiered stands wrap the entire field, with openings in the corner where people still stream in. Entrepreneurs are already moving through aisles, hawking food, drinks, and even tiny flags marked with fire or water sigils.

Like this is a festival and not a death match.

Though I do my best to shove the fear aside, ice floods my veins. Too much rides on today's outcome.

Our future. Our very lives. Our existence as we know it.

Above the stands, even the sky is thick with onlookers. Tirene's winged people hover, accompanied by others on the backs of gracefully gliding alicorns.

A thrilling sight to many.

But one that churns my stomach.

Just last night, I pleaded with the dragons to stay far away from today's fight. After Ziva's threats, I couldn't put them at risk.

I'm still terrified. I feel their absence like a phantom limb and miss the reassurance that proximity to their massive, powerful bodies provides.

How much will we lose today?

The arena stretches before me, an open expanse of hard-packed earth ringed by layers upon layers of spectators. Their excitement envelops me like an oppressive blanket, thick and suffocating. The gods' section gleams with an unnatural light.

Crystals grow, radiating from each deity.

An active harvest blooming right in front of everyone. And yet, no one thinks twice about it. No one questions the gods and their actions.

My stomach flips at the sight, disgust tightening my lips. What they're doing is vile.

Movement catches my attention. A flash of black clothing and predatory grace.

Sterling is heading for the center of the arena toward a strange ornate weapon rack. Just from a first glance, I can tell that no human crafted these weapons. Must be a "gift" from the gods, which means I should keep my distance.

No gift from the deities comes without a price.

To continue the ruse, I head for the god-fashioned weapons despite the sword, daggers, and bow already in my possession. I force myself to breathe, pushing aside the tide of noise and the swirling anxieties that threaten to drown me.

My heart pounds a frantic rhythm, yet I focus only on him, my tether amidst the chaos, as I cross the field.

Sterling's gaze never falters.

It's as if the world has fallen away, leaving only the two of us against the spectacle the gods have orchestrated.

His magic swells, infusing the air with cool anticipation. His intense eyes lock onto mine, piercing through the noise and doubt and igniting warmth in my chest.

There's something feral about him. Primal.

His magic, his very essence, calls to me even as terror constricts my lungs.

The crowd's chanting begins to rise again. It grows louder and louder as they holler his name and mine with thunderous fervor. People I've never met are taking sides in this debacle. Do they even know what they're cheering for?

Probably not.

But they will.

Soon.

The question is, will they still choose a side when they learn the stakes?

Between us, at the center of the field, the godly weapons in the rack gleam. Swords, axes, spears, bows...blue and red of each to indicate the element it was created from. Offerings from Ziva and Rivlan. My eyes land on the elegant fire blade meant for me, its hilt wrapped with intricate motifs of phoenix feathers.

A beautiful trap.

I clench my jaw before returning my attention to the gods.

Zeru lounges in his seat while stars eddy around him like a dazzling but dangerous mantle of power.

He's toned down his appearance to better pass as human. Bronze gold skin, sparkling white teeth, square jawline. A swirling design of deep purples and blacks and streaks of yellow, blue, and pink adorn his robes, as if the seamstress captured the cosmos and manipulated it into fabric.

Nyc sits on Zeru's left. The goddess has smooth dark skin, and an aura of darkness surrounds her. It's difficult to discern her features until she turns and I catch a glimpse of her profile.

Ziva's scarlet robe is a flickering flame, dancing up and down her body, lashing out at any who come too close. Hallr, seated next to her, doesn't seem to care. The God of Mountains ignores her flame, his caramel skin covered in granite gray robes.

Other gods fill the stands, some who I recognize and others I don't.

The Devoted, seated along the bottom row as close as they can get to the gods, touch their star-marks with reverence. Nobles and commoners alike crane their necks to witness the unfolding drama, waiting to hear from their gods most likely for the first time in their lives.

The gods we're defying.

Fear rushes through me like wind over a drought-stricken field. Yet amidst the terror, within the storm of my uncertainty, a flicker of excitement ignites.

Sterling strides closer.

A feral grin breaks across his face.

The raw power radiating from him steals my breath. Tiny hairs prickle on the back of my neck. Even the roar of the crowd—an irrelevant backdrop to the connection we share—fades as I approach him.

Time distorts around us, drawing out the moment.

Heart thundering inside my chest, wings raised with

anticipation, we wait. As champions, we face the gods and the desperate hopes of our people. Our magic billows, fire meeting water in the heart of this arena, poised to defy the predatory whims of the deities who dare to manipulate us.

The chanting resumes as people shout our names and cry out to the gods. I remember standing before my people during my coronation. How they reacted to my words, to my speech. But now isn't the time for words.

A hushed silence descends over the crowd.

No more waiting. It's time for action.

CHAPTER FIFTY-FOUR
STERLING

The amphitheater thrums as the crowd chants, the stands packed with bodies as I head for the middle of the arena to start the fight. Over the stands, throngs of Tirenese people fly and hover, waiting to see what will happen with their monarchs. Alicorns dot the skies, and people from various kingdoms jostle for a good view.

The dragons are visibly absent. Though Lark sent them away because of Ziva's threats, I wouldn't be surprised if they're somewhere nearby but out of sight.

Through the roars of the crowd, Lark moves with the dignity of a queen and the resolve of a warrior, each step bringing her closer to our shared destiny. Her golden eyes lock onto mine with an intensity that steals my breath.

She's fucking magnificent.

In this moment, with thousands of eyes upon us and deities looming from their crystal-lined dais, I can think only of how much has changed since we met. How Lark has transformed from a sharp-tongued fledgling to a queen who faces gods without flinching. A woman who stands toe-to-toe with the universe itself and refuses to bow. The spark that once flickered inside her has spread into a raging inferno.

Pride that borders on pain swells in my chest.

I've known warriors, kings, men and women who commanded respect through fear or birthright. But Lark commands it through the sheer force of who she is.

And she chose me. Despite my betrayal. Despite our foundation being built on lies. Despite all my fuck ups. She still chose me.

We meet in the center of the arena where the weapon rack of beautiful blades forged by divine hands glints in the morning light, each imbued with power matching our magical affinities.

Tools of slaughter dressed as gifts.

A glaive of ice, a long swordlike blade attached to a pole as long as my wingspan and marked with Rivlan's sigil, catches the sun, gleaming with deadly intent.

Its power calls to mine.

Repulsed and angry, my magic flares before I can control it. There's a twitch along Lark's jaw that lets me know she's just as disgusted. She turns away from the weapons, raising her face to the gods.

I turn with her, ignoring the rack.

Zeru rises to his feet, sending the Devoted huddled on the stands below the gods into a fanatic frenzy of fawning. Stars dance around him in a dazzling display of power. The other gods lean forward, waiting for him to say or do something.

They have no idea what's coming.

A strange sensation creeps over me, raising the hairs on the back of my neck. As if someone's watching us. Which is weird, because everyone *is* watching us. We're putting on a show for the entire world.

Goose bumps cover Lark's arms, and she casts a subtle glance at me. She feels it too.

"We need to get Zeru to admit why we're all here." I hope the gods can't hear me shouting over the roar of the crowd.

Lark's lips curl into a smile that's both beautiful and dangerous, her eyes alight with malicious intent. "Then let's piss him off. Gods hate it when their toys don't behave."

We survey the stands, our hands clasped tightly together. I feel the weight of divine attention pressing down on us from the raised dais. Zeru's starlight gaze burns with impatience. Rivlan, dressed in a flowing white tunic and white breeches, tracks our every move, features so tense he could be chiseled from stone. Ziva's charcoal black eyes watch Lark with an emotion I can't quite parse.

I lift my foot and kick the weapon rack over with a single decisive motion. Sacred weapons clatter across the dirt, their metallic song echoing through the now silent arena.

The crowd's collective intake of breath feels like a physical force against my skin.

"We won't be playing your game!" I point directly at Zeru, abandoning all pretense of reverence. "This spectacle is built on lies and threats."

Zeru pulsates with anger, his form fluctuating between a golden human appearance and glimpses of his cosmic reality, a being of stars and void, ancient beyond comprehension. "The covenant dictates—"

"That covenant is between gods." My nerves tingle with reckless satisfaction at the shock that flutters across his perfect features as I cut him off. "No human signed it. We're not bound by your arrangements."

"You came willingly." Stars swirl around Zeru like a mane. "Champions must be willing participants. That is the law."

"Willing, my ass." Lark's laugh is sharp enough to cut glass. "You threatened to sink Tirene beneath the waves if we refused. You threatened to kill every man, woman, and child in the palace. Every animal, including my beloved dragons. You said you'd erase us from existence, including the island itself. That's the only reason we're here today."

The gods glance at each other, but only Zeru and Rivlan, both angry and indignant, seem affected by her words. The others simply stare with open curiosity, like they're eager to see how this plays out.

The crowd's whispers grow louder while an undercurrent of unease spreads through the stands. Faces stamped with rising confusion and concern shift toward each other, seeking answers.

"Is that true?" An elderly Meridian nobleman with salt-and-pepper hair curled into perfect rings stands on shaky legs to address Zeru. "Did your gods threaten to destroy their kingdom? Their people? That's genocide!"

Before Zeru can respond, I press further. "We don't know what the inter-deity conflict is or who's fighting who. Yet we're supposed to be your champions? How can I possibly choose a side when I don't know what the sides are? You have set it up so I might be fighting against my own best interests, against those of all mortals."

The murmurs in the crowd become louder.

Devotion, carefully cultivated over centuries, begins to waver in the face of uncomfortable questions. The invisible tributaries of faith that feed into the glittering formations beside the gods' seats slow and thin.

Zeru's perfect features contort with fury. "You speak of things you cannot understand. You stand on a precipice of knowledge not meant for your kind."

"And yet here we are because you and your kind forced us." Lark's gesture encompasses us and the pile of discarded gifts. "Not as pawns, but as players. Not as champions, but as accusers."

"We do so because we understand more than you wanted us to." I lift my arm and my magic surges stronger than ever, as if my defiance of Rivlan somehow unlocked new channels of power.

Water rises from the ground in crystalline patterns, identical to the formations that started appearing in temples across the world. The same ones that began growing around the arena once the gods arrived. They stand on display, refracting sunlight into rainbow ribbons across the dirt.

Gasps rise from the crowd.

They've seen these formations before. In their places of worship, in sacred groves, beside altars where they've knelt in prayer.

"For too long, these crystals have been growing in your temples. They appear where prayer is strongest, where devotion flows most freely." Lark's eyes sweep across the amphitheater. "Perhaps you were told they were signs of divine favor."

"They are harvesting equipment." I scowl, my voice hard with certainty. "The gods have been fighting each other, and that conflict is what caused the strange occurrences you've all witnessed. Temples moving overnight, sacred waters transforming into crystal, divine animals attacking villages. In order to stop those happenings, we agreed to fight in this match. Until we learned that by doing so, we would be hosting a feast for the gods."

Lark's wings shift, the gold streaks gleaming. "They manufactured this battle to frighten you into praying harder, into devoting yourselves more completely. Because the gods gain power from your faith and fear. They feed on us. On our prayers. And by making things worse for us, they receive even more devotion, more food, more power."

"Lies!" Zeru's stars swirl in a violent path around him, mocking the human form he's trying to maintain. "These misguided fools are trying to sway you from the proper path of devotion."

Beside him, the other gods shift uncomfortably, some avoiding the direct gaze of the crowd, others staring defiantly back. Only Rivlan stares directly at me, his eyes unreadable.

"You are nothing without us." I point at Zeru directly. "Divine parasites feeding on human devotion."

"Preposterous!" Zeru's voice booms across the arena. "We shaped this world. We granted you magic. We—"

"Look for yourselves!" I gesture at the crystalline formations situated near the gods' section. "Those crystals were growing and pulsing when you entered the arena, when the crowd gasped in awe at your divine presence. But they've been still since we began speaking. Since the truth pushed your faithful audience toward doubt instead of devotion. The harvest slowed, and so did the growth of the crystals."

Lark steps forward, her eyes flashing gold as her fire magic responds to her emotions. "Let me demonstrate. Join me, people of Tirene and beyond, as I pray to Aletheia, Goddess of Light and Truth!" She points to the goddess in the stands whose porcelain skin contrasts with chestnut hair and bright green eyes.

A murmur runs through the crowd, and heads swivel to study the formations with anxious eyes.

Lark lifts her hands skyward. "Great Aletheia, reveal whether what we speak is truth. Show your faithful followers the reality of divine hunger!"

The people rise, lips moving as they pray.

The crystals beside Aletheia, a goddess who has remained silent throughout our confrontation, begin to pulse. Light trickles through them. Before the crowd's astonished eyes, they grow, extending delicate, transparent branches that reach toward Lark and the spectators like hungry leeches.

The reaction is immediate.

Gasps of horror. Cries of betrayal.

Prayers die on trembling lips.

Aletheia herself says nothing, but her sad, serene expression speaks volumes. She does not deny our accusations. The Goddess of Light and Truth cannot lie, not through words or actions.

Instead, she sits still, her alabaster skin shining brighter as she's fed.

"Enough! What does it matter if we draw strength from your devotion? It is the natural order. Gods rule. Humans serve. You exist to sustain us." Zeru's naked admission sends shock sweeping through the crowd.

Even the doubters gape in horror.

Time slows as the people process the deity's words.

Zeru's eyes become incandescent with rage.

Then his fury explodes.

The irate god slams his foot down, creating a forceful wave that crashes over everyone in the arena. The stands groan in protest. "We were here first. We shaped this world. You know nothing of what we are, what we've sacrificed!"

My own anger courses through me, heating my blood. "We know that you've pushed us too far by forcing us to kill each other." I gesture between Lark and myself. "That's too much to ask. We will not. Fucking. Do it."

Zeru thrusts a finger in our direction. "You are bound by the covenant. You will fight."

White-hot miniature stars spiral across the stadium.

The screaming crowd ducks in horror.

I cock my head to the side, sharing a look with Lark. "Are you a willing participant? Ready to fight as a champion in this death match?"

Lark lifts her chin, eyes burning gold with power and defiance. "I am most definitely not willing. I was pushed into this farce under threat of genocide against my people."

"As was I." I turn back to face Zeru. "The covenant

requires willing champions. Since we don't meet the criteria, can't we withdraw our consent?"

Though I don't know why I bother attempting to clarify. It's not as if the gods are particularly trustworthy.

Zeru's perfect face contorts with mounting fury. "If you will not fight for the gods, then you will fight the gods themselves."

The crowd scrambles in terror, people pushing and shoving against each other in an attempt to flee. Children cry out, clinging to their parents. Wings flare in panic as some try to fly skyward only to hit an invisible barrier that now encases the entire arena.

"We expected as much." Lark holds out her hand, slender fingers steady despite everything. "Ready to merge our powers and show them who they're playing with?"

If this is a bluff to get the God of the Heavens to stand down, it's a damn good one.

Zeru's fury falters for a heartbeat, uncertainty flickering across his features. The gods shift nervously, exchanging glances that contain entire conversations.

Their sudden apprehension isn't lost on the crowd.

The mortals pause their efforts to escape and watch with renewed interest.

"You cannot." There's a note in Zeru's voice I've never heard before. Fear. "The convergence of opposing elements during a Champions Match is forbidden."

"Oh, I assure you, we can." Lark's smile is lethal.

Our magics, more powerful than ever before, begin to mingle. The air around us shimmers with heat and moisture, creating a hazy aura that sparkles with possibility. This is what Bastian called our "long shot." The loophole in the covenant he'd discovered in his research.

If Lark and I merge, we become one champion instead of two.

If one dies, we both die.

Neither can win...which means no gods can claim victory through us. Our union nullifies the covenant, rendering their divine game unplayable. It doesn't solve the larger issue. They could still force us into a fight.

But our union buys us time.

It gives us leverage.

And keeps the lesser gods frozen in their seats, all eyeing Zeru.

Zeru raises his hand, comet-fueled fire gathering at his fingertips. "Stop this abomination!"

I pull Lark closer, feeling her wings unfurl against my own as we stand shoulder to shoulder, facing Zeru's wrath. Water and fire rise around us in a spiraling vortex of elemental fury. Not as opposing forces, but as complementary ones stronger together than apart.

Just like us.

Zeru's swirling ball of cosmic energy jets toward us, destroying everything in its wake.

Chapter Fifty-Five
Rose

I hide under the wooden seats of the big arena. People shout all around me. Weapons clash and magic ripples through the air like a giant storm just out of reach. I know I should be brave like Lark or Uncle Agnar, but I'm so scared.

Tears stream down my cheeks as I squeeze Kin tight against my shoulder. My friend's tiny fire warms me, but I still feel like I'm drowning in panic.

I should've stayed with Mama.

She said we had to meet up with everyone else in case we had to leave in a hurry. My mama won't be happy when she realizes I've left her side. But I want to be near Lark in case she needs me.

Noise wraps around me like Uncle Agnar's coat, too big and too heavy. It's hard to breathe. To get enough air. All the people are talking about things I don't understand. I peek through the slats with wide eyes and watch the gods yell at Lark and Knox. Uncle Agnar instructed me to stay behind in the city today. But I didn't listen to him either.

Now I really wish I had.

Kin hovers near my head, the flame flickering in a crazy

sort of dance. The warm glow contrasts with the cold running through my bones. As I cover my face with my hands, I can feel Kin's heat growing.

"Not now." I press my palms to my eyes. I can't afford to cry. Tears won't do me any good. Crying won't help Lark or Knox or Uncle Agnar. It won't help anyone.

But Kin keeps pulsing.

Three big flashes. Then three small. And then three more big ones.

Just when I think the flashing has stopped, it happens again.

Three big, three small, three big. A pause. Then again.

I know that pattern. It means something...something big.

"Save our souls," I whisper.

That lesson is one I will never forget. Uncle Agnar's told me lots of stories. Tales of bravery about my great grandfather, who used to travel the world and knew all kinds of things.

S-O-S was the signal people would send when they were stuck or needed aid.

"How do I signal, Kin?"

Kin cocoons me, and the hug chases away the cold, making me all warm and bright.

I'm not afraid anymore.

With a deep breath, I close my eyes, pushing past the last little bits of my fear. The flame offers me comfort.

And something else. Just a flutter at first, like Mama's wings when I scare her.

Then it gets bigger.

And bigger.

My eyes pop open.

"Lark will be so happy!"

So happy, in fact, that surely she won't be upset with me for sneaking in.

CHAPTER FIFTY-SIX
LARK

We brace for impact.

As Zeru's comet hurtles toward us, my skin prickles with the approaching heat. My magic rises instinctively to meet it, all fear forgotten as the battle begins.

A big enough explosion could knock it away, but I doubt I could accomplish that in time. Instead, I thicken the fire on my right wing, shifting to shield Sterling and myself with it.

An earthen mound shoots skyward, flinging the comet into the heavens where it belongs.

"Did you think we'd let you have all the fun?"

I know that voice.

Agnar charges out onto the arena floor, coppery hair tied back, face set with fierce determination that can't quite hide the reckless grin beneath. "I didn't expect these bastards to play by the rules. If they don't have to, we don't have to either."

In true Agnar fashion, he raises one hand and gives Zeru the middle finger.

I'm not sure whether to laugh or scream at the crazy bastard for having such a blatant death wish. The impulse to protect him wars with the overwhelming relief of having reinforcements. My heart twists with both emotions, settling on neither as I open my mouth to respond.

Words die in my throat as more figures emerge from around the stands.

Bastian crosses the field with the grace of a soldier, eyes burning with protective fury. Leesa walks beside him, dark golden blond hair braided and ready for battle.

My stomach knots, fear taking root for my very pregnant, very magicless sister.

Behind them, as formal and composed as if he were attending a council meeting, Rafe strides forward, strapped to the teeth with weapons.

"It's a family affair now." Leesa bumps my shoulder with hers. There's a bow in her hands and a full quiver on her back. On her hip is the magic-imbued sword. At least she came armed. "The baby and I won't survive if we don't end this, so don't give me shit about being pregnant."

With a heavy sigh, I clamp my mouth shut, the argument dying on my lips. She has a point.

"You really thought we'd let you do this alone?" Bastian clasps Sterling's forearm before addressing me, the usual warmth missing from his eyes. "After everything we've been through?"

They're here.

They've walked into the path of divine wrath.

For us.

The realization, both terrifying and heartening, hits hard.

Sterling's hand finds mine, our fingers intertwining as naturally as breathing. "While we had to make a show as the named champions, I'm so fucking glad to have you all here."

"Think we scared them?" Agnar raises his eyebrows.

The earth wall still stands between us and the gods' section, but it won't hold forever.

Cracks are already forming.

"Six mortals putting all their secrets on display? Probably. They should be shaking in their seats." Despite his calm demeanor, there's a tremor in Rafe's voice.

"They are scared." I remember Zeru's expression just before he attacked. "I saw it in Zeru's eyes. He's angry, but also afraid of what we can do."

They all gawk at me.

"Why would gods fear humans?" Leesa's brow furrows in confusion. "They're immortal, near-omnipotent beings who've shaped our world since its creation."

I shake my head. "They're not entirely immortal, remember? Narc's dead. He was mid-resurrection when I incinerated him after my blood dripped on his remains."

Pride gleams in Sterling's eyes. "And that was before you improved upon your strength with the guardian training."

"So what you're saying," Agnar's blue eyes glow with maniacal glee, "is that we might actually stand a chance against them."

"Sterling is stronger than ever. I am too. We might only be six mortals standing against gods, but together we're more powerful than any of them want us to know. That's why Zeru attacked. He's afraid of what we might become if we fully merge our elements."

Sterling nods, his expression shifting into a grim mask of resolve. "Five mortals and one guardian. A person who is halfway between the gods and humans."

There's a brief silence as we all absorb this. Sterling has never fully claimed this identity before, this liminal state between mortal and divine. It changes things, knowing one of our own straddles that boundary.

Agnar throws back his head and laughs. A sound of pure, reckless defiance that rings out across the arena floor. "I like our odds, brother." He claps Sterling on the shoulder.

A sharp crack splits the air.

The earthen wall Agnar created shatters, spewing chunks of compacted soil.

From the stands, Zeru glares. His form expands to become vaster than the stars. More remote. Almost too alien for human minds to comprehend.

"Once again, mortals fail to understand." His voice is no longer a single sound but a convergence of pitches that make my teeth ache and my bones vibrate. The air around him bends and warps, our realm struggling to contain his rage. "The covenant is clear. Champions will fight, one way or another."

As he speaks, the other gods begin to vacate their seats. They don't walk or fly.

They simply cease to be in one place and appear in another, materializing in front of us in a loose arc.

Valk, Goddess of War, lands with the cry of thousands of ravens, which suddenly fill the air above the field. Gone is the thin woman who sat quietly in the stands. Now she's a veritable mountain, her strength obvious even with much of her body covered in metal armor.

When Hallr lurches forward, the ground trembles in response to his presence. Terro joins him, the God of Earth a formidable force draped in moss-colored robes that end at the knee. Thick leather bracers cover his muscular arms.

Nyc, a vast pillar of darkness, stands silent. If she's moving, I can't tell.

In sharp contrast, the flames wreathing Ziva snap and crackle with eagerness.

The air shimmers, making me think Gallera, Goddess of Air, is somewhere among them as well.

Others join their side of the field, gods whose names I know from childhood prayers and myths, their true forms far more terrible than any statue or painting could depict.

Above us, the air flickers and tears. From behind the swirling energy, creatures begin to manifest. Twisted amalgamations of light and star-filled skies. Creatures from the heavens or below. Some I have no name for.

One, a twisting, shadowy, smoky...thing, reminds me way too much of the drachen.

Others are known sacred animals to the gods, like the ravens are to Valk. Sylphs, cave cats, golems, what appears to be an entire family of pangolins, and stallions with spear-like horns and sharp fangs.

Too many nightmarish creatures to count.

The sea on the far side of the arena heaves as tentacles as wide as barrels lift from the water.

Above the ravens, the sky darkens and clouds form. In response, angry eyes glare down on us.

As if fighting a bunch of pissed off gods wasn't enough.

In the stands, the crowd erupts in aghast screams as the cosmic horror streaks toward us. Tendrils whip out, scarring the field. An opening forms in the blob, and a hissing roar echoes out. My lungs shake while a wave of nausea ripples through me.

Agnar twirls a finger, forming a massive ball of muddy earth and hurling it down the monster's throat. "Oh, shut your yap!"

And just like that, the first colossal creature is defeated.

Choking on the mud or pinned into place by the weight of it.

Animals, gods, and monsters of the deep race toward us.

"Merge." Bastian bends over to pick up a heavy shield from the tipped over rack. "All of us, now! It's our only chance."

Normally this many people merging would require a ritual and Fusion Root Vine tea to help facilitate the bond. Except we've already merged together for sparring. Our powers know each other. Agnar's earth, Bastian's fire, Rafe's air, Sterling's water. My own flames burn higher and brighter than ever before, and with my expanding power, I can now merge with another fire elemental while protecting us both from any dangerous repercussions.

We choose to stand together, not from fear or obligation, but from love.

It's time to show the gods what that kind of power can do.

CHAPTER FIFTY-SEVEN
STERLING

Our magic rushes together like rivers converging into a single devastating flood. Fire, water, earth, and air amplifying and building into something that makes my very bones hum.

I've never felt anything like this before, not even when Lark and I merged with the others in the past.

This is different. Vaster. More practiced.

Five consciousnesses touching at the edges while remaining distinct. The sensation is at once intoxicating and terrifying, like flying through a hailstorm.

Through this connection, I feel Lark's fierce determination, Bastian's protective fury, Agnar's reckless courage, and even Rafe's calculating precision. All of it feeds into a swirling vortex of power with me at its center.

Though Leesa doesn't have access to her magic and isn't part of the merge, she stands with us shoulder to shoulder, her face a mask of firm resolve as she wields her fire magic-imbued sword.

From the corner of my eye, I flinch as Agnar's rebuilt barrier begins to crack under the pressure of divine power. Our initial line of defense, already failing.

Earth responds with a thought, solidifying the wall yet again.

A second wall shoots up on the other side. Ice forms over the barriers, rising higher, growing thicker, stiffening and reinforcing the earth. Then I angle them, creating a funnel that leads straight to us.

A killing ground.

In the air above us, a monstrosity that defies description crawls through a wound in reality.

Six limbs jut out at odd angles, supporting a torso that folds in on itself. The fucker's face, if you can call it that, resembles shattered glass caught in a moment of explosion, each shard reflecting a different aspect of divine fury. Its movements are fluid yet wrong, like a predator from a world with different physical laws. I've never read about anything like it in our bestiaries or histories.

Agnar readies his sword, flexing his fingers on the hilt. "What the actual fuck?"

I shudder when the entity's power washes over me. "It's a god." The creature's broken-glass face shifts in my direction. "One we've never seen before."

The thing lunges, covering ground faster than seems possible. At the last second, it springs into the air, intending to land on top of us. Broken glass flares wide, maw opening to bite and tear.

"It's the God of Broken Things! That's just one of his shattered pieces. There are more." Bastian's eyes widen with recognition. "More broken pieces than stars in the sky, the books say. His name is impossible for humans to pronounce. He's taken on this form for battle."

Lark calmly follows its moves.

In the blink of an eye, a white-blue haze forms overhead. Fire, the kind used to make steel, creates a protective dome around us.

The monstrosity burns without a sound, disintegrating into fine ash.

Lark blows the gray powder from her sleeves and shakes it from her hair. "Agnar, Leesa, Rafe, protect our sides. I'll make sure nothing gets the drop on us from above. Sterling, we'll keep them lined up for you."

Amazing. Woman.

She thinks of everything.

My love for her courses through my veins and warms my heart, and I can't help the smile that spreads across my face despite our shitty situation.

I stalk forward, drawing on our merged power. "Got it, love."

Water answers my call, not as a gentle stream but as a torrent of raw potential. It crystallizes into a blade of ice so cold it shines blue-white in the arena's sunlight. This weapon is an extension of my arm, the manifestation of my will. Something I learned from Lark and her wings of fire.

Filling the area between me and the opening where the gods' minions are charging with lava mist is as simple as thinking. Fire, water, air, and earth meld together. The watery air hides the earth and fire, which explode as soon as they're touched.

Valk's horned war horses go down first. Their shrill shrieks vibrate through my skull in a direct assault on my nervous system. My vision blurs, and I stagger back a step, fighting to maintain focus.

Obsidian cave cats, Nyc's favored beasts, attempt to race along the earthen walls. Until I shroud them in slick ice to hold them captive. As soon as their claws start to sink in, they're blasted away. The sylphs, Gallera's nearly invisible spirits of air, attempt to get close, but the overwhelming heat of Lark's dome keeps them back.

None of this stops the gods.

Valk charges forward, double-headed war axe held high. The detonating mist doesn't even slow her down. Nor do the explosions that destroy her ravens and Hallr's golems.

She's on me.

I meet her charge, ducking under the initial strike and bringing my ice-blade up in a sweeping arc. The edge, honed to molecular perfection by my enhanced magic, slices through the handle of her weapon.

The axe head spins away, eliciting a string of curses from Agnar.

The Goddess of War doesn't hesitate. Her beheaded axe handle morphs into a halberd over my shoulder. She yanks the weapon back.

Crazy bitch plans to skewer me.

There's no time to dodge.

Ice forms in a smooth curve along my shoulder and neck. The god's weapon slips along it. Caught off guard when her strike doesn't penetrate, Valk stumbles.

I take that moment to blast her with a cyclone of warm, wet air.

She's flung backward.

Right into one of the grasping tentacles of Rivlan's kraken, who crawled out of the ocean.

Hook filled sucker cups latch onto Valk. A second tentacle wraps around its prey.

The goddess is lifted away—screaming as those hooks carve holes into her flesh—and dragged into the water.

Hallr lunges forward next. He almost comes across as an old, ancient human, save for the granite legs that propel him through the mist.

I raise my sword, ready to take on his rocky skin.

But Hallr doesn't come close enough to engage. Instead, he reaches down, then throws something at me.

Stones?

No. As the rocky projectiles close in, they expand.

Rock golems.

This low, they're not affected by Lark's fire dome.

But, thanks to the merge, Lark isn't the only one who can use her flames. Just as I would have done with water, I create a wall of fire. It's not as potent or as hot as Lark's.

But it's close enough.

Though these creatures don't seem to care about the fire. They fly right through the wall I've summoned, skin glowing red as their stone bodies absorb the heat.

No doubt Hallr planned that.

Rearing back, I conjure up another wall.

This time, it's a mix of water and air, both as cold as I can make them.

The golems shatter with high-pitched screams. Bits fly in every direction, including toward Hallr, who raises his arms to protect himself.

"Behind you!"

Leesa's warning is almost too late as the ground crumbles under my feet.

Forming steps conjured from ice, I climb up and out of the way while hunkering low to avoid the flock of ravens trying to find a way to get down to us.

A pack of Terro's pangolins tunnels out of the ground. Muck and dirt stick to their hairy sides, their long, sharp claws still covered in grass and mud from their digging.

I spin, but I'm a heartbeat too slow.

Two pangolins reach out for me, and claws the length of my forearm close in.

Pangolin heads, necks, and backs are shielded by scaled skin so thick and durable, it would make for great armor. Though hunting them is useless. They're nearly impervious to heat, cold, and physical attacks.

A sudden gust of wind howls.

The startled pangolins curl into tight balls.

The wind forces them out of the hole like corks from shaken beer barrels. Spinning, they fly into the air, through Lark's dome, and into the murder of crows before disappearing from sight.

"Thanks." I salute Rafe before shifting to confront the next threat.

"Left!" Lark slashes an arm my way, and I duck without hesitation.

A stream of her fire roars over my head, so close it singes my hair. A winged horror diving toward us is engulfed in flames, its feathered body, too many wings, and too few limbs consumed in an instant.

The freaky fuck plummets, a wailing comet of burning flesh that smashes into the arena floor and lies twitching.

"They're starting to work together." Leesa kicks a tiny creature, the remains of a sylph, from the back of the winged creature. "This thing guarded against the fire so the others could enter through the dome."

Her words are barely out of her mouth before a portal opens between us.

Without thinking, I cover the portal in ice as Leesa and I jump clear of it.

Is this what being a god feels like?

The thought is both exhilarating and terrifying.

And so wrong.

A creature slips through the ice and past my guard. The thing has too many mouths, each lined with grinding, gnashing teeth that move independently. It's on me before I can react, one of its mouths latching onto my shoulder. Razor-sharp teeth sink through cloth and armor to find the flesh beneath.

Pain explodes through me, white-hot and all-consuming.

My concentration shatters.

The water I was manipulating crashes to the ground in a useless splash, and a strangled cry rips from my throat. Through the haze of agony, I feel a cool, familiar presence brushing against my consciousness.

Lark.

Her mind touches mine through our merged magic. *"Sterling! Are you all right?"*

"I'll be fine. I swear. But you'd better take control of the merge."

Black ichor sprays across my face as the creature explodes, the substance burning where it touches my skin.

I wipe the mess away with my sleeve, already searching for the next threat. The explosion has cleared a circle around us, the divine creatures thrown back or temporarily destroyed.

But it's only a respite, not a victory.

Around us, more rifts open. Within the walls we've built.

Through those rifts, more horrors line up to enter our world in an endless queue of divine vengeance.

And we're weakening.

I can feel that truth through our connection. The strain of maintaining such power is costing all of us. Rafe's wind has become a fraction of its normal strength. Agnar's earth barriers crumble under renewed assault, no longer rising as solidly as before. Bastian's flames dim as exhaustion sets in, the wall of fire he creates to block a charging horde of multi-legged abominations barely charring their chitinous hides.

Even Lark's fire, usually so vibrant and uncontainable, begins to waver against the onslaught.

My own magic is increasingly difficult to control. Where before water answered my call with eager precision, now it responds sluggishly, requiring more effort for diminishing returns.

The wound in my shoulder throbs with each heartbeat.

Blood soaks my sleeve and drips from my fingertips, loosening my grip on the weapons I form.

Is this Rivlan's attack on us?

Doesn't fucking matter who's responsible at this point.

We're losing ground with each passing second. The circle of cleared space around us grows smaller as divine beasts press in from all sides.

My vision blurs at the edges, fatigue and blood loss taking their toll. I force myself to focus, to keep fighting even as my body screams for rest.

We will not die today. Not on my watch.

CHAPTER FIFTY-EIGHT
THE CHRONIMŪRTI

The three Gods of Time convene in a chamber filled with whispers and currents. Their ancient forms flicker like half-remembered dreams, casting shadows that stretch beyond the very fabric of existence.

In front of them, the water in the small pool swirls, humming with energy. Each ripple tells a story, past, present, and future. The fabric of fate woven in currents of water and light.

Below, a woman stands next to a man, their hands clasped and lifted to the sky.

Chronoth peers into the water, his fingers skimming the surface. Shadows pass over his angular features as he contemplates the events of both mortals and deities as though he's seeking patterns in the disarray.

Leaning against the smooth stone wall, Chronir vibrates with impatient energy. He grips a shard of ancient stone and rolls it between his fingers, each motion cracking the very air around him. "This is new."

Chronoth calls forth images of the realm, maddening and heartbreaking visions of chaos where mortal lives intertwine and bend under divine weight. "Only the mortals. The gods are the same as they always were."

"There was a time when they were not gods." Chronira glances back toward the pool, a determined light gleaming in her eyes. "They are shaped by their stories, not just their powers."

Chronoth's brow furrows, an old worry passing over his features. "The gods know their own pasts."

Calm and unwavering, Chronira observes the tension between her fellow gods with a mix of wisdom and warning. She stands at a distance, watching the water as images swirl and shift in frenzied patterns. The thread in front of her is stacked with possibilities.

Man and woman defiantly upright.

Man and woman dead.

Man and woman kneeling, heads bowed.

Man and woman fighting.

A little girl crying.

An island on fire.

An island consumed with waves.

A woman covered in flames, burning the island with the man at her feet.

"But the mortals do not." Chronira tears her gaze away from the endless outcomes. "They've lost their knowledge. And the gods want to keep it that way."

Chronir exhales, crossing his arms as he relents. "And will you share with the gods the secret you've been keeping?"

"There are always consequences." Chronira stares at the growing stack of what-ifs. There's more now, due to her brother's question. "That might be of great benefit. To see what is yet to come."

As the currents of water swirl anew, the boundaries of time bend, and with it, a whisper of fate shifts around them.

The Gods of Time prepare for whatever tumultuous possibilities lie ahead. It is time to intervene.

~

Sterling

Too far. I've come too fucking far to die today.

I'm pinned to the ground, unable to move. The darkness at the edges of my vision transforms into a void, blotting out everything except Lark's desperate face. My lungs burn for air that won't come. A blur of motion comes into view.

Beady black eyes. Smooth, scaly body. Razor-sharp teeth.

A snakelike creature, thicker than a human, crushes me, cutting off my air. A rugeru. Zeru's hideous monsters.

The creature opens its mouth. Wider. Then even wider. Dozens of hissing black snakes spew from the rugeru's mouth.

They slither as one toward Lark and block her way to me.

Lark's mouth forms my name, her eyes blazing gold with desperate fury. She carves through a mass of the writhing horrors, her fire consuming everything in her path.

The flames don't burn her. Rather, she becomes the flames.

Agnar sprints behind her, hair matted with sweat and something darker, less human. His face contorts with effort as he splits the earth to clear Lark's path.

He stumbles.

A claw-like appendage from a creature I can't see slashes across his thigh. Suddenly vulnerable, he falls face first, arms flailing.

Bastian's head whips around, his expression frozen in horror as a barbed beast lunges toward Agnar.

Leesa, sweat pouring down her face, draws an arrow from her quiver and nocks it with fluid precision.

I swallow hard, my memory shifting to my mother's crumpled form in the courtyard. The thought comes with perfect clarity as the edges of my world collapse inward.

My screaming lungs spasm and pull. Nothing happens. No air.

Black serpentine eyes are still locked on me.

Then the pressure vanishes.

Air rushes into my starved lungs. I suck in a ragged breath. Then another. Each desperate gasp is more painful than the last. The arena tilts and sways around me.

Through watering eyes, I get a glimpse of the dead rugeru that grappled me.

Someone stands between me and the creature.

"Rivlan." The word is torn from my abused throat.

The god turns, fierce determination carved into every line of his face. "Get up. This battle has only just begun."

My shock rattles through the temporary, merge-induced connection, jolting everyone.

"Why?" The question encompasses more than I have breath to articulate.

Why help me? Why now? Why rebel against his fellow gods again?

I stagger to my feet, my legs threatening to buckle beneath me. Lark catches me, hauling me upright.

"Because I do believe in you." Rivlan nods to Lark before gesturing toward the others.

Agnar struggling to rise.

Bastian and Rafe standing back-to-back against a tide of abominations.

Leesa releasing arrows as fast as she can find a target.

"All of you. In humans." He holds his hand out, and a streak of sparkling blue appears. The glaive, his gift to me before we revolted. "You deserve this. Use it and magnify your strength."

Despite my earlier reservations, something in his eyes compels me to trust him.

I accept the glaive, drawing on reserves of strength I didn't know I possessed. My guardian magic responds more readily, and water answers my call, spiraling around my arms and crystallizing into bracers of ice so cold they smoke in the arena air.

Another figure emerges.

The throng of divine creatures parts, ash settling amidst swirls of concentrated heat.

Ziva's wrapped in living flame, weapons of fire materializing from her hands as she advances.

Her eyes meet mine, then seek out Lark's. "We will not be killing dragons. Or mortals."

Lark freezes in shock, her gaze locked on her patron goddess.

The moment of distraction nearly costs her as a multi-limbed horror lunges toward her exposed back.

I shout a warning.

Too late.

A shadow detaches from the screaming crowd, materializing behind Lark with lightning speed. Nyc seizes the creature, her fingers lengthening and her claws extending as she rips it apart with casual strength.

The darkness rippling around her like a living cloak consumes the flailing monster. "I got you into this mess. My family is in your debt."

Behind her, Mar emerges from her shadows. Nyc's daughter, the Goddess of Dreams and Visions. An aura of light surrounds her, illuminating delicate features and hair so pale it's almost white. The creatures that approach Mar seem to forget what they're doing and turn on each other in their confusion.

Distrust trickles through the connection I share with the others.

But so does a sliver of hope.

Something stirs within me.

The exhaustion that dragged at my limbs fades, replaced by a gush of energy that tingles my skin. My wounds start to heal, and the pain recedes, becoming distant and unimportant. The others straighten, their movements becoming more fluid, more certain.

Nyc swells, the edges of her darkness flaring and swallowing a pack of cave cats. When they emerge again, they're facing the opposite direction. With snarling roars, they charge into the fray, attacking another family of pangolins.

With the gods' intervention, the battle shifts.

Where before we were pushed back, now we advance, blazing a trail through divine creatures that are suddenly less sure, less coordinated.

Rivlan and I move as a unit, my ice complementing his water in ways I never imagined possible. He pulls the liquid from their bodies, and I freeze it.

Lark and Ziva are twin vortexes of heat and flame that consume everything in their paths, leaving nothing but ash in their wakes.

That kindling of hope flickers in my chest.

With gods fighting alongside us, we might actually stand a chance. This crazy, desperate gamble might pay off after all.

Thank you.

The prayer slips out reflexively, and a sudden realization hits me. We can bolster the gods on our side by praying to them.

I start with the prayer I learned as a child. "Praise Rivlan, God of Water, Source of Life."

Next to me, Rivlan's waters run faster.

Lark catches on, lips moving as she murmurs a prayer to Ziva. The others follow suit.

Our powers amplify.

Devotion pours from each of us.

The creatures fall back, cowering in the face of our revival.

In the stands, Zeru rises to his full height, his form oscillating between human and something far more terrible, far more alien.

Silent explosions of stars burst around him. The creatures on the arena floor respond to his rage, their attacks becoming more coordinated and brutal. "Advance! Kill the heretics!"

The beasts surge forward in a wave of chitinous limbs and gaping maws. Even with the rebel gods fighting alongside us, we're forced back step-by-step. Our connection starts to weaken. The merge can only hold for so long.

Rafe falls out first.

The merge breaks, then reforms as the remaining people reach out again.

Rivlan pivots toward me, his watery features troubled. "Something's wrong. The balance is shifting."

I spear another beast that leaps toward us. "What do you mean?"

"Zeru is pulling on more power than should be possible." Rivlan's form ripples as if he's trying to discern the problem. "No. That's not him. It's from something beyond—"

He vanishes.

Simply gone between one heartbeat and the next.

I stare at the empty space where he stood, my mind refusing to process what my eyes are communicating.

Then Ziva disappears, mid-swing, her fiery weapon clattering to the ground before dissolving into embers.

Nyc and Mar follow.

The same phenomenon spreads through the stands like a

wave. Zeru goes first. Then the gods who remain. All gone in an instant, like smoke before a windstorm.

The arena falls silent, everyone, mortal and monster alike, frozen in disbelief.

"What the fuck?" Agnar breaks the quiet, his voice carrying across the sudden stillness. "I was just getting my third wind!"

His outburst releases the tension. The crowd in the stands erupts into panicked conversation, nobles and commoners gesturing to the empty spaces where gods had been seconds before. On the arena floor, the creatures, baffled by their masters' disappearances, become erratic and uncoordinated.

Lark appears at my side, her eyes bewildered. "What just happened? Should— ?"

Before she can finish, one of the larger beasts, a thing with too many limbs and a mouth that could swallow me whole, regains its purpose and charges.

"We keep fighting." I push through the fatigue seeping into my bones and threatening to overwhelm me. "Because they are." Pulling deep on my guardian magic, I strengthen the merge.

In the back of my mind, a strange presence looms. One with a singular purpose that makes absolutely no sense.

We're coming.

CHAPTER FIFTY-NINE
LARK

With each swing of my fire blade, my arms scream. My muscles burn hotter than the flames I struggle to conjure. Sweat beads on my brow and drips down my face. Between my shoulders and down my back. Blood and ichor drench the arena floor, the remains of twisted divine creatures scattered like broken dolls across the once-pristine dirt.

Beside me, Sterling's ice shatters against the hide of a multi-limbed horror, the fragments melting in the light of a sun that's way too bright for such a dark moment.

I drag myself forward, each step an act of pure will on legs as heavy and wobbly as filled waterskins. There is no fucking way I'll give up.

The fire still burns within me.

The divine creature in front of us, another rugeru that's spewing green flames, lunges with uncanny speed.

My fire blade flickers dangerously as I bring it up to block the attack, the flames barely maintaining their form.

I don't need the flame.

Sharp steel is enough.

The impact reverberates through my exhausted arms and

rattles me all the way to my bones. I push back against the creature's incredible strength, my boots sliding through the gore-slicked dirt.

A sudden tickle at the back of my mind almost distracts me. Almost.

Something is coming.

No. Someone.

I don't have time to dwell on it. There are already too many beasts trying to kill me.

"Lark!" Though he's only yards away, Bastian's voice is distant. His own fire, usually so vibrant, sputters in erratic bursts as he defends Leesa, who has relied solely on her weapons in this battle.

Her face is ghost white, loose tendrils of dark golden blond hair plastered to her forehead with sweat. The quiver on her back is empty. Even this far away, her heaving gasps reach me.

Impotent rage wells up in me. If only I had more power. Wasn't nearing burnout. If only—

Sterling passes the lead of the merge to me.

I blast the rugeru away with an arctic wind that leaves it in a stupor. Then I turn to protect my siblings.

With a desperate surge, I slice through the vini's limb, knocking it away from Leesa, who can now barely lift her fire magic-imbued sword.

The creepy jackhole bellows out a sound no earthly being could create.

The high frequency vibrates through my teeth and causes my vision to swim. Putrid black gore sprays across my face. The substance burns like acid where it touches my skin. I stagger back, wiping the caustic goo away with my sleeve.

Across the arena, Agnar stands with his back to the wall, his makeshift barricade of earth barely keeping a wave of chitinous horrors at bay. "Get back! I can't hold them much longer."

A dozen civilians who'd bravely, or foolishly, left the relative safety of the stands to join our fight when the gods disappeared cower behind him. Their weapons—fists, ceremonial swords taken from fallen guards, even a nobleman's cane—are pitiful against the nightmares we face.

They weren't supposed to get involved.

Instead of two sides battling each other, the fight has transformed into an all-out melee. No clear lines of engagement exist, which heightens the difficulty of keeping civilians safe.

But it's their decision.

I'm in no position to tell people they can't join this battle. Not when their own families are being threatened, same as mine.

From overhead, scores of Tirenese rain down elemental attacks to protect the magic-less foreigners. Heated swords cut through flesh. Timed blasts choke opponents. Dust and dirt fill eyes. Water slicks the ground in front of our enemies yet doesn't hinder us.

A few clusters of people work together with merged power.

Apparently, some folks listened to us when we sent those training manuals.

Rafe appears at my side, chin lifted in defiance despite the exhaustion evident in every line of his body. His air magic manages only to buffet the approaching monsters rather than repel them.

Still, flinging dust in their eyes is enough to slow them down and screw up their aim. "We need to regroup. Central position. We'll last longer together."

And maybe coax the monsters away from the civilians.

I nod, too winded to speak, already searching for Sterling.

He's surrounded by three creatures, each more horrific than the last. Blood streams from a deep gash across his forehead, turning one side of his face into a crimson mask. His wings are extended for balance, several feathers bent or broken.

Like me, his magic no longer cloaks him. The water only envelops his arms, while I confine my fire to my wings.

"Sterling!" My voice cracks with the effort to be heard over the fighting. "Fall back!"

His gaze slides toward me, his brown eyes meeting mine for just a heartbeat. Long enough for me to appreciate the grim determination there, the love, the apology. He knows, as I do, that we're losing. That everything we've done, everything we've sacrificed, might not be enough.

A burst of emotions threatens to undo me.

Pure, unadulterated rejection of loss, and a raging desire to fight, to incinerate, to rip enemies apart with teeth and claws.

I know that rage.

So like my own.

A grin splits my lips, baring my teeth as the urge to bite and burn fills my throat. My entire body vibrates with savage glee. "Dragons!"

A shadow passes overhead.

Massive. Familiar.

And furious. So. Fucking. Furious.

My heart leaps.

My dragons came.

I'd sent them away, ordered them to safety. They were supposed to be far away from here, protected from divine wrath. Yet they've come to dive toward the battlefield with their talons extended and their wings folded for speed. Three of them wheel above the arena, scales flashing shades of emerald, sapphire, and black.

Fire erupts from Ryu's maw, and the stream of liquid flame engulfs a cluster of divine creatures. The monsters shriek, their otherworldly flesh blackening and bubbling. The mighty blue dragon lands, but only for a second. Just long enough to snatch up a clawful of rock golems.

Then he takes to the skies again. The air pressure changes as he beats his massive wings, creating a downdraft that forces the lighter creatures to the ground. Rendering them vulnerable.

Rubble rains down.

Broken parts of the golem fall strategically on the heads of our enemies.

Mygist seizes a particularly large abomination in his claws, lifting the thrashing creature high above the arena before releasing it.

The beast falls, hitting the ground with a sickening crack. Its body shatters on impact.

Tanwen circles lower, his green scales glinting as he lands beside Sterling. He opens his mouth, spewing red-orange fire and swinging his clubbed tail like a thresher.

They're risking everything to help us. To defend their homeland and the people they willingly share it with.

My chest constricts with a tangle of emotions.

Gratitude. Fear. Love. Despair. Too many to separate and name.

They merge with the emotions of the dragons. Rage, anger, glee, territorial and protective instincts.

Above it all, bloodlust.

If we fail, they'll die too. Everything I love, everyone I've fought to protect, will be lost.

A moment of warning is all I get as Ryu dives low again.

I peer up into his open maw. As the largest of the dragons, his teeth are longer than my legs. And I'm staring right down his throat as fire boils up from it.

Mygist is right behind him.

Nailah is on his left.

Three dragons wide. Enough to cover the fighting arena.

Inside me, hope battles desperation, both fighting for dominance.

As a plan formulates in my head, I cup my mouth. "Come to me! Huddle up!"

Sterling flies to me, leaving Tanwen to his own devices.

Rafe ducks low behind me. Bastian and Agnar carry Leesa as they sprint toward us.

I can only hope I have enough magic left to do what needs to be done.

Dragonfire, hotter than any elemental magic, hits the field like a river. Earth starts to boil and blaze.

Dragonfire is indiscriminate. It destroys everything while it's being channeled. Only a fire-wielding dragoncaller has a chance of surviving.

I've done it before. When I wasn't worn out from fighting.

I take a deep breath and wish for the best.

Power gushes toward me as Agnar, Rafe, Bastian, and Sterling give me everything they have left. My entire body trembles with exertion. The edges of my vision turn white.

Still, I reach deeper. To that second fire I have.

Phoenix fire.

I wrap every human in those flames as the river of dragonfire hits us.

With a trembling heart, I wait. I counted how many groups I covered. Hopefully the numbers will match after the dragons pass.

We're like rocks on the beach as the tide of destruction surges around us. My hair, clothes, and mouth are all instantly dried as the flame passes over.

Sacred animals and divine monsters alike fall screaming, the fire pouring over them like water.

I pivot, keeping that wave in sight. At every pool of phoenix fire wrapped around our allies, I reach out. With my arms turning to lead and my mind screaming with exhaustion, I grab the dragonfire and part it.

Over. And over. And over.

My eyes burn, but I dare not blink.

The fire on my wings snuffs out as I lose control over it.

The dragons sweep overhead, flames streaming from their mouths. I search the sky ahead of them, finding every stream of phoenix fire by feel and parting the dragonfire to protect the people inside.

Once Ryu, Mygist, and Nailah reach the end of the field and ascend into the sky, the dragonfire hits the ocean and fizzles out.

Thirty. Seven.

I deflected dragonfire thirty-seven times.

The same number of groups I covered.

My knees buckle, and I crumple to the ground. Vision wavering, nerves shrieking, I don't understand what's happening until Rafe rolls me onto my side.

I'd collapsed beside him.

"Lark! Are you okay?"

I can hear his voice but can no longer sense him in my mind. The merge is broken.

I'm spent.

Overhead, I feel the pride and joy of my dragons. Pride in me. In my abilities. They'd trusted me to keep everyone safe.

By some miracle, I did.

My vision swims, and my head throbs. A tangle of voices blur together nearby.

Gentle hands wrap around me and lift me into a sitting position. "Talk to me, love. Tell me you're all right."

I blink, Sterling's face coming into focus as he crouches beside me. "Yeah. Just need...a minute."

"I didn't know that was possible." Agnar kneels beside us. "We should all be dead."

A hand settles on my shoulder, and I peer up to see Leesa holding a waterskin in her other hand. "Drink up. It's Fusion Root Vine tea. There's plenty for all of us."

Leave it to my sister to come prepared. I have no idea where she stashed the tea during our battle, but I'm too tired to ask.

I smile my thanks, take a long drink, then hand the container to Leesa. "You next."

She accepts the tea, drinks some, and passes it to Bastian.

"Better?" Sterling skims his knuckles across my cheek, eyes shining with concern.

"Much better." I lean over and brush a kiss across his lips. "Help me up?"

We stand, not bothering to wipe the dirt and ash and gore from our clothes.

I spare a moment to scan the crowd outside the arena. Some people have fled. Others who helped fight mill about. Some remain in the stands.

A strange sound rends the air. A booming, cracking noise from far above, like thunder but deeper and more resonant. I glance up, past the wheeling dragons to the sky beyond.

Though clear and blue directly overhead, the edges of the heavens look...distorted somehow, as if something massive is pressing against our reality.

The sound comes again, louder this time. A tremor runs through the ground beneath my feet.

Bastian's eyes widen with alarm as he follows my gaze upward. "What is that?"

I shake my head, mud squelching with the movements.

Then an awful suspicion forms in my mind. "It sounds like what we heard in the portal outside the realm of the gods as they were fighting. Except worse."

Sterling's brow furrows. Dried blood smears his forehead, and he waves away my concern when I reach for the already-clotting gash. "I thought they couldn't fight each other so long as we're still their champions."

Another tremor, stronger this time, nearly knocks me back down.

"Supposedly, they can't." Bastian passes the tea to Rafe. "Not with each other. If they're fighting something, it has to be something outside the pantheon."

Fantastic.

"Fuck." Agnar rises from where he'd been silently catching his breath. "So we stopped one war just for them to start another? Bastards."

Several rifts form across the field as the air warps and bends.

Creatures with too many eyes and limbs poke their heads out and peer around. Their grotesque features tilt upward as if listening to voices only they can hear.

Movement at the far edge of the arena catches my eye.

A figure striding calmly through the devastation as if taking a pleasant morning stroll. Tall, muscular, with golden hair that glows with its own light and eyes the color of distant stars.

The Guardian.

He struts past creatures and humans alike, and none of them seem to notice him. As if he's not really here.

Just like when he appeared to us at the masquerade.

My heart stutters in my chest. His appearance can only mean one thing. The gods have sent reinforcements.

Whatever temporary advantage the dragons gave us is about to be obliterated. "Sterling!"

He whips around, his bloodied face a mask of exhaustion and pain. His gaze tracks mine, landing on the approaching figure. His shoulders slump for just a moment, like he's recognizing that the battle is truly lost.

Then, with a fierceness in his eyes and stubborn defiance, he straightens again.

I push through the fatigue, through the pain, and force my legs to move. My wings strain against my back, aching to extend fully but too weak to do so. I stand a few paces from Sterling, ready to defend him and the others with whatever magic I can muster.

Bastian appears at my other side, Leesa just behind him. Rafe and Agnar move to complete our defensive circle, the civilians they were protecting running to huddle in our center.

The Guardian continues his unhurried advance, his perfect features arranged in an expression of mild interest, as if we're an experiment with unexpected results. He carries a gleaming lance in one hand and a sword that pulses with strange light in the other.

"Seriously?" A drop of fresh blood trickles from the wound on Sterling's forehead. "Now?"

"Now." The Guardian hefts the lance, muscles rippling beneath his flawless skin.

In one fluid motion, he hurls the weapon directly at Sterling.

Pure terror wraps around my heart and squeezes. I forget how to breathe.

My husband is going to die.

CHAPTER SIXTY
LARK

I try to move, to throw myself in the weapon's path, to burn it to ash. But my exhausted body betrays me.

The lance soars over Sterling's shoulder—missing him by a hair—and continues its deadly flight.

It strikes a massive tentacled creature that had been crawling out of a portal behind us, piercing straight through its chest. The monster convulses once, twice, then collapses into a heap of twitching limbs.

Sterling staggers, knees buckling.

The Guardian crosses the remaining distance in three long strides, seizing Sterling's arm and hauling him upright with supernatural strength. "On your feet, son. It's not over."

All I can do is gape at him, uncomprehending.

Did he just...help us?

The Guardian, staunchest defender of the gods, Zeru's most loyal servant?

He meets my gaze, his starry eyes unreadable. "Yes, Queen Lark, I am helping you. For now." He surveys the battlefield, his expression hardening. "The situation has...evolved."

Another crack—the loudest yet—booms from above.

Trees shake. Clouds form and dissipate. A rainbow sprouts and disappears as quickly as it arrives.

The creatures surrounding us pause again, as if receiving new instructions.

"The portals are unattended. Unfocused. You will see things humans were never meant to see." The Guardian lifts his hand, and by magic, his lance is clasped within his fingers once again. "Were never supposed to find in the mortal realm. And most of them will hunger for your flesh. For any physical flesh."

I don't understand what he means, but there's no time to ask.

Sterling somehow raises his glaive. "To me!"

The stunned humans rush toward the only hope of survival left.

We gather in the center of the arena. Mortals and now two guardians.

Even with his help, we're outnumbered and outpowered. Already exhausted and burned out.

Swarming from all sides, the new creatures attack with renewed ferocity.

The Guardian wades into the thicket of monstrosities, his glowing sword cutting through divine skin as if it were nothing but parchment.

I fight mechanically now, my body operating on instinct rather than conscious thought. My fire comes in weak, sputtering bursts, barely hot enough to singe the monsters' hides. Each time I call on my magic, the response is weaker, the well of my power nearly dry.

A bugle splits the air, and I could weep with relief at the sound.

The dragons have returned.

In moments, they appear, already tearing through the creatures with brutal savagery.

For every beast we destroy, though, two more materialize from the rifts that continue to open around the arena's perimeter. A never-ending horde of monsters.

A barbed appendage penetrates Sterling's defenses and slashes across his torso. The blow should kill him.

He staggers but doesn't fall, tumbling forward with a defiant roar. Blood streams from the wound. His flickering ice blade, though nearly transparent, is still sharp enough to sever the creature's attacking limb.

But he can't keep this up.

None of us can.

Our eyes—Sterling's and mine— meet across the chaos, and a moment of terrible clarity passes between us.

We've failed.

Revealing the truth about the gods wasn't enough. Their power runs too deep. The creatures they've set against us are too strong, too numerous.

I'm sorry, I mouth.

I will him to understand everything I don't have the strength or time to say. Sorry for not being enough, for not saving them, for the future we'll never have.

Our merge has collapsed completely. I can no longer feel him in my mind. We're isolated in our own exhaustion and despair.

I gather the last remnants of my energy, forcing my fire blade to reform one final time. If this is the end, I'll go down fighting. For Sterling. For our friends. For the hatchlings. For the dragons circling desperately overhead. For Leesa's unborn child. For Tirene. For everyone.

Just as my power reaches its absolute limit, a sound rises above the chaos. Not the terrible booming from above, not the shrieks of monsters or the clash of weapons, but something else entirely.

A song.

Clear and pure, a child's voice lifts in melody.

Not the same melody Rose hummed to the hatchlings, but eerily similar to that lullaby of protection and love.

A fresh wave of terror raises the hairs on my arms.

How can Rose be here? She was supposed to be safe, far away from the arena. Inside the capital with the alicorns and the families and protected by the army in our desperate attempt to save the Tirenese people from total erasure. Ready to flee in case we fail.

When we fail.

The song grows louder, more confident. Stronger.

I turn, searching for its source, and spot Kin instead. The flame familiar is dancing through the air between the arena floor and stands.

The small flame expands, dividing into beams of light that extend outward like sun rays. The beams that split from the original spin on their own. A chain of glowing orbs spreads out, flanking Kin.

Within each one, a vision forms.

Scenes from across the kingdoms. Northern temples in Meridia, where priests stand with outstretched arms. Southern villages in Aclaris, where farmers pause in their fields. The capital of Tirene, where alicorns and dragons stand ready to fly. Glimpses of countless other kingdoms, other lands. And in each vision, voices join Rose's song. First children, then adults, then entire communities raise their voices in harmony.

The wind sweeping through the arena carries the combined melody.

It smells of honeysuckle and wood fires and dying fir, scents of home and hearth and hope. The creatures falter, shrinking back from the musical wind as it swirls around us, bringing with it a strength I believed lost forever.

My fire flickers, then steadies, burning brighter as the wind caresses it. I feel Sterling's presence again, faint but growing stronger. Our connection reestablishes itself as if nurtured by the song.

How? Why? What's happening?

Then a screech splits the sky. High and piercing and somehow majestic.

From beyond the arena wall, bright flame erupts. Spots dance across my vision. Through the afterimage, a bird of inconceivable beauty comes into view, its wings trailing fire as it banks over the arena. Each feather shimmers with colors no painter could capture, its crest a crown of living flame.

A phoenix.

But they're supposed to be gone.

I saw them in my vision in the Hidden Valley. Watched the story of the wounded princess who saved the phoenix chicks, whose blood and tears mingled with theirs, and who gained the gift of phoenix fire that also burns in my heart. Learned about my dragoncaller heritage, my ability to feel and share emotions with animals, and my healing tears.

But to meet a living phoenix, here, now...

Another joins it, slightly smaller but no less magnificent, its tail a comet-streak across the blue sky.

Their emotions drift over me. They're not angry, not filled with rage. But they are determined, and they're sad things had to happen like this.

Together, they plunge toward the battlefield, their blazing wings scattering the divine creatures like smoke before a storm. The monsters that try to stand against them are consumed by phoenix fire. Not just burned but unmade, as if their very essence is incompatible with the phoenixes' flame.

At that, the remaining creatures flee through their portals, back to wherever they came from.

The crowd, which has been alternating between terrified screams and stunned silence, falls completely quiet. All eyes track the flaming birds as they wheel overhead. Even the dragons pause in their attacks, hovering respectfully as the phoenixes dance through the air.

I drop to my knees, my legs giving out as emotions overwhelm me.

My legacy. The dragons. And the phoenixes.

They're so happy they were called back. That the song was finally sung again. They've been waiting.

All of them.

In the sudden silence, a warm laugh bubbles up from somewhere near the arena wall, followed by the enthusiastic clapping of small hands. "I knew you'd be happy!" Rose's voice carries clearly across the field, innocent and delighted.

She's standing beside a section of collapsed seating, Kin hovering above her shoulder. Her blond hair is tangled, her face smudged with dirt, but her smile is radiant as she watches the phoenixes circle overhead. She claps again and again, completely unconcerned by the battlefield around her, the monsters retreating from the phoenixes' light, or the recovering fighters struggling to their feet.

Rose raises her arms to the sky as if greeting old friends, and the phoenixes respond, dipping lower in acknowledgment. As I watch this child—this remarkable, precious child who somehow called creatures of legend back into our world through nothing more than song and belief— my heart swells with a hope I thought long extinguished.

But the battle isn't over.

The booming sounds from above continue, the rifts still stand open around the arena's edge, and a few of the divine creatures, though cowering now in the shadows, remain. But in this moment, as the phoenixes soar above a battlefield where minutes ago we faced certain death, I allow myself to believe that, perhaps, we haven't failed.

Perhaps we've only just begun to fight.

CHAPTER SIXTY-ONE
LARK

The fabric of reality shifts as the gods materialize once more, their forms condensing from nothing into something.

First comes Zeru. He's different. Calmer, with his starlight dimmed enough to identify his features. The constellation across his chest is a faded map rather than a burning declaration of power. His eyes, once swirling galaxies, now hold the dull gleam of distant stars viewed through cloud cover.

More gods take form beside him, each one manifesting with less flourish than before. Valk, whose presence once made the ground tremble with anticipated bloodshed, stands with her shoulders slightly bowed. The others—Ziva, Hallr, Mar, Nyc, and the rest—all appear less...intense.

They've given up their human facades and reverted back to their original, more elemental forms.

A shiver ghosts through me as I stare in disbelief, unable to process what I'm witnessing.

My body still thrums with battle-readiness, fire coiled just beneath my skin and ready to burst forth at the slightest provocation. Something about the return of the phoenixes has revitalized me. At this distance, I know I can incinerate at least two of these gods before anyone can stop me.

Zeru will be my first target.

Then Valk.

The two strongest. The two who are clearly not on our side.

Whether it'll be effective or not remains to be seen. But I won't go down without continuing to fight.

Sterling stands beside me, teetering on the edge of exhaustion.

When Zeru moves, every muscle in my body tenses.

But the god doesn't attack.

He doesn't summon star-fire or command more creatures from the rifts. Instead, his gaze sweeps over our ragged band of fighters before landing on Sterling and me. And then, impossibly, inconceivably, he inclines his golden head.

A bow.

Not the cursory nod one might give a lesser being, but the deliberate acknowledgment of equals, perhaps even superiors.

The other gods follow suit, bending in gestures of respect that feel utterly alien coming from beings who, not so long ago, were trying to eradicate us.

Beside me, Bastian inhales sharply. Agnar mutters something that sounds suspiciously like a string of expletives. Leesa's hand finds mine and squeezes with trembling fingers.

My jaw hurts, and I realize it's because it's hanging open.

This isn't just us winning. This is…surrender.

The gods are surrendering.

To us.

And that's infinitely more terrifying, because I don't understand why.

The space between Sterling and Agnar distorts, water condensing from the air itself to form a familiar figure. Rivlan materializes in his translucent, watery form.

Agnar leaps back a pace, reaching for a weapon he no longer holds. "You could warn a man..."

Sterling's expression remains neutral, but his tension is palpable. His magic is a living, breathing entity, edging toward me in case we need to merge. "What's happened?"

Rivlan tilts his head thoughtfully, his watery form catching the light in ways that create prisms across his features. "Nothing that concerns you directly. But the gods, all of us, have been reminded of certain truths."

The cryptic response does nothing to ease the knot of suspicion in my chest. "Truths about what?"

"Time." Rivlan's form ripples, the motion reminiscent of a shrug, though far more fluid. "Beginnings. And endings."

At these words, the other gods shift uneasily, their perfect forms glimmering as if they're struggling to maintain coherence. Even Zeru's starlight flickers.

"The Gods of Time." Bastian leans close to my ear, his voice tinged with academic fascination despite our dire circumstances. "I'm betting they met with the Chronimūrti."

I have no idea who he's talking about.

So I just nod as if that makes sense.

Rivlan gives him a strained smile, an expression that somehow manages to be both approving and wary. Then he pivots to face the stands, where thousands of spectators remain frozen in various states of shock, confusion, and dawning hope. "The war is over. The harvesting of mortal devotion ends. Mortals and gods are both essential parts of the tapestry. We do not hunt each other."

Ziva steps away from the line of deities. She closes her obsidian eyes and bows her head.

I find myself inclining my own head, my body responding before my mind can catch up. Between us is everything left unsaid. Her choice to ally with Zeru, my rebellion against divine authority, the moment she turned against her own kind to fight beside us.

Head still down, she whispers up to me. "I never would have harmed you. Or the dragons."

I nod again, throat too dry for words, heart too full of contradictory emotions.

Somehow, I believe her.

Strange, after everything, but I do.

The goddess who chose me as her faction's champion, who gifted me with fire magic stronger than any other in generations, would not have destroyed me even at Zeru's command. "Allegiances shift. I know something about that."

All too much.

How many times had I fought Sterling, only to fall in love with him? How fiercely did I hate the royalty of Tirene, only to become their queen?

Loyalties change.

Circumstances demand it.

"Yes. They do." A complex mixture of regret and respect laces her tone. She is an ancient, powerful being, yet in this moment, she looks almost vulnerable. A goddess who chose a side and must live with the consequences, just as I have.

"Be well, Lark Axton." Her form is already beginning to unravel at the edges. "Fire Queen."

Before I can respond to the new title, she dissolves into pure flame, the heat of her passing washing over me like a desert wind. A single ember lingers for a moment, suspended in air, before drifting upward to join the phoenixes in their aerial dance.

My skin tingles with the aftereffects of divine presence.

I've barely taken a breath when darkness pools at my feet, rising in sinuous tendrils to form another figure. Nyc, Goddess of Night, is so dark I can only discern the edges of her matronly form and the motion of her arms as they cross over her ample chest.

"You've grown." There's maternal pride in her voice. The words feel heavy, significant in ways I can't fully grasp. Her unseen eyes assess me, not as a queen or a champion, but as something more fundamental.

"We all have." I think of Sterling, Bastian, Agnar, Leesa. All of us forced to become more than we were by circumstances beyond our control.

She lifts her head, displaying a pointed chin and full cheeks. Her black eyes are hidden, yet I feel the weight of them searching my own. "I am...sorry."

"So am I." The words surprise me as they leave my lips, but I realize they're true.

I'm sorry for many things. I'm sorry that I will never again trust the gods with the innocent faith I once had. Sorry that I now see their flaws, their petty rivalries, their willingness to sacrifice mortals for their own gain. Sorry for the loss of something I never knew I valued until it was gone. What is seen can never be unseen.

The comfort of believing in benevolent beings watching over us

Nyc is silent for a long while. Then she inclines her head, a movement so subtle it might be imagined. "The darkness watches over those who walk in light as well." With those cryptic words, she melts back into the shadows at my feet.

I stand alone again, surrounded by the aftermath of battle but somehow isolated in a bubble of strange calm.

Though I'm not truly alone.

I sense Sterling before I see him, standing a few paces off, arms crossed over his chest. He hasn't interfered with these divine audiences, but he's been watching, ready to step in if needed. His wings are folded against his back, his posture alert despite the exhaustion evident in every line of his body.

Beyond him, Elijah Durand weaves through the crowd of brave mortals who joined our fight. He's taking names, promising help, triaging wounded. His natural authority is apparent even as he limps from an injury to his calf.

Sterling crosses the space between us with fluid grace. He pulls me close, his arms encircling me with careful strength, and rests his chin on the top of my head.

I exhale into the rhythm of our hearts beating against each other's chests and breathe in the familiar scent of him. Sweat and battlefield grime, yes, but beneath that, there's something uniquely Sterling. Leather and soap and a hint of spice.

Home.

My arms tighten around his waist, holding on as if he might dissolve like Ziva if I let go.

"So," Sterling tips his head down, hands sliding to my lower back, fingers interlacing just above my hips, "were you scared?"

I scoff, though my heart has barely slowed from the bone-deep terror of facing godly wrath. "Oh, please."

"Yeah." His lips quirk into that half-smile I love so much. "Me neither."

We gently touch our foreheads together and keep ourselves there, sharing breath, sharing space. Somehow, the gesture is more intimate than a kiss. A reconnection that reaches beyond the physical.

"Want to crown me king and start our honeymoon?" He's so casual, he might be suggesting we get something to eat.

I pull back a few inches, fighting a smile. "Oh, I don't know. I need to wash my hair, and—"

"Read a history book?" His eyes dance with humor despite the fatigue shadowing them.

I meet his gaze directly, and our playfulness fades into something more serious. "I think maybe I can be a good queen without doing all the things I hate."

He lifts a brow. "You think?"

"Maybe there's need for a warrior queen." The words feel right as I say them. Not a reluctant ruler bound by duty, but a fighter who defends her people with sword and fire alike.

"There's always need for warrior women." Sterling bends toward my lips. "Especially for me."

My heart swells with emotions too complex to name. "I'm sorry about the guardian thing," I whisper against his mouth. "We're together, even if it's just for one lifetime."

His hands tighten on my waist. "I didn't want to be a guardian if it meant centuries without you. Maybe there's a way—"

A huffing, irritated breath interrupts us.

"You two are exhausting." The Guardian towers nearby, leaning on his sword with his perfect features arranged in an expression of supreme annoyance. "Haven't you read the addendum to the covenant? Either of you?" His stare scolds us, as if we're naughty children.

Sterling and I exchange a slow glance before shaking our heads.

I ask the question for both of us. "There's an addendum?"

"Of course there is." He huffs the reply, as if irritated by our ignorance.

But how were we supposed to know such a thing existed? No one offered that information up. We just took the integrity and words of the gods at face value, even while fighting against them.

Beside me, Sterling practically vibrates with anger, and my own ire heats my blood.

Gods, I swear. Far too many of them are pustulant wounds on the ass of humanity.

"Well, we didn't know about it," Sterling all but growls.

"Shocking." The Guardian's dry tone could wither crops, and I reach out and grab Sterling's arm to keep him in check.

"The addendum states mortals named as champions shall be elevated to guardian status."

I frown. "But we didn't fight each other."

The Guardian turns to Sterling. "She's very focused on fighting. Watch out for her. Oh wait, you're married. Too late for you, buddy. You're stuck with her." His lips split in a wry grin that's so uncharacteristic I blink to ensure I haven't imagined it. "Were you named as a champion? Both of you?"

We nod.

"The covenant says nothing about fighting in a Champions Death Match. It says 'named champion.'" He closes his sky blue eyes, pinching the bridge of his nose with long, elegant fingers. "'Named champions shall be elevated.' No loopholes on that one."

My heart skips a beat as I process his words. In our defense, we did just finish fighting against gods and creatures not of this realm. And succeed in changing the entire world.

We're really fucking tired.

Uncertainty flashes across Sterling's face. "We're...both guardians?"

The Guardian snorts in amusement.

The implications begin to sink in. It will take a long time to absorb everything we've just learned.

Of course, we now have a long time. A *very* long time.

"How much longer of a lifespan do guardians have?" I don't even try to mask the awe in my voice.

The Guardian straightens, his galaxy-filled eyes distant with memory. "It depends. Personally, I remember when your Queen Aero flung Narc out of the sky."

My breath catches. According to the histories, that was three hundred years ago. Give or take. "You were there?"

His slight nod carries the weight of ages, of centuries witnessed and endured.

Sterling studies him with newfound interest. "Why were you elevated?"

The Guardian meets his gaze, pain flickering behind his eyes. Without a word, he pivots and stalks away, his perfect posture betraying nothing of his thoughts.

Sterling and I stare at each other in thick silence, trying to acclimate to the stunning news. Then with a grin that breaks through his exhaustion like sun through storm clouds, he swings an arm over my shoulder. "I still think we should go ahead and start our honeymoon."

"Do you think it's really over?" The question tumbles out of my mouth without thought.

Sterling's arm tightens around my shoulders. "Well, we do still have a new covenant to hammer out with the gods. And we have to take into consideration not just Tirene, and not just now, but all the kingdoms for the rest of time."

My stomach clenches. My face must betray my unease because he laughs.

"Don't worry." He kisses the corner of my mouth. "We'll make it work. I know a thing or two about contracts."

I smile up at him, struck by the simple confidence in his voice. Not arrogance, just the steady certainty of a man who knows his capabilities and the strength of those who stand by him.

"He always was better with a pen than a sword."

The voice comes from behind us, unexpectedly close. I turn to find Agnar grinning through the dirt and blood that streaks his battle-scarred face. His coppery hair is matted to his forehead, one sleeve of his uniform torn away completely to reveal a hastily bandaged arm. Despite it all, his blue eyes sparkle with their usual mischief.

"Eavesdropping?" Sterling glares, but there's no bite to his words. Just the opposite, actually. His voice warms with affection for his oldest friend.

"Call it 'tactical information gathering.'" Agnar winks. "Besides, you two are the least subtle pair in all of Tirene. You practically broadcast your conversations to the entire kingdom."

Before I can retort, more figures approach.

Leesa rests one hand over her abdomen protectively. The other clutches her phoenix sword. Bastian, as always, stands beside her, his hazel eyes watchful as they roam the crowd. Helene joins us, her glossy black braid unraveling in a rare show of vulnerability. Upon his arrival, Rafe lifts his pointed chin in his usual arrogant fashion.

And behind them, more come.

The butcher whose cleaver had proven useless against divine hide but who had fought anyway. A noblewoman with a torn silk gown and determined eyes. A palace guard with a broken arm who had continued defending civilians one-handed. The merchant who had transformed his food cart, brought to make money selling to the audience from the safety of the stands, into a barricade.

So many faces, all bearing the marks of battle, all alive when they shouldn't be.

My throat tightens with an emotion I can't quite name.

Pride, perhaps. Or gratitude. Or maybe it's simpler than that. The pure, uncomplicated joy of not being alone in this strange new world we've created.

Without warning, Sterling releases my hand and takes three quick strides toward Agnar. He grabs his friend by the shoulders and yanks him into a fierce soldier's embrace. Agnar freezes for a heartbeat before returning the gesture, hands slapping Sterling's back.

Tears stream down Leesa's cheeks as she starts to giggle. Bastian pulls her close before drawing me into a group hug. Leesa grabs my hand, and I rest my head on my brother's chest, reveling in the warmth of family.

"Love you, my brother, but whatever you do," Agnar's voice is muffled against Sterling's shoulder, "please don't kiss me."

Sterling's laugh is rusty but genuine. "When you learn how to train a hunting hawk properly, I'll kiss you."

Agnar draws back entirely, his expression morphing into exaggerated outrage. "I trained hawks when I was eight years old."

"Yes." Sterling nods, his voice dry as desert sand. "Poorly."

"Oh. My. Gods." Agnar flings his hands up. "When did you become a master hawker?"

"Don't need to be a master to be better than you." Sterling tosses a grin my way. Despite everything, my heart flutters. The familiar banter sounds so normal, so wonderfully ordinary amidst the extraordinary circumstances, that I can't help but smile back.

Ordinary sounds absolutely perfect right about now.

Chapter Sixty-Two

Sterling

Dawn breaks over Tirene in ribbons of gold and amber, catching on the palace spires like fire. The day is far from ordinary.

We never considered how badly our race to sneak everyone out of the palace, so they'd be ready to flee to the far reaches of the world if necessary, would affect our ability to hold today's scheduled coronation.

Rhiann is helping Lark ready the throne room and work on her speech. I stand before the full-length mirror in our bedchamber, dragging a finger over the faint pink scar on my forehead from the battle. Getting used to healing overnight will take some time.

I try not to fidget as three attendants fuss over the final adjustments to my formal attire.

The fabric is heavier than anything I've worn before. The deep blue silk embroidered with silver thread matches my wings and trousers and is lined with enough official symbols to make a military uniform look understated.

My hands may be steady, but my stomach knots with a strange mix of anticipation and disbelief.

In three hours, I'll be crowned King of Tirene, tasked with reigning over my kingdom beside Lark.

Me.

The younger son. The soldier who once slept in tents and barracks and ate whatever was slopped onto a tin plate. The prince who posed as an instructor to gain a young woman's trust, kidnapped her, and later married her.

I think I started falling for Lark that first day she smacked into me at Flighthaven. And I've fallen harder, more deeply in love with her, every second of every day after that.

That incredible woman.

She's mine.

For several mortal lifetimes and then some.

Hard to believe it's been three days since we faced the gods in the arena. Three days since Rose somehow summoned phoenixes back into our world. Three days since we learned that Lark and I are both guardians, neither fully mortal nor divine, but something in between, with centuries stretching before us instead of decades.

Two days since we started working on drawing up a new covenant with the gods. Something we only finished last night and still haven't signed. That will happen later today.

Meaning the gods will be attending my coronation in person.

Not the most thrilling thought after all the shit they put us through.

The door swings open with unnecessary force, banging against the wall and sending the attendants scurrying away like startled birds.

Agnar strides in, his uniform pristine for once, his battle-scarred face split by a grin that's equal parts up-to-no-good and proud. "Look at you!" He circles me with an exaggerated appraising eye. "All dressed up like a proper royal instead of the dirt-covered recruit I had to teach which end of a sword to hold."

"You never taught me which end of a sword to hold." I'm grateful for the familiar rhythm of our banter. "If I'd relied on your instruction, I'd have been stabbing people with the pommel."

"Effective in certain situations." Agnar reaches up to adjust my collar, somehow managing to make it more crooked in the process. "Your hair looks like someone's been threading their fingers through it. The queen, perhaps?"

Oh, she'd done more than that. She'd pulled it, raked her nails over my scalp, over my back. Wrapped her perfect legs around my waist and screamed my name as I fucked her against the wall.

My blood heats, and I run my tongue over my teeth before deflecting the question. "She's been preoccupied with her own preparations."

"Preparations, hmm? Whatever you say." He pats my cheek, smirking while continuing to orbit me, pretending to help while actually creating more work for the hovering attendants. "At least you'll only have to change once. Lark has to do this twice today."

"Three times." I smooth down a fold in my sleeve that Agnar has just crumpled. "She's insisting on armor for the covenant signing."

Agnar's eyebrows lift, and then he nods approvingly. "Smart woman. Never negotiate without armor, literal or figurative." His expression softens. "You got lucky there, my friend."

"I know." I know this with a certainty that runs bone-deep. Finding Lark in the middle of war and chaos, falling in love despite every obstacle placed in our path...it feels like the one miracle I never thought to pray for.

Agnar moves to the window, leaning against the ornate

frame as he surveys the gathering crowds below. "Speaking of which..." He nods toward a cluster of cloaked figures drifting through the throng.

My coronation has drawn people from every corner of Tirene and beyond. Nobles in finery that could feed a village for a year, merchants hoping to capitalize on the festivities, ordinary citizens wanting to glimpse their new monarchs.

But woven among them, meandering with a strange awkwardness that catches the eye, are many of the gods.

"Gods trying to be subtle." I join him at the window, watching the divine beings attempt to blend with their mortal counterparts. "Failing magnificently. Rivlan's idea of blending in needs work. You'd think the God of Water would blend like it was second nature."

I point to the god's familiar form. His cloak ripples even when there's no breeze, the fabric occasionally becoming transparent at the edges.

The gods' movements are too fluid in some ways, too stiff in others, as if they're unused to navigating dense crowds.

Or walking. I can't believe Ziva is so bad at it. She keeps forgetting to shuffle her "feet" and just moves her body forward instead. Even Nyc is better than that.

"Still, he's better than Zeru." Agnar points to a tall figure leaving a literal trail of stardust in his wake. The glittering motes hang in the air for several seconds before fading. "He's literally trailing stardust. Subtle as a siege weapon."

Behind the God of the Heavens, men and women step into the motes, trying to catch them on their hair, wings, and clothing.

How easily humans adapt to the impossible. Just days ago, we were fighting for our lives against divine wrath. Now we're critiquing gods' disguises as if commenting on a poorly chosen hat at a social gathering.

The door opens again, more gently this time. Bastian

enters, his arms laden with scrolls. His formal attire looks rumpled, as though he's been wearing it while hunched over a desk all night. "Final draft of the covenant. Thought you'd want to see it before—"

As he attempts to deposit the scrolls on a side table, his foot catches on the rug's edge and pitches him forward. The scrolls tumble from his grasp in a cascade of parchment.

"Careful there." Agnar's hand shoots out, steadying Bastian before he can complete his fall. The scrolls aren't so lucky. They scatter across the floor in every direction. "How's my favorite scholar holding up?"

Bastian blinks, his gaze still distant as he bends to retrieve the fallen documents. "Leesa's fine. Still a little nauseous at times, but good otherwise."

"I meant you." Agnar pats him on the shoulder and crouches down to help collect the scrolls.

Bastian doesn't seem to register the words. His focus is entirely on his pregnant love and soon-to-be wife. It's been like this for days, his usual sharp intellect softened by concern and adoration.

"Her morning sickness is..." He pauses, distress flashing across his features. Then he manages a wan smile. "Well, Rose's flame familiar helps. Something about the song it hums. It's the only way she can sleep for more than a couple hours at a stretch."

I move to join the scroll-gathering effort, noting the dark circles under Bastian's eyes. Thankfully, the healers assured us that the fighting didn't affect Leesa's pregnancy and that her morning sickness isn't unusual.

"How's the wedding planning going?" I change the subject to something that might wake him from his distraction.

The effect is immediate. Bastian's expression brightens, a smile transforming his tired face. "We've decided on a small ceremony, just family and close friends. Like what you and Lark did. After everything," he makes a sweeping gesture to encompass the battle, the upheaval, and the uncertain future, "we don't want to wait."

"Good." I clap him on the shoulder. "Life's too short." The irony of these words coming from my newly guardian lips twists something in my chest.

A knock at the door interrupts us before Bastian can respond, and Lark appears in the doorway. Her hair is partially styled for the ceremony, dark waves pinned up on one side while the rest cascades over her shoulder. She's wearing a simple robe rather than her formal attire—clearly in mid-preparation—but her eyes gleam with excitement.

My heartrate quickens at the sight of her, white-hot need rushing through my blood. Judging from Agnar's raised eyebrow and the slight curl of his lip, he didn't miss my reaction.

Observant bastard.

"Come look at this." Lark motions for us to follow, bouncing on her toes in a way that makes me want to cancel the damn coronation and spend the entire day alone with her in bed.

Bastian's already gravitating toward the door. "At what?"

Lark's excitement is infectious. So much so, Agnar doesn't even mock her half-finished appearance.

"Just come!" She turns and disappears out the door, expecting us to obey.

We exchange curious glances before abandoning the scrolls and trailing after her. She leads us through the palace's winding hallways, past flustered servants preparing for the day's events, up a staircase I haven't used in ages, and finally to a heavy door set with silver filigree.

I realize where she's leading us before we even get there. The gift room. Where foreign dignitaries' presents were sorted and catalogued. It feels like a lifetime ago that we were here.

And found Rivlan's present.

She pushes the door open, and we all freeze in the threshold, unable to process what's happening.

Diamonds.

Thousands upon thousands of diamonds, piled knee-high across the entire floor of the spacious chamber. They catch the morning light streaming through high windows, fracturing it into countless rainbow shards that waltz across the walls. And still more pour in tiny waterfalls flowing from nowhere, depositing additional gems onto the glittering mounds.

"What in the three hells?" Agnar's gaping mouth and wide eyes pretty much sum up my own reaction.

"The maids came to tell me when the diamonds spilled out from under the door." Lark steps carefully into the room. "They had to sweep them up and store them in buckets."

I follow her, shuffling my way through the diamonds and their eerie crystalline sounds. Atop the largest pile sits a note, beribboned with tiny streams of red and green water that twine around the parchment like living veins. Lark plucks it up, the water-ribbons parting to allow her fingers access.

"'There is more where this came from. I will show you.'" She turns the note over, though we all know who sent it. "Rivlan."

"The gift of magic," Bastian breathes, understanding dawning in his eyes. "Enough for...everyone?"

"Enough for everyone in the world to have one." The implications slowly unfurl in my mind.

Not just nobles or those born with natural talent. Not just the Tirenese. Everyone. This will settle the political rumblings that are still transpiring. The worry that Tirene has grown stronger while the rest of the kingdoms remain weak.

"We'll need to establish a distribution system." Bastian

nods toward the diamonds, already thinking like the administrator he's becoming. "Criteria for who receives them first, training programs for proper use."

"And security." Agnar pops a diamond into the air, catching it in his hand. "These would be worth killing for."

A cough from the doorway draws our attention. Rafe stands there, his formal council attire impeccable, dark brown wings partially extended behind him. His pointed chin lifts in his usual aristocratic manner, but there's genuine respect in his caramel-colored eyes as he surveys us.

"It's almost time. The guests are being seated. The gods are arriving." He pauses. Then, with uncharacteristic gentleness, he smiles. "You have about twenty minutes, Your Majesties."

The weight of those words settles over me like my coronation robes, heavy with responsibility and expectation. But unlike the robes, this weight doesn't feel like a burden.

It feels like purpose. Like a future worth fighting for. "We'll be there soon." I give Lark's hand one final squeeze before releasing it.

Together, we step out of the diamond-filled room, leaving footprints in the glittering wealth that will soon change the world. Today, I'll be crowned. Today, we'll sign a new covenant with the gods. Today, everything changes.

Again.

CHAPTER SIXTY-THREE
LARK

Tirene's great hall breathes with silent anticipation, sunlight filtering through stained glass to paint the assembled dignitaries in pools of jewel-toned light. I stand tall despite the weight of my ceremonial gown.

My gaze drifts across the space, taking in the faces of those who've traveled from every corner of our world to witness this moment. The Tír Ríogan delegation sits in places of honor, their sea-weathered faces beaming with genuine pleasure. Their kingdom has much to gain from our new alliance, and their smiles convey they know it.

Even Kamor's representatives appear pleased, or at least as pleased as their perpetually stern expressions allow. Just months ago, we were enemies. Now they watch with careful respect as their former adversary is about to crown a king. Their heavy formal clothing looks uncomfortable in our mild winter, but they wear their discomfort with dignity.

The world has changed so quickly that sometimes I wonder if I'm dreaming.

My heart soars as I spot two familiar faces among the attendants.

Theo Everheart and Abel Rummon—my two closest still living friends from Flighthaven—stand together near the back, their simple clothing marking them as out of place among the finery. My guess is I have Helene to thank for sending them invitations.

Theo's grin lights up his whole face when he catches my eye, dimples popping and blue eyes twinkling. Beside him, Abel is a little more reserved, but his smile is sincere. He's grown a full beard, the dark hair covering half of the ebony skin of his face. They watched me fall on my ass so many times in training and helped me survive the rigorous classes at Aclarian flight academy.

Today, they're watching me crown my king.

To my right stand Helene and Elijah, acting as witnesses for the noble houses. Helene's glossy black hair is loose for once, hanging down her back in waves. She may be caustic and difficult at times, but she represents what remains of Aclarian nobility with unflinching poise.

Beside her, Elijah's husky build is draped in formal attire that doesn't quite disguise the warrior beneath. His brown eyes continually scan the crowd, his training first to be a flyer at Flighthaven and then as a guard in Windmyre never quite forgotten even in this ceremonial moment.

The master of ceremonies steps forward, his staff striking the marble floor three times, the sound echoing through the now silent hall.

Sterling approaches from the side entrance, his movements precise and measured. The silver of his wings catch the light filtering through the windows, creating an almost ethereal effect as he strides toward me.

My breath hitches. Not just because of how incredible he looks in his formal attire, but because of what his presence here means.

As Sterling draws near, Agnar leans in from his position at

his side, murmuring something that makes Sterling's lips twitch with suppressed laughter.

I can't hear the words, but Sterling's eyes meet mine, dancing with amusement as he mouths, *Tell you later*.

The music swells, signaling the next phase of the ceremony.

Sterling stops before me, his posture straight and proud. Unlike me, he was born to this, raised as royalty, trained in the subtle language of court and crown. Yet he kneels before me without hesitation, his head bowing in a gesture of respect that tightens my throat with emotion.

My fingers close around the king's crown, a masterpiece of silver and sapphire that complements the colors of his wings. "Knox Sterling Barda," I use his full name as tradition demands, "do you swear to uphold the laws of Tirene, to protect its people, and to rule with justice and mercy for as long as you shall live? Do you pledge yourself to the service of this kingdom, placing its needs above your own desires, defending it against all threats, known and unknown?"

His eyes never stray from mine, steady and certain. "I, Knox Sterling Barda, do so swear to govern the people of Tirene justly..."

He continues reciting the same pledge I made before becoming queen, maintaining eye contact the entire time.

Once he finishes, I ask one final question.

"And do you accept the crown of Tirene, with all its burdens and privileges, as equal partner to its queen, bound by duty and honor to the end of your days?"

A smile meant only for me touches his lips. "I so accept."

I lift the crown high so all can see it gleaming in the light, then slowly lower it onto his head. The metal settles into place, and something shifts in the air as everyone takes an anticipatory breath.

"Rise, King Knox Sterling Barda." My voice carries to the

farthest corners of the room, letting everyone know how proud and happy I am, how excited. "First of your name, King of Tirene, Protector of the Realm, Guardian of the Western Seas."

Sterling rises, transformed by the simple addition of a circlet of metal, yet unchanged in all the ways that matter. He faces the assembled crowd, standing tall beside me.

The master of ceremonies strikes his staff again, and the hall erupts in cheers and applause that wash over us like a tide.

In the midst of the thunderous approval, Sterling leans close, his lips brushing my ear. "I know you're happy to divide half the responsibility with me. Don't even try to deny it."

A grin breaks free, and I shift so only he can see my expression. "You know me too well. And yes, I think I'll let you handle all the public speaking from now on."

His eyes crinkle, and his mouth twitches with suppressed laughter, warming my heart.

The master of ceremonies steps forward once more, gesturing toward the great doors that lead to the balcony overlooking the central courtyard where thousands more have gathered. We join hands, our fingers intertwining with easy, practiced familiarity, and move forward together.

Before us, Rose appears as if by magic, blond hair bouncing with each step as she scatters petals from a woven basket. Kin dances overhead, pulsating with warm light that grows brighter with each passing moment. The child struts with absolute confidence, as if leading kings and queens through crowds of nobility is something she does every day.

As we glide toward the balcony doors, the roar from outside grows louder. Like approaching thunder, only continuous.

The noise announces the people of Tirene, who've congregated to view their new king.

My people. Our people.

The thought has my hand tightening around Sterling's, and he squeezes back in silent understanding.

We reach the balcony, its stone balustrade carved with the ancient symbols of Tirene's founding. The mass of expectant onlookers that fill the courtyard spill into the streets beyond.

The sight steals my breath.

Not because I've never dealt with crowds like this before, but because these people gaze at us with eyes that sparkle with anticipation.

Hope.

They're practically vibrating with it.

After months of fear, after generations of war, after the gods' manipulations, after everything we've endured, they still believe in the possibility of something better.

And standing here with Sterling's hand warm in mine, so do I.

I step to the edge of the balcony and grip the stone balustrade with my free hand.

The sea of faces watches us. Waiting. Sterling's steady presence serves as an anchor in a storm I no longer need to weather. I raise my hands, and the crowd falls into an expectant hush that presses against my skin more heavily than any silence I've ever known.

"People of Tirene." My voice is carried by artful magic that Rafe has woven into the air around the balcony. "I present to you King Knox Sterling Barda, first of his name, your rightful sovereign and my equal in all things."

Sterling steps forward to stand beside me, his wings halfway extended in a subtle display of strength and pride that makes my heart swell.

The crowd's response is immediate and overwhelming. The roar of approval hits us like a physical force, vibrating through the stone beneath our feet. Names become chants,

chants become songs, and the current of unbridled joy beneath it all brings unexpected tears to my eyes.

From the palace rooftops, roars join the chorus.

Dragons perch on every available surface, their scales glinting like living jewels in the midday sun. Dame occupies the highest spire, her wings spread wide as she joins the chorus, her hatchlings clustered tight around her front leg. Chirean is next to her, scaled snout pointing to the sky as he bugles.

Dozens of others join her, creating a harmonious crooning that reverberates through my chest. Some dragons are unfamiliar to me, visitors from other kingdoms, perhaps, or wild ones drawn by some instinct to witness this pivotal moment of change.

The singing of dragons mingles with the cheers of humans below, creating a symphony that feels ancient and new all at once. These creatures, so long hunted and feared, now perch openly on the palace roofs in celebration.

Every dragon here represents a future that wasn't guaranteed, a life that might have been extinguished if things had gone differently in that arena.

Beyond them, I catch a glimmer of fiery colors. Phoenixes. The view overwhelms me.

At my feet, Rose twirls in a circle, her basket empty of petals but her joy undiminished. Kin pulses above her shoulder in time with the dragons' song, creating its own melody in perfect harmony. The tiny flame has grown since the fight in the arena, its light steadier, its movements more purposeful.

Something about it reminds me of the phoenixes. "I think your familiar is singing."

Rose beams up at me, her blue eyes wide with delight. "It's a phoenix song. They're happy we're all together."

Sterling's fingers interlace with mine in a gesture that feels more binding than any ceremony we've just completed.

A king and queen. Husband and wife. Guardians. Warrior and diplomat. Partners. Lovers. Soulmates.

Forever.

That word has new meaning now that we understand just how long our lives might stretch. The thought is both terrifying and exhilarating.

"They love you." Sterling dips his chin toward the people still chanting our names. "They believe in what we're building."

I stroke a thumb over his hand, watching as the crowd below continues to surge with excitement. People are throwing flowers, releasing tiny floating lanterns that drift skyward, and embracing strangers in shared joy. Their adulation washes over us in waves, not just for what we represent as rulers, but for what we've done.

The realization hits me with unexpected force.

Everything we've worked for, everything we've fought for, bled for, lost loved ones for, nearly died ourselves for...is actually happening. This isn't some distant dream or desperate hope, but reality unfolding before our eyes. The kingdoms united, the gods subdued, our people free from divine predation, and a future stretching before us like an open road.

"We did it." My words end on a breathless note.

Sterling slips an arm around my waist, drawing me against his side. "We're just getting started." There's no pressure in his tone, just promise.

I lean into him, allowing myself to fully experience the weight of the moment. For the first time since I can remember, I feel no urgency, no impending threat lurking just beyond the horizon.

There will be challenges, of course.

Rebuilding always takes longer than destruction. Trust must be earned anew each day. Peace requires vigilance.

But standing here, with Sterling's heartbeat steady against my shoulder and Rose dancing at our feet and dragons singing overhead and our friends smiling around us, I let myself believe in the future we've created.

A future where my family is safe, where children will be born into peace rather than war, where dragons and phoenixes and humans coexist in harmony, where gods no longer prey on mortal fear.

A future worth living for.

A future worth ruling for.

A future worth loving.

The End

Acknowledgments

I enjoy a variety of different genres, but romance owns my heart, with fantasy a close runner-up. Getting the opportunity to combine my two favorites into a single story makes me a very happy writer.

As all writers know, the amount of work involved in creating a book from that first inkling of an idea up through final publication is no joke. The journey requires the support of a lot of people, and I'd be remiss if I didn't express my appreciation.

Thanks to my editing team for helping me make the book stronger and for bonding with me over Merriam-Webster's odd, hyphen-phobic ways (resecured, MW? Really?),

Shout out to my cover artist, because no one should ever be subjected to my art-challenged creations.

A huge thank you to RoseHarbor Publishing for making my dream come true by taking a chance on a new author.

Beta readers, I appreciate your enthusiasm and feedback so very much. Also, thanks to the small group of writers that adopted me into their fold and shared their knowledge along the way.

I'm so incredibly grateful to my family and friends for

standing by me while I pursue my dream. Much love to you all, muah!

A final shout out to you, the reader, for downloading my book and granting me the gift of your attention and time. I appreciate each and every one of you!

Nina

About Nina Frost

Nina Frost's passion for creating stories began in elementary school when she started rewriting the book endings that made her cry. She loves fantasy worlds, laugh-out-loud banter, plucky heroines who never give up, and the infuriating yet irresistible heroes who fall head over heels for them.

A native Californian, Nina spends most of her non-writing time outdoors, enjoying the sunny weather while periodically bemoaning the lack of seasons. She enjoys reading, waterfall hikes, and couch surfing with her husband, kids, and fur babies.

Discover more about Nina Frost on her website.
www.AuthorNinaFrost.com

Connect with Nina online

facebook.com/authorninafrost

instagram.com/authorninafrost

tiktok.com/@authorninafrost

Printed in Dunstable, United Kingdom

73899284R00291